PALM BEACH COUNTY
LIBRARY SYSTEM
3650 Summit Boulevard
West Palm Beach, FL   33406-4198

DOWN
A
DARK RIVER

Down A Dark River

AN INSPECTOR CORRAVAN MYSTERY

Karen Odden

NEW YORK

Published in the United States by Crooked Lane Books, an imprint of The Quick Brown Fox & Company LLC.

Crooked Lane Books and its logo are trademarks of The Quick Brown Fox & Company LLC.

Library of Congress Cataloging-in-Publication data available upon request.

ISBN (hardcover): 978-1-64385-869-2
ISBN (ebook): 978-1-64385-870-8

Cover design by Melanie Sun

Printed in the United States.

www.crookedlanebooks.com

Crooked Lane Books
34 West 27th St., 10th Floor
New York, NY 10001

First Edition: November 2021

10 9 8 7 6 5 4 3 2 1

To George, Julia, and Kyle, always

KEY

⭐ Scotland Yard
⬛ Wapping Station

Chapter 1

London
April 1878

Most of us Yard men would say that over time we develop an extra sense for danger close at hand. For me, the earliest glimmer of it appeared when I was still new to Lambeth division, wearing a scratchy blue coat with shoulders a few inches wider than my own, and I felt my way for the first time down a shadowed alley, truncheon in hand, braced for whatever skulked around the corner.

After a dozen years of policing, I liked to believe my instinct had been honed to a keen blade. That I'd seen enough London crime not to be surprised by much. That I could sense the approach of something especially vicious by a prickling along my arms or a tightening below my ribs.

But that Tuesday morning, I never saw it coming. A case with a murderer as hell-bent on destruction as the mythical three-headed monster Ellén Trechend roaring out of its cave. All I saw, at half past eight that rainy morning in early April, was young Inspector Stiles. He knocked and poked his head into my hole of an office, as he'd done dozens of times before.

"Inspector Corravan." His voice was subdued, and his brown eyes lacked their usual spark.

I looked up from some notes I was making about a missing wife. I was two days behind on my diary, and in the wake of last year's scandal, the new Yard director, Howard Vincent, was a stickler for keeping proper records in case anyone from the Parliamentary

Review Commission wanted to see them at a moment's notice. "What is it?"

"The River Police found a dead woman downstream from Wapping. They just sent word, and Vincent wants us both to go."

The thought of a dead woman was unpleasant, certainly, but it was the other part of Stiles's remark that surprised me into silence—because River men never asked for help from the Yard if they could avoid it. Not to mention that Blair had been the superintendent for fifteen years and knew more about the Thames than anyone. Why would he need us? And I could imagine the look he'd give when he saw that it was I who'd been dispatched. Besides, what was Director Vincent doing, sending us off to other divisions? Every one of us already had too many cases, including me—one of which was the missing Mrs. Beckford, which I might manage to resolve by the end of the day, so long as I didn't get sidetracked. And I was keen to find her. Missing people claw at my nerves even worse than dead ones.

I snorted my annoyance, and Stiles looked apologetic. "The chap said there's something peculiar."

As I plucked my overcoat off the rack, Stiles took my old black umbrella out of the stand and offered it to me. That was Stiles, doing his best to keep me from catching my death, even when I barked at him. I grasped the handle and grunted my thanks.

We walked toward Whitehall Place, our umbrellas braced against the rain, and I sent a sideways look at Stiles, who was tugging his hat more firmly onto his head. I was his senior by almost a decade, having served in uniform in Lambeth for nearly three years, the River Police for four, and here as a plainclothes detective at the Yard for five. When he came to the Yard eighteen months ago, Stiles had been an above-average policeman, with hands as quick as most boxers I'd fought, a willingness to learn, and an amiable manner that put witnesses at ease. But he'd been uncertain with me at first, a little nervous. And then the trial last autumn had been hell, with crowds outside the Yard every morning screaming how we were frauds and cheats, and we all deserved hanging or worse. I could tell it ate at Stiles, but we kept our heads down and resolved six cases in three months—an outcome I liked to think encouraged the Review Commission to let the Yard remain open for a while longer. So we'd been through enough together that now he was like a sturdy skiff, still bobbing in my wake but, to my secret satisfaction, not about to be easily overturned by anything.

"Mr. Quartermain was in with the director first thing this morning," Stiles said once we settled into a cab.

Of all the members of the Review Commission, Quartermain was the most critical of the Yard. He believed all policework should be done by men in uniform—partly because the uniform deterred criminals and partly because our plain clothes provided what he called "corrupting opportunities."

"Hmph."

"I've heard he's in favor of cutting us back further," Stiles ventured.

"He's trying to make a name for himself at our expense," I said sourly. "The public likes the sound of a clean sweep after a scandal."

"It feels rotten, though. It isn't fair to keep tarring us all with the same brush."

I agreed; it was unjust. Only three inspectors—Druscovich, Meiklejohn, and Palmer—had been found guilty of helping criminals evade capture in exchange for substantial bribes, but the press was all too willing to blame the entire Yard. I had a feeling this was why Director Vincent had assigned me—one of the two remaining senior inspectors—the task of finding the missing Madeline Beckford. It wasn't lost on him that Stephen Beckford was a respected gentleman from Mayfair and a partner in a significant shipping concern. Restoring his wife to him might make it into the newspapers, if there was still one willing to publish anything good about us.

The rain had stopped, though the wind gusted, and we hurried from the cab into the River Police station, a brick building that loomed over the warehouses on either side. The clerk told us that Blair was on the dock, so we dropped our umbrellas in a stand and made our way out back. It was nearly nine o'clock in the morning, but the sun was invisible behind the clouds dragging their dark shadows across the Thames. The breeze buffeted us with the smells of fish and brine and spice. Blair stood at the very end of the wooden pier, his back to us, his coat flapping in the wind, his head turned to the left, downstream. As our boots thumped closer on the water-soaked boards, he peered over his shoulder. Catching my eye, he stiffened and turned away, planting his feet across the middle of the dock so neither of us could stand beside him.

There was a time when Blair and I would have stood shoulder to shoulder on a case. A time when I craved Blair's good opinion more than anyone's—and for four years he'd given it to me, along with training and advice and introductions to people he thought I should know. But things happen, and when I asked for a transfer to the Yard, Blair took it badly. He sneered at me for my presumptuousness, ripped into me for my arrogance, and cursed me for being disloyal, while I held my tongue. I had my reasons for leaving Wapping, but they were best kept to myself. Once at the Yard, I didn't have much to do with Blair, but the past few years when we happened to be in the same room, Blair pointedly ignored me. So my insides felt like a reef knot pulled tight as Stiles and I walked the last few steps.

"Superintendent," I said.

Blair gave a phlegmy sniff in reply, and behind his back, Stiles shot me a questioning glance, which I ignored.

Beside Blair lay the simple canvas-and-poles stretcher we used to remove bodies from the river to the station. His eyes still focused downstream, he said, "They're towing her in."

I had a sudden, absurd vision of the dead body being towed through the water behind one of the River Police boats. "The body?" I asked.

"She was found in a lighter," Blair replied.

Ah. A lighter.

Now I wondered if Blair had in fact requested me specifically. Before I was a policeman, I'd been a lighterman for hire, and, as a result, I was uncommonly familiar with the fleets of small boats used for carrying cargo from dock to ship and back.

The three of us stood silently shivering in our coats. At last a gap appeared in the traffic, and the River Police boat emerged, its prow pushing through a web of scrap and refuse. It eased toward the dock, two men navigating against the current. On a towline lurched the lighter, a rough blanket covering what lay in the bottom.

"Who found her?" I asked.

"A riverman," Blair replied. "About a quarter past six. By Limehouse Basin."

Just over two miles downstream, near the West India Docks.

The boats drew close. One of the men was new to me, but with a feeling of relief, I recognized the other as Andrews. A good man, fifteen years older than I, smart and trustworthy. I tipped my hat so he could see my face, and his surprise was followed by a warm smile. "Hullo, Mickey," he said, his eyes darting toward Blair to assess how he was taking my presence.

"Good to see you, Andrews," I replied.

He maneuvered the boat to within inches. The other man flipped the black fenders over the sides and threw the line to me. I tied up, my hands moving automatically around the cleat while my eyes scanned the boat. It was just your average lighter, low-slung, broad across, more weathered than most, but with no obvious identifying marks.

Andrews removed the two rocks weighting the blanket. In the moment before he pulled it away from her face, I wondered if by some coincidence the victim might be Madeline Beckford. But it wasn't. This woman was a few years younger, no more than twenty years of age. Her chin was dropped to the side, and her dark hair fell in waves across her breast.

"For God's sake," I muttered. "She looks asleep."

Then Andrews drew away the blanket to reveal the rest of her. Her wrists were bound with rope, and a good amount of blood stained the upper half of her skirts, which appeared torn.

Something inside me hardened with the force of a slammed door, like it always did.

"Ach," Stiles said softly.

But it didn't look to me as though the amount of blood she'd lost would be enough to kill her. So how had she died? A blow to her head? There was no sign of blood amid the hair. Perhaps she'd been killed elsewhere and laid in the boat. But why would someone bother doing that?

Her being in a lighter was peculiar, as Stiles said. But more than that, she was not the sort of person we usually pulled out of the Thames. Her dress was of dark blue brocade, which I recognized because my Belinda had one of a similar fabric. The bodice was embroidered with silvery threads, and the ripped skirt revealed the shimmering undergarments that probably cost a small fortune. In short, she was no female mud lark who'd been scrounging along

the riverbanks for bits of coal or scrap. And she was no prostitute either. That type wouldn't have a dress like this unless it was
stolen—and one look at the snug fit of the bodice told me it likely
belonged to the wearer. Though her hair was mussed, it had been
done in an elaborate style, formed into thick brown coils that fell
over her shoulder, the way Belinda sometimes wore hers.

"Look at her hands," Stiles murmured to me.

Her skin was pale and soft, the fingernails clean. No doubt
about it. She was the wife or daughter of someone of means, which
meant they'd be looking for her and holding the police accountable. I looked again, closely: no rings. No necklace, no earrings.

I said to Stiles, "Where's the jewelry?"

He looked startled, and then chagrined. "Of course. I didn't
think of that."

Blair spoke up: "There's a few splats on her dress, but she was
never in the water."

Yes, the hem of her dress was clean. Someone had put her in
this boat—carried her to it—possibly even placed her in alive.

I bent over the stretcher and unfurled the canvas, so it lay flat
between the two poles. God knows how many times I'd done that.

"Get her out of there," Blair said.

Andrews scooped up the body, and Stiles took her from his
arms. "She's stiffish," he said and laid her on the stretcher before
picking up the ends of two poles as Andrews took the others.

"You look over the boat," Blair said to me and strode up the
pier in their wake.

Well, it was no more than I'd expected.

I stepped in, taking care where I put my feet.

The sweeps used for steering were absent, but the boat seemed
intact. Some pinkish petals and twigs floated in an inch of water,
but that was probably rainwater, not a leak. I bent over the bow
to look for numbers, letters, or any of the symbols I'd recognize, burned into the sides below the gunwales, but I found none.
There were no clusters of interior scratches, meaning it probably
wasn't a company boat, which handled one or two sizes of packages repeatedly.

Shifting my weight, I stepped over the center thwart toward
the stern and bent to check the exterior and the transom for nicks
or markings. Still nothing. The four thwarts—all present and

intact—met the sides, and their grooves hadn't been reinforced to accommodate heavier-than-usual loads. The metal cleats were solid, but if they'd borne manufacturers' marks, these had been effaced. Finally, I bent over and sniffed. A tea or tobacco manufacturer's wares will taint the wood, but I smelled only moldering planks.

A few hard drops of rain pelted my back. With nothing more to be discovered here, I headed into the station. As I hurried up the pier, I scanned the quay and felt a flash of relief that I saw no one. Even a novice newspaperman would have sensed a story here.

As I entered, a young sergeant gave a respectful bob of his head and gestured down the hall. "Second door, Inspector."

The young woman's body lay prone on a worn wooden table. My eyes were drawn to a white sliver of skin amid her skirts. The cloth had been sliced crudely all the way to the waist.

Stiles was standing at some distance, trying to keep a wretched look off his face. I could read his thoughts as if they'd been printed on his forehead: Had the murderer raped her before he killed her?

The young woman was perhaps five foot three or four. Slender, but not underfed. Seven and a half or eight stone. Her face was pale, with a patrician nose, fine dark brows, and a well-formed chin; but her mouth was raw at the corners, as if she'd been gagged, and it wore the rictus I associated with death. I examined the bodice and saw pearls among the silver threads. This dress probably cost more than I made in five years.

Someone had removed the ropes that bound her wrists and positioned her arms to reveal several fairly deep cuts, crusted with blood, across the skin on her forearms. I bent closer. These cuts were clean, probably made by a blade, and likely the source of the blood on the skirts.

Blair drew back her curls and pointed to the throat, with purplish-brown marks. I put my hands close; the murderer's hands were about the size of mine. Doubtless a large man.

"Can't tell if he choked her first, or if he cut her when she was still alive," Blair said.

"Why wouldn't he have just dumped her body in the river?" Andrews asked.

"Mebbe he meant to, but she landed in the boat," Jenkins said behind me.

"She was laid out too nicely for that." I turned. "Unless you moved her."

Jenkins put up a hand in denial. "Didn't touch her. Just put the blanket over her to be decent."

"He might've killed her in the boat," Blair said. "But why float her down the river?"

Andrews shrugged. "P'rhaps didn't want to be bothered with moving her."

"It looks like she's wearing her own clothes," Stiles interjected.

He was thinking of a case from last month, with a man who made a shopgirl change her clothes before he killed her. It was one of the reasons we hadn't initially identified the body. We'd been looking for a girl in a green dress, and she was wearing black mourning, two sizes too large.

I nodded. "The dress fits her. She's wealthy."

Blair's mouth twitched irritably. "Did you find anything on the boat?"

I shook my head. "Nothing above the waterline."

He coughed to clear his throat. "Well, the Yard'll hear about this sort of missing woman quicker than anyone else."

Only then, with a flash of annoyance, did I realize that this might have been another reason he'd wanted me here—to serve as a messenger boy back to the Yard—because public opinion notwithstanding, people still came to us to find missing friends and relatives.

Blair turned to Jenkins. "Ask Charlie Dower to come in for a sketch. Then he can make copies to take round to the other divisions while Corravan takes her to the morgue."

I wasn't Blair's to command, but I didn't balk, partly because I'd have chosen to go to the morgue anyway. If I went alone, so much the better.

Jenkins returned with Dower, a short, sturdy man of about forty. He was one of the desk clerks and a good hand with a pencil. He had a habit of humming as he drew, off-key measures of music hall songs. Tilting his head back, he flashed a smile up at me. "Hullo, Inspector. A pleasure."

"Hullo, Charlie."

He studied the woman for a moment before nudging her chin. I was standing on the opposite side of the table, and the movement revealed a flicker of silver in the hair at the back of her neck.

"Wait." I pointed. "Look there."

Blair came to my side, bent down, and squinted. "I see." His thick fingers took a moment to untangle it.

"What is it?" Stiles asked.

Blair laid it on the table. As if in answer to our prayers, on a thin chain hung a heart-shaped locket bearing a scrolled monogram: "R A E," with the "A" larger, for her surname. I pushed the tiny button at the side. The locket sprang open to reveal a picture of a young man. Light hair, a close-mouthed smile. *Smug,* I thought. *But handsome. Perhaps a brother, but probably a sweetheart.*

We could have Charlie Dower not only depict the woman but also reproduce an enlarged image of the small, delicate photograph. With the initials from the locket and some luck, we'd discover who she was within a day or so.

"This bloke'll know who she is," Blair said.

Stiles winced, his sympathy evident on his face. He was thinking that if this man loved her, her brutal death would all but kill him.

Into my mind unbidden came a vision of Belinda's beautiful hazel eyes, her dark hair, and her hand on my left cheek drawing me close for a kiss.

I turned abruptly and made my way back out to the pier for some air.

CHAPTER 2

I had Stiles wait for copies of Charlie's drawings, so he could deliver them to the Metropolitan Police divisions in the wealthier areas of London. Meanwhile, I took the first copies of both sketches for myself and went to the morgue. I waited for the examiner to share his findings, so it was nearly two o'clock when I entered the Yard.

Sergeant Connell motioned me over to his desk. "What'd Blair want with you?"

"A dead woman, about twenty, well-to-do. Choked to death. They found her floating down the river in a lighter."

His eyes widened. "Cor, like a bit o' cargo? That's bloody strange." He nodded toward Director Vincent's closed door. "Might be her father in there. Daughter's missing since last night. He brought a picture."

"What's his name?"

"Albert. Or mebbe Alfred. He's a judge." He dragged out the last word in a way that told me the man had not endeared himself to Sergeant Connell.

Albert or Alfred. Either way, an "A". And a judge, so he was likely well-off. Those two pieces fit. I nodded. "Might be."

I went to my office to remove my coat. If Archibald Bowden were still our director, I'd have gone straight to his office and knocked, wet coat, filthy shoes, and all. But Vincent was a different sort of man. He was my age, young for the post at just thirty years old, the second son of a baronet, and a former correspondent for the *Daily Telegraph*. What's more, he'd never spent a day in uniform, while most of us had spent a few years in the rougher divisions—Lambeth, Stepney, or the Chapel. Vincent's appointment after the bribery scandal had given rise to grumbles that he must be someone's favorite nephew. To go along with his neat waistcoat and shined shoes, he had a way of speaking that was different from most of us who'd been raised working class. Still, I'm not one of those who thinks that a bit of public-school polish means a man's a fool. What bothered me was how Vincent was more concerned with kowtowing to the Review Commission than with making it so we didn't all have dozens of cases on our desks. During the three months since he'd arrived, I had mostly stayed out of his way.

I pulled an old rag out of a drawer and swiped at my shoes and the bottoms of my trousers before I went to Vincent's door. Through the mottled glass, I saw two figures. The director was sitting behind his desk, while the judge seemed to overflow the leather armchair reserved for guests. I heard a low rumbling voice but couldn't make out the words.

I knocked, and Vincent answered, a frown coming over his features when he saw me.

"Could I speak with you a moment?" I flicked my gaze toward the judge and back. As I said, Vincent isn't a fool. He caught my meaning.

"Of course." He turned his head. "Excuse me, Your Honor."

We went to my office, and I shut the door behind us.

He surveyed the clutter but said nothing as he rested his fingertips on the top slat of a chair stacked with case files. His gaze, steady and observant, met mine across the desk. "What did you find?"

I took both drawings from my pocket, unfolded the soft creases, and laid them on the desk, the sketch of the young woman on top. "Connell said the judge brought a photograph of his missing daughter. This is the dead woman they found on the river this morning. Do you think it's her?"

He let out an audible exhale. "There's a strong resemblance." His fingertips drew the man's portrait out from behind hers. "Who's this?"

"His picture was in her locket." Briefly, I relayed the events of the morning, concluding with her initials.

"They match," Vincent acknowledged. "Was she—" he hesitated, chose the polite alternative, "—outraged before she was killed?"

"No. Although her skirts were cut to the waist, as if he thought about it." I paused. "The examiner said she died of choking, and the cuts on her wrists happened after. I went to the morgue and sent Stiles over to Marylebone, Chelsea, and Mayfair with sketches."

"Only those three?"

"They were the most likely, but it seems he needn't have bothered." I nodded in the direction of Vincent's office. "Who's he?"

"Matthew Albert, of Portman Square, in Mayfair."

Despite myself, I started. My missing woman Mrs. Beckford lived not an eighth of a mile from there. That part of Mayfair wasn't the usual breeding ground for crime. Then again, London was changing.

Vincent was staring at the sketch of the dead woman. "Assuming she's our victim, her name is Rose."

"R". That made two of the three initials correct.

"She's twenty, unmarried, and attended the annual ball at Lord Harvey's last night." Vincent pushed the heel of his hand into the middle of his brow, as if he had a sudden pain.

I wondered what aspect of this case upset him especially. It might be that this young woman was from his own class and could have been someone he knew.

He dropped his hand to his side. "We need to keep this quiet. We can't have the press trumpeting that we're failing to keep our young ladies safe, on top of everything else."

True, but that wasn't the only reason to keep it away from the papers. A single headline could turn this case into a bloody circus, with people peppering us with clues, ninety-nine percent of which would steer us astray.

"I doubt the papers know," I said. "The quay was empty."

"Well, that's something." Vincent still looked grim. "The photograph he brought is a good one. But be prudent. Please make absolutely certain."

As if I wouldn't.

"No doubt he'll have questions. It's better you answer them." Vincent led the way back to his office, took a fortifying inhale, and opened the door.

The judge was a large man, running to fat, though the cut of his clothes worked to conceal it. His thick forearm held a silver frame against his waistcoat. His polished shoes caught my eye. He hadn't walked anywhere outdoors today, that much was certain.

Vincent stood beside his desk. "Your Honor, I'd like to introduce Chief Inspector Michael Corravan. He was called to the River Police this morning."

The judge frowned.

Vincent continued: "Please show the inspector your photograph."

The judge didn't rise, so I stepped forward to take it. The weight of the frame told me this was solid silver, not plate. And the photograph was one of the new expensive kind, tinted with colors. I studied the picture for a long moment—the nose, the chin, the brows, her mouth. Making allowances for the way death altered faces, this was the dead woman.

I looked up. "I'm very sorry. This morning, a woman was found dead on the river. Your photograph tells me it's your daughter."

"Don't be a fool," he said, his voice surly. "She'd never go near the river."

This sort of hostility didn't get my hackles up anymore. "She wore a heart-shaped locket, about so big," I put my thumb and forefinger an inch or so apart, "with the monogram 'R A E'."

"To my point." He waved a hand. "She doesn't own such a thing."

I set aside the fact that the initials matched.

"She was dressed in a fancy gown, of dark blue brocade with silver threads," I continued. "There were pearls sewn into the bodice, sleeves that just covered her shoulders, and the skirt had a train."

This punctured the man's confidence at last. He blinked several times, rapidly. "She has a dress like that. It came from Worth's." His voice faded. "In Paris. On the Rue de la Paix."

It's peculiar the details that come to people's minds in those first minutes. But I understood. He was clinging to what he knew to be true, in the face of something he couldn't imagine.

He swallowed visibly. "How?"

I paused to see if Vincent would answer.

"I asked *how*." The judge's eyes sparked with anger. "Tell me, man. Or don't you bloody know?"

I kept my voice even. "She was choked and put into a small boat, which was found near Limehouse Basin. We don't think she suffered." That last was a lie, but I said it anyway.

He went white to the lips. And then two red spots appeared, one in each cheek. "I must see her. I'm not telling her mother, until I do."

"I'll have one of the sergeants take you," Vincent said.

So Vincent wanted me to stay here.

I said to the judge: "I'll need to ask you some questions."

Vincent gave a warning cough to catch my eye. He shook his head, and I felt a prickle of irritation. I hadn't planned to ask questions *now*. I can be tactless, but I'm not heartless. The judge was in such shock that I'd get nothing useful out of him anyway.

The judge appeared not to have heard me. He pushed himself up from the chair and put out his hand for the frame, which I returned. An umbrella with a fine ivory handle stood beside the door. As he left the room, I picked up the umbrella, planning to hand it to him outside.

"Did you bring a carriage, Your Honor?" Vincent asked.

The judge halted, struggled to recollect, then nodded.

As we made our way through the central room, I motioned to Sergeant Philips, who leaped up from his desk and put on his coat. While Vincent steered the judge through the door, I asked Philips to take the judge to the morgue, confirm the woman's identity, and be sure he arrived home safely. Vincent held the carriage door for the judge and stepped back, and as Philips climbed in, I tucked the umbrella near the judge's feet. "May I call on you tomorrow, sir?"

The judge looked at me blankly, as if he were seeing me for the first time. As I suppose he was. Time would always be divided into Before he began to take in his daughter's death and After.

But the judge surprised me. His expression hardened. "No. Not tomorrow. Tonight. Just give me time to go to the morgue and tell her mother."

So it begins, I thought. The uneven waves of grief and rage and pain. And a desire for justice. Especially for a judge, that desire might be the ballast that kept him upright through the coming weeks.

As the carriage disappeared into the swarm of black cabs heading north, I wondered how Rose's mother would take the news. I always felt worse for the mothers.

At the door, Vincent stood waiting with his hands clasped behind him. "He's the sort who won't rest until he knows who did this. You should probably call first thing tomorrow."

"He asked me to call this evening." I pulled the door open for Vincent to pass through.

He led the way to his office. "You must find out who her young man is. But I didn't want to put ideas in the judge's head."

"Someone will know him. Her maid, or a friend."

"Just so." He nodded. "Make this case your chief concern. Set aside the rest of them for now." Perhaps I grimaced, for he asked, "How many others do you have?"

"Near thirty-five."

"Thirty-five?" His eyebrows rose. But when I said nothing by way of excuse or explanation, he tapped a few papers on his tidy desk so the corners aligned. "Very well. Give some of the more hopeful ones to Mr. Stiles. It will be good for him to have something new. He seems a bit lackluster."

Stiles didn't seem lackluster to me, and the last thing he needed was a stack of my unsolved cases. However, I wasn't going to say so.

Nor was I going to tell Vincent that I wasn't going to abandon Mrs. Beckford on his command. Her trail had gone cold, but it had warmed up again yesterday when a crossing sweep told me he'd seen a policeman trying to subdue a woman matching Mrs. Beckford's description a few weeks ago. Against all odds, she might not be dead, and this might be my chance to find her. If my attempt today came to nothing—well, then I'd do as Vincent asked.

I replied, "Yes, sir."

I left the Yard a few minutes later, planning to stop for a belated lunch on my way to the asylum where I hoped to find my missing woman. But there was a break in the rain, and I leaned against the rough stone wall and looked down at the Thames. Sometime during the night, Rose Albert might have floated past this curve.

Some people say the Thames is the lifeblood of the city, and in certain lights I can see it, on those days when the breeze blows just the right way and shards of sunlight brighten the waves stirred up by boats carrying the foodstuffs and mail, textiles and machines that make our modern life what it is. But me? I say it's mostly a cesspool, a receptacle for the entire city's detritus, complete with entrails and rotting corpses. And fight as you might, it corrupts the people who work on it. That filth had lapped my shoes when I worked at Wapping. But what does it say about me that when I left, I made it only as far as the Yard, less than a furlong from the embankment? My desk happens to face west, and on days like this, it's easy to imagine the Thames as a live serpent, filthy and slithering at my back.

The smell rising from the muddy shallows was a vile mixture of refuse and rotten fish. Along the river moved tugs large and small, steam-powered boats, and rowed skiffs. Moored in front of me were sailboats and schooners, the masts forming an oscillating calligraphy against the clouds. Distant lightning flashed, glimmering on the far reaches where the river headed out to sea. I counted—one-one-thousand, two-one-thousand, three-one-thousand, four-one-thousand . . .

Nothing. Perhaps it was too far.

Only when I turned away did I hear it, above the clanking of metal, the rumble of the boats, and the men's shouts on the wharves. Thunder rolling in from the east, low and savage.

A storm was on its way to the valley. It would be here soon.

CHAPTER 3

Belinda has her own particular surmise about why cases involving missing people bother me so—namely, because my own mother vanished when I was eleven.

Now, I'm the first to admit Belinda is clever about people. Once in a while I'll talk with her about my work, and although mostly she just listens with that look that tells me she understands what I mean without my having to be overly particular about how I say it, every so often she'll offer an insight about someone involved that strikes like a wave across the beam, rolling me sideways.

But in this instance, she's mistaken.

To me, it's the uncertainty that's so disturbing. That is, a dead body lying in front of you, whether it's been knifed in an alley or pulled from a boat, is a horrible thing. However, a dead body is *certain*, and once you've seen it, you've faced the worst. But a missing person? Your imagination can take the most violent, depraved acts and multiply them endlessly until the moment she is found. Meanwhile, it's all dread and doubt, with that sick clutch at your insides every time it seems you've found her, only to discover you haven't.

I'd been searching for Madeline Beckford for three weeks, since her husband had called at the Yard to report her missing. In my office, he'd explained, wretchedly and with some mortification, that over the past several months, his wife had given way to "peculiarities" that verged on delusions. Finally, one cold March night, she'd had a tantrum and fled the house wearing only a brown silk dress. He'd spent two days making discreet inquiries of friends before coming to us. I let him see my annoyance at the delay. Any fool knows we stand a better chance of finding someone if we're called in promptly. He defended his actions by saying that he wanted to save her from embarrassment when she returned.

I'm not one to accept unquestioningly what I'm told by anyone, particularly by husbands about their wives and vice versa. Still, I felt for the man, who seemed sincerely torn about how best to protect her. Naturally, I verified his account with others, including his brother, a friend, and a doctor, who provided yet more shocking examples of Mrs. Beckford's "peculiarities." It made me wonder, Was Mr. Beckford unaware of them? Or was he just downplaying his wife's strange behavior, so as not to disgrace her, or himself? Either way, I'd spent three weeks placing advertisements and inquiring at police divisions, hospitals, and train stations in expanding circles around Mayfair. Only yesterday had I discovered where she might be—and that for half a crown I could go in and get her.

Which brought me, coins in pocket, to the Holmdel Lunatic Asylum for the Poor.

The female attendant on the madwomen's ward was squat and red-haired and smelled of gin, like a character in a jailhouse sketch by Dickens. She led me down a hallway that reeked of piss and opened the small judas window in one of the wooden doors. I peered through it into the rotten little room. A young woman sat grimly motionless on top of what passed for a sleeping pallet. A stained straitjacket held her arms crossed over her chest. What I could see of her dress was torn and filthy, but—I felt a small bubble of hope—it appeared to be a brown silk gown.

"How long has she been here?" I asked.

The attendant sniffed and wiped her nose with her sleeve. "I dunno."

I glared down from my height. "A week or a month or a year?"

"Summat less'n a month," she grumbled. "A const'ble brought her. Found 'er in the street."

"Let me in," I said.

"Keys're kept at the end of the 'all," she muttered and shuffled off in that direction.

Through the square window, I called "Mrs. Beckford" twice—the first time gently so as not to frighten her, and the second more loudly so she might hear me above the moans and cries echoing along the corridor—but she did not move her eyes from a spot on the wall.

If she'd been in her right mind when she arrived, she wasn't now. But who could blame her? A single day would be a horror, and she'd been here for weeks with no idea if she'd ever escape. That alone would have turned me into a raving lunatic.

As I waited for the attendant, my eyes adjusted to the semidarkness, and I could see the woman more clearly—her snarled brown hair, a fragile white ankle, her bare toes. The space between her pallet and wall was just wide enough for a metal pail, which probably served as a chamber pot. Along the lower margin of the wall sped a rat, its body round, its tail long and straight as a blade.

I'd been in asylums before, but none so grim as this. My friend James Everett, a medical man who treated diseases of the mind, ran a quiet ward at St. Anne's Hospital, where soothing yellow walls were adorned with paintings of flowers. Very few patients were in restraints, and the nurses were chosen for their gentle manners.

The attendant returned swinging a ring of keys, the metallic *ping-ping* setting off a range of hopeful cries from behind other doors. She laughed uproariously, and I had a sudden longing to serve some of her cruelty back to her in the shape of a shaking. But if nothing else, the trial last fall and its ugly aftermath had taught me prudence, and my task was to get Mrs. Beckford out without having to use time-consuming legal methods.

She picked through the keys until she found the one she wanted. "She ain't goin' to talk to you. She ain't talked sense since she come."

She dragged open the door, then closed it behind us.

The damp air stank of rotten plaster and the woman's unwashed body. Cockroaches scattered in front of my boots as I approached the pallet and knelt beside her. Tiny bugs moved along her neck at the edge of the straitjacket, but she did not appear to notice.

I touched her arm. Still she did not move. I reached a hand and gently brushed aside her hair, so I could better see her face. She shrank from my touch, and her mouth tightened into a suspicious knot. But making allowances for the time she'd been in this hellish hole, she resembled the portrait hanging in her husband's study: blue eyes, a mole by her left temple, a smallish nose, and light brown hair. The only difference was the absence of a shy smile. There was a grim set to her cracked lips.

"This portrait was done last year," her husband had said, his voice pained as we gazed up at it. "She was so sweet and perfectly sane when I married her. You can see it in her face."

I'd made no reply. My first thought was that when admitting patients, James has always insisted that the countenance provides no evidence of madness or sanity. I'd witnessed myself how one of his patients with doe-like brown eyes and a gentle smile had stabbed a nurse with a fork. My second thought, as I had studied Mrs. Beckford's portrait, was that I knew from Belinda's painful experience how people's characters can change drastically, and sometimes not of their own volition.

"Mrs. Beckford?" I said, for the third time. "I'm an inspector with the Metropolitan Police, and I've come to get you out of here."

Her body twitched, rustling the pallet underneath her, but her eyes remained vacant.

And then, quietly, I tried her Christian name: "Madeline?"

Her eyes darted to my face. What I saw there—the desperation of a hunted animal, not a mad one—made me flinch. Not wanting to lose her, I held her gaze and spoke without turning my head. "Release her."

The attendant crouched and untied the straps, jerking the straitjacket off. Still the woman did not move. Cautiously, I put my hands on her sleeves. Under the filthy silk, her arms were like the bones of a bird, and her whole demeanor was at odds with what I'd been told about her viciousness, her tantrums, and her lasciviousness.

"How long has she been wrapped?" I asked.

Sullenly: "Since two days after she come. We had to. She was havin' fits."

"What do you mean, fits?"

"Fits!" the attendant snapped. "Ravin' and screechin' and wrivin' about! So we put 'er in a jacket, and she shut her hole."

"How has she been eating, without her hands?"

A hesitation. "I feed her soup."

I turned. There was no light of humanity in those piggish eyes. I could just imagine how much of the soup made it into her mouth as opposed to Mrs. Beckford's.

I picked the unresisting woman up, one arm around her back and the other under her knees. She couldn't have weighed seven stone.

"Unlock the door."

The attendant held out her open palm and raised her eyebrows.

Awkwardly, I slung Mrs. Beckford over my shoulder and reached into my pocket, withdrawing a half crown and depositing it in her grimy hand.

She slid the coin through her fingers as dexterously as a magician and ran her tongue along the edge. Finding it satisfactory, she dropped it into the pocket of her soiled apron, unlocked the door, and pushed it open for us to pass through. Once I gained the hallway, I strode toward the front door, dropped a second coin into the palm of the guard, and reached the pavement, where I gulped the comparatively fresh air.

Upon hailing a cab, I placed Mrs. Beckford inside as gently as I could, and beside me she hunched, staring mutely again. The journey proceeded at a painful crawl among the carriages and costermongers' wagons, and I felt a rising impatience. But she seemed devoid of anticipation or interest. Her arms remained wrapped around herself, as if she were still in the straitjacket or simply cold.

The cab crossed Willis Lane and continued onto her street. Anticipating Mr. Beckford's relief and his wife's thankfulness, I said with no small satisfaction, "Mrs. Beckford, you're almost home."

She turned to look. The misting rain blurred the view, but the light of the gas lamps shone upon the wet wrought-iron fence that ran along the row of terraced houses, at the end of which stood hers. From the windows came the pleasant glow of lit fireplaces and electrified lamps—signs of prosperity and comfort. Surely her experience at Holmdel would cause her to appreciate her home, and whatever had caused her to flee could be put right somehow.

I saw on her face the struggle she made to recall herself to the present, and as she recognized where she was, her eyes widened and her mouth opened in a silent scream. Flinging her arms out, she snatched up the truncheon I'd laid on the cushion and whirled it toward my face. Instinctively, my hand came up, and the wood hit my palm with a force that speared pain up my arm. I seized the weapon, flinging it to the floor, and she launched toward me, her hands coming like claws, one set of nails raking my cheek, the other clutching at my hair, ripping some from my scalp. I grasped her arms, though in the same second, I was mindful of not wanting to hurt her. Her screams began in earnest, as loud as a River Police siren, like the howling of a creature being whipped. Both arms straining in spasms, she freed her left hand. I caught it and wrapped my arms around her, holding her body close against my own.

One thing was certain—I couldn't leave her here. I kicked the wall of the cab, and shouted, "Driver! Go on to St. Anne's Hospital!"

The wheels slowed to a halt. He either didn't hear me or thought he'd misheard.

Her thin arm started to slither out from under mine.

I tightened my grasp and kicked again at the side of the cab. "For God's sake, man! To St. Anne's Hospital! Go!"

Chapter 4

The moment the carriage turned off her street, Mrs. Beckford ceased struggling. And within another few minutes, she returned to her rigid, silent state. Several times she clenched her shoulders, as if to pull away from me.

Very well. I'd release her from my grasp, so long as she didn't try to claw me again.

I set my boot on the truncheon rolling about and warily loosened my fingers. She scrambled to the opposite corner, her eyes fixed on me accusingly, her half-open mouth revealing the edges of her teeth. With each breath came a peculiar gurgle in her throat. As the cab jostled over the cobbles, my eyes never left her. If she attacked me again as we drew up to my friend's hospital, I'd be ready.

My scalp was tingling, and something dripped down my cheek. I put my fingertips to my cheek, and they came away bloody. Not just drops, but a smear of red. I stifled a curse and pressed the heel of my hand to the cut, which was starting to sting.

It was obvious she wasn't going back into that house without a fight—and if we forced her, God knows what would happen.

In her eyes, a fierce, bright shine spoke of something more than fear. I'd known fear for years, had learned to fold it into quarters like a handkerchief, to carry it with me, wear it close, tucked in a pocket. But this was desperation. That shine was as clear as words spoken aloud: like a wolf caught in a trap, she was willing to chew off her own limb if it meant escaping with her life.

The realization brought a prickle of heat down my arms, all the way to my hands, and my spine sought the cushion behind me. Fifteen years ago, I'd fled Whitechapel with nothing but a sack of clothes, a few shillings, and my fists—because I wouldn't have lived through the night if I hadn't.

Was this what those blazing eyes were trying to tell me? That her life depended on staying out of that house?

We watched each other silently—with unwavering suspicion on her part and an evolving sympathy and curiosity on mine— until we drew up to the hospital. St. Anne's was a brown brick building, three stories high, with large windows and a clock up top that showed a quarter to six. The black wrought-iron gate that separated the building from the street wasn't all that different from the one at her house, and by the gas lamp outside the carriage, I saw her stiffen with alarm.

"Madeline," I said, remembering how she'd responded to her name, "this is a hospital. A good one, not like Holmdel. My friend is a doctor, and you'll have a clean bed and warm food and kind nurses."

Her expression remained distrustful, but she didn't bolt or come at me. One hand grasped the windowsill and the other held a thin clump of my black hair in a fist in her lap.

One of the hospital caretakers came through the gate and approached the carriage. He held an umbrella over his head, so I saw who it was only when he tilted it back.

I leaned forward. "Hello, Owen."

His eyes widened at my appearance and that of Madeline— but I gave him a sharp look, and he said pleasantly, "Why, Mr. Corravan. What can I do for you?"

"Could you ask Dr. Everett to come out here, please?"

"Of course."

He vanished, and in a few minutes, my friend's shorter and sturdier figure appeared under the same black umbrella, which he angled back to reveal his pleasant mien, a head of thick graying hair, and a tidy mustache and beard. He wasn't wearing his silver-rimmed reading spectacles, so I could plainly see his eyes, bright with curiosity.

"Corravan."

Though he asked me years ago to call him James, he always called me by my surname. He claimed it suited me, especially on those days when I was in what he called my "predatory humor," stalking around in my black overcoat like a crow of the genus *Corvus*.

"James." I nodded toward Madeline.

He peered into the carriage and said softly, "Oh my."

I stepped out, under the protection of his umbrella, leaving Madeline inside.

He inspected my cheek. "Owen said you looked as though you'd been in a fight. Did *she* do that?"

"After she tried to bash my head with my truncheon." I put my fingertips gingerly to the wound. I was still bleeding, though less than before.

The corner of his mouth twitched. "Well, I'm glad to see you could defend yourself. She must weigh at least half of what you do."

"Oh, shut your head."

"Where did you find your fearsome adversary?"

"I brought her out of Holmdel less than an hour ago. She's been there for weeks."

At that, all signs of humor vanished from his face. "I'll have the nurses prepare a bed. Who is her nearest relation?"

I hesitated. "It's complicated."

He looked askance.

"I tried to take her home. That's why she did this." I gestured to my face. "We pulled up to the door, and she fought like a cat caught in a bloody pillowcase."

"But she was fine until then?"

"Fine?" I pulled a face. "She sat stiff as wood, arms wrapped around her, as if she was still in a straitjacket."

His mouth tightened at the word, as I knew it would. "Very well. Go wash up. I'll examine her, and then you can illuminate me." Relieved, I headed up the path. James might jest about *my* injuries, but I could trust him to do everything possible for her. Behind me, I heard the cab door open, and James's voice, soothing, courteous, charming: "Hello, my dear. Why don't you come out of there . . ."

★ ★ ★

It took James a good while to settle Madeline in the ward, long enough for me to wash my face, pace about his office with its books and anatomical models, and gather my thoughts, which had altered over the past two hours. Until now, I had largely accepted the accounts of Beckford, his brother Robert, his friend Speare, and the doctor who had been treating Mrs. Beckford because they had verified one another without being too perfectly similar. All had described her increasingly odd behavior and had been unable to name a reasonable cause. But Madeline's panicked desperation at her house and her relative calm as we drew up to the hospital didn't fit easily with the men's accounts. Either she was wholly delusional or there was another piece to her story. With this new murder case to work, I didn't have time to uncover the truth. But eventually she'd be capable of explaining herself. I only needed to convince James to let her stay here, *sub rosa*, until then. He would resist because admitting her without her husband's consent was illegal. But I had known James a long time, and I had some idea of what might sway him.

James came into his office carrying tea for himself and coffee for me. I wrapped my hands around the proffered cup, feeling the stiffness in my knuckles, always worse when it rained. James once said it was from my years of boxing, adding disapprovingly that I deserved the pain for engaging in that sort of mercenary savagery in the first place.

He took the chair behind his desk.

"How is she?" I asked.

"Disturbed, certainly. Her brain function is irregular, and she has a cluster of primary and secondary symptoms."

"Has she said anything?"

"Not a word." He frowned. "Who is she, and why was she lodged at Holmdel?"

"Three weeks ago," I began, "her husband, Stephen Beckford, came to the Yard to report her missing."

"Beckford." He shifted in his chair. "Of Beckford Imports?"

"You know him?"

"We're not acquainted. But the family funded a new surgery at St. Bartholomew's. They named it in honor of their family solicitor, I think it was. The Griffiths Wing."

"They must think a good deal of their solicitor," I said.

"Or they want to avoid others requesting donations," James replied dryly. "But continue. How long had Mrs. Beckford been missing?"

"Two days."

He looked dubious. "Why wait? Had she done this sort of thing before?"

I drank and relished the coffee warming my insides. "Before I tell you, I want you to know I've never seen her before today. All I knew is what I've been told by various people. The stories correspond, but—"

"She might give a different account." He gave me a shrewd look. "I can tell you feel sorry for her, no matter what she did to your face."

"Well, yes," I admitted. "But I'll tell you everything, and you can decide for yourself." I set the cup on the desk. "Every Wednesday night, Beckford and his friend Speare go to Clavell's and the theater. Speare writes reviews for the *Turnbook*."

James sipped his tea. "A respectable journal."

"The two of them had returned to Beckford's house at around half past eleven, as usual, to find Madeline waiting up in the library with a fire. On what Beckford called her happy days, they would have a glass of wine all together. But this time was different. Beckford says she was distraught and began to accuse him of all manner of unkindness—none of it true. Speare says he was shocked and embarrassed. Got himself away as quickly as he could."

"What sort of unkindness?"

"According to Beckford, looking through her mail and gossiping about her to the servants, but Speare said she made outrageous accusations—stealing her jewelry, trying to poison her, dismissing her favorite maid to torment her. He also said she came at Beckford with her fingernails ready to scratch."

James looked quizzical. "Beckford didn't tell you that?"

I shook my head. "I think he was mortified. Tried to tell me as little as possible, while wanting me to understand she might be in danger."

James ran his thumb and forefinger along the edge of his desk, as if creasing a tablecloth. "How long have they been married?"

"A little over a year—after a relatively short courtship—six months, something like that. He said since their wedding, she'd changed from an agreeable, affectionate creature—his words—to one who seemed determined to be unhappy and resentful despite all his efforts."

Blowing rain struck James's window with a sudden patter. I rose and looked out onto the darkened, bricked courtyard. The wind was whipping a bare elm's thin branches, and they made me think of Madeline Beckford's arms flailing against me. I winced. I'd probably terrified her by holding her close. God knows, that wasn't what I'd intended.

"Corravan."

I turned back to him. "What?"

"I asked what efforts Beckford made to please her. Did he say?"

"Oh. He bought a piano she wanted and found a young man from the Royal Academy to give her lessons. He introduced her to his friends' wives. He took her out driving in a new carriage he bought for her." I left the window and sat back in my chair. "He said he would have done anything she asked, but most days she didn't seem to care for much."

"Apathy and low spirits."

"I suppose."

"What's your general impression of Beckford? Is he the sort who inspires aversion? A drunkard? Coarse in his sensibilities?"

"I've seen no evidence of it." I shrugged. "He strikes me as a decent fellow, a bit bewildered by his wife, as most men are, I suppose. He's more concerned with what society will think than I would be. But I haven't seen any brutishness in him."

"Is there any chance he committed her to Holmdel in lieu of divorce?" James had received visits from several men who sought to end their marriages this way.

"No. She was brought in by a policeman. But according to Speare, Beckford might have legal grounds. One night, when Beckford left the room, Madeline threw herself at Speare, kissed him on the mouth and drew his hands to her breasts."

My friend's gray eyebrows rose over the rims of his spectacles. "Adultery?"

"He told me Madeline has been lascivious toward several of Beckford's other friends, too. At the time it made me wonder if she might have left for a lover."

"Hm."

"I also spoke to Beckford's brother Robert. He thinks Stephen married Madeline partly because he felt sorry for her. Both her parents are dead, and she was living with an aunt. Robert says he found her temperamental and melancholy even before the wedding."

"So the seeds of a nervous disorder were already present," James mused. "And you spoke with her doctor. What was his name?"

"Willis. He told me that Madeline had become progressively erratic over the past few months, and at one point, she had bitten her husband. Beckford hadn't told me that either, but the next time I saw him, he admitted—reluctantly—that it was true."

James's eyebrows rose again. "*Bitten* him. Where?"

I gestured to my right forearm. "About here. But it had been a week or so, and the mark was gone."

His fingertips on the rim, James slowly rotated his cup, until the handle was parallel to the desk edge. "Did the people at the asylum remark on her behavior?"

"Apparently she came in raving and thrashing about. They put her in a straitjacket to calm her down."

A grimace. "How long did that take?"

"A few days." I paused. "When I first saw Mrs. Beckford, she was sitting on the floor. She didn't respond to me at all until I called her by her given name. Then I saw the terror in her eyes."

"Hm." He frowned. "When precisely did she attack you? Had you pulled up to the house?"

"Not quite. We were on her street."

He removed his spectacles and rubbed at them with a white handkerchief. "So it might not be something connected with her own house, per se. It could be that she's terrified of something connected with a place nearby."

"I suppose," I admitted.

He laid his spectacles on the table with a sigh. "Well, your story doesn't surprise me. It fits with what I've seen so far. She is evidently suffering from delusions due to regressive hysteria."

"Regressive hysteria," I repeated.

"The patient reverts to childish behaviors. Biting. Scratching. Not speaking. A lack of language is what distinguishes the infant."

"But James, she's exhausted. Probably tried to stay awake the whole time, so the rats wouldn't bite her."

He fidgeted irritably. "That is how you would diagnose her? Excessive fatigue?"

"Oh, for God's sake, James. I'm not trying to diagnose her! I'm just saying there could be another possibility. What if she ran out of the house because she was legitimately frightened?"

"But that's not what Mr. Speare said," he objected. "He said she came at Beckford, ready to attack. That sounds like anger, not fear."

"He might've been mistaken," I said, but the protest sounded weak even to my ears.

"And you're gathering this from 'the terror in her eyes,'" he said mockingly. "Bah! She hasn't given you a word of explanation, whereas you have the stories of three—no, four—different men, including a doctor, that corroborate one another." I opened my mouth to reply, but he held up a hand. "I know you believe there is a logical reason for every peculiar behavior. But that is simply not true, Corravan. Madness *does* exist—"

"I *know* that."

"—organic madness—as real as any splanchnic disease—that disorganizes the brain and misdirects its responses. And in Mrs. Beckford's case, I suspect her terror does not correlate with anything in the real world."

"Then why did she behave one way at her house but another when we arrived here?" I argued. "She was utterly different when we pulled up to your gate. Wary, but calm."

He spread his hands. "That could imply some logic. But then why did she fight off the nurses just now? Why did she fling her soup at the wall? I'm certain she's hungry."

Soup.

I sat forward. "That's what they fed her in Holmdel, James. What if it made her sick? You've told me yourself that the senses of smell and taste are our strongest connections to memories."

His expression underwent a subtle change, and I pressed my advantage.

"What if we force her back home, and she runs again—only this time we don't find her until it's too late? Or she attacks her husband with more than her fingernails and ends up on trial for murder? What good does that serve anyone?"

He opened his desk drawer and drew out a paper that he used for admissions. "I can admit her, of course, but you'll need to call round to Beckford and tell him she's here. She should remain, at least for a week or two, until we can help restore her reason."

"No, James. That's not what we should do at all."

He pinched the top of his nose between his thumb and forefinger. "I *knew* you'd want this. But it's not legal. And aside from that, the poor man is no doubt worried sick about her."

"But he'll retrieve her out of embarrassment. A man like him would die before letting anyone find out his wife is mentally diseased."

"Well, a husband's rights supersede a doctor's. There's nothing I can do."

Before his resolve hardened, I switched to a different tack. "What if—against all appearances—Beckford is abusing her? Do you want to take the chance of returning his wife to him?" Last year James had been compelled by the law to return a young woman to her brute of a husband, who'd immediately beaten her to death.

His eyes flashed with resentment. "Stop fishing in my pond, Corravan. The thought of Mrs. Watts still torments me."

"So what's the harm in keeping her for a few days?" I urged. "Let her recover. Eventually she'll talk, and you can determine what to do. In the meantime, she's safe."

He glowered. "You realize the hospital could dismiss me for thwarting the law."

"You're not thwarting the law," I retorted. "I am. You can say I told you I found her on the street."

His fingers nudged the corners of the admission form until, like the teacup handle, it lined up with the edge of his desk. I kept my mouth shut and waited. Finally, he looked up, his expression pained. "We both know, given what you did for me, I can hardly refuse you."

That took all the iron out of me. "I wasn't thinking of that at all," I said, momentarily ashamed for pushing so hard. "You don't owe me. You've done plenty in return." My voice roughened over those words, and he gave a faint nod of acknowledgment. "But this isn't for me, James. There's more to her story. She just needs a chance to tell it."

A long look. "Very well. I'll give her three days." He slid the paper back into the drawer. "You're correct about one thing. She's ravaged by what she's been through."

I pushed my hat onto my head. "I'll stop in tomorrow to see how she is."

"*Cave quid vis,*" he muttered sourly.

It was James's habit to resort to his Latin when he wanted the last word in an argument. But this was also his way of saying he wouldn't hold my winning it against me.

As I reached the curb, I gazed up at the lit windows of the women's ward and imagined a nurse scrubbing a splotch of soup from the wall and Madeline curled into a ball in a bed nearby.

Surely if the poor woman could distinguish between her house and here, she could distinguish between Holmdel and here. Or she would soon enough.

I turned away feeling unsettled. Usually I'd take satisfaction at having found a missing person, of being able to remove a file from my desk. But what if Madeline didn't speak before the three days were over?

Well, at least I'd retrieved her. James would do his best.

And now I could go see the judge.

CHAPTER 5

The Alberts' house was an elegant three-story on a well-kept street, situated between two others of the exact same type, with mullioned bay windows and rounded stone steps rising to the door. As I approached, my thoughts darted to other cases that began in homes like these. One from last May: a beautiful bored young woman who stirred up a jealous rage between two suitors, one of whom subsequently murdered her in the carriage belonging to the other. Another, from two years earlier: an MP's son, abducted from outside his gambling club, whose corpse was missing a finger that once sported a gold-and-diamond ring. Invariably the parents would tell me the victim was a wonderful person, beloved by friends; modest and kind (in the case of the daughters) or clever and good-natured (sons); and unfailingly generous to her maid/his valet. As the truth emerged, it inevitably proved James's thesis that there are four motives for murder: fear, revenge, passion, and greed. Cases involving the progeny of well-to-do families tend toward the latter two. In Rose Albert's case, it could well be either, or both.

I climbed the steps and raised the knocker.

A maid showed me into the judge's study, a spacious room with a fireplace, shelves of leather-bound books, and two desks, one large and one small. The judge stood beside the larger one, its green leather surface stacked with papers and books. Gone was the stunned look I'd seen at the Yard. His face was flushed, his jaw rigid, his eyes cold.

Was he angry about what had happened to his daughter, or angry at my presence? It wouldn't be the first time someone forgot that they'd asked me to come at a particular time.

"Good evening, Judge."

He scrutinized me. "You're the Yard man. Corbin."

"Corravan. Michael Corravan."

"What happened to your face?"

I'd almost forgotten the scratches. "Nothing. I fell."

His mouth pursed with annoyance. "I suppose you want to begin by probing into our private concerns."

You'd have thought I was swindling him out of money instead of discovering who killed his daughter. But this is the shape that some people's grief takes.

Calmly, I replied, "I do have some questions. My first is, Had she or anyone in the family received any threats?"

"Threats?" He drew back. "You mean a threat to her person— and a demand . . ."

I nodded. But I already saw my answer.

"God, no." He shook his head so vigorously the pale flesh under his chin swayed. "Nothing like that."

"All right. Then I'd like to ask you about Miss Albert. I know this is difficult." I paused. "But believe me, I am on your side."

He considered that, muttered an acknowledgment, sat down in one leather chair beside the fireplace, and waved me into the other.

"You must tell me precisely how she died," he said. "Don't spare my feelings. I've no need of that."

People say this, often, and I rarely take them at their word. Words such as "suffocated," "raped," and "strangled" raise pictures in the mind that last for years. I avoid the words when I can and choose gentler versions of them when I can't. However, being a judge, this man had the power to discover anything I could tell him. Better to have him hear most of the truth from me, so he didn't think me a liar.

I kept my eyes on his. "As I said before, according to the examiner, she was choked. Her wrists were bound and her forearms cut, but there wasn't much blood, which suggests he did that after she died. There were no signs of struggle, and nothing to indicate he assaulted her in any other way."

His face paled and two red spots appeared on his cheeks, as they had at the Yard.

I could see him assembling the image. As much to steer him away from it as to gather information, I decided to broach a question. An easy one, to begin: "Tell me about your daughter. How old was she?"

His right hand twisted a ring on his left pinky, so the black stone vanished, reappeared, vanished again.

"She didn't have any enemies," he said. "That's where these things often begin, don't they? But she's just a girl."

"Begging your pardon, but often it isn't an enemy who does something like this. It could be an unsuccessful suitor, a jealous friend, even someone who admired her from afar and fancied that he'd been rejected." I observed a skeptical frown beginning to form, and I added, "I've seen all of those before."

"Well." He huffed. "Rose isn't flirtatious. She's never done anything to incite someone to violence."

"All right. Then could you tell me about her friends? Who might she talk to, if she were afraid or worried?"

His hand flicked dismissively. "What would she have to be worried about?"

To break this unhelpful pattern, I took out my pencil and pocketbook and found a fresh page. "Let's begin with last night. Was she home?"

"I already told that man Vincent. She was at Lord Harvey's. She left our house around two o'clock with Lucy, to prepare and dress. You know how long it takes young ladies."

Having never been a young lady, and never having had sisters, much less those who went to fancy parties, I didn't. But I said only, "Is Lucy another daughter?"

He frowned. "Her maid."

My heart lifted, hearing that Rose had taken a maid with her. I'd ask to see her next. "How long has Lucy been with you?"

"Six years. Her previous employer wrote her an impeccable character." He shook his head. "Not a cross word between them."

There never was. "When did the ball begin?"

"Nine o'clock, with supper and dancing." He plucked at the end of the leather chair arm. "Rose was staying the night. It's too much trouble to come home, and it gives them time to gossip afterward, I suppose."

He still spoke of her in the present tense, so I fell in with it.

"The Harveys' daughter is a particular friend?"

"Yes. Edith. The Harveys' second daughter. The first is unmarried and abroad for a year."

"I see." I jotted the name down in my book. "And did Lucy come home?"

He nodded. "Before supper. Said Rose was dressed."

"Is Rose engaged to be married?"

"No." He turned up his broad palm. "Oh, she has plenty of suitors. Young men standing in line at balls to sign her dance card, sending her absurd bouquets of flowers . . ."

He spoke with paternal pride, until he halted, dropping his hand limply back onto the chair arm. His face went slack as he remembered that this would no longer be true. I gave him a moment, for I knew this ripple of acceptance of his daughter's death was only the first of many that would go on for weeks, even months.

At last I murmured, "You said she had many suitors."

He turned to stare into the fireplace. The flames illuminated the lines around his mouth, between his brows, across his forehead. "Her mother would remember their names. But she's overcome with grief and cannot be disturbed."

"Does Rose have any siblings?"

"Two brothers. Hugh and Peter, both at university." His expression changed again.

He's just remembered he'll have to tell them, I thought. "And the last time they were home?"

He glared. "Surely you don't suspect them of—"

"No, I only wondered if she might have confided in either of—"

"They haven't been home since Christmas. Neither is the type to correspond." A log cracked in the fireplace and drew his gaze. The fingertips of his left hand clawed the end of the chair's arm. It must be a habit of his, like turning the ring, for the leather looked worn.

Now would have been the moment for me to pull out the sketch of the man in the locket, but I left it in my pocket, partly because I guessed the maid would recognize him, and partly because if the judge didn't know about the locket, chances are he didn't know the man was courting her. And I wanted to speak to him before the judge did.

"Did the Thames have any special significance for your daughter or your family?" I asked.

He dragged his attention away from the fire. "The Thames?"

"It's strange that she was in a boat." I thought of what Sergeant Connell said about her being like a bit of cargo.

He looked nonplussed. "I can't think of any reason it would mean anything special. She's seen it, of course. Not that it's much to see."

"Is anyone in your family a merchant, for example, or invested in any of the industries with warehouses along the wharves?"

"Nothing like that." He rested a heavy elbow on the leather chair arm, denting it, and kneaded his eyebrow between his thumb and forefinger. "My first thought was my own cases. Verdicts that made people angry. But my cases in recent months have been ordinary, with reasonable resolutions." He turned his palm up again. "And if someone felt he'd been badly served, why wouldn't he attack me? Or one of my clerks, for that matter? We'd be easier to find, for one thing."

"Have any of your cases in the past several years, say, had anything to do with the Thames or companies on it?"

His eyebrows rose. "Oh, I suppose if you look hard enough, probably a quarter of my cases have *something* to do with the Thames. Warehouses, shipping companies, anything manufactured, the mails, the unions, taxation . . ."

"Any that gave rise to especial bitterness toward you?"

I waited as he groped backward in his memory, and at last he said, "Well, last year there was a case concerning a tea company."

It happens sometimes that a possible motive appears early on, tempting as a well-baited hook. I knew better than to leap at it. Nevertheless, I asked for the particulars.

"You know about the Food and Drugs Acts," he replied.

"Yes, of course."

"Last year, the Yellow Star Tea Company was accused of adulterating their tea, and under the new law, they were found guilty and fined. They *claimed* that a single batch of tea had been doctored without their knowledge and the Custom House inspectors tipped to arrive that particular day." The judge shook his head. "But they'd cut their tea with hawthorn leaves and sand before, and in the end, they had to take responsibility for the goods in their warehouse."

I noted the name of the company in my pocketbook. "And when was this?"

He considered. "Last September, I believe. Early September."

"Any other cases that stand out in your mind?"

A log snapped, and his shoulders convulsed involuntarily. "I'll think on it."

There was a knock at the door, and a maid appeared. "Begging pardon, Judge, but Mrs. Albert asks that you come straightaway."

We both stood.

"Let me know what you need," he said brusquely. "Money. Information. Anything. Find out who did this. We won't sleep until we know." He brushed past me and was at the door before I reminded him that I wanted to speak with Lucy.

He turned back, his eyes narrowing, as if considering any potential damage this might do. But after a moment, he nodded. "Mary, show the inspector to the parlor and fetch Lucy."

As he left, I turned to Mary, whose eyes were red-rimmed and frightened.

"I imagine this is terrible for all of you," I said.

"Wretched," she whispered. She led me to the next room and bobbed a curtsy.

There was no fire in this room, and the air held a chill. I wished I could have stayed in the study. No doubt the judge didn't want me snooping about his desk. But my feet were cold, and I hadn't eaten anything but two pieces of bread with butter all day.

I would have done a lot for another hot cup of coffee.

★ ★ ★

"You wished to see me?"

I turned.

My first thought was that Lucy was not attractive. Perhaps thirty years of age, of medium height, with a square jaw, mouse-brown hair, a sharp nose, and a strained expression. But as she came forward, I saw that her eyes were a beautiful shade of gray, fringed with dark lashes, and she was examining me thoughtfully. With relief I saw this was someone who had her wits about her. Someone who could be helpful to me, if I could gain her trust.

"You're Lucy?"

"Lucy Marling."

"Inspector Corravan." I crossed behind her and closed the door. "Could we sit? I might want to write some notes."

We took the chairs by the unlit fireplace, and I waited while she adjusted her skirts. I knew that Lucy would probably be released from service, as there were no other sisters, so she would need a good character from the Albert family in order to find another position as a lady's maid. She would only tell me the truth if she believed I would not betray her confidences to the judge or his wife.

I began my usual speech: "Often in these cases, out of love and affection, the family and friends are concerned to protect the victim's character." I raised a hand to forestall the familiar protest. "An instinct I wholly understand. But sometimes as they describe the victim's virtues, they forget to mention peculiarities of temperament or habit, which are in fact most helpful. They emerge after it is too late." I paused. "For example, two years ago, a wealthy young man went missing. He was found murdered in Whitechapel three days later. Had his friends only told us that he went to boxing clubs, we'd have known where to look, and he might still be alive."

Her eyes widened.

"Not that Miss Albert visited boxing clubs, of course," I added, with my usual haste.

She said nothing, only looked away, as if she'd spied something out of place on the fireplace mantel and needed to study it.

"Miss Marling," I said pointedly.

Her eyes returned to mine, with an intensity about them that seemed at odds with her wandering gaze.

"What you say here will never be repeated," I continued. "You won't suffer for speaking honestly. If, however, I find that you knew information that you did not give me—"

Color came into her cheeks. "I quite understand," she said, in a tone of rebuke. "Of course I will help you."

"In my experience, a maid often knows things about her mistress. For example, if her mistress carries on a private correspondence, or has a weakness for wine, or recently quarreled with a friend."

Very deliberately she looked away, then back at me, and then away again, so insistently that I turned in my chair to see the object of her interest. But there was only an elegant metal latticework above the fireplace—on the wall shared with the judge's study.

My eyes darted back to find her nodding, and her chest rose and fell with a relieved breath. "Please, what questions can I answer for you, Mr., er—"

"Corravan."

"Like the birds?"

"Well, no." I spelled it for her. "It's from the Gaelic, O Corra Ban. A common surname in County Armagh."

She smiled briefly. "My grandmother was from Dungannon."

Both towns were west of Belfast and within a day's drive of Lough Neagh.

I let a moment pass so as not to seem abrupt, but before I could steer the conversation into the proper channel, she bent her head over the pouch at her waist, saying, "Oh, you needn't put your pocketbook away. I know writing helps me remember things properly."

I stared in surprise, for I hadn't taken my pocketbook out.

From her pouch emerged a pencil, which she took in her right hand as she stretched her left hand toward me.

She'd come prepared, I realized, my pulse quickening at the thought of the information she seemed intent upon conveying.

"Thank you." I fumbled in my pocket. "I do prefer to write things down." I opened to a fresh page and handed the book to her.

"Now, most useful for me to know," I said, mindful of the need to both hold a normal conversation and give her time to write, "are, first, aspects of character. Was she easy to work for, or was she spoiled and selfish? How did she spend her leisure time? Was she in love? Was there anyone who might wish her ill? Who were her closest friends? You may address any of these questions, in any particular order. Whatever you think most important."

"Oh, goodness. All of that?" She began to jot some notes on the page. "She wasn't difficult at all. I know people tend to speak well of the dead, but she truly was a young woman of fine character. Rather serious, although she did love to read novels, both English and French." She considered a moment, then made another note in the book as she continued, "She played piano beautifully, and it was her solace, for sometimes she worried about her mother, who has been ill." She was still writing as she concluded.

Not wanting to let too much silence fall, I asked, "Have you been told how Miss Albert died?"

The pencil paused, and her eyes met mine. "We were told she was found in a small boat on the river."

"That is true," I said. I didn't want to reveal the specifics of her cut skirts, but I added, "Some aspects of the attack suggested it might have stemmed from . . . a thwarted passion."

Her lips parted and her cheeks paled so quickly I thought she might faint. The pencil fell to the carpet, and I retrieved it. She took it back with trembling fingers. Whatever deception Lucy was enacting for the benefit of her employers, her horror was not part of it. "I see," she whispered.

"I'm sorry," I said. "But this is why I wanted to know particularly about her suitors."

The pencil quivered in her hand. "She—well, there were several last year, but none that seemed very serious. The usual sorts."

"The usual sorts?"

"Second sons, looking to trade their titles for a fortune. Dissolute fops who lose money at cards or the racetrack. Young men who flirt thoughtlessly." Her lip curled. "Miss Albert had an eye for spotting them. But I can't imagine any of them doing something like this."

"There was no one she admired in particular?" I drew the man's sketch from my pocket and unfolded it, turning it toward her, so she could see.

She drew in a quick breath and made another note on the page. "Not that I recall. But Lady Edith might know. She's her closest friend."

I refolded the sketch and stowed it back in my pocket. "Lady Edith Harvey. The party was at her house, wasn't it?"

"Yes."

She bent her head and wrote a few more lines. I was becoming desperately curious and had to resist the urge to reach for my book. The more she wrote, the better for me. I still needed to keep up the pretense of conversation.

"Please tell me about last night," I said. "I want to be sure I understand. When did you arrive and leave?"

The pencil continued across the page. "We arrived sometime before three o'clock, and I left at half past six. Miss Rose wanted to be sure I left before dark, as I was walking."

"She wouldn't have the carriage bring you home?"

She looked up in surprise. "Oh, she would have, but I prefer to walk. It's not far, and it was a nice evening."

"It was raining," I reminded her.

"It was only sprinkling, and I had an umbrella. I enjoy the fresh air."

So Lucy snatched at liberty once in a while, like all of us.

"And when you left, Miss Albert was planning to stay the night?"

She nodded. "I said goodbye to her, and she said she would be home tomorrow. Well," she corrected herself, "today."

So the last Lucy saw of her was at half past six.

"Can you think of anything else I should know? Anyone who might have been angry with her? Anything that might help me find out who did this?"

The two vertical creases between her brows deepened. "No. I'm afraid not." But as she spoke, she wrote one last line. "I should return upstairs. There is a great deal to do, in preparation for the funeral."

I stood.

"Good luck, Inspector," she said and handed me the notebook.

I glanced down. She'd filled nearly two pages in her tidy, slanted script.

"Thank you," I said sincerely. "You've been most helpful."

"I hope so." Her eyes were moist with tears, and her voice caught. "Miss Albert didn't deserve it. Not that anyone would, but . . ."

"I understand," I replied. "One more thing. Where can I find the Harveys?"

"Greyson Square, here in Mayfair. Number 4."

★ ★ ★

I waited until I was at a pub, with some shepherd's pie and a cup of strong coffee in front of me, before I opened my notebook and read what she'd written:

Rose neither spoiled nor selfish. Noble character, intelligent and devotedly loyal to friends. Could be outspoken, blunt on occasion. May have offended someone? Unhappy and angry about constant squabbling among family members.

Mrs. A in bed with ailments, some feigned for attention. Iron heiress, money in trust established by her father prior to marriage.

The judge and Mrs. A estranged. Possibly a mistress?

Sons Peter and Hugh at Cambridge. Hugh caught last year cheating on exams.

Ask Lady Edith abt Anthony Thurgood, man in your drawing.

Ask AT abt Sir Percy Dukehart, R didn't like or trust him.

For God's sake. Squabbling, adultery, cheating, distrust, all in one family. More intrigue than in one of Belinda's novels. I reread Lucy's notes twice to be sure I understood them all.

As I closed my pocketbook, I was struck with admiration—for Lucy's powers of observation, her ability to provide the most salient facts, and her skill in managing two trains of thought simultaneously. If she were a man, I might have asked her if she were interested in a career at the Yard.

CHAPTER 6

The next morning when I finished breakfast, it was only half past eight, which usually would be too early to intrude upon the Harvey family. But these weren't ordinary circumstances, and I have been called worse things than rude, so I started out. As I drew near Mayfair, curiosity made me detour past the Beckford house, my steps slowing as I turned off Kinsley Lane and walked beside the iron fence. Like all the other houses on this street, it was quiet, with a few lights behind the sheers. Nothing amiss at all.

Except, of course, that the mistress was in hospital and the husband had no idea.

I continued on my way.

The exterior of the Harvey residence in Mayfair was very much like the Albert and Beckford houses, although Grayson Square had an enclosed park with a manicured lawn and gardens in the middle. But as I stepped inside the Harveys' foyer, I noted differences. The rugs seemed thicker under my feet, the chandelier sparkled more brilliantly, and the gilt frames around the portraits were suitably heavy for male ancestors who appeared weighed down with wisdom and dignity. Belinda might have described it as the difference between old money and new.

I was told the family wasn't finished with breakfast yet, but Lady Edith would see me shortly. I was taken to the parlor, and within minutes a young woman of about twenty entered the room with her aunt, Lady Harvey, a dark-haired woman of thirty-five or so with a sour expression, a set of spectacles on a gold chain, and bony, ringless fingers.

At first, Lady Edith made me think of a good-natured puppy. Rather plump, with toffee-colored hair and large brown eyes that were red and swollen with weeping. A crumpled handkerchief wadded in her hand was as obvious a sign of misery as a property in a play. But the grief in Lady Edith's face seemed sincere. Lady Harvey gestured for me to sit down, and so we all did. I saw them both take note of my wounded face, but they were too well bred to comment.

"I gather that you've heard about Miss Albert," I began.

Lady Edith nodded, and tears welled up. "We heard last night."

"I understand you two were friends."

"She was my dearest friend," she managed chokingly. "She truly was."

"My dear, try to control yourself. Hysterics won't help the inspector." Lady Harvey leaned toward me, and in her eyes—no tears there, I noticed—was the gleam of sly interest veiled by simpering sympathy. "What happened to poor Miss Albert? All we know is it was something dreadful. Was it an accident?"

"I can't say much yet," I explained stiffly. "But, no, it doesn't appear to be an accident."

Lady Harvey sat back, dissatisfied.

Lady Edith's eyes were fearful. "Did he hurt her very badly, before she died?"

That question told me she loved her friend, and I told a lie I've squared with my conscience plenty often: "We don't think so."

A glimmer of relief. "I just can't imagine anyone wanting to hurt her—"

Lady Harvey gave a derisive snort.

At that, Lady Edith whirled. "Aunt Louisa! I know you didn't like her, but she's *gone*, and I don't want you sniffing at everything I say. It's *unkind*. And whatever you think, Rose was my *friend*, and I—I want to talk to the inspector alone."

I looked at her in some surprise. Not such a puppy after all.

Lady Harvey drew herself up. "There can be nothing you would say to the inspector that—"

"But in fact, I would much prefer it," I broke in. "In cases such as these, the more unique accounts I hear, the better. Would it be possible for me to speak with you afterward, Lady Harvey?"

The expression on her face could have curdled milk. But she rose and left the room, closing the door behind her with exaggerated, offended care.

I turned back to Lady Edith, who had risen several notches in my estimation. "I'm sorry about Miss Albert, truly."

She slumped in her chair, as if the spine she'd momentarily shown had deserted her. Her chin trembled. "Oh, Inspector. Have you ever lost a friend? Someone you trusted?"

My breath caught. I might have nodded out of sympathy. But, in fact, I'd been nearly Lady Edith's age when my closest friend, Pat Doyle, died. "Yes, I have."

"It's the strangest thing, isn't it?" Her eyes filled with tears again. "Rose and I told each other everything important. And I keep thinking I'll feel better if I can only tell her what's happened, but after a moment I remember she's not here to tell." In a whisper, she added, "You must think I sound mad."

"Not at all," I assured her. "It takes time to get over the shock."

A grateful nod. "What happened to her? Please, Inspector. What I've been imagining is beyond dreadful."

The softness in those brown eyes warned me. I couldn't tell her everything, but I would tell her something. "She was attacked and put into a small boat, which, as far as we can tell, drifted down the Thames and was caught in the shallows early yesterday."

"They put her into a *boat*? In the middle of the night?" Her expression was horrified. "She must have frozen! Or—or was she already . . ."

Hastily, I steered the conversation away. "We still aren't sure. But she was dressed in a blue brocade gown, with pearls and—"

"Oh, yes," she broke in with an eager look. "That's the dress she wore to our party."

I drew out my pocketbook, relieved that she was amenable to being redirected. Now to begin with a few uncomplicated questions. "Were there many people at your party? Did you have all your friends and acquaintances?"

The tension eased from her face. "Certainly not *all* of them. Perhaps two hundred people, for dancing and dinner. And cards in the smoking room for the gentlemen who preferred not to dance."

"Who did you dance with?"

Her eyes widened. "Is that important?"

"It might be," I said. "Anything you can tell me about that evening might matter."

She thought back. "Well, I danced with Lord Blanford and Mr. Wallis . . . and . . . and James Branden." Her cheeks grew pink with a telltale blush.

"Is he a particular friend of the family?" I asked innocently.

"He's a beau of mine. Rose liked him very much."

"And did Miss Albert dance most of the night?"

"Of course! She's always one of the prettiest in the room." She said this without a note of jealousy.

"Who were her partners?"

She looked disconcerted. "Well—I can't remember all of them—but her dance card might be upstairs."

My heart jumped. Later, I'd ask to see the room where Rose had stayed, but Lady Edith was doing very well here. "That would be helpful, if it could be brought down."

Lady Edith went to the wall beside the fireplace and pulled a velvet cord. A moment later, the maid who appeared was sent to retrieve the dance card.

I asked, "What time did you last see Miss Albert?"

Her answer came hesitantly. "Perhaps just before two. The room was still crowded, but I saw her speaking with Mr. Haverling, by the pillar near the alcove."

I scribbled down the name. "Who is Mr. Haverling? One of her suitors?"

A tiny smile. "No. He's a dear, but he must be at least forty-five. He's her family solicitor, and ours as well."

Ah, the family solicitor. So were he and Rose making pleasant conversation or discussing a legal matter?

The maid returned with the card.

"Thank you, Hester." Lady Edith handed it to me.

Every line was filled. Rose didn't dance with any man more than once, and the name Anthony Thurgood did not appear.

But I would wait to ask Lady Edith about him. "Could you show me where the ball was held?"

"Of course. The decorations are being dismantled, but I can show you the room."

I followed her out into a hallway and through a pair of enormous carved doors. Coming toward us were two men carrying wooden music stands, and I stepped out of their way. The room was at least sixty feet long, with a high ceiling painted with naked pink cherubs and winding vines and whatnot. At the far end, a cluster of chairs stood among some greenery. On the left wall, four sets of French doors led out onto balconies, and halfway down the right was an alcove flanked by marble pillars.

Lady Edith crossed the room and positioned herself with her back against one of them. "Rose was standing here, and Mr. Haverling was facing her."

"Could you tell what they were talking about? Whether it was merely pleasantries, or something more significant?"

"I was dancing and only caught a glimpse of them." Her voice broke. "She looked rather serious, but not upset or angry."

I would definitely be speaking with Mr. Haverling.

"And what time did you come upstairs?" I asked.

"Around four o'clock. Her room was dark, so I let her alone and went to sleep."

"Could you show me her room?"

"Of course." She took a few steps toward the front staircase and then halted, her expression uncertain and apologetic, and I liked her all the better for her transparency.

"Take me up the servants' staircase," I suggested. "I'd like to see it."

Relief flashed across her face, followed by a small grateful smile. "It's quicker, anyway," she said and led me upstairs and then to the second closed door on the hall. "This is where Rose stayed."

"May I?" I turned the handle.

It was a pretty room, with peach papered walls and a high ceiling edged in white trim. The furniture was bare of objects, and the bed stripped, leaving no sign of Rose's presence. I stifled my disappointment.

"The maids cleaned it," Lady Edith said. "But here are her things."

An elegant satchel stood on a chest at the foot of the bed. I unbuckled it and rooted around inside, finding nothing unusual, mostly silken undergarments. I looked up to find Lady Edith flushing a deep crimson.

I closed the satchel. "Where are her clothes from home?"

She opened the armoire. "Here's her day dress." She looked around the room. "The only thing missing is her wrap."

"What sort was it?"

"A cape trimmed with mink. There was no reason for her to wear it downstairs, of course."

"Is it possible someone took it?"

Her eyes widened. "Of course not! Our servants are honest. And besides—well, they wouldn't risk it."

So it was likely Rose had come up here to fetch her wrap, which meant she wasn't taken from the house without warning.

"And her jewelry?" I asked. "Did she wear it, or was it brought over?"

She drew a sharp gasp, her eyes widened, and both hands went to her mouth.

I waited a moment. "Lady Edith?"

"Was she still wearing the necklace?" she whispered.

"We found a silver locket with her initials. Is that what you mean?"

She shook her head vehemently, went to the writing desk, took out a piece of paper, and dipped a pen in an inkwell. She sketched deftly, then turned the paper toward me. "It looked like this. Pearls and small sapphires, here along the chain." She pointed to them with the nib of the pen and then to the pendant the size of a shilling. "And this is a sapphire, with diamonds all the way around."

I shook my head. "She wasn't wearing that when we found her."

She uttered a soft moan as the pen fell from her fingers, releasing a blob of ink, and she groped backward for a chair.

Mystified by her distress, I ventured, "I expect it was valuable."

She drew a breath. "Yes. Not that it matters, but it was mine."

I started. "*Yours?*"

"It went perfectly with her dress." She looked at me pleadingly. "I wore her jewelry sometimes, too."

This complicated everything.

Had the necklace been what the man was truly after—and was it just Rose's bad luck that she was wearing it? Had she been murdered to hide the thief's identity? But then why the cut skirts and the boat?

My heart sank at the thought of the number of people at the party who might have been tempted to steal it from around Miss Albert's slender neck.

"Did you lend anything else? Earrings or a bracelet?"

She shook her head, her forehead screwed up in distress. "It wasn't that sort of necklace. You wore it alone."

"Do you have any idea, exactly, how much it was worth?"

She flushed. "I—I'm not sure. At least several hundred pounds, I expect. My grandfather purchased it years ago."

"And there's no chance Rose left it here in the room?"

"I don't think so. One of the maids would have mentioned finding it. As I said, they're all very trustworthy."

Several hundred pounds trustworthy?

"Do you have a photograph of it?" I asked, hardly daring to hope.

"No, but there's a painting." She led me back downstairs, through the foyer, and across the way into a different parlor. This one was a delicate green, with flowery curtains and the sort of chairs that I'd never dare put my full weight onto. She pointed to the portrait above the fireplace.

"My grandmother," she said.

The necklace was stunning, even in the painting. I compared it with the drawing in my hand. It was a fair copy.

I held up the paper. "May I keep this?"

"Of course." She laid her hand on my arm and begged, "Please don't tell anyone it's gone. It may turn up."

I stared. "Won't your family ask about it?"

She shook her head. "I don't think so. We're all so completely stunned about Rose. Besides, I'm not sure my parents even saw her, once she'd dressed. They may not know she was wearing it."

I tucked the drawing into my pocket as we walked back to the parlor. "I assume you have footmen who might have seen her leave."

"Mr. Dilts and Mr. Greene. I'll send for them."

Within minutes, they appeared, a matched pair, tall with brown hair.

"Did either of you see Miss Albert leave the party?" I asked.

In unison: "No, Inspector."

"And at least one of you was at the front door the entire time?"

They nodded.

Then how the devil did she get out of the house? And when? And what would have lured her away from the party, caused her to come upstairs, fetch her wrap, and dodge out of the house by a back door?

"But she did receive a message, late," Mr. Dilts volunteered uncertainly.

Lady Edith looked surprised. "A message?"

"A carriage pulled up, and I took the envelope." He flushed. "P'rhaps I should have brought it to Lady Harvey. But the man said it was urgent, and he gave me a crown to deliver it to Miss Albert directly."

"Where did you find Miss Albert, to give it to her?" I asked.

"I'd seen her go upstairs not long before." His flush deepened. "Her light was on, so I guessed she was still awake, and I slid the letter under her door."

"And there was no letter found among her things?" I asked. "No envelope?"

Mr. Dilts looked at Lady Edith, who called for the maid Hester, and I asked the question again.

"No, sir. She must 'a took it with her," she replied obligingly.

"Was there a fireplace in her room?"

Hester looked disconcerted. "O' course, sir. But I didn't see even a scrap of paper among the ashes. Honestly, sir. I'd 'a noticed."

"All right."

A message Rose either burned thoroughly or took with her. A message from whom?

Everyone left us then, and I drew out the sketch of Anthony Thurgood, unfolded it, and handed it to Lady Edith. "She had a picture of this man in her locket. Would you say it's a good likeness?"

She gasped and tears welled and rolled unheeded down her cheeks. At last she answered, "Yes. That's Anthony."

"Was he at the party?"

"No." Her chin trembled.

"Were they—sincerely attached?"

She gulped. "They were secretly engaged."

Secretly engaged? That could lead to all sorts of trouble.

Lady Edith pressed her handkerchief to her eyes, then wadded it into her right fist. "Her father doesn't like him. But Rose's birthday is in two months. She was to inherit some money, and they could be married."

"What's your opinion of him? Anthony Thurgood? Is he a good sort?"

"Oh, yes!" she said earnestly. "They've known each other for years. He's a true gentleman."

"Do you think he's heard of her death?" I asked.

"Oh!" Her expression grew horrified. "I—I suppose he hasn't! Her family wouldn't—I wonder if—if I should—"

"I'll be tactful," I broke in. "Where can I find him?"

"He belongs to the Pemberton Club, just off of Pall Mall," she said. "He might be there later. I don't know where he lives."

The Pemberton Club, for young, prosperous, working City men.

"Poor, poor Anthony," she whispered.

"I'll see him as soon as I can," I promised. "Could I speak with your aunt now?"

She pressed the handkerchief to her mouth and hurried out of the room.

★　★　★

Lady Harvey perched on her chair as warily as a squirrel with a nut. "I don't know why you'd bother with me. I'm only an old maiden aunt. No doubt you'll have pried everything useful out of my niece."

God help me.

Into my mind came the thought of Stiles. He'd have charmed her within minutes. I adjusted my expression and did my best.

"Lady Harvey, as I am sure you know, sometimes people can see only a friend's best qualities. It takes someone wiser, someone at a distance, to give an unbiased account of her true character."

The stern lines around her mouth softened.

"I've heard that Miss Albert could be outspoken," I hinted.

She snicked her tongue against the roof of her mouth. "If by outspoken you mean selfish and flirtatious, yes." She pinched at her skirt, adjusting its folds. "That girl tried to ruin my niece's life."

"Ruin her life?" That wasn't Lady Edith's impression. The disparity set off a burning prickle at the back of my neck.

"Yes, ruin." Her dark eyes snapped. "A girl like Edith? She's amiable enough, but she's no beauty."

My, what a loving aunt, I thought.

"Which is why," she continued, "last year, we were all delighted that Sir Percy Dukehart showed such interest. He danced with her at least twice at every ball, paid calls, even remembered her birthday. And then suddenly, one night, Rose resolved to lure him away. She danced and flirted and sat whispering to him in a quiet corner, and Sir Percy never came near Edith again. My niece still has no idea of that woman's disloyalty and defends her at every turn." She clenched her bony hands. "Mind you, Rose didn't care for Sir Percy—oh no! She just couldn't bear the idea that my niece would be engaged first. Little minx."

That certainly didn't correspond to Lucy's report of Rose's character. However, I knew better than to express disbelief. "That *does* sound selfish."

"Yes. It is." Her mouth puckered like a drawstring bag pulled tight. "Of course, Rose ignored him afterward. Now the poor man is going to be snared by that awful Melinda Fenton."

I noted down her name. "When is the last time you saw Miss Albert at the ball?"

She sniffed. "Perhaps midnight. I don't recall. She was nothing to notice, you understand. Plenty were more beautifully dressed."

I closed my pocketbook. "You've been so helpful, Lady Harvey. Most people aren't nearly as observant."

She thawed another degree. "Thank you."

"One last question. Do you know where I might find Mr. Haverling?"

She raised her eyebrows. "Goodness, why do you want to see him?"

Her disdainful tone told me what she thought of the solicitor.

"According to your niece, he spoke with Miss Albert."

"I'll fetch you the address." She returned a moment later with a paper. I thanked her profusely, and she bid me goodbye.

I went straight to Mr. Haverling's chambers, where I learned he arrived at his desk early in the morning but departed by eleven for his appointments. From there, I went to the Dukeharts', but Sir Percy was also unavailable—though it took the butler nearly twenty minutes to ascertain this fact. I left a message that I would return the next morning and that Sir Percy should not depart until

I'd spoken with him. It was too early to seek Mr. Thurgood at his club, and I'd forgotten to ask where he worked. So with these three men unavailable, the easiest plan was to examine the motive as conspicuous as a fish flailing at the end of a line. I patted the pocket with Lady Edith's sketch of the necklace. It was time to visit a jeweler I knew.

CHAPTER 7

Philip Durrell—born Philippe d'Airelle, native of Marseilles—owned a jewelry store on Dowell Street in Hatton Garden. We'd become acquainted when I'd recovered some stolen jewelry for him, and we became friends when Jack "Bones" Brogan, head of a ruthless gang in Seven Dials, wanted to buy a necklace for half its value, and I convinced him otherwise. In exchange, whenever I needed to know anything about jewelry, I came to Philip.

I rang the bell to be admitted. A new young woman opened the door. She wore a ready smile that broke and re-formed uncertainly.

I kept forgetting about the scratches on my face.

"May I help you?" she asked.

"I'm Inspector Corravan from Scotland Yard. Is Mr. Durrell in?"

She took a quick breath in and blinked before answering. "Of course. Won't you sit down?" She gestured toward a gilt chair. It was one of those spindly ones, like at the Harveys', so I remained standing.

A moment later, Philip came toward me with both hands out in welcome. Just under forty, his black hair still dark at the temples, with a waistline that betrayed his love of fine food, he was impeccably dressed down to his polished shoes. *"Michel, mon ami!"* He took notice of my face but only raised one black eyebrow. "Come in, come in."

I followed him through a heavy wooden door, past the workshop where two men bent over tables, their hands occupied with silver tools. Philip's office was meticulously tidy, with a gilt-edged desk, a Turkish carpet, and an enormous cabinet whose drawers were labeled in a code only he understood.

"Some coffee?" he asked.

Through the closed door, I heard the bell ring. Mindful that I was potentially keeping him from a customer, I refused.

"Is something wrong?" he asked, a note of anxiety in his voice.

I hastened to reassure him. "No, no. Nothing to do with you personally—or I assume not." I took Lady Edith's drawing out of my pocket. "Do you recognize this?"

He put on his spectacles, studied the paper for a moment, and looked up in surprise. "It's the Thierry necklace, owned by the Harvey family. Why do you ask?"

I sat back in my chair. "It's gone missing."

He sucked in his breath.

"And what's more," I continued, "the last person to wear it was a woman who was murdered after the Harvey ball on Monday evening. I think it was taken off her body, but I'm not sure if she was murdered for the necklace—or if the necklace was merely a—a—"

"An afterthought?" He blew out his breath in a disbelieving puff and removed his spectacles. "*Non.* There's no possibility whatever this necklace was an afterthought."

"How much is it worth?"

"Something between two thousand and twenty-five hundred pounds."

My mouth went dry. One could build a house for that sum. "Are you sure?"

"Yes. Why?"

"Lady Edith said she thought it was worth several hundred."

"Perhaps so, in the '40s when her grandfather took advantage of some fool who'd lost a fortune in the railway shares and was desperate for ready money." Both eyebrows rose and his chin dropped. "I never told you that."

I nodded my assurance.

"Even then it was underpriced," Philip continued. "Especially given its provenance."

"Why? Who owned it?"

"One of Count Thierry's mistresses, a courtesan and friend of Joséphine de Beauharnais." He went to his bookshelf. "*Attends.* I can show you better than that sketch." He ran his forefinger along the spines and pulled down a thick book. On the cover, the title was stamped in gold: *Couillard, Paris.*

"How do you say that?" I asked.

"Coo-ee-yar," he pronounced. "Pierre Couillard studied with Nitot."

"Who?"

He sat down in his chair, put his spectacles back on, and began turning pages. I watched his hands—small and nimble. Jeweler's hands. From where I sat, I could see page after page of drawings of elaborate necklaces, coronets, earrings, bracelets, and rings. "Marie-Étienne Nitot and his son François began the jewelry firm of Chaumet in 1780. They were the official jewelers to Napoleon. I had one of their daggers in the front case last year." He looked up. "You admired it."

"I remember."

"Pierre Couillard apprenticed with Nitot for a while and then opened his own firm in 1804. His son, and then his son, carried it on. They still have their shop near the Place Vendôme." He paused to study a page.

"Is that the necklace?" I asked, leaning over.

"No. Just one of my favorites." He turned another page. "Ah! Here it is."

On the left page was a block of printed matter, in French. On the right was a colored drawing of the piece. The date was underneath: *1810.*

Now I could see how elaborate it was, and the pendant appeared even larger. "The sapphire is enormous. Is that why it's so expensive?"

"Well, partly. But the workmanship is exquisite." He pointed. "These are sapphires from India. But they're cabochon, a special cut." He made an inverted cup with his hand. "Rounded, rather than faceted. Couillard was known for using cabochon stones in his work. And the diamonds here are set in a technique called 'pavé.' Like cobblestones on a street, fit closely together, *comme ça,*" he interlocked his fingers, "so each adds to another's brilliance. It's extraordinary work."

I pushed the book toward him. "And Lady Edith lent this out like an umbrella."

"Well, according to you, she didn't know its value." He replaced the volume on his shelf.

"What could someone do with a necklace like this?" I asked. "Once he'd taken it?"

"What could someone do?" His eyebrows shot up. "I've no idea. It could never be worn in public. It's far too well known. And it couldn't be sold legitimately. It would be recognized in an instant by any jeweler who could afford to purchase it, and he'd contact the police."

"Assuming he had any ethics," I said.

"Pah! Even without them." He shook his head. "A jeweler would report it, so he could claim the reward."

"Perhaps so," I admitted. "But if a jeweler contacted his local division, I wouldn't necessarily have heard at the Yard."

He rolled his silver jeweler's loupe between his palms. "There are those who help families sell off their jewels discreetly. The thief might inquire of them."

"But if the thief knew he couldn't sell it whole, who'd break it apart for him?"

His eyes flashed. "*Merde!* No one of any reputation! To do such a thing would be like—like cutting a Renaissance painting into strips!"

"But it could be done."

He spread his hands. "*Mais, oui.* Any jeweler could dismantle it and recut the stones, so they'd be unrecognizable."

"Who'd do it?"

He pressed his lips into a thin line.

"Philip, I won't cause them trouble. I'm only looking for the murderer."

His sigh expanded and deflated his entire ribcage. "There is someone who will know if the necklace has appeared. I'll ask."

"Thank you, my friend." I stood up. "Let me know what you hear from your man."

CHAPTER 8

By the time I returned to the Yard, it was nearly four o'clock. Sergeant Cole stopped me on the way in with a letter, and as I recognized Ma Doyle's handwriting, my insides clenched in preparation for a blow. The last time Ma had sent me a message at work, back when I was on the River Police, was the day Pat had been killed. I tore open the note, ripping the paper in my haste, and had to piece the sentences together: "Mickey, could you come see me, soon as you can? Not to worry. We're all grand. Ma."

My sudden, sharp fear dulled, but still, it had to be something important. I usually took Sunday tea with the Doyles at least once a month, and I'd planned to go this week. But whatever Ma needed didn't sound like it could wait. I headed back out and found a cab to Leman Street, where I disembarked and walked east, crossing over into the Chapel. It was easier and shorter to walk to the Doyles' house than to direct a cab down the few navigable streets.

When my real ma vanished, I was not quite twelve. For the first few weeks, while I searched Whitechapel for her, friends looked after me. But soon I realized it wasn't fair to take food out of their mouths when my ma had taught me reading and ciphering, and I was strong for my age. So I took to star-glazing for a man in Chicksand Street. Johnny—the crow—would keep watch while I'd break into a shop, sliding the blade of my knife along a window's edge to form cracks in the shape of a star, and soundlessly removing the pane. Then Danny would take everything worth stealing. What we brought in was usually enough for food in our bellies and a corner to sleep in.

Things went on that way for a while until one day, I came upon three ratbags beating a fourth lad in an alley. I might've walked by, except that they were calling him "dirty Irish." I don't even remember whipping out my knife, but I found myself holding the tallest one from behind, the blade pressed against his throat, and me hissing in his ear, "Let him bloody be, or I'll cut you."

All of them froze. We stood measuring one another, until the one I gripped said a surly, "A' right."

"Now, git on. All of ye," I said. I took my knife from the tall one's throat and shoved him. But maybe because my thoughts were on the bloke in the dirt, I didn't push as hard as I should have. His hand slashed a blade toward my face, and it seared my forehead. But my knife was still at the ready, and I stabbed his shoulder hard enough that he screamed and dropped to the stones. Then the one with the cap was on me, his fist flying toward my head. I ducked and spun, coming round as he pummeled my back with blows heavy and hard enough to halt my breath, but my knife, reaching low, found his thigh.

And they were gone, shouting curses as they went.

Bent over, with my hands on my knees, I gulped for breath. The boy was bleeding from his nose and mouth but more angry than afraid. "Bloody buggers," he spat. As I straightened, he studied my forehead. He was about my age, a few inches shorter but sturdy. "M' name's Pat Doyle, and that's bad," he said, tapping his own head above his eye. "Come on. My ma'll fix us."

As I followed him down narrow alleys, jiggering left and right, he asked where I lived and how I learned to handle a knife like that. When I merely shrugged, he gave a sidelong look out of eyes as Irish blue as my own and let me be. Finally we reached a shop with a set of stairs leading to the living space above. After his ma had seen to our cuts, he asked if I could stay for dinner, and then, later, if I could stay, just for a while. I could tell this troubled Mrs. Doyle.

"Don't worry, mum," I said. "I don't need charity. I'm all right."

She tipped her head. "How old are you?"

"'Round fifteen," I hedged.

"You say you're all right," she said. "Doin' what?"

When I didn't answer, her face fell and she sighed.

"Please, Ma. I'd be dead as Francis, if it warn't for 'im," Pat said soberly.

After a minute, she pulled Pat close, kissed him hard on his forehead, and nodded at me. "Thank you for taking care of my boy. Couldn't'a borne to lose him."

After supper, as the fire died down, we gathered around the bed she shared with the twins, Elsie and Colin, and she related one of the legends of the warrior Cú Chulainn. My mother was Irish, too, but I'd never heard any of the old stories. Over the years, Ma Doyle told us about Lugaid, Abhartach and the banshees, and the fairies and Johnny Freel, and though Pat and I would smile indulgently, pretending the tales were just for the twins, I loved hearing them. Her voice lilted the words into the air, and they hung there for us, sparkling as spinning coins. If I have any ability whatever to tell a story, it comes from her.

Moving in with the Doyles put an end to my star-glazing. Ma Doyle made that clear from the start. But she hadn't flourished in Whitechapel by sitting about, and her children did their part. I was expected to work in the shop, run errands, teach Elsie her sums. I might groan about sweeping the floors and toting heavy bags of tea from the wharf to the storeroom, but I took a secret pride and pleasure in it, too, knowing that I was no burden.

A year or so later, two of Ma Doyle's nephews were finally old enough to help with the shop, so Pat and I went to find work at the docks. We loaded cargo for ten hours at a time until I was promoted to lighterman, moving cargo by small boat. It was hard work, but it changed me into a young man who could sling a hundred pounds from a dock to a deck without thinking about it. And maybe that was a good thing, and maybe not. Because one day, Seamus O'Hagan came down to the docks, saw me carrying one of the burlap bags of tea over my shoulder, and asked if I wanted to make some extra money.

"Doing what?"

"Fightin'." His dark eyes held mine. "You done much?"

"No."

"Willin' to learn?"

By then I worked it out that he was talking about bare-knuckles boxing. It was dead illegal, and when the police raided the places, they put the boys away for weeks in rotten Chapel prisons. With me being Irish, they'd be twice as glad to do it. "How much?"

"Share of the profits. I'll guarantee a quid a week to start." He spat his tobacco to the side. "Bein' new, and with those shoulders, those hands, you'll make more."

Four quid each month?

I didn't even try to hide how much I wanted that money. I knew what it would mean. To Ma Doyle. To me. To all of us. He saw it in my eyes and smiled.

"Why me?" I pointed my chin toward the docks where dozens of other men were working, most of them stronger than I was, though they were older, too.

He handed me a scrap of pasteboard with an address. "Don't say nothin' to no one. Just come tonight at half past eight."

I didn't like the looks of him. His eyes were like a snake's, hard and shining, but I was only seventeen, and his choosing me out of the lot pleased me more than it should have.

The whole rest of the day the pasteboard burned in my pocket. At six o'clock I told myself I wasn't going. I'd fought plenty on the streets, but I didn't know anything about fighting in a ring. And it could be a trap. I could get killed. Knifed. Left for dead, with nobody knowing where I was. And I knew nothing about this man O'Hagan. I'd never heard of him. I wished I could ask around about him. But that would have tipped my hand.

At half past seven, I saw Ma worrying over the sums in her books and decided I'd go. What was the harm? If I didn't like what I saw, I'd leave.

At eight o'clock, I remembered the snaky glint in O'Hagan's eyes and changed my mind again.

But then I watched little Elsie mending her skirt with bits of thread and her single precious needle that she secured every night in a scrap of brown felt, saw Pat run his crust of bread round the edges of his plate to sop up every last drop of gravy, thought about what Ma Doyle had done, taking me in, probably saving my life—and quarter past eight saw me out the door.

Sometimes I still wonder what my life would be if I hadn't.

Bare-knuckles boxing clubs are dark, ugly underground lairs, filled with the smell of rotgut and sweat and more blood than a dirt floor can soak up. But it was intoxicating, entering that room, seeing men eyeing me sideways, and then, as O'Hagan came to greet me, looking me over with what appeared to be approval. The air was charged with men greedy for a fight and for betting.

O'Hagan put me in the ring, and I won three matches out of three that night, against blokes who were smaller than I was. The odds were in their favor, though, because I was new. I won two quid six that night, and I was hooked. Easiest money I ever saw.

I did that for nearly a year.

Until one afternoon, O'Hagan told me he needed me to throw a match. Lose on purpose.

"What the hell? Why?" I demanded. Truth be told, I had lost only one match ever, and I was proud of my record. My fists were fast, I'd never been knocked on my head, and I was large and strong enough to take on almost anybody.

"Odds are no good anymore. You win so much, nobody'll bet against you." He spat tobacco at my feet. "You ain't makin' me money. Gotta do sumpin' to change 't."

I hated the idea. Still, last month the Doyles' roof had leaked so badly that the rain had come through, moldering the rug and falling down into the storeroom, spoiling three barrels of tea. I planned on putting this month's boxing money towards a new roof. By the time I was standing outside the ring, I'd reconciled myself to throwing the match, just this once.

O'Hagan had put me up against a tall, wiry kid named Devlin who looked a lot like I did when I first came. In another year or two, he'd fill out and be a good, dependable fighter. But just watching the way his bare shoulders moved, I knew he was no match for me now. One of the other fighters, Murphy, tapped me before I stepped out and muttered, "Make sure you get in a punch or two so it's not obvious."

Startled, I turned. "What?"

His snort ended in a mocking grin. "You think you were winnin' your first matches by yourself?"

The words hit me like a blow, hollowed me out.

His eyes widened. "Jaysus. You're more fool than I took you for."

The shame of it rolled over me like a tide. Had I won *any* of those early matches on my own? Surely I had! The look of approval on O'Hagan's face when I beat Joe Kelly and Tommy Mackey and Lem Shanahan . . .

Yet perhaps not. As I caught sight of O'Hagan sliding past the bookie, nudging him with an elbow, the cold truth hit me: I was nothing but a beast to be worked, a means to fill their pockets. And for a second, I thought to myself, *It needs to be just business for you too, Mickey. Just do what you're supposed to do. Lose the match, collect your money. Then you can get out for good.*

But when I got into the ring, I was stupid. I try not to judge myself too harshly now; I was young, hot-tempered, and hurting with mortification. Within ten seconds, my intention to throw the match was gone. Devlin swung a good first punch, and I went after him with everything I had. If it had been a day I was tired from working the docks, he might have managed to land a few blows. But that night, Devlin didn't stand a chance. He was on the ground in twenty seconds, back up, then motionless on his back another minute after that.

With the back of my hand, I wiped the corner of my lip, tasted salt and blood, and looked over at O'Hagan. He stood against the wall with his arms across his chest, his expression stony. Turning aside, he spat tobacco out of his mouth.

I knew what I'd done. Still, I'd earned him plenty. I figured he'd give me another chance, like he'd done when I lost to Gahan. I approached him, and under cover of wiping my face as I put my shirt back on, I muttered, "I'll throw the next one."

"Get the hell out."

Suddenly Ma Doyle's face appeared in my mind. I knew exactly how she'd look when I told her my boxing money had evaporated. Disappointed, though she'd try not to let me see. I felt a wave of remorse. "Look, I'll throw it next time, I swear."

"I said, get out." His face was implacable.

Surprised, I blurted, "But—but I need the money—"

"You fecking idjit!" he hissed. "I'm short on earnings this month, and now I'm even shorter."

I blew out my breath and drew myself up. "What about my quid for this week?"

He barked a laugh. "You're lucky I don't beat the shite out of you. Now, for the last time, get out!"

Stunned by how quickly everything had changed, I climbed out of that hole and went home.

When I told Ma Doyle what happened, her jaw slacked with dismay, just as I knew it would. But a moment later, she patted my arm. "We'll manage the money, Mickey. I just don't want him coming after *you*." She sighed. "It's a bloody hard line he took, to toss a boy after one mistake, after all this time. But some folks are made of granite. Ye can't move 'em, no matter what you say."

"I *told* him I'd throw the next one. Hell, I'd throw any match he wants, now that I know everyone does it."

She clicked her tongue against the roof of her mouth. "Well, the O'Hagans have always been rubbish Irish. No loyalty to them."

And as she used to say, loyalty was what separated the potatoes from the rot.

By the next morning, my shock had worn off and been replaced by anger. For days after, I had raging fantasies of revenge, of reporting O'Hagan to the police, of running him up against the granite force of the law. Ma caught me meditating on it, and she asked, "What has you scowlin' so?"

I was on the floor, a chair turned over in front of me, reattaching a wooden leg. "Nothin'."

She put a hand under my chin to make me look up at her.

"O'Hagan. Wish I could hurt him back," I admitted.

Ma looked troubled. "Ach. Mickey, you know better. That's how you'll end up dead." Her expression softened, and she knelt beside me. "I know it hurts, but he's not worth it. He wasn't anythin'—wasn't family, wasn't a friend." She shook her head. "We both know he didn't do right by ye. But I'm glad you're done with it. Something else'll come along. You'll see."

Her words comforted me, and my anger began to subside.

That might have been the end of it, except two days later the police raided the boxing hall, arresting the lot of them, including O'Hagan. They relished catching one Irishman with his hands dirty and a pile of money and books that implicated another dozen. O'Hagan figured I'd been the one to rat him out for revenge, and the afternoon he was put in prison, Ma Doyle found me at the docks and thrust some coins into one hand and a sack with my clothes and some food into the other.

"O'Hagan's passed the word you ratted on him."

"But I didn't!" I protested.

"You swear?" She gazed up at me searchingly.

"I swear! I know you were right. Revenge isn't worth dying for!"

She sighed with relief. "Then, God willin', the truth'll out someday. But you need to go tonight, Mickey. Send word where I can reach you." She gave me a quick embrace, a murmured blessing, and a push toward Leman Street, from whence I found my way down to Lambeth, where my size and strength proved to be assets in the Metropolitan Police, too.

Once in uniform, I was able to ask a few discreet questions. I learned that young Devlin didn't recover from the fight, not right away. His father discovered how he'd been injured, and it was he who'd reported O'Hagan to the police. I sent word into the Chapel, and eventually a message came back from O'Hagan conceding I was probably telling the truth, but he still blamed me for beating Devlin in the first place. That was over a decade ago, and we'd never exchanged a word since. Still, an unspoken deal had emerged. He knew I could've arrested him a dozen times over, but I hadn't. And I'd been in and out of the Chapel dozens of times since then without incident. However, there were those who believed I'd been an Irish rat and would have enjoyed knocking me about. So whenever I crossed Leman Street, I kept my hand near my truncheon.

★   ★   ★

I pushed open the door to the store, where as usual half a dozen customers gathered. Mrs. Wynn caught sight of me, and her face broke into a smile, which I returned, but I didn't want to embark on a conversation. A quick glance around told me Ma wasn't here, but I caught Elsie's eye behind the counter, and she flashed a smile.

"Is Ma in back?" I mouthed, nodding toward the storeroom. She shook her head and pointed at the ceiling. I exited and headed up the stairs, turned my key in the lock, and let myself in.

"Ma?" I called out.

She came out of the bedroom, both her hands out to me. "Why, Mickey. Thanks for coming."

"Is everything all right?"

Her hazel eyes widened. "Oh, aye. Like I wrote, we're all grand."

Her words rolled a hot wave of relief over me.

"But Lord, Mickey, what happened to your face?" She stood and turned my chin toward the window. "You ha'n't been boxing again, have you?"

"Of course not!" I bent over to kiss her cheek. "It's nothing. I'm fine."

She gave an appraising look, as she used to when I'd come home scraped up, but she relented. "All right, then." She held me close for a few seconds past when I'd have released her. I felt a softening inside me and—why not admit it?—a relief at being held by the closest thing I had to a mother on this earth. I gave her one final pat on the shoulder and pulled away to unbutton my coat. I studied her covertly as I hung it on the wooden rack. Her coppery hair was thinning slightly at the temples, and her round face had a few more wrinkles, but she looked well for all that. Whitechapel has a way of breaking people, but Ma Doyle wasn't the sort who broke. She thrived, both because her shop sold candles and sundries at a fair price and because Ma Doyle knew how to offer tea and sympathy without giving offense.

"Can I fetch you a cup o'?" she asked. "It's cold in here. The wind's comin' straight through the glass." As I followed her into the kitchen, she added, "Were you on the river today?"

The question startled me. "I was yesterday. Why?"

"You smell of it. Like when you and Pat used to work at the docks."

I studied her for a moment. She didn't often mention Pat, but his name slipped out as if she'd been prepared to say it. I raised my sleeve to my face and sniffed. "Ach, I do. Sorry." I took out two clean cups and saucers from the shelf as she put the water on to boil.

She peered up at me. "You look tired," she said. "Wraithy."

"I'm all right, Ma." I leaned against the wall. "I'm glad to see you—you know I am—but what's the matter?"

"Let's fix our tea, and then I'll tell ye."

The kettle whistled, and she brewed the tea strong to stand up to the milk. We carried the cups back to the chairs, and after a hot gulp spread warmth into my belly, I settled the cup in the saucer and waited.

Her brow furrowed with something between perplexity and a sort of practicality that I recognized. It meant that she had a problem, she'd worked out a solution, and that solution involved me. "It's my sister's boy. You remember Aileen passed five years back."

I didn't realize it had been that long, but I nodded.

"Well, her husband died last month, and so Harry's come down to live wi' me."

I raised my chin toward the back bedroom. "Is he here?"

"Nae. I sent him out with Colin, so I could talk to ye first." She sighed. "I thought him being here would be fine, but it ain't."

"Why not?"

She shook her head. "He doesn't belong in Whitechapel, Mickey. He wasn't here two days 'afore I knew that."

"Is he too good for it?" My voice had an edge.

"N-a-e." She drew out the syllable as she leaned back in her chair. "He's just . . . well, he's clever, like you, only not clever enough to hide it." She gave a rueful smile, but then the humor vanished from her face, leaving only concern. She held her tea carefully in her lap, with both hands. "I hate to ask it. You already do so much, Mickey. Don't think I don't see you slipping summat to Elsie and Colin when you come."

I closed my eyes briefly and shook my head. "Spare coins, Ma." I sipped at the tea, which was beginning to cool. "What can I do? Talk to Harry? Perhaps give him some advice?"

"Well . . ." She hesitated. "I was hopin' you might keep him with you for a bit."

The tea went down the wrong way, and it took me half a minute to stop coughing. "Ma, I'm hardly ever home. I can't just adopt a boy—"

"He's not a *boy*. Leastwise, he's near to sixteen, though he doesn't look it from sartin angles. Can't you keep him," she tipped her chin in the general direction of the Yard, "find him some copying, or messenger work, till we figure summat else for him?" Her brow furrowed. "He's already been beat twice. You know how it is."

Yes, I knew. Pat and Francis had both died in the Chapel, and they were smart and tough enough to have a fighting chance. I also knew it was more than fair, Ma asking me to keep Harry for a while, after she'd kept me for years. For most people in the Chapel, sleep and food and safety and work were like four aces, held close to take a fat pot in a fast-paced game. But from the first night I entered her house, Ma had made it clear that game wasn't played at her table. She'd dealt all four aces into my palm, the same as she dealt them to Pat and Elsie and Colin, never once making me feel like she regretted taking me in, no matter how many times she had to reuse the leaves for tea.

I managed a smile. "Don't worry, Ma. I'll figure out something." I set aside the cup and saucer and stood to retrieve my coat from the rack.

She stood as well, looking up at me with a face full of affection. "Thank you, Mickey. I wouldn't ask, if I could think of summat else."

"When do you want to send him?"

"Tomorrow, around midday." She hesitated. "Mind you, he ain't much to look at, but he's a good sort, once you talk to him."

"Don't worry, Ma," I said again. I settled a kiss on her cheek and opened the door. "We'll be fine."

★ ★ ★

When I arrived back at the Yard, there was a messenger, just arrived, with a note addressed to me:

Quiet but better. Was expecting you today. James.

I heard the rebuke and let out a groan as I checked the clock. Half past six. How was it so late? And I still needed to find Anthony Thurgood at his club.

In that moment, I made a decision. The case of Madeline Beckford was officially solved; she'd been found. All that remained was to wait for her to talk. No doubt it would be best if I visited her regularly, convinced her to trust me. But with Vincent pressing me on the Albert murder, I had no time. My eyes sought Stiles. He was just the person for such a task. Pretty young maids and old harridans, they all unbent for him. James had met him several times and found him a smart, likable young man.

"Stiles," I said. "Come outside for a minute."

Obligingly, he set aside some papers and took up his coat.

We stepped into the darkening yard. The sounds of wheels and horseshoes came through the arch. It wasn't raining, but the cobblestones were shiny, and light from the sconces seemed to reflect from one to the next.

Pavé, I thought. *Like the diamonds.*

"Is something the matter?" Stiles asked curiously.

Briefly, I explained how I'd found Madeline Beckford and why I'd taken her to the hospital instead of home.

"She isn't talking at all?"

There was an odd note in his voice, and I guessed why. He was loyal, but he was also more conscientious about rules than I was. "Not yet," I said. "I just want to buy her some time."

"I understand."

"Vincent told me to concentrate on the murder of the judge's daughter." I paused. "He suggested I give you some of my unsolved cases. I didn't agree to that."

He let me see his relief.

"But I was hoping you might see Madeline in my stead." I rocked back on my right heel. "I need to see Anthony Thurgood at his club tonight. The man in the locket."

"All right," he said amiably. "I'll see her before I go home."

Grateful for his willingness, I nodded my thanks and added, "I doubt Thurgood knows Rose is dead. They were privately engaged, but he's not on speaking terms with the family."

"Poor bloke." Stiles winced. "I don't envy you breaking the news to him."

I didn't tell him that of the two, I'd rather face a grieving lover than Madeline Beckford. It wasn't because she'd attacked me. That was nothing. There was something about her desperation that edged too close to memories that I'd rather let lie.

CHAPTER 9

From St. James Street, I walked east on Pall Mall toward Trafalgar Square, looking up at the flags of the gentlemen's clubs. The Army and Navy. The Marlborough. The Guards'. The Oxford and Cambridge, for alumni of those esteemed universities. The Athenaeum, with its Doric columns, where James belonged.

The entrance to the Pemberton Club was around the corner on Wincher, and when I climbed the steps, I saw the brass placard below the lamp to the right of the door: "Members Only. Others Please Apply to the Side." Below was a neat arrow pointing to the right.

I went around the corner a second time and rang the bell.

"Inspector Corravan, from Scotland Yard," I said to the man who opened the door. "May I ask your name?"

He frowned. "It's Loomis. What can I do for you?"

"Is Mr. Anthony Thurgood here? It's important business."

"I'll see if he's in." He pointed to a wooden ladder-back chair and headed down the hallway.

I ignored his gesture and followed in his wake. Through the open door, I glimpsed a billiard room with wooden panels, a marble-edged fireplace, and oil paintings hung at regular intervals. A chortling laugh, the click of one ball hitting another, and the smell of cigar smoke wafted out as the door closed behind him.

It was only a few minutes before Loomis reemerged, followed by a young man who resembled the portrait. Mr. Thurgood was perhaps five and twenty years of age, tall and fair, wearing clothes that were proper but not showy. He had a pleasant face, a high brow, and a small scar on his chin. His expression was open and forthright, and he politely stubbed out his cigar in an ashtray before he approached me. What had appeared as smirky in the portrait was in person a modest, close-lipped smile. If he had killed Rose Albert, he was a superb actor, but my guess was he hadn't even heard the news of her death.

"I'm Anthony Thurgood. May I help you?" he asked.

"Inspector Corravan. Is there somewhere we can talk privately?"

His smile faded, and his expression became wary. "Very well," he said shortly. "Come through."

He led me to a room not much bigger than my office at the Yard. It was cold, for the hearth was empty. The wool carpet had worn spots where the threads showed through. Two lamps shed soft light upon an elaborately framed map of Africa on the wall.

He stood facing me. "Loomis said you were Scotland Yard. What do you want?"

"When is the last time you communicated with Miss Rose Albert?"

His eyes flashed. "That is a private matter. Who asked you to—"

"I'm not here on anyone's behalf," I broke in. "And I'm not here to cause trouble for you. But something's happened, and I need to know when and where you last spoke with her."

He sat down in one of the leather chairs, his eyes steady on mine. "I saw her three days ago. We met in the park. Why?"

I sat, too. "Did you send her a message at the Harveys' party two nights ago?"

"Of course not!" His brows lowered into a scowl. "Why do you ask?"

I couldn't put it off any longer. "Mr. Thurgood, Miss Albert was found yesterday morning, in a small boat, on the Thames River. She'd been killed, sometime after two o'clock in the morning, after she left the party at the Harveys' house."

He froze, with his lips parted, and his pupils went wide and dark, a marker that is difficult to feign.

"I'm very sorry," I said.

His chest heaved with quickened breaths. "You're mistaken. She spent the night with Edith."

"I'm afraid not. Her father has identified her."

His eyes suddenly sparked with fury. "Is this his idea of a joke? Because he found out about us?"

I shook my head. "This is no joke."

His chin came up. "Show me your identification."

I drew out my warrant and gave it to him. He studied it, and his whole body slumped. As he dropped his head into his hands, my warrant fell to the floor. "Oh dear God. Oh dear God." When he raised his eyes again, they were brimming with tears, and he suddenly looked very young. "How did she die? Did they hurt her?"

I didn't hesitate. "We believe she was unconscious."

"How?" It came out breathlessly, a dead syllable.

"She was choked."

A rasp came from the back of his throat.

The door opened with a high, dry creak. A short man with a round face, holding a cigar in his right hand, appeared in the doorway. "I say, Tony, is everything all right?" He had a naturally cheerful countenance, but as he looked from Mr. Thurgood to me, his expression became mistrustful. "What's this about?"

"It's Rose, Sam," Mr. Thurgood said. "This man says she's dead."

He looked as stunned as Mr. Thurgood. "My God. What happened? I'd no idea she was even ill." Sam closed the store, snuffed his cigar in an ashtray, and pulled a chair near his friend.

"She wasn't ill. She was killed the night before last," I answered, when it became clear that Mr. Thurgood wasn't going to explain. "I'm from the Yard."

Sam's face was incredulous. "Who'd want to kill her?"

"We're not sure," I said. "She was wearing a very expensive necklace that she'd borrowed from Lady Edith Harvey for the night, and it could have been a theft. But that doesn't explain why someone would take her to the Thames and put her in a boat."

"A *boat*?" Sam stared. "What sort of boat?"

"A small lighter boat. Such as rivermen use to move cargo."

Sam blinked several times rapidly, opened his mouth, and then shut it again.

"Were either of you at the Harveys' party on Monday night, even for a short while?" I asked.

"What? No." Mr. Thurgood shook his head. "Rose and I weren't appearing anywhere in public together. We didn't want anyone to suspect."

"Where were you?" I asked.

"Two nights ago?" He strained to remember. "I—I was here. I think."

"He was here. We were playing cards," Sam supplied.

Mr. Thurgood's expression grew desperate. "Look here, are you *certain* it was her? There could be no mistake?"

I wished I could answer differently. "I'm sorry. They found her locket, with the initials, and your picture inside. That's what helped us identify her."

"Was it silver?" Mr. Thurgood's jaw sagged, and he swallowed hard. "Heart-shaped? With her initials?"

I nodded.

"I gave her that." He dropped his head into his hands again, letting out a low, feral moan. "Did this happen because she promised herself to me?"

"I don't think this had anything to do with you," I replied. "But I have questions I need to ask."

Sam's hand came up and rested on Mr. Thurgood's shoulder.

"Can you think of anyone who would have wanted to hurt her?" I asked.

Mr. Thurgood's head was still down, but he turned it from side to side.

"I'd like you to tell me about Rose—how you met, and what sort of plans you had," I said.

He looked up at that and glanced over at his friend.

Sam rose and gave his friend's shoulder a squeeze. "I'll be in the smoking room." He closed the door quietly behind him.

Mr. Thurgood's eyes were suddenly wet, his lips trembled, and his jaw clenched trying to hold them still. Tears spilled in uneven traces down his cheeks. "This entire past year, we'd been trying to solve our problems—trying to figure out how we could marry, how we would manage, where we would live—my God, those weren't *problems*!"

Yes, death had a way of making every other consideration seem small.

"Mr. Thurgood, I know the last thing you want to do is talk to me. But with every passing hour, the chances of learning who did this wane. I need your help. I didn't know her—and you knew her better than anyone. So I need details."

He looked incredulous. "Details?"

"Yes."

He let out a bark of a laugh. "You mean like she took marmalade on her toast? Or she played the piano like an angel? Or just finished reading *Anna Karenina*?" His voice rose in anger. "What sort of detail can I tell you that will bring her back? You tell me that, and I'll bloody give it to you!" And then his head dropped a third time, and his narrow shoulders shook with sobs. "Oh, God. Just leave me alone!"

The raw pain in his voice put my heart into my throat. This was one of the worst parts about investigating murders, asking people to speak logically when they were still feeling the first violent stabs of grief.

"All right," I said quietly. "Where can I find you tomorrow morning?"

"Twenty-two Snowden." It came out between gasping breaths. "Top floor."

I stood. "Thank you, Mr. Thurgood. I'm very, very sorry."

I told Loomis to fetch Mr. Thurgood's friend for him and left. On the street, the night air drove its chill straight into my bones.

I'd be willing to swear that Mr. Thurgood had nothing to do with Rose's death. I was beginning to believe Philip had been right. Despite the peculiar display the killer had made of Rose, the motive had to be the Thierry necklace.

I was tempted to visit Philip again in the morning, except I'd been told to call upon Mr. Haverling early, and I'd made appointments with Sir Percy and now Anthony Thurgood. Perhaps afterward. And I'd send a note to the River Police to inquire if anything had been discovered once they took the lighter out of the water.

I trudged home and fell into bed, my sleep broken by uneasy dreams.

CHAPTER 10

Twenty years ago, after the portion of the Fleet River running along Farrington Street was covered over to make space for railway tracks, parts of Soho were rebuilt with long streets filled with two-story terraced houses, having shared walls and no pavements, so the doors opened right onto the cobbles. My house in Soho was in the middle of one of those long streets, and though it was small, it was plenty for me, with a kitchen and a fair-sized room with a hearth downstairs and two bedrooms up. Ma Doyle had helped me furnish the place, so it wasn't as spare as I'd have left it. In what she called the parlor, I had three comfortable chairs and some tables, a bookshelf, and two pictures. My kitchen had shelves filled with dishes and the like, and we'd fitted both bedrooms with beds and washstands. I'd even put a stove in my bedroom. Still, my room was cold in the mornings.

Bracing myself, I pushed aside the bedclothes and, shivering, pulled on my trousers and shirt before washing my face. Hastily, I fixed myself coffee, drinking it black and as hot as I could take it before I stepped out into the chill air.

Rather than going to the Yard, I went straight to Mr. Haverling's rooms. The curtains were open behind the diamond-paned windows, revealing several sources of lamplight and the purplish shadows of people moving about.

The door opened as I lifted my hand to the brass knocker, and a young man on his way out directed me upstairs. When I gave my name to the clerk, I was shown immediately to a back office, as if I were expected. Three windows dropped the pale morning light upon a wooden desk, enormous and tidy, and a figure stepped away from a bookshelf to greet me. He was a tall man—as tall as I—but gaunt, and he moved deliberately, with a cane in his right hand to counter a pronounced limp.

"Mr. Corravan, I am Edgar Haverling."

Despite what I'd heard from Lady Edith, he did not strike me as "a dear." He had shrewd, penetrating brown eyes under thick brows, graying hair, and thin lips, as if they were perpetually sealed against betraying a confidence. He remained standing and did not ask me to sit down.

"You're here about Rose," he said.

So I'd missed my chance to see his first reaction.

"You've heard, then," I said.

"Her father sent for me yesterday." A tremor shook his frame, down to the knobby fingers holding his cane.

No, he might not be "a dear," but he had a heart, and quite suddenly, I wanted to gain this man's confidence.

But before I could speak, he said deliberately, "Mr. Corravan, as a solicitor, charged with administering trusts and drafting wills and such, my chief stock in trade is my discretion."

My heart sank. "I understand, but in—"

"As the Albert family's solicitor—in this office—I must adhere to that role." There was an odd tone in his voice, and he reached for his coat. "Therefore, let us go for a walk."

My head snapped back, as if to dodge a surprise left cross out of nowhere. I stared dumbly as he headed for the threshold, then replaced my hat and hurried after him, wondering if I'd understood. Did the very act of leaving his office free him from his usual constraints? Well, that was a peculiar notion, but I would abide by it. As we descended the stair to the street, I realized that like Rose's maid Lucy, Mr. Haverling had anticipated this meeting. No doubt he planned to provide information to a certain limit, which I would press. But for now, I'd see where he led us.

"Lincoln's Inn Fields?" he asked.

"Of course."

With his limp, he walked slowly but seemingly without pain. Or perhaps he was accustomed to an old injury. "Do you have any notion yet as to who killed her?" he asked, his eyes on the pavement in front of his feet.

"Are we speaking in confidence?"

"We are, Mr. Corravan," he replied soberly.

"I'm gratified."

"Your character was verified by someone I trust."

I eyed him for several steps, but that hawkish profile gave away nothing—except that there was no point in asking.

"All right." I would give him a bit of truth and hope for an even exchange, like twenty-one shillings for a pound sterling. "Lady Edith told me you spoke with Rose at the ball."

"Yes."

The wariness of the syllable warned me that the topic of their conversation was too valuable a coin to ask for just yet. Well, I'd lay out a shilling or two. "Do you remember the necklace she was wearing?"

He shot me a sideways glance. "The Thierry necklace."

"When we found her body, it was gone."

That news caused an infinitesimal hitch in his step.

"The judge didn't tell you?" I asked.

"He did not."

"So far as I know, Lady Edith hasn't called attention to having lent it. She is hoping it was—er, misplaced."

He gave me an incredulous look, and I snorted softly in agreement.

"Ahem," he coughed. "And you think Rose was killed for it?"

"I don't know. It's worth several thousand pounds, and any of the two hundred guests could have seen it." I paused. "I'm doing my best to search for it quietly. But—frankly—the murder makes little sense. Why not just demand the necklace—wear a mask to hide his identity—and let her go?"

"Just so! Why create such a spectacle?" His eyes were intent. "The boat as an *ekkyklema*."

"An *ekkyklema*?" I'd never heard the term.

"In Greek tragedy, it's how a murder was revealed. The dead body was rolled onto the stage on a wheeled board. For example, Eurydice in Sophocles's *Antigone*." We paused at a corner, where he deliberately placed the ferrule of his cane into a small divot in the pavement.

"I've been wondering about Miss Albert's possible ties to the river," I said. "Do you know about a case involving the Yellow Star Tea Company?"

We stepped off the curb. "Yes, and the judge reminded me of it. But the owner, Quinn, is a lawful businessman. He paid the modest fine and hired extra guards to prevent further mischief. It was months ago. I can't see its relevance."

I was inclined to agree, and the case dropped down my list of motives.

At the corner of Lincoln's Inn Fields, Haverling pivoted right to take the perimeter. To my mind, it was his turn to lay down a few shillings, and as we passed a branching path, he said, "Rose would have reached her majority in a few weeks, and her aunt Lyvina willed her a birthday gift. Rose wanted to clarify the conditions for receiving it. There is only one, which is that the funds be placed in a trust for her, which her future husband cannot touch."

"Because otherwise, any money she brings to the marriage . . ."

"Becomes the property of her husband, yes," he finished.

"Is the sum worth killing for?"

"Well, it's not insubstantial. The shares and investments are valued at approximately fifteen hundred pounds."

Less than the necklace, but still six times my annual salary.

"If Rose doesn't claim the inheritance, it goes to her younger brother, Peter." He raised a hand. "And before you ask, he—" He paused and considered his words. "He plans to obtain a living with the Church."

I frowned. "That's not an alibi. Trains run frequently from Cambridge. He could get to London and back in an afternoon."

"He's weak-willed. Nervous. Trust me, he doesn't have it in him."

"What about her other brother, Hugh? Did the aunt leave anything to him?"

His lip curled. "He'd never see a farthing. She didn't care for him."

Clearly Mr. Haverling didn't either. "Was that all you talked about? Her inheritance?"

"That was the only topic of substance." He turned off the perimeter toward the middle of the park. It was cool under the trees, and there was a rich, loamy smell. "Mr. Corravan, I'm the last one to tell a man how to proceed. But have you considered that the two crimes—the theft and the attack—might not be related?"

"The two don't fit together easily in my mind either," I acknowledged. "It seems a thief would be as stealthy as possible, and the murderer could hardly have called more attention to himself. But it seems an unlikely coincidence otherwise."

"I suppose so," he said heavily.

We walked on, circumnavigating a garden that would be filled with roses in June but at the moment held only bare sticks and placards with Latin names.

"What can you tell me about Anthony Thurgood?" I asked. I watched him carefully as I added, "I understand they were secretly engaged." His response would indicate how far Rose Albert had taken him into her confidence.

He appeared relieved. "Indeed, they were. Have you spoken with him?"

"Only briefly, last night. When I see him again, I'd like to know if I can trust him."

"Rose could only have loved a man of character," Mr. Haverling said. "He is an architect, you know, for one of the building firms. He loved Rose sincerely. I think whatever he tells you is the truth, so far as he knows it."

"All right."

He paused where two paths met under the trees and gazed up at the branches. "In the course of your investigation, you may discover unpleasant truths about the family."

Here it is, I thought. *The pound sterling.*

"I'd ask you," he murmured, "to be discreet with what you discover. Rose didn't approve of her family's behavior, but she wouldn't want her death to bring it all to light."

"Well, I won't report anything irrelevant, but often the truth will out, as they say."

His expression grew bleak. "Do you believe that? *I* don't. To my mind, the idea of a single truth that will naturally emerge is suitable only for idealists and scholars. For the rest of us, a partial truth is sometimes the best we can achieve."

"Sometimes," I agreed. "But I tend to poke around until I stop finding new facts."

"Yes, I imagine you do," he said dryly and sighed. "Well, if you uncover a rumor that the judge has had a long-standing affair with the actress Marie Dupré, you needn't continue to poke around, as you say. It's true."

"Did Rose know?"

"Yes. But I doubt it's relevant. Marie has been his mistress for years now." He scraped his cane absently across the gravel. "You may also discover that Hugh spends his allowance gambling and carousing, and if it weren't for his grandfather's legacy, he'd be thrown out of Cambridge. And Rose's mother has affairs with her medical men. Three, so far."

"Anything else?" I asked mildly.

His eyes met mine. "Isn't that quite enough?"

There was yet another question, but I took my time in framing it, for it had become clear to me that Mr. Haverling felt affection for Rose, if for no one else in the family. "What sort of person was Miss Albert? Can you think of anyone who'd have wanted to hurt her?"

As he turned to gaze at the church across the way, the bells began to toll the hour. He waited until they'd finished. When at last he spoke, his voice trembled: "She was one of the finest young women I've ever known. Intelligent, candid, loyal to a fault. The world has lost a light, Mr. Corravan." He met my gaze, and I saw his eyes were moist. "I am paid to be her family's solicitor. But I am proud to say I earned the right to call her my friend."

The depth of his feelings left me without words.

"Good day, Mr. Corravan." He nodded farewell, and I watched as he made his way to the margin of the Fields.

I followed slowly, reflecting on all I'd learned.

This conversation had nudged me away from the necklace and back to something closer to home for Rose—especially that phrase "loyal to a fault," so at odds with Lady Harvey's story about Rose's duplicity toward Lady Edith.

Well, perhaps Sir Percy would enlighten me.

CHAPTER 11

I was shown into a room where Sir Percy sat among the stale odors of the previous night's scotch and cigars.

My first thought was that women would find him handsome. Tall and lean, with dark hair, high cheekbones, a well-cut mouth, and a jaded expression in his gray eyes. He reminded me of a painting of a Greek tyrant that Belinda had once shown me in the National Gallery. In my mind, I set his visage beside Lady Edith's sweet round face, but I couldn't make them fit together at all.

We sat in two chairs upholstered in crimson velvet, and he drew out a polished silver case, offered a cigarette to me, which I declined, and lit one. His fingers were long and elegant, like the rest of him, and did not tremble.

I began: "Have you heard the news about Miss Albert?"

His expression was instantly sorrowful. "It's awful, isn't it?" He tapped the cigarette into a green glass ashtray at his elbow. "I'd just seen her the night before. It's the strangest thing to think that's the last time I'll ever see her. She was quite beautiful."

But he said it as if he were praising a museum piece. There was no hint of the thwarted lover here. "You speak as if you admired her."

He puffed on the cigarette before he answered. "Well, I've only met her a few times, but she seemed a good sort. And she could play the piano astonishingly well. No tinkling or crashing through chords."

"So you would say you were friends," I said. This did not match what Lucy Marling had led me to believe, or what Lady Harvey had said.

"Acquaintances, rather. She's a close friend of the Harvey family—and *I'm* a close friend of the Harveys." He waved the cigarette. "So I've seen her a few times at their house, the way people do."

His manner was as decently regretful as you'd expect from someone who was sorry that a woman had died, but he wasn't pretending to be terribly grieved, which is what I'd have expected if he felt guilty. Still, I sensed he wasn't being truthful.

I shifted against the back cushion. "On the night of the party, did you happen to notice what she was wearing?"

His eyebrows arched upward. "What she was wearing? That's really not in my line, I'm afraid."

"So you don't remember her jewelry?"

There was no spark of interest. Only puzzlement. He tapped his cigarette into the tray, and his gaze flicked to the clock reflexively. "No, but you could ask Edith. She'll know."

"Can you think of anyone who might want to hurt Miss Albert?"

"Sorry. Didn't know her well enough for that sort of confidence. Everyone's ready to claim a friend. Admitting that someone is an enemy is much more intimate, don't you think?" He pointed the cigarette at me. "So I'd say Edith is probably the best person to ask about that, too."

"One more thing," I said. "What do you think of Mr. Haverling?"

He barked a genuine laugh. "*Haverling?* You can't think *he* had anything to do with this!"

When I didn't answer, he smirked and stubbed out his cigarette. "I've spoken with him only once or twice in my life. He's deplorably stiff. Humorless. Taciturn. But I suppose that's a good thing in a solicitor."

"And what time did you leave the Harveys' party?"

He smiled serenely. "Couldn't say. I was quite drunk, you see. It's one of my several vices. But I left with my friend Andrew Pascal. He'll vouch for me, as can my butler, Warner." He tipped his head toward the door. "You can ask him on your way out."

I took the hint, bid him goodbye, and found Warner waiting for me. He confirmed that he'd waited up for Sir Percy on Monday night—he didn't look particularly happy about it—and it had been after three o'clock when he'd seen Sir Percy to bed.

I kept my voice low. "How was Sir Percy when he arrived home?"

Warner's lips pressed closed in disapproval.

"Soused?" I asked.

A wordless nod.

"Standing?"

He sighed. "Barely."

Then he bid me good morning.

I had a feeling there was something to Lady Harvey's story about Rose and Sir Percy, but it seemed unlikely it had been Sir Percy's hands around Rose's neck. Still, I would follow Lucy's direction and ask Mr. Thurgood about him.

★ ★ ★

Twenty-two Snowden was one in a row of a dozen old houses in the process of being renovated into flats. The square foyer was crowded with coatracks, umbrella stands, and tables littered with newspapers and packages. I climbed the three flights up and knocked.

The door opened, and Mr. Thurgood stood before me in the shirt and trousers he'd worn the previous night. He looked exhausted, and his eyes were red-rimmed. But he nodded civilly and led me to a sitting room that faced the street.

He gave me my choice of two leather chairs, and after I sat, he took the other. "I'm sorry I was rude."

"It was terrible news."

He nodded, mutely. Through the window came the sounds of carriages, horses, hammering, and workmen's shouts.

He rubbed the heels of his hands into his eyes. "I need a drink. Will you have one?"

I hadn't taken spirits in months, but the question still tugged at me both ways, made me want a drink and made me cringe, remembering where even one could lead. "Not for me."

He poured himself one finger of scotch from a decanter on the sideboard and came back to me. His hands were shaking as he took a sip.

I could smell notes of wood smoke. Good scotch. I swallowed down the spittle that came to my mouth.

"Tell me about Rose. When did you first meet?" I asked.

He rolled the glass between his palms. "Two years ago, at Lord Lewis's party. To raise money for one of his wife's charities."

"At his house?"

"Yes. I danced with Rose twice, and then she asked me to take her out onto the balcony, so she wouldn't have to dance with Lord Wallace." He gave a brief, pained smile. "She had a way of doing that."

Of ducking a commitment? I wondered. "Of doing what, precisely?"

"Of not suffering fools. Lord Wallace is a drunken boor whose hands go where they shouldn't." He set down his glass. "But she'd inconvenience herself in all sorts of ways for the people she loved." His voice dropped. "Even if they didn't deserve it."

"I've heard about her family—the actress and the doctors and the gambling."

He nodded bleakly.

"Tell me more about you and Rose. When would you meet?"

He blew out a sigh. "Oh, I'd escort her home after her piano lesson. I'd see her at parties. I'd call at her house."

"But I thought you kept your attachment secret."

"Not at first." He took up the glass and swallowed the remainder. "I was just one of a half dozen blokes. But at some point, her father *did* notice and told Rose he'd never give his consent."

"What did he have against you?"

He waved his glass in a semicircle toward the room. "This. I'm decidedly middle class."

"It's not as though the judge has a title," I said.

"Precisely. Which is why he wanted one for his daughter."

"Ah."

"In a few weeks, she'd inherit some money from an aunt," he continued. "With what I make at Barry and Banks, it's enough for us to marry, and then she would come to live with me."

His expression changed as if he was retreating into memory, and I wasn't ready to lose him yet. "Lady Edith said she and Rose were in the habit of wearing each other's jewelry. Is that true?"

His right shoulder rose and fell. "I suppose. Rose lent her some jeweled combs once. Why?"

Instead of answering, I asked the question I'd saved for last: "And what can you tell me about Sir Percy Dukehart?"

It was as if the air in the room had suddenly thickened. He stood and poured himself another scotch, keeping his back to me. "Why do you ask?"

"I heard that Rose didn't trust him. But I also heard that Rose and he were briefly flirtatious."

He gave a snort and went to the window.

"Mr. Thurgood." I rose and stood at his elbow. "Did any affection ever exist between Sir Percy and Rose?"

"No." His answer was decisive.

"Did Rose know something about him that left him open to blackmail?"

He tensed, and I knew I'd guessed correctly. His fingers were white around the glass.

"Mr. Thurgood."

"She told me in confidence," he muttered. "I'm not breaking it."

I scuffed one heel against the floor. "I've seen men kill for far less than social and financial ruin. Do you know Sir Percy well enough to swear that he wouldn't hurt Rose, or pay someone else to do it?" He turned to me, his expression full of horror, and I pressed my advantage. "Does Sir Percy have a mistress? A gambling habit? What is it? I'm not leaving until you tell me."

"You're rather a bully, aren't you?" he snapped.

I squirmed inwardly but remained silent.

He spun back to the window. "He prefers men."

In Sir Percy's circles, it would be fodder for relentless gossip, though it mattered little to me. "How did Rose know?"

"She was in a maze at a garden party last year, and she came upon him—with someone." He drained the glass and glowered at me. "There. I've betrayed her. Are you satisfied?"

I let that go. "Did Sir Percy know she knew?"

"That is why he stopped courting Edith." My mystification must have been evident, for he sighed and continued. "Edith has a dowry of ten thousand pounds per annum. But Percy would've made her life a misery. So Rose promised Percy she wouldn't tell anyone what she knew, so long as he stopped pursuing Edith, which he did. Afterward people said Rose had stolen Edith's beau." He dropped his glass onto the wooden sill with a muted clank. "It was wretched, all the gossip. But Rose couldn't clear her own name without humiliating Edith, and she knew the fuss would die down eventually."

So Rose had borne social ridicule for her friend's sake. "Does Edith know all this?" I asked.

He hesitated. "I'm not sure Edith was told the particulars about Percy's predilections. But she knows Rose was trying to protect her."

"And Sir Percy is pursuing Melinda Fenton now."

"Her father owns copper mines. Poor girl." He said it without irony.

"Would Sir Percy kill Rose to keep her from telling Miss Fenton?"

He shook his head. "Word is he pursues these women to pacify his mother. He has no intention of catching any of them. Why would he?"

Perhaps because he needs the money, I thought. *Or the veneer of respectability, if rumors about him—and his friend Andrew?—are circulating.*

I plucked my hat from the table. "I'll find whoever did this."

He didn't reply.

As I reached the door, I heard his voice behind me.

"I'd trade," he said hoarsely. I turned and saw his eyes, full of agony. "I'd undergo *anything* she did, to keep her alive. I *loved* her."

Into my mind came the image of Belinda instead of Rose in that boat, and something clogged my throat and kept me from replying.

He turned back to the window, and I shut the door behind me. The carpet on the stairs muted my footsteps. From the flat on the lower floor came the clink of metal pots, the murmur of voices, a laugh.

I took a deep breath as I reached the street.

My suspect list was growing: the hundreds of party guests who saw the necklace; Sir Percy, with a wealthy marriage to lose; Rose's brother Peter; and, though unlikely, the judge because Rose knew about his mistress. Years ago, I might have discounted the possibility that a father would kill his own daughter to protect himself, but I'd seen it before. Never mind that the father had been the one to report her missing and seemed shocked at her death.

I'd seen that before, too.

CHAPTER 12

It was after four o'clock when I finally returned to the Yard.

Sergeant Cole beckoned me toward the front desk. "Inspector, you have a visitor. Been here since eleven. Says you were expecting him." He raised an eyebrow. "Name's Harry."

Ma's nephew. I'd completely forgotten.

Damn everything.

"Where?" I asked.

Cole pointed toward the side hallway. I rounded the corner and saw the boy sitting on the bench, his head tipped back against the wall, his eyes closed.

Ma was right. He wasn't much to look at. Lanky, with dark hair that fell unevenly across his forehead, a pale face with a pointy chin, and slender hands that lay listlessly on the hat in his lap. His woolen coat had been good when it was new, and his boots were scuffed but stout. As I drew close, I saw he had dark lashes that would have been pretty on a girl. His left cheek bore remnants of bruises, and I remembered Ma saying he'd been beaten twice.

I took care to scrape my heels as I approached, so I wouldn't startle him, and he opened his eyes. They were brown, and after he took me in, they narrowed in annoyance.

"Harry Lish?" I asked.

A sullen look. "I suppose you're Mr. Corravan."

His voice was at that awkward stage, breaking high then low. But I understood immediately what Ma had meant about him not belonging in Whitechapel. His enunciation betrayed public schooling, and his manner was what Belinda would call refined.

I nodded. "Come with me, lad. Sorry to keep you waiting."

He stood up stiffly, and I wondered if he had injuries other than the ones on his face, or if he was just sore from sitting on that bench all day.

We entered my office, and he looked about. Suddenly I was aware of what it must look like to a stranger. Stacks of papers, two plain chairs in front of a scratched desk, a window too filthy to let in much light. The look on his face was more curious than disdainful—but still, I didn't care for the scrutiny.

"Sit," I said, gesturing toward the empty chair.

He sat down on the edge, his hat again in his lap. His gaze was steady, not challenging exactly, but not lacking in confidence either. He didn't look like someone who would put up with being beaten if he could help it.

"Tell me about yourself," I said.

His narrow shoulders rose and fell. "I imagine you know the salient facts. My mother died five years ago, and my father five weeks ago. I've come from Leeds to live with my aunt, but she doesn't want me."

"It's not that she doesn't *want* you," I retorted. "Ma Doyle is as generous as they come. She just thinks you don't belong in Whitechapel. And my guess is she's right about that."

At my sharp tone, his prickliness wilted, and he looked down at his hands. "I suppose," he said wearily. "But I haven't anywhere else to go."

"She thinks you might do well here," I said.

He looked up at me. "Do you have people other than police working here? I only saw one boy the whole time I was waiting."

"A few, yes. Messengers, mostly."

"Oh."

"Do you have any idea what sort of work you'd like?" I leaned back. "I don't suppose you want to be an inspector."

"No, I want to be a doctor. I want to help people."

I tried to pretend that didn't rankle. I liked to think I *did* help people. But the news of the Yard scandal had no doubt made the front page of the Leeds papers, too. "All right, then," I said. "What can you do?"

"Well, the usual, I suppose. Writing and ciphering. And I took a prize last year for reading the *Aeneid*." When I didn't reply, he added condescendingly: "It's a poem by Virgil. In Latin."

My annoyance flared. "There's no cause for that. I'm trying to help you."

His cheeks colored, and he looked away.

And then came a loud feminine shriek from the main room, followed by a string of what sounded like French, broken by sobs.

"Where's Landau?" Sergeant Cole's voice boomed over the woman's cries.

"Not here," replied Mansel, the clerk. "She'll just have to wait 'til he's back."

"What's wrong with her?" Harry asked.

"I don't know. I don't speak French," I replied.

Harry's pointy chin tilted. "I do."

I was already rising from my chair. "Would you talk to her?"

He followed me to the woman, who was about five-and-twenty, with dark hair, and a look of terror on her face. Her eyes darted between Harry and me as we approached.

"*Pardon, madame. Je parle français,*" the boy began.

With an expression of immense relief, she broke into yet another torrent of breathless French. It sounded like nothing on earth to me, but as Sergeant Cole, Mansel, and I watched, the boy listened, nodded, and patted her hand, which clutched his like a lifeline.

Finally, as she wound down, he turned to me. "She and her husband were at Piccadilly train station when two men approached them. One had a knife that he poked at her husband's side, like this," he demonstrated, "and the other held her by the arm and dragged her away, saying that if she screamed, her husband would be killed. So she went silently. Then he put her into a railway carriage—one of the second-class carriages—and waited until it pulled away. She got off at the next stop and asked a hansom cab to bring her to the police."

"In French?"

"*La police* is the same," he said simply.

"Ask her about the two men. What did they look like? English or French? Did she recognize either? And what's her name?"

Harry issued a series of questions, after which she spoke at length, gesturing all the while, though her hands trembled.

He relayed her answers. "Her name is Madame Thérèse Bonavelle, and her husband's name is Édouard. They just arrived from France three days ago and are spending time with friends here. She didn't recognize either man, but one spoke to them immediately in French, so they must have guessed she and her husband were from France. From their accent, she's sure they're not English. They were both shorter than you, with dark hair and plain clothes, perhaps thirty years old. One had a mustache and beard, and the other only a mustache, but he had a red mark here," he pointed to his right cheek, "and wore a cap pulled down."

I nodded approvingly at her and turned to the sergeant. "Can you give Harry materials to write all that down? I'll send someone to Piccadilly right now to see if anyone saw anything or remembers the two men who took a third man with them." I paused as the sergeant handed some paper and a pencil to Harry. "Could she give us a description of her husband?"

He turned back to the woman and spoke briefly. In response, she pulled out a locket and opened it. *Thank God for lockets*, I thought. She gave it to Harry, who handed it to me. Inside were a brown curl and a miniature. This was more than we usually had to go on when looking for missing persons.

As Inspector Leigh headed off to Piccadilly with the locket, the woman sat back against the wall to wait, and I steered Harry back into the hallway where I'd first found him. "Why didn't you mention you could speak French?"

He met my gaze. "You didn't ask."

I rolled my eyes. "Sometimes it is the responsibility of the person being questioned to volunteer helpful information."

He looked abashed. "Honestly, I didn't think it would matter." I waited for more. "Oh—and I know how to ride and care for horses. I learned that on a farm in Leeds."

"You're a horseman?"

"Not really. But I like treating them. The veterinary let me assist when he had to stitch a mare once." He paused. "I helped when she foaled."

Then I remembered he wanted to be a doctor. He knew Latin. Was a tad pretentious.

A bell tinkled in my brain.

James Everett might get on with this boy very well. Not to mention I'd planned to stop at the hospital anyway.

"Well, then," I said. "Where are your things?"

"Just here." He gestured toward a valise under the bench.

That was all he owned?

Pity for the boy pinched at me. I remembered what it was like to carry so little, to wish I had more than a single case tethering me to the world. But instinctively I knew he'd feel humiliated by my sympathy. So I said only, "Let's find some supper, and then there's someone I want you to meet."

CHAPTER 13

At a pub, over some pie, I told Harry we'd be stopping at St. Anne's Hospital on the way home.

He frowned suspiciously. "Why?"

"For two reasons. One of them is that my friend James Everett runs a ward there. He's a doctor who reads Latin, and I think you two might get on."

"So you'll push me off on him, then?" he asked.

I swallowed the pie in my mouth. "If you want to put it so. But you'll need to do something during the day, and you'd like that better than being a messenger boy at the Yard, wouldn't you?"

That won a small nod.

"If you hate it—well, we'll find something else."

Our pies eaten, I set a few coins beside my plate, and we started for the hospital.

"You said there were two reasons," Harry said, trotting to keep up with me.

"What? Oh—there's a patient I want to see."

I walked faster, partly to keep him from asking any more questions, and within a few minutes, we reached the gate. I rang the bell, and Owen appeared. "Ah, Inspector Corravan!"

"Hello, Owen. This is Harry Lish."

"Evening," Owen said pleasantly.

"Is Dr. Everett still here?" I asked.

"On the ward probably, but he should be done soon."

We found James in his office. He was making notes for a patient's file and asked us to wait. Harry inched toward the leather-bound books on the shelves and scrutinized the anatomical model of the heart until his eye was caught by a framed diagrammatic sketch of a head on the wall. He walked toward it as if mesmerized.

At last James laid aside his pen. "Hello, Corravan. Stiles is here, so I wasn't expecting to see you." He gazed at Harry, who stood raptly before the illustration. "And who is this?"

"Harry Lish," I said. "Ma Doyle's nephew."

Harry didn't even turn.

"Ah," James said. "How is Mary? The last I saw her was at Christmas."

"She's fine. Wondered if I might find some useful employment for him, but there's nothing at the Yard. However, he can write and cipher and knows Latin and French. Wants to be a doctor."

"Hm." James rose and crossed the room to stand beside Harry. "What do you think of it? A friend and I composed it together."

Harry looked uncertain, but James smiled encouragingly.

"Well," Harry said. "It's *much* better than the ones I've seen in books. You've not only all the bones and muscles but the nerves, too, and the cavities, all together—and labeled so clearly."

He couldn't have said anything that would please James more. The charm of it was, Harry was sincere.

"Would you like to see the hospital?" James asked. "Corravan was exactly right to bring you here. I can always use an observant young man, if you've any interest in patients."

Harry's eyes widened. "Yes, sir."

"Follow me," James said. "One of my students will show you about."

Harry shoved his valise behind a chair and departed with James, who returned a few moments later with a bemused look. "When did this happen?"

"Ma sent for me yesterday. His mother's dead, his father died recently, and Ma's his closest relation, or at least the only one who'd take him. But Whitechapel doesn't suit him."

"No, it wouldn't," James said decidedly and sat back down behind his desk. "So you are to play nursemaid."

"Hardly." I took my usual chair. "He's sort of a prig, and prickly. Thought you two would get on." I gave a sly grin.

"He's a clever lad, and you shouldn't hold his book learning against him," James retorted.

I leaned back into the cushion, which rustled behind me. "Can you truly find something for him to do here?"

"Of course. I can have him write up patient notes and assist the students." He lifted his hands from the arms of the chair, resettled them. "Speaking of cases, I imagine you want to hear about Mrs. Beckford."

I stifled a yawn. "Yes—although I'm not sure how much time I can devote to her. That's why I sent Stiles. Vincent has assigned me a peculiar case of murder."

"What do you mean by peculiar?" he asked. Murderers were the topic of an entire chapter in the book he was writing about disorganizations of the brain.

I gave him a quick summary, and as I concluded, he let out a low whistle, removed his spectacles, and polished them with his white handkerchief. "Rather like poor Aslaug."

"Who?"

"She was the Viking wife of Ragnar, a legendary Danish king," he said. "The Norsemen often placed their royal or wealthy dead in boats, along with their valuables." He replaced his spectacles and peered over them. "You *should* remember. Belinda took you to see *The Tragedy of Aslaug and Ragnar* last year at the Criterion, in one of her bootless attempts to civilize you. I suppose you slept through it."

I snorted. "Never mind that. Tell me about Mrs. Beckford."

James's eyes gleamed. It was clear that Madeline had become more interesting since her arrival.

"Well, I still believe her mind is disordered, but not in the usual way, or for the usual reasons." He leaned forward. "Did Mr. Beckford ever mention his wife speaking French?"

"Not that I remember."

"Nothing about a French governess, or time spent in France?"

"No."

He wore his triumphant three-corner smile. "She hasn't spoken a word during her waking hours. But she's done something I've never seen before. The first night, she uttered noises in her sleep. The nurses always transcribe any spoken words, but the nurse couldn't decipher more than garbled noises." He reached for a desk drawer and pulled it open. "However, while Mrs. Beckford napped today, a different nurse realized she was speaking—in *French*."

This was an unexpected development. "Did you ask her where she learned it?"

His eyes widened in alarm. "Of course not! Introducing the workings of her sleeping mind to her woken self could muddle everything! Not to mention the poor woman will feel she can't go to sleep for fear she'll reveal something she doesn't intend."

"Well, what did she say?"

"Nurse Aimes isn't fluent, but she picked up a few bits. I'll read it."

He consulted the paper he'd taken from the drawer. "I wish she'd made a record of the original French, but instead, she translated it as well as she could."

"It's better than nothing."

"Quite." He adjusted his spectacles. "Here it is: 'I'm sorry, I'm sorry, I saw.'" He glanced up. "The last word was unclear." I nodded, and his eyes dropped back to the paper. "The other three words she could make out were 'kitchen,' 'knife,' and the name 'Pierre.' And then Mrs. Beckford woke screaming, and the nurse administered a sedative to calm her."

"So now we must learn who Pierre is," I said softly. "And why she's sorry and what the devil she saw."

"Well, that's *your* task. *I've* discovered that she speaks French. Surely that's worth something."

I admitted it was.

He folded up the paper and slid it back into the drawer. "And Harry speaks French?"

"Fluently, yes."

"Perhaps, eventually, I might borrow him for a few nights."

Apparently, James had decided that Mrs. Beckford would be staying.

I concealed my relief. "So long as Harry's willing," I agreed.

There was a knock at the door.

"Come in," James called.

Stiles appeared, and his eyes widened as he saw me. "Oh, hullo! I didn't know you were here."

"I'm just waiting for Harry," I said.

"I saw him with the young doctor," Stiles said with a grin. "They're visiting all the patients on the men's ward, with Harry asking plenty of questions."

"I'll bring him to your place tonight, after he's finished here," James said. "No reason to hurry him."

"I was planning to stop at Belinda's," I said.

"Well, I *could* take him home with me," James said dubiously.

"No, I'll see him at home." I didn't want to miss my Thursday evening with Belinda, but I didn't want Harry to feel unwanted either. I shrugged into my coat and nodded farewell as Stiles held the door open for us.

I waited until we reached the street to ask how Mrs. Beckford was.

"I didn't see her when she first came, so I can't rightly compare, but they say she's better. She's eating and sleeping now." Stiles drew on a pair of gloves. "She's skittish as a colt, though."

It was growing dark, and the wind was beginning to howl around the corners. I pulled my hat lower on my head and balled my hands inside my pockets.

"Inspector, I'm sorry if I seemed reluctant to visit Mrs. Beckford."

I concealed my surprise. He'd seemed willing, to me.

"I had a—a reason." He looked embarrassed. Then his face became resolute. "When you told me about Mrs. Beckford not speaking—well, it reminded me of my sister Cathy."

My steps slowed. "I didn't know you had a sister."

He looked uncomfortable. "Three of them, actually. Beg pardon."

"Not at all."

"She's married now, with a son." He cleared his throat. "But when she was thirteen, her best mate Lily slipped in the street, and a cart full of hay backed over her, killing her. Cathy saw the whole thing."

The horrifying image leaped into my mind; I could tell by Stiles's bleak face it was in his, too. "Cathy didn't say a word for two weeks, would scarcely eat or drink." His eyes were sober. "She'd wake in the night, screaming and thrashing about. We'd all take turns keeping watch and holding her. After a while, it seemed to pass. But she still jumped at every little sound. That's what Mrs. Beckford's like." We began to walk again. "Dr. Everett said it would be best if she could see me every day. Then she'll talk to me when she's ready."

"Every day?" I repeated, chagrined. "But you have plenty—"

"I don't mind!" he broke in. "If there'd been anybody who knew how to help Cathy, I'd have wanted him to."

I shook my head. "You're a good man, Stiles."

He flushed. "And I—well, I want to meet Mr. Beckford."

We'd reached the corner where we'd go opposite ways, so we halted.

"What reason could we give?" I asked. "He's not going to like his case getting handed off."

He had his answer ready: "We can tell him I found a railway porter who saw her on a train leaving London, and I'll try to pick up her trail."

I frowned. "But Stiles, the case is solved. It's bad enough *I'm* keeping it from Vincent. If he found out that you're taking time off your other cases to—"

"He *won't*. Besides, the case isn't really solved. Not until we know what made her run in the first place." His expression was earnest. "Perhaps someone will tell me something they forgot to mention to you." He grinned. "Or I could make friends with one of the maids. You always say they know things."

"That's true," I allowed. "And it might be a good way for you to meet a nice girl."

He looked alarmed. "I wouldn't—I mean, I'm not looking to—" And then he saw I was chaffing him.

"We can go tomorrow morning," I said. "I'll tell him I'm still searching hospitals and asylums. We'll say you're an expert on trains. Study your *Bradshaw's* tonight. The towns on each line, the timetables. Make sure your story's convincing."

He looked startled for a moment, then took a long breath in. "I'll do that."

We bid each other good night, and while I waited to cross the busy street, I watched him walk north with his easy rolling gait. I thought about his entire family taking turns to keep vigil over his sister, and it struck me, not for the first time, that Stiles and I had very different pasts. Perhaps that's why he was less wary and watchful than I was. Quicker to laugh. I could already imagine him talking to a maid at the Beckfords' house, making her smile, gaining her confidence. He had a way of listening to a witness so attentively, he wouldn't see a freight train roaring through the room.

While I tended to let my eyes flick around to every moving thing, just in case.

Chapter 14

I made my way to Belinda's house in Belgravia.

Other men might have called her my mistress. But I didn't think of her that way, primarily because neither of us was, or had ever been, married—and Belinda didn't want to be. Besides, far from being a kept woman, she could have kept *me*. Born Belinda Gale, daughter of a wealthy gentleman, she wrote novels and plays and had made more money in seven years than I would ever make as an inspector. Several nights a week, she entertained at home. Writers and artists, scientists and musicians all attended her soirees. But Thursday evening was always ours. And I needed to see her tonight. Badly. It had only been two days since Rose's body was found, but it seemed much longer, and Belinda had a way of reassuring me that behind every crime was a true story, as discoverable and logical as the one that led to the burglary at her home nearly three years ago, when we met.

I had arrived that night to find the wood-paneled library upended. The only object still in place was an enormous desk, inlaid with brown leather, which took up the middle of the room. The window facing the street had large panes—one of which was broken, which is why the curtains billowed and rippled in the breeze. The electrified chandelier overhead swung gently, flinging light around the room. The wall of bookshelves had been emptied, the contents thrown on the floor. Papers, newspapers, writing instruments, and inkwells were everywhere. The intruder had been desperately looking for something—or intent on wanton destruction.

Standing amid the chaos, I wondered what the man of the house did for work, when I heard behind me: "Obviously, someone entered through the window."

It was a woman's voice, low and musical. I turned to find the source, and from a Queen Anne–style chair in the corner rose a woman of about my age, tall and slender, with pale skin and expressive, watchful eyes. Her hair was dark brown and pulled into a net at the back of her head, to keep it out of the way. She was dressed in a gray silk dress, and she looked much like any well-to-do wife of a barrister, or a businessman, or a banker.

She came toward me through the wavering light. "My name is Mrs. Gale."

I surveyed the room. "And this is your husband's library? Is he at home?"

"It is *my* library," she corrected me. "And my husband is not at home because I do not have one."

I am accustomed to people correcting me, with either annoyance or disdain, which I resent, though I try not to show it. But her voice held a note of wry humor, and my only feeling was a peculiar elation that she was unmarried—which was ridiculously presumptuous. Nevertheless, to my mind came the image of her dressed in much less, with her dark hair down around her shoulders. Heat rose to my cheeks, which she misinterpreted. A shallow dimple appeared. "Don't be embarrassed, Inspector. It's not the first time someone has overestimated my husband."

"Underestimated you, you mean."

A smile tucked the corners of her mouth, and a few wrinkles appeared at the sides of her beautiful hazel eyes. And for several seconds, I found myself uncharacteristically tongue-tied and unable to present a coherent thought.

Fortunately, her case was easily solved. It took only a fortnight to discover the culprit, the leader of a fervent religious group that objected to the presence of the firebrand Annie Besant at Belinda's evening gatherings, after which I had no reason to see her ever again. Except that by the end of those two weeks, I was falling desperately in love with her. She took my attentions lightly for months, until the day I asked her if she would engage herself to me. That was when she explained her qualms about marrying: her beautiful, brilliant mother went mad three years after marriage, and Belinda and her father lived in a state of perpetual worry and heartbreak for twelve years until the poor woman hanged herself. As a result, before he died, Belinda's father had cautioned her repeatedly against taking the irrevocable step of marriage—eliciting a vow from his deathbed that she would allocate at least several years to ascertain the stability of a man's character and always keep her trust fund in her own name. Belinda made me swear we would be discreet, and our companionship had unfolded, slowly, until now, when she kept her Thursday nights for me, and I kept my promise to her, having revealed our attachment to James, with her permission, and to no one else.

By the light coming from a gas lamp, I used my key to let myself in the back entrance. I'd barely closed the door behind me when she was in my arms, whispering my name.

★　★　★

We had dined by the fire, and now I sat on the divan, a cup of coffee warm in my hands. Though Belinda had drawn the heavy patterned drapes, I could hear rain slapping at the windows.

"Is the coffee hot enough?"

I turned to see Belinda standing there like a ghost, in that white lace peignoir she wore to bed, when she wore anything. With a start, I realized she'd styled her dark hair in a way that looked a good deal like Rose's.

"What's the matter?" she asked. "You have a peculiar look on your face."

I didn't answer, and she held out a hand. "It's getting cold, even with the fire. Come back to bed, Michael."

She's the only one who calls me that, and I've always liked the way my name sounds when it comes off her tongue. I'm Mickey or Inspector or Corravan with everyone else.

I shook my head. "I can't stay tonight, love. I don't want the boy there alone." And I knew damn well if I got into her bed again, I wouldn't leave.

"All right. But bring him next time. I'm curious to meet him, after what you've told me." She curled up beside me, extricated the cup from my hand to take a sip for herself, and gave it back. "Now tell me why you have that expression on your face."

This was a game we played sometimes. The novelist in her poked at me, wanting to discover my movements, turn the events of my day into the beginning, middle, or end of a story. Sometimes I'd talk to her about a case, although usually I'd wait until I was near to solving it, preferring not to display my initial fumbling and stupidity. So I didn't want to tell her about Rose Albert. However, I knew she hated it when I was too secretive. I had to give her something, and fortunately I had an incident at hand:

"I saw Blair on Tuesday. At Wapping."

Merely seeing the immediate sympathy in her eyes caused my discomfort to resurface in a way that made me want to squirm.

"Did he speak to you?" she asked.

"Not much. I wasn't there long. I think he wanted me there to look at a lighter." I paused and added dryly, "And to make clear how much he still despises me."

She gave me a keen look, but her voice was gentle. "If he despised you, he wouldn't have cared that you left. And it's been a long time, Michael. The fact that he asked for you . . . perhaps he's coming around to forgiving your defection." She smiled. "Although why he thinks the Yard and Wapping are on different sides remains a mystery to me."

"Well, I'm not sure he *did* ask for me. It's just a guess." I shrugged. "He might have said more if Stiles hadn't been there. It was bloody awkward." A short laugh escaped. "Poor Stiles. He picked up on Blair's cold shoulder straight away. Wasn't sure what to make of it."

She rested her arm along the back of the couch. "Did you explain?"

"No."

She shook her head bemusedly as I took a sip of the coffee.

It was lukewarm, and I must have grimaced because she reached to take the cup. "I'll get us more."

I could feel her holding back the advice she'd offered more than once: that I should someday talk openly to Blair about why I left. But Belinda didn't know the entire story. I'd told her I left Wapping because I discovered some of the River Police had been taking bribes from the officers at Custom House, knocking them about when they didn't pay, and I didn't want to get caught up in it.

The truth was, I hadn't left because of the bribes. I didn't take them myself, but I understood it was the way things were done on the river. I'd left because I was nearly certain that Blair—who valued loyalty above all else—had lied to protect two of his River Police men, Pye and Wick, who'd done more than knock about one of the Custom House officers, a man named Kevin Walsh. They'd murdered him. But there was nothing I could do about it. The proof I had wouldn't stand up in court, not against the word of Blair, Pye, and Wick. So I had left Wapping, letting Blair think I went to the Yard because I was—as he put it—getting above myself and being a disloyal Paddy.

Sometimes I let my mind play with the possibility that Blair was innocent. That Pye had lied about Blair giving him and Wick false alibis. That Belinda was right and I *could* clear the air—or at least make Blair think less badly of me—by telling him the truth about why I left. The difficulty was, if he was innocent, he'd rightfully be insulted that I'd ask if he'd lied to cover up a murder. He'd despise me for *that* act of disloyalty, so I wouldn't gain much.

However, most of the time I accepted what was likely the ugly truth. I knew Blair well enough to believe he'd protect Pye and Wick, especially as, practically speaking, letting them stand trial for murder wouldn't do anything for Kevin Walsh and would merely lose Blair two experienced men who knew the river. And if Blair was guilty, he couldn't admit it. A murderer could be charged for decades after the crime. No, there was no possibility I could broach the topic. Not even now.

Belinda returned with two cups of steaming coffee this time, instead of one for us to share, her expression as understanding as if she'd followed my train of thought, right along with me, to the unhappy conclusion I arrived at every time. "I'm sorry, Michael."

The warmth in her eyes and the curve of her soft mouth made my heart turn over in my chest.

Thank God for her, I thought, not for the first time.

"It matters less than it once did." I took the cups carefully from her hands, set them on the table, pulled her into my arms, and buried my hands in her hair.

James and Harry would just have to wait.

CHAPTER 15

When I arrived at the Beckfords', Stiles was already there, waiting at a discreet distance. I rang the bell, and the butler Quincy—a stolid, taciturn man—opened the door. Upon recognizing me, his usually expressionless face betrayed dismay and concern, which roused my curiosity. But he hastily smoothed away the signs of disquiet and brought us into the study.

Stephen Beckford and I had spoken at least half a dozen times, and this is where we'd met on each occasion. A fireplace bordered and manteled in veined white marble filled a fair portion of one wall. A desk occupied a corner, and in the center of an enormous Turkish carpet stood a round table with a green felt surface for cards. The room smelled of cigars. That morning, both brothers—Stephen and Robert—were present. They looked very much alike, though Stephen was older by a year. They were both above average height, clean-shaven, and what most would find handsome, with high foreheads, light brown wavy hair, and brown eyes under well-shaped brows. Robert remained seated, but Stephen rose with a hopeful expression. His right fingers twitched at the front of his coat. "Inspector Corravan." He turned to his brother. "You remember Robert."

I nodded a greeting.

"Is there any news?" Stephen asked.

"Possibly," I said, feeling less comfortable at my deception, now that we were face-to-face. Stephen's face was pleasant, though his smile seemed strained, and there was a tension about his frame.

I gestured to Stiles. "I want to introduce you to Inspector Stiles. He may have found a clue to Mrs. Beckford's whereabouts."

Stephen looked at me with concern. "Are you giving up the case, then?"

"No," I said. "But Stiles is better than *Bradshaw's* for knowing branch lines and closures, and he knows most of the porters and railway servants at the stations."

"Ah." Stephen gestured toward a group of four chairs near the window, and we all sat.

Stiles spoke up: "I found someone who thought he saw your wife board a train out of London."

"And you only discovered this now?" Robert broke in.

"Inspector Corravan spoke with people at railway stations soon after she vanished, and no one remembered seeing her." Stiles's tone was apologetic. "Yesterday I was at Euston on another matter and found a porter who was absent that day. This man remembered someone matching your wife's description. He noticed her because she wasn't wearing a wrap and seemed upset. She departed from track seven at around six in the morning, just after he began his shift. That track services trains for Birmingham on the London and Northwestern, and it wasn't an express."

Stephen's brow furrowed. "So she's left London."

Stiles nodded. "Can you think of any place she'd go? Perhaps someone she knows out that way?"

"What are the towns?"

Stiles replied obligingly: "Boxmoor, Bletchley, Wolston, Berkhamsted, Rugby, Coventry, Birmingham . . ."

Stephen shook his head. "I don't know. I believe she had some distant relations near Bletchley or thereabouts—on her mother's side."

He'd never mentioned them before. But I kept my expression bland.

Stiles drew out his pocketbook and a stub of pencil. "Do you know their surname?"

Stephen shook his head. "She seldom spoke of them. Bronwell. Bromwell, something like that."

Stiles made a careful notation. "Another thing. Could you tell me, does your wife speak any other languages? Possibly French?"

"French?" Stephen considered it. "Well, a few phrases, the way we all do. But not fluently. Why?"

"The porter thought she sounded foreign," Stiles said.

"Probably just garbled," Robert said. "She wasn't in her right mind."

Stephen shot a look at his brother. A warning at his brother's derisive tone? Robert's shoulders twitched, and he sat back in his chair, fiddling with a ruby ring.

Stiles made another note in his book.

A plain-faced, thin maid of about twenty-five entered and placed a silver tray loaded with cups and a shining urn of coffee on the side table. "Shall I pour, sir?"

Robert scowled. "We didn't ring."

Her blue eyes blinked in confusion. "I beg pardon. Mrs. Wilkins said I was to bring coffee when—"

"It's all right, Harriet," Stephen interrupted mildly and turned to us. "Would you like some?"

I refused, but to my surprise, Stiles said, "Yes, please. Kind of you. I've a chill this morning."

"Seems odd that the porter suddenly remembered her," Robert spoke up.

"And how would she pay for her ticket?" Stephen added.

"I wondered that myself," Stiles said. "Did she have anything that she could pawn? A ring or a brooch?"

"Her wedding ring, I suppose." Stephen sighed, a forlorn look on his face. "I hope she wouldn't do that."

Stiles put out his hand for the coffee and smiled at Harriet, who returned the smile weakly. Clearly Robert had flustered her, and her work-worn hand shook as she passed the cup and saucer to Stiles. Some coffee would have fallen onto the carpet had Stiles not slid his sleeve underneath it unobtrusively, catching the drops on his cuff.

Harriet's expression was stricken.

"It's my fault," Stiles said quickly. "My mum always said I was clumsy."

"It'll come out with salt." Harriet's voice was breathless.

Stiles gave her a ghost of a wink, enough to reassure her, and she looked grateful.

"That will be all," said Stephen. As she left the room, he turned to me. "Are you still looking here in the city?"

I nodded. "The advertisements have yielded nothing. I've been searching establishments, working outward from here. It takes time."

Stephen placed a hand over his eyes. When he finally dropped it, his expression was somber. "We'll continue to pray for her safe return."

"One other thing," Stiles said. "Have you had any problems with servants the past twelve-month? Kitchen staff, or any of the footmen?"

I knew what he was thinking: *kitchen, knife, Pierre.*

Stephen looked thoughtful before answering. "Well—yes, rather. We had to let three of our servants go nearly . . . oh . . ." Stephen looked as if for confirmation at Robert. "It was June or July of last year, I believe."

This was yet more new information, although it seemed there might be a nugget of truth to it.

"Oh? Why was that?" Stiles asked.

"Well, the footman decided to return to the country. He said the London air didn't agree with him. And the two maids . . ." He shook his head ruefully. "They were young and rather flighty, I'm afraid. Our housekeeper, Mrs. Wilkins, caught them several times lying abed and dawdling at the shops when they should have been working."

"Do you recall their names?" Stiles asked.

"Er." Stephen looked vaguely flummoxed.

"Mrs. Wilkins would know, but she's away," Robert replied.

"Ah," Stiles said and made a note in his book. "I can come back this afternoon to ask."

"No, no," Stephen said. "I remember. Joseph Towne, Ellie Price, and . . . er, Annie McKay."

Robert fidgeted in his chair. "You'll begin searching for Madeline in the towns up north, then?"

Stiles seemed not to notice the attempt to steer the conversation but nodded obligingly and set his half-drunk cup on the tray. "There's a train leaving at the top of the hour, and I don't want to miss it."

We bid the brothers goodbye, and I followed Stiles out to the street. The day was cool, with a damp air that chilled my bare neck and hands. The street was mostly empty, except for a few solitary men—one of whom was tall, with a firm stride, and thick hair prematurely gone silver. I recognized him, but I couldn't think of why.

Five more paces, then I looked over my shoulder, in time to see the man start up the steps to Stephen Beckford's door.

Ah, I thought. *So that is who Quincy expected when he opened the door to us.*

Stiles was saying, "Robert was making Stephen uneasy. And did you notice Harriet?"

"The maid?" I raised an eyebrow, teasingly. "Yes, she seemed sweet."

His mouth quirked briefly. "She went pale as a ghost when she looked at Robert, and at one point he stared at her, as if he was giving her a warning."

Not for the first time I thought it was often better to have two sets of eyes in the room. "You think you might become friendly with her?"

He looked uncomfortable. "Well, I don't want to pretend to like her, just to get her to talk to me."

"Stiles, I'm not saying you should profess love to the woman. Can you arrange to meet her, when she's off work, take her for tea?"

"Of course. But I'd have to tell her straight out that I had some questions for her."

I merely grunted in reply because suddenly I remembered who the silver-haired man was. "She wasn't supposed to bring the coffee for us."

"What?"

I jerked my head backward toward the house. "Mr. Taft, a private detective of sorts. He specializes in finding people . . . although not always to their benefit. We just passed him."

Stiles stopped in his tracks. "A private detective? Why would— does Beckford think we're not doing our jobs properly?"

I shrugged. "He might."

Stiles's brows were knit so tightly they almost touched. "Was Stephen's manner different than other times you've seen him?"

"A bit edgy. Said things he hadn't before. He's never mentioned relations in Bletchley."

"Yes. They weren't in your notes," Stiles said. "I sensed he wasn't being truthful."

I hid the smile tugging at my mouth. "You acted as if he'd just given you the best clue yet."

He gave a sudden sneeze, pulled out his handkerchief, and swiped at his nose. "I've been looking into Beckford's affairs. Did you know their shipping company isn't doing as well as it once was? Last month there was an incident involving pirates in the Indian Ocean."

"What would that have to do with Madeline?"

He heard the skepticism in my voice and gave an easy smile. "I'm just looking for anything out of the ordinary. And did you notice Harriet said that Mrs. Wilkins asked her to bring the coffee, but then Robert said she was away?"

I hadn't noticed the disparity at the time, but Stiles was right. "Robert was trying to keep Stephen from talking about the servants."

"I wonder if it's because they're in enough financial difficulties that they're not paying servants their wages."

"Hmph." I nodded. "Could be why those three left."

We paused together at the corner before we parted. "I'm on my way to Wapping, to see if they found out anything about the lighter," I said. "I'll ask about the Beckfords' company for you. Blair might have heard something, if they're in trouble."

"Thank you," he said and began to turn away.

"You don't trust them, do you?" I asked.

He met my gaze, and his young face was somber. "I see Madeline every day. I don't know if they're responsible, but that sort of raw fear has a cause."

He has a point, I thought as I watched him walk away. And in my experience, raw fear leaves little room for dissembling. It usually points close to the truth.

CHAPTER 16

The River Police division seemed surprisingly empty for a Friday afternoon.

At the front desk sat young Sergeant Mason, and his face lit up when he saw me. "Inspector Corravan! Hullo!"

"How are you, Mason? How's the missus?"

His mouth screwed sideways, like he was trying not to smile but couldn't help it. "She's aw'right. Just had twins on Saturday."

"Good lord, that woman's a wonder."

His grin broke out. "B'lieve me, I know. 'M luckier than I deserve."

"Corravan." Blair stood in the door of his office.

"Say hello to her for me, would you?" I said to Mason and headed toward Blair.

"Your director sent you?" he asked.

"No," I replied, surprised. I began to close the door, but he waved for me to leave it open, making it clear I wouldn't be here long.

He winced as he sank into his chair, and despite his hostility, pity twinged at me. He wasn't young anymore, and he worked hard.

He didn't invite me to sit, so I remained standing. "Why would Vincent send me?"

He snorted. "Damned if *I* know why the Commission has him overseeing me."

My mind leaped back to that first morning here at Wapping. My impression from Stiles had been that Blair had *requested* some Yard men, but perhaps I'd misunderstood. Or Stiles had misunderstood Vincent.

Blair saw my perplexity. "They didn't just reorganize the Yard," he spat. "When Vincent came in, the Commission told me I have to notify him of any murders that come through here. Doesn't accomplish a whit except make everything take twice as long."

Well, that explained why Stiles and I had been sent. But I wasn't about to be drawn into a discussion about it.

When I remained silent, Blair lifted his hands from the chair arms and slapped them back down with an air of resignation. "Any idea yet why she was killed?"

I gave him a brief outline of what we'd uncovered thus far, ending with the possibility that the necklace might have been the motive. "We haven't discovered a firm connection to the river yet."

He rubbed a hand over his mouth. "We pulled the boat and cleaned the bottom. There's a 'T' burned into it."

"A 'T,'" I repeated, sketching the letter in the air. "You're sure. Couldn't be an 'X'?" The shipping company of Wilmot Helmswirth marked their lighter boats with that letter, though usually they burned it on the port side.

He scowled. "See it for yourself. I was thinking it could be Terrington's, if they've started marking theirs. They're upstream, and they've got enough boats that somebody could take one without it being noticed."

His expression hinted at a reason buried underneath the guess. Terrington's was one of the most successful merchants of textiles—cloth, lace, and the like. But there were plenty of merchants with names that began with the letter "T."

He pursed his lips and cocked his head. "Was planning to send a man up the wharves to see if anybody had a boat missing. Figured I'd have him start there." He looked at me aslant. "Unless you want to go."

I felt like a fish that was being offered bait. I didn't object, but I wanted to know whatever Blair knew. "Why Terrington's? Any circumstances out of the ordinary?"

"'Any circumstances out of the ordinary?'" He mimicked my tone. "Jesus, Corravan. Vincent's public school airs rubbing off on ye?"

I let that go. "Why Terrington's?"

He leaned back in his chair, his thick fingers rapping a restless tattoo on the chair arms. "Six months back Terrington's was caught weighting their bolts."

Adding sand to the tube around which the cloth or lace was wound was a common trick to boost the price. "I heard. Someone tipped Customs, didn't they?" I asked.

He nodded.

"Preston's?" That was Terrington's biggest rival.

"That's what people figured. And then last month one of Preston's docks was torched, along with four of their lighters." He picked up a pencil, tapped the end on the desk, waiting for me to follow his thought.

"Do the Alberts have a connection to either of the merchants?"

He rocked sideways, and the chair creaked in protest. "I don't know. Might be something."

I took a backward step, with the feeling of wanting more distance from the problem in front of me. Here I'd been speaking to jewelers and tracking down all the people in Rose's life—and her murder might be the result of a textile company feud? Had the judge ever presided over a case involving Terrington's or Preston's? Or did the judge own shares in either of them?

That might be a question for Mr. Haverling.

"There's something else." Blair set down the pencil. "We found a scrap of a silk slipper caught on a spear of wood, like it was ripped off in a struggle. Means she was probably alive when she was put in."

There was a cough at the door.

We both turned.

It was a young sergeant in uniform, looking anxiously at Blair. "Sergeant Wickley asked me to fetch you to the London Docks. They've seized one of the boats. Guns under the gin barrels, just like they said. Bill o' lading says Belgium."

My ears pricked. Guns bound for Belgium?

Blair stood up and pulled his coat off a peg on the wall.

I raised a detaining hand into the air. "Wait. I have a question for you. Won't take a minute."

The sergeant hesitated, then, at Blair's nod, left us alone.

"What can you tell me about Beckford Imports?" I asked.

He looked up from buttoning his coat, glaring with resentment at the thought I'd been keeping something from him. "Why? You got reason to think maybe this lighter could be one of *theirs?*"

"No. Different case entirely. Beckford's wife went missing a few weeks ago." I paused. "I heard pirates attacked one of their ships a few months back."

His expression altered, and in his eyes was a flicker of something—interest, perhaps, or just the memory of the days when I'd come into this very office and tell him some odd fact I'd found. After a moment, he nodded cautiously. "Two of their ships, last December, near the Maldives."

"Anything else?"

He shook his head. "The business is sound, so far as I've heard."

I nodded my thanks. "I'll visit the wharves in the next couple of days. But where's the boat? I want to look at the mark."

"In the shed. We lock it now." He pulled open a drawer and handed me a key. "Turn it back when you're done."

I followed him out onto the rain-soaked wooden pier, where he departed with the sergeant, and went to the long shed, turned the key in the padlock, and opened the door. The air inside was as musty and moldy as I remembered. Through the dirty windows came a gray light that revealed two tattered canvas stretchers and shelves full of tools, extra parts for police boats, and the like. Most of them were in rusty heaps. Rain leaked through the metal roof, and rats scurried at my step. I wondered, briefly, if there was really a need to lock the shed.

The boat hung from two hooks. As Blair said, the "T" was burned into a plank at the bottom of the boat, close to the centerline. I crouched down to look at the rest of the bottom but could see no other mark. I examined the "T" closely. The lines were sloppy as if hand-done, with an uneven, bowed line for the top of the "T" and a thickening at the bottom of the letter. But it was unmistakably a "T," not an "X."

I left the shed, returned the key, and turned west for the hospital, my thoughts darting around in circles. Until an hour ago, I'd been following two possibilities—that Rose Albert's murder had to do with either her personally or the Thierry necklace—with a case involving the judge a plausible third. But what if the boat was a means of conveying a message from one merchant to another? And Rose's dead body was just a way to make that message clear? The thought that a young woman had been used for such a purpose made my insides churn.

The rain slid down the back of my neck because, as usual, I'd forgotten my umbrella at the Yard. A chill, half from cold, half from fatigue, slithered along my bones. I'd fetch Harry from the hospital, go home, and get myself to bed as soon as I decently could.

CHAPTER 17

Saturday morning when I woke, Harry's bed was made, yesterday's shirt hung from a nail in the wall, and he had already left to spend the day at the hospital. After gulping down some coffee and a slice of bread with butter, I headed to the river.

Terrington's warehouse was a prosperous affair, made of sturdy red bricks and with plenty of windows. I asked the foreman about the "T" on the lighter boat, but he said they didn't mark their boats that way, and he showed me the small brass tags screwed into the port side. I hadn't seen screw holes on the lighter we found, and these boats were in much better repair. The Preston Company's lighters were slightly larger and had five thwarts rather than four. I stopped in at the Yellow Star Tea Company, on the off chance, but they marked their lighter boats with numbers carved along the prow. If Rose Albert's murder indeed had anything to do with these companies, the boat provided no obvious link. I spent another few hours walking up and down the wharves inspecting lighter boats, to no avail. In all likelihood, the boat belonged to a riverman for daily hire. The theory that the necklace was the cause of Rose Albert's murder began to reemerge as the most likely. Still, I'd check the wharves on the other side of the river tomorrow or the next day, just to be sure.

It was well past three o'clock when I found a pub where I could eat and read the papers. I took my time about it, and then, as dusk fell, I walked the half mile to the hospital.

James wasn't in, but Harry was in James's office, tucked into an armchair and reading a thick volume. I reminded him that we were dining at Belinda's, and we didn't want to be late.

He rose with a scowl and buttoned up his coat. "I don't understand why I'm going at all. I'm sure you'd rather I didn't, and I'd rather stay here and—"

"Belinda wants to meet you," I interrupted. "She said so."

"Why?"

"Because she's that sort of person," I said. "Don't worry, you'll like her, much better than you like me. Now stop complaining. You have to eat dinner, so you might as well try to enjoy it, and I'll thank you to be polite, as she's probably gone to some trouble about it."

He rolled his eyes, said not another word, and kept a sulky half step behind me the whole way to Belgravia.

When we arrived, Belinda opened the door herself. Harry muttered a greeting under his breath, but rather than taking offense at his rudeness, Belinda treated him as if she found him delightful. Within minutes, he began to thaw, and by the time we were seated at Belinda's elegant table, he was behaving civilly enough. She was dressed to please any man—and certainly a fifteen-year-old boy—in a lovely olive silk that warmed her complexion and brought out the green in her eyes. She asked him what he thought of London, whether he'd been to any of the museums yet, whether he liked his work at the hospital. She was genuinely interested—it's the novelist in her—but the effect was flattering, and Harry was succumbing to her charm. Finally she asked what he was reading now.

His eyes brightened. "Mostly what I find on Dr. Everett's shelves. I just began a wonderful treatise by a medical man named Carpenter."

"William Carpenter, the physiologist?"

With almost malicious pleasure, I watched as Harry's fork dropped with a clatter onto his plate. He snatched it up, flushing, and looked at me suspiciously. I raised my hands in a gesture of denial.

"He's a friend of mine," Belinda continued as if she hadn't noticed. "Perhaps you'd like to meet him."

"Oh," Harry said breathlessly. "Well, I would—but only after I finish his book. It's rather dense going."

"Well, he's rather dense too. Quite oblivious in company." Her dimple appeared. "And when you're not reading medical treatises, what do you enjoy?"

"Oh, I enjoy novels." He added with apologetic haste: "But I—I don't think I've read any of yours yet."

"That's all right. Whose do you prefer?"

"Well, Wilkie Collins. *The Moonstone* is one of my favorites." She smiled.

Harry's eyes widened. "You know him, too?"

"We're acquainted. The artist Henry Charles Brandling was a friend of my father's. Henry accompanied Wilkie on a tour of Cornwall years ago."

His capitulation was complete. He sat back in his chair, open-mouthed.

She smoothed the napkin in her lap. "After dinner, I'll show you the library. You're welcome to borrow anything I have, with only a few exceptions."

"Thank you," he said with some difficulty and then turned what was left of his attention to the fish, which seemed to be slipping about his plate under his fork and knife.

"And where were you today?" she asked me.

"Out and about."

Her eyes flashed surprise at my evasion, but after a moment, she turned to Harry. "Have you been to see the river yet?"

"Yes, on Thursday." Harry gave up on the fish and laid his silver utensils aside. "I thought it was ugly. Made me think about the name. There's a Middle English word, *temese*, that means 'dark,' and the Celts called the river *Tamesas*." A glance, half-defiant, in my direction before looking back at her. "I think words are interesting, the way they cross languages."

"And the word *tamas* means 'darkness' in Sanskrit." She rested her silver on her plate. "Sometimes *tamas* is translated as 'indifference,' which feels appropriate to me. I find the Thames cold and impervious to human suffering."

"It isn't a person," I said.

"It feels like one to me," she retorted. "It's as much a part of the city as anyone."

"And what is the city but the people," Harry added.

She smiled. "'His heart's his mouth: What his breast forges . . .'"

"'That his tongue must vent,'" Harry finished.

She turned to me. "It's from Shakespeare's *Coriolanus.*"

I grunted. "Of course it is."

★   ★   ★

When we finished our trifle, Belinda rose from the table, and we proceeded to the library. She pressed the switch on the wall to light the chandelier.

"Cor," Harry said under his breath and scanned the shelves. "Are these all yours?"

"Many of them were my father's before he died." She touched his shoulder. "Why don't you see if there's something you'd like to borrow?"

He muttered his thanks without taking his eyes off the volumes. Belinda and I headed to the parlor and took our usual places on the divan in front of the fire. She removed her slippers and curled her feet underneath her, graceful as a cat.

"He's a very interesting young man," she said.

I grimaced. "I suppose. He doesn't have much to say to me, but he and James get on like a house afire. And he's fallen hard for you."

"The two of you don't get on because you're too much alike," she said.

A chuckle escaped.

She gave me an odd look. "Why do you laugh?"

I stared, incredulous. "Belinda, he's been through years of schooling. I don't speak French, and I've certainly never taken a prize for my Latin. I don't even like to read, except the papers, and he'd rather do that than anything. He wants to be a doctor, and I'd take up—well, anything before I'd work in a hospital. And I'm quite certain he wouldn't fare too well in a boxing ring or on the docks."

Her eyebrows rose. "Do you really need me to tell you what I see?"

"Yes."

"I see a boy who is clever, proud, and stubborn. Not to mention both of his parents are gone, and he's coming out of Whitechapel with next to nothing." I stiffened at her pointed tone. "My guess is that Mary Doyle thought you'd be the one person who *would* understand him."

"Plenty of people come out of Whitechapel without much."

"For goodness' sake, Michael." She huffed in mild exasperation. "Did it ever occur to you that Mary wasn't doing this only for Harry? She probably worries about you being alone."

"I don't need company."

"Perhaps not, but—"

"Besides, I don't have time for him."

She drew back at my sharp tone. A searching look and then: "You were down on the river today, weren't you?"

Sometimes I'd give a good deal for her to have less intuition. "For a while."

"Don't make me drag it out of you, Michael. That's the second time in a week, and you despite going there. What is it?" She wound a curl of hair around her finger. "Is it a new case?"

"Just another one of many." I pulled one of the stiff tasseled pillows out from behind me and pushed it aside. "Tell me what's happening with the governess and the little French brat."

A flash of resentment came into her eyes. "Don't do that."

"What?"

"Put me off, of course! As if I could be distracted simply by you asking about my novel. Why won't you tell me what's bothering you?"

"Your story is more interesting," I replied, hoping she'd laugh and let it go.

She fixed her eyes on the fire, a frown creasing the skin between her brows and frustration compressing her mouth.

I felt a wave of irritation. Yes, I was unsettled, but I didn't want to part on a quarrel, and Harry and I would leave soon. "It's nothing," I said. "I have a pile of cases on my desk, and I don't like it."

She turned back and propped her head on her hand. "But you always have a pile of cases. Is everything all right with the Doyles? Elsie and Colin?"

Harry's excited voice came from the doorway. "I found this!" We turned to see him holding a book, his eyes bright. "I've been wanting to read it for ages." He turned the spine toward us. "Darwin's *On the Origin of Species*. Is it truly all right for me to borrow?"

"Of course." Belinda smiled.

But the excitement slid off his face as he looked from Belinda to me and realized something was amiss. Before the silence became uncomfortable, I pushed myself to standing and bent over, brushing her cheek with my lips. "It's time we were going. You stay here where it's warm. Good night, Bel."

"Good night." Her tone was remote, and I knew exactly what that tilt of her chin meant. "Goodbye, Harry," she said more warmly. "I hope I see you again soon."

After the cozy parlor, the hallway was cold by comparison, and I shivered as we headed down the stairs and past the kitchen. Harry trailed me silently. These nights with Belinda were the most wonderful few hours of my week. And yet as I let us out the back door, locking it carefully behind, I had a sensation of relief. I loved Belinda—of course I did. But she liked to haul thoughts and feelings out into the light to examine them, and sometimes mine were wily and furtive and wanted to be left alone in the dark.

Chapter 18

First thing Monday morning, I found an envelope that had been slid under my door. Inside was a card that held two lines, in Philip Durrell's tidy script: "*237 Stafford. Go early. Ask for Walter. Trust him.*"

I found the address easily, though it wasn't the jeweler's shop I expected. It was a private house. At a few minutes after eight, I rang the bell and waited.

A curtain at the front window swayed, and after a moment I heard the turn of a key in the lock. The door opened to reveal a thin stooped man of about sixty-five, with a shock of white hair. He studied me for a moment, his pale blue eyes keen.

"Good morning. I'm Inspector Corravan. Philip told me to ask for Walter."

The tension eased around his mouth, and he waved me inside and shut the door. "There is no Walter. That is just so I'd know it was you. My name is Benjamin Fiedler. I thought meeting here would provide the most privacy."

He led me into an impeccably furnished parlor, and we sat. In situations like this, when I have no idea at all what someone might say, and unsure of what I might be expected to know, I keep my mouth shut and wait.

He rested his knobby hands on his knees and studied me. After a moment, he said abruptly, "Philip wouldn't tell me what you'd done to deserve the level of trust he has for you."

I gave a look of apology. "Well, if he wouldn't tell you, I'm afraid I can't either."

"Hmm." Another pause, his eyes on me, unblinking as a bird's. "I won't reveal who gave me this information. Indeed, I wouldn't be meeting you except that Philip said it was a matter of life and death." His mouth twitched, as if he doubted the truth of that.

I kept silent.

His words came as if rehearsed: "The Thierry necklace will shortly be found, safe and entire, at the Harveys' house."

He saw my surprise. Though his mouth had clamped shut, suggesting he'd say nothing more, I felt compelled to ask: "Did someone bring it—or stones from it—to you to sell?"

"No."

"But the person went to someone you know," I guessed.

He frowned unhappily. "Philip assured me you wouldn't press. Is it not enough to know that it will be returned?"

I sat back in my chair, thinking hard. The necklace must have been taken by someone and not merely misplaced or lost. But that still didn't answer the question of whether the thief had taken it from around Rose's neck or whether she had left it behind at the Harveys'.

"Trust him," Philip had written. He meant not only that I could trust what Benjamin would tell me but also that Benjamin would be discreet.

"Like you," I gestured with an open hand, "I am limited in what I can say. But I will tell you what I can, so you'll understand why I need to know."

A cautious nod.

"Lady Edith Harvey lent the necklace to a friend for the party. The young woman left the Harveys' party and was found murdered the next morning. She wasn't wearing the necklace when we found her."

His eyes widened, and his word came out in a hoarse whisper: "Oh."

"Philip is certain the necklace was the motive for her death," I continued, "but I'm not. What I need to know is whether the victim left the house still wearing the necklace and the thief took it from her, or whether she left it behind. I'm sure you can understand why that's important."

He answered slowly. "If she left the necklace behind, she was killed for a different reason."

I nodded.

He blinked several times, thinking for a long minute. "If I tell you that the young woman left the necklace behind, would that be sufficient?"

"I would appreciate if you could tell me why you think so." I paused. "I won't repeat it."

"Very well." He interlaced his fingers. "The morning after the party, the necklace was found in one of the upstairs rooms, by someone who took it and gave it to someone else, who brought it to an unscrupulous jeweler who deals in stolen goods."

"Go on."

Perhaps he was reassured that I didn't ask for any names, for his manner eased. "The jeweler recognized the piece immediately, but he agreed to take it apart, cut the stones, and return part of the profit. You see, even removed from their settings, the gems are recognizable. And there is one stone in particular—the pendant sapphire—that is of a very unusual color and size." He paused. "A deal was struck, and the person agreed to return the next day. But the jeweler guessed the family would pay a higher reward for the necklace than he could earn by selling the individual stones, and selling those stones would take months. He would be required to dribble them into the market and take the considerable risk of being caught. So instead, the jeweler planned to contact the family, naming the person who brought the necklace to him as the thief."

I noticed Mr. Fiedler was careful not to reveal the person's sex. "But that didn't happen."

He shook his head. "An assistant in the shop understood what the jeweler was planning. He thought it was a dirty trick, so before the person brought the necklace back, the assistant came to me to ask what he should do. I told him that he should warn the person immediately, spiking the jeweler's gun. Last night, the necklace was returned, intact, to someone who could replace it in the house."

A maid, most likely. Or a footman.

He sighed heavily. "Mr. Corravan, most of us are honest men, pursuing an honest trade."

"I understand." I put on my hat and stood. "One more thing. How often would stones like those in the necklace come on the market legitimately? Once a year?"

"Once a decade, if that." He walked me to the door and said good-bye. Standing alone on the pavement, eyeing the morning bustle of pedestrians and carts and carriages, I gave a groan of disappointment.

I hadn't realized how much I'd wanted the motive to be uncomplicated theft.

★   ★   ★

I spent the next few hours down at the docks on the other side of the river, asking about the "T" on the bottom of the boat, to no end. Finally, I headed to the Yard, where a message awaited: *"I must speak with you urgently at my office. Haverling."*

I had a feeling I knew what he would say, but I went. Immediately upon arriving, I was ushered into his office, though he remained seated behind his desk.

"Please." He gestured toward the chair opposite. "I beg your pardon for not rising, but my leg is giving me trouble."

"I'm sorry to hear that." The leather chair creaked underneath me.

He folded his hands deliberately. "I wish to convey that you need not pursue the matter of the necklace anymore. It has been found." As he observed my expression, his own altered. "But you already know that."

"I only just heard today, from a confidential source."

He swallowed. "So the necklace was a red herring."

"A what?"

"A kipper. A fish cured in brine." He gave a wave of his hand. "The scent is so strong that it can distract a hound from the scent of a hare, even temporarily. It's used in training the dogs, you see."

A short laugh escaped me. "So I'm the hound."

He looked apologetic. "Anyone would have thought the necklace was the hare, Mr. Corravan. As you said, it's an unlikely coincidence otherwise."

"But now I need to find the proper hare."

He spread his hands. "I am at your disposal."

I sat forward. "The fact that she was put into a lighter boat surely means something. Does the Albert family have any special interest in the Thames? Perhaps in a company such as Terrington's or Preston's, whose warehouses are on the river?"

He frowned. "Textiles?" He shook his head. "Not that I know of. But . . ."

I held my breath.

"Rose's grandfather made his money in steel, and his two daughters, Rose's mother and her aunt Lyvina, were given significant shares in the Baldwin Company. Rose's inheritance would have included some of her aunt's."

"Baldwin," I repeated, sifting through my memory for what I knew of them. "They supply materials for buildings and railways."

"And bridges," he added. "Baldwin's just obtained a contract for two bridges west of Chelsea Reach."

My ears pricked. Those city contracts were coveted and lucrative. There had been several scandals on occasions when they'd been obtained through bribes or other inducements.

"Does the judge control Mrs. Albert's shares?"

"Naturally. Although by a special provision they revert to her if the judge's death precedes hers."

"And what is Aunt Lyvina's surname?" I asked.

"Baldwin. She never married."

A knock at the door, and a young man put his head in. "Mr. Haverling, I've your next appointment."

I pushed myself out of the chair, and we bid each other goodbye.

The building contracts for the city were awarded by the office of the Home Secretary, the third most powerful office of the government. Had the judge, seeking to inflate the price of his shares, influenced a cabinet member in order to obtain that contract? And was Rose murdered because she had discovered what he'd done?

This was no small hare. The thought of investigating someone in the Home Secretary's office for corruption, much less murder, brought to mind a picture of a bloody enormous tiger whirling on me, its claws unsheathed and its teeth shining like knives.

CHAPTER 19

James sent a note to the effect that Harry would spend the next few nights at the hospital, so he could monitor Madeline as she slept.

I woke up alone on Tuesday morning, made myself a strong cup of coffee, and drank it hot while I dressed and arranged my thoughts. As often happens, a good night's sleep had renewed my spirits and produced some ideas about people I might ask about whether the judge or Baldwin's had exerted improper influence on the Home Secretary's office. Thus I was almost cheerful as I reached the Yard. I might even have been humming under my breath.

Until I saw Stiles waiting for me at the door. He had a rigid set to his shoulders and wore a wretched expression.

I felt my grin fade as I approached. "Stiles. What is it?"

"There's been another one."

"Another what?"

"Another dead woman in a boat." His face looked gray in the morning light. "Vincent says we're to go to Wapping."

★　★　★

One day, when I was eighteen, working as a lighterman, I fell out of the boat. As the current pulled me sideways and down, the icy river shocked me stiff, and the gray world trembled and vanished as I sank.

Old Tim Miller was close enough to see it happen, so when I surfaced, sputtering and flailing, there was his long oar a few feet in front of me. Hand over hand, he hauled me toward him till he could grab my shirt and drag me aboard, where I sat shivering and retching river water. His mouth was a rictus over his black teeth. "River a'most got y' thar." And from that day on, my thoughts were irrevocably changed. My original concern, to transfer the most cargo the quickest so as to earn the most pay, had altered to include preserving my life while doing it.

The appearance of a second victim reoriented me the same way. The fairly straightforward question, *Who killed Rose?* became overlaid by others: Why these two women? What did they have in common? Was the fact that they were both found dead on Tuesday morning part of a pattern? Or coincidence? And given what Haverling had told me, did both of their families have connections to Baldwin's, or someone in government?

My thoughts in tumult, I went to my office, removed my coat, and sat at my desk. I took up the folder of notes I had compiled about Rose and the necklace and the judge and saw it for what it was: a stack of paper that might contain a few pieces of useful information, relevant in hindsight, but by and large, I could toss most of it in the dustbin. I dropped my head into my hands.

And then a chill raced along my bones.

Le Loup, I thought. *The Wolf.*

Le Loup was what drove me to drink spirits so hard that afterward I promised Belinda I wouldn't touch them ever again.

I hadn't even noticed that Stiles had followed me into my office. Now he stood looking down at me from the other side of the desk. "I thought of him too, Inspector. But these women weren't clawed or left in alleys." He shook his head determinedly, though there was uncertainty in his eyes.

Stiles and I had worked on the case last fall. The first murder happened on a Saturday night, during the second week of the Yard trial. Two more murders followed on subsequent Saturdays. The man killed women who worked at music halls and theaters in Soho, strangling them and putting claw marks all over their bodies. The women looked nothing alike, had never known one another, and were aged eighteen to thirty-two. Why those three? Why the scratches?

To make it worse, a greasy newspaperman named John Fishel got hold of the story. After the first murder, he found two witnesses who, after being plied with whiskey, claimed they'd seen a suspicious-looking Frenchman near the music hall. The next day the *Beacon* printed "FRENCHMAN MURDERS INNOCENT WOMAN" on its front page, which spurred attacks on French stores and churches and only added to our caseload. After the second murder, Fishel saw the claw marks and crafted the headline "LE LOUP TERRORIZES SOHO." And after the third, "YARD SHIELDS LE LOUP! CORRUPTION CONTINUES!" That was the worst week I can remember, with crowds of people outside the Yard screaming and threatening to kill us.

And then the murders stopped. I'd like to think Le Loup ceased killing because he was afraid Stiles and I were on the verge of catching him. But we weren't even close.

Stiles broke the silence. "Rose Albert isn't a music hall girl."

I didn't answer.

The image in my mind was no longer a tiger; it was a wolf, laughing, his teeth bared and bloody.

And, given my utter failure last time, what were my chances of catching him—or a man like him—now?

★　★　★

We didn't talk much as we set off for the dock at Wapping.

This time Blair had three of his own men with him. They greeted us with silent nods while Blair ignored us, his eyes narrowed against the wind, watching. The cold wind sheared right through me, and I was relieved when the police boat appeared a few minutes later. From the dock, I could see this lighter was less weather-beaten than the first and slightly longer. This time, no one had covered the woman with a blanket.

The connection to Rose's murder was obvious. This woman, fair-haired and pretty, was slightly younger, but she wore a dress for evening. Her hands were bound, and her skirts were sliced and bloody near the waist. At the bottom of the boat were sodden leaves and petals, which made me think of James's comparison to the Viking funeral. The debris might have been intended to represent valuables.

Stiles muttered into my ear. "She's a mite younger, but . . ."

"I know."

There was dread in his eyes. Probably the same dread he saw in mine.

Dread that this was a second instance of a new, modern kind of London crime. Something more virulent than simple murder. And we at the Yard weren't ready for it.

Chapter 20

Identifying the second murdered woman took three days because of a misunderstanding.

Jane Dorstone had been visiting friends, the Leverings, where she planned to stay until Thursday. But she had left them, unexpectedly, after the theater on Monday night. So while Jane's parents assumed she was with the Leverings, the Leverings believed Jane was home. On Thursday, when the Dorstones realized Jane was missing, Mr. Dorstone went promptly to the Mayfair division, and, at Vincent's request, they brought him to us without telling him that his daughter might be dead.

Vincent and I received Mr. Dorstone together in his office. Vincent sat behind his desk, of course; I stood by the bookshelf, from where I could observe Jane's father.

He was a tall, slender, rather effete sort of man with a weak mouth and chin. After he sank into a chair, he tugged first at one cuff and then the other, as if he wanted to pull them farther over his wrists, though the tailor had made them fashionably long.

"I'm sorry to ask you to repeat your account for us," Vincent said. "How did you discover your daughter was missing?"

Mr. Dorstone stroked his mustache with one forefinger before answering. "We received a note at breakfast from Isabella. It was addressed to Jane, which was peculiar because Jane was to stay with her until today. So my wife opened it."

"Do you have it with you?" I asked.

He pawed at both inside pockets but came up empty-handed and appeared distressed. "Sorry—sorry. But I remember what it said. Isabella asked if Jane could accompany her to a luncheon tomorrow. And she asked about Sidney."

"Sidney?"

He looked uncomfortable. "My son. He's—er, been ill. Isabella is fond of him."

"How old is Sidney?" I asked, imagining a younger brother.

Mr. Dorstone stroked his mustache again. "Twenty-five."

Not the answer I'd expected, and my ears pricked to the tone in his voice: guilty, with an undertone of defiance. I'd have to find out more about the brother.

"What did you do after reading Isabella's letter?" Vincent asked.

"I went to the Leverings' house, of course." His head tipped at an angle, as if his world was askew and he was trying to set it straight. "Isabella said Jane left on Monday night, directly from the theater. My carriage drew up, and the driver handed her a message."

"*Your* carriage?" Vincent echoed.

"Yes." His voice cracked. "Isabella was certain of it. We keep our carriage at a livery down the street. Someone must have taken it out, though it's been returned."

We would need to know when, but Mr. Dorstone wasn't the one to ask. I slipped in my question: "What is the livery address?"

"Marlton Yews, number 20. It's at the corner."

"Do you have a usual driver?" I asked.

"Joseph. But it was his night off."

"So you were home?"

"Well, no. I went to my club, as usual, by cab." He frowned worriedly. "Look here, there's no need to ask questions of Joseph. He wouldn't hurt Jane for the world."

"Of course not," Vincent replied.

"Which show did they see?" I asked.

Mr. Dorstone stared. "Why on earth would that matter?"

"He means which theater," Vincent interposed. "So we know where she disappeared."

"Oh." He looked nonplussed. "Er—I don't know. Something new. *Uncommon Courtship*, I think."

"*A Most Unlikely Courtship*," Vincent said to me. "It's at the Winchester." He turned back to Mr. Dorstone. "And where do the Leverings live?"

"Redding Street, number 14."

In Mayfair. Another connection to Rose.

"Could you please tell us about your daughter?" I asked gently. "How old was she?"

I almost bit my tongue at the "was" I'd let slip, but he appeared not to notice.

"She's seventeen."

"And what does she look like?"

"Blond hair, very pretty. Gray eyes. About so tall," he gestured to his shoulder.

"What did she wear to the theater?"

He looked at me blankly. "Oh, I've no idea. Isabella might know."

"And how does she occupy herself?" I asked.

He shook his head. "I don't know. She makes calls. She goes to church every Sunday, of course. She enjoys reading."

Rose had liked to read. But that hardly ranked as even a tenuous connection.

"Which church do you attend?"

"St. Martin in the Fields." The steepled church in Trafalgar Square.

"And is your daughter engaged?" I asked.

A brief hesitation. "No-o-o." The syllable stretched long.

"Mr. Dorstone," Vincent interjected. "Is there anyone who ever formed an attachment to *her*, welcome or otherwise?"

He sighed. "She refused Samuel Gordon when he asked for her hand last year; I believe he was unhappy about it. And now it seems Robert Eddington is on the verge of proposing. That is, he has shown every sign, but he hasn't asked her yet, and it would be humiliating for her to—to—"

"We won't say a word," Vincent promised.

"Besides which, both of them are very proper young men." He frowned. "And she certainly isn't the sort to run off to Scotland. She isn't silly."

There was a silence, and then Vincent withdrew the sketch of our second victim and slid it across the desk. "Mr. Dorstone, is this your daughter?"

He stared at the drawing and then looked from me to Vincent. "Look here," his voice wobbled. "What sort of game are you playing?"

"Mr. Dorstone." Vincent's voice was sober. "There's no game. If this *is* your daughter—and mind, it *is* just a drawing—she was found dead, in a boat, on the Thames on Tuesday morning."

That blow silenced him, and he sank back into the chair, his face frozen.

I felt the stab of sympathy I always have at this moment.

"Before we can be sure," Vincent added, "we'll ask you to identify her at the morgue." He paused. "I'm very sorry. So very sorry. It's a terrible thing."

Mr. Dorstone's head snapped up. "Oh, it isn't her," he said, with absolute certainty.

There was a long silence, and at last Vincent stood up. "Mr. Dorstone, I pray that is so. But then it's another young woman's family that I need to notify. Could you please come with me?"

"Of course! Her poor family." He rose and followed Vincent out the door with alacrity.

Neither of them gave me a backward look.

Which was fine. I knew where I'd be the rest of the day.

I went to my office to get my coat.

Bold, I thought, as I headed out. Temporarily stealing the father's carriage. So is that how he took Rose, too? Pulled up in a carriage she'd recognize? And what sort of message had Jane received that would cause her to leave her friends so abruptly? That her brother Sidney was ill? Had that been how the murderer had lured Rose as well? Told her someone was ill—perhaps her mother?

I needed to talk to Isabella Levering, and I wanted to do it before she heard that her friend Jane had died.

We'd already lost three days.

CHAPTER 21

Isabella Levering looked to be about eighteen. She had an ivory complexion, a small nose and mouth, and a chin like an inverted triangle. It's the kind of face that people say is elegant and fashionable, though it makes me think of a cat. But thank God, Isabella's character seemed neither sly nor kittenish; her blue eyes were serious and her manner constrained. She fiddled with the fabric of her skirt, repeatedly drawing it together in pleats between her fingers.

While I'd been given permission to question her alone, the parlor door had been left ajar for propriety's sake.

"Miss Levering," I began. "You sent a letter to Jane this morning."

She nodded.

"But you knew she'd left you Monday night, on an urgent matter. Why would you wait so long to write to her? Were you not concerned?"

I heard her inhale, and her small white teeth caught her lower lip.

"You have an idea where she went, don't you?" I asked.

Her expression was pleading. She wanted to help me, but she was also trying to be a loyal friend.

"I'll tell Miss Dorstone that I pressed you *insistently*," I said. "She can blame me."

Her gaze darted to the open door, and her voice dropped to just above a whisper. "The message was from Sidney. He asked her to come."

"Come where?"

Her eyes widened. "I thought you knew. He's in a—a sanatorium."

"A sanatorium," I repeated. Well, that might explain Mr. Dorstone's discomfort. "How long has he been there?"

"A little over a year, though he came home at Christmas."

"Do you think Jane was telling you the truth?"

"Oh, yes! She looked worried and sad, and when she looks like that, it's usually about him."

"Does her brother write to her often?"

Her gaze slid away.

"Miss Levering?"

She sighed. "He sends the letters here, and I pass them to her."

"Which sanatorium is it?" I asked, praying that it was somewhere close.

"Seddon Hall, in Surrey."

My heart jumped. I knew of the place. It had been in all the papers several years before, when it was established by a medical man who, having made his money selling pills and ointments, wanted to offer a place of rest for those suffering from tuberculosis, consumption, and nervous ailments. Believing that the yearlong miasma in the Thames Valley brewed disease, he built his sanatorium beyond its reach but still close enough to be convenient to London by train. Jane could have been there and back in a matter of hours.

"Her mother would be furious," she continued. "Sometimes Jane tells her mother that she's staying here so she can visit him. Her aunt Mary lives in the next town."

"Why is Sidney in a sanatorium?"

Her pained expression could mean only one thing.

"Did he try to destroy himself?" I asked.

"He cut his wrists," she whispered.

My mind jumped to the cuts on Rose and Jane, just above the wrists.

She leaned forward with that pleading look again. "He wrote to Jane in August, begging to see her, but her mother hid the letter, and Jane didn't even know he'd written. So when his message arrived this time . . ."

"Of course," I said. "She had to go."

"You *must* understand, Inspector. He's *not* insane. And he's not weak like Jane's mother says. He just thinks too much."

I heard the voice of a devoted sister in those words. "Jane is very fond of him, isn't she?"

"Of course!" Miss Levering's hands were knotted so hard the knuckles were white. "He's a wonderful person. Brilliant and kind and—and he shouldn't be in there."

The tremble in her voice told me that Jane wasn't the only one who loved him.

Something nagged at me—a connection my mind was trying to make—but Miss Levering was looking at me expectantly, and I steered my thoughts back to the questions at hand.

"When Jane visited Sidney, did she usually stay for several days?"

"Two days at most, which is why I thought it safe to send the letter this morning."

I took out my pocketbook, scribbled a few notes, and looked up. "One other thing. Was Miss Dorstone wearing any special jewelry the night you went to the theater?"

It was a slim chance, but there was no harm in asking. Perhaps the person who had killed Rose and Jane had first taken notice of them because of it.

She nodded. "A cameo brooch that belonged to her grand-mother. She always wore that."

"But nothing expensive?"

"No. Jane wasn't much for gemstones."

I closed my pocketbook and rose. "Thank you, Miss Levering. You've been very patient."

Her fingers were twisting at each other. "When you see Jane, please tell her to visit me immediately. I hate being caught out like this."

I put on my hat to cover my guilt at deceiving her, bid her a hasty goodbye, and made my way to the street. As I walked toward the livery, I replayed the conversation in my mind, paus-ing at the moment when Miss Levering described Jane's affection toward her brother. The connection my brain had been trying to make was this: Jane was loyal to her brother the way Rose was loyal to her friend Lady Edith. I couldn't see how that would be of interest to a murderer, but in addition to them both being young, attractive women, loyalty was another of the slender threads linking them.

A thicker thread was that both women lived in Mayfair. And then it occurred to me: Mrs. Beckford lived in Mayfair as well. And the night she ran out, she was dressed in a beautiful gown; she was only a few years older and pretty, the way Rose and Jane were. So was there a chance that Madeline had been the murderer's first intended victim but had managed to escape?

The thought halted my steps in the middle of the pavement.

What day of the week had Madeline vanished? It was a Wednesday, wasn't it?

I pulled out my pocketbook and searched feverishly through my notes. Yes, it was Wednesday, the night Beckford always went to his club and the theater with his friend Speare. My momentary consternation diminished, I replaced my pocketbook and walked on. With each step it seemed less plausible Madeline was connected to Rose and Jane. The traits they had in common were shared by hundreds of other women in Mayfair. Madeline was married, not engaged secretly or otherwise, and according to her husband, Madeline had run out of the house of her own accord, not been lured away by a cab driver. She'd been mentally disturbed for weeks before the attack, unlike Rose and Jane. And how would Madeline have escaped a powerful man, who was able to overpower these other women?

Frustrated, I scrubbed a hand over my scalp. It was wildly unlikely—and in any event, impossible to find any meaningful connections to the other victims until Madeline began speaking.

And for now, I had plenty of people to see.

Sidney Dorstone, naturally.

Perhaps also Aunt Mary.

But first, the driver of the carriage.

CHAPTER 22

The livery in Marlton Yews looked large enough to house a dozen horses and four or five carriages. Entering through the side door, I found four men playing cards at a rickety wooden table. At each man's left elbow sat a small pile of coins; at each man's right hand was a tankard of ale, no doubt from the pub directly across the way.

I entered and introduced myself. "I have some questions about the Dorstone carriage. It went missing for a while on Monday night."

They looked at one another and then up at me. "Dunno," one man answered for all of them. "Warn't any o' us."

"I just want to know what time it left and came back. Can you help me there?"

Still no answer. They studied their cards.

I leaned between two of them, putting my hands on the table. "It won't hurt you to have a Yard man in your debt. And I'll buy your pints."

The thin one with brown hair met my gaze: "I come back from drivin' Mr. Swales to Euston at ha' past nine, and it was gone."

"When did you leave to pick up Mr. Swales?"

His eyes slid away guiltily, and he muttered, "Seven, or there'bouts, an' it were here."

It took no more than twenty minutes to drive to Euston, which probably meant he picked up a fare on his return journey, using his employer's horses. But I merely thanked him and nodded approvingly, and he looked relieved.

"And when did any of you see it again?" I asked.

The man to his left grunted. "I got here next morning just 'afore six and saw it."

The first man spoke up again: "There was a man 'anging about Monday." He thrust his chin toward the pub. "Stood by the door, watchin'. Sumpin made me think 'e warn't from 'ere."

"What did he look like?"

"About as tall and broad as you, mebbe forty-some, dark hair, so long." He gestured to the top of his shoulders and then tapped his cheek. "Thick beard."

"Do you think he might have been the one to take the carriage?"

He thrust out his lower lip. "Mebbe. He was lookin'."

"Yer might try askin' over at the pub," the fourth man hinted. "Might be he got thirsty."

"Might be." I turned away.

The pub stank of spilled beer and burned onions, but there was a barkeep with a watchful eye. Just the sort who's useful. He greeted me as I approached. He took in my slightly crinkled ear; his eyes darted to my hands, then to my belt where I keep my truncheon, and a satisfied expression came over his face. He knew what I was, but he didn't seem bothered. I ordered a pint and asked about the man the driver had seen.

"Dunno his name, but I remember him," he replied forthrightly. "Two days in a row he come. Bought two tanks o' ale, made 'em last. Plunked hi'self right there by the winda'."

I went over to the chair. My view was straight into the large door of the livery, where the carriages rolled out.

"Anything else you remember about him?" I asked.

"Had a bad cough. Gurgly, like he got consumption or sumpin'. My uncle had it, 's how I know."

I finished my pint, ordered four more for the men in the livery, and prepared to leave.

The barkeep crooked a finger at me and leaned in. "You a boxer?"

My heart gave a quick thud. "I was, once.

"Any thought o' gettin' back to it?"

I shook my head. "Never."

He appraised my shoulders and hands. "Can find you good money."

A sudden heat flared at the back of my neck. "Nah. Thanks."

This man was another Seamus O'Hagan, taking me for a beast to be worked.

Suddenly it occurred to me that this dark-haired man, tall and broad, might be doing the ugly bidding of someone else, someone with more power, and with more at stake.

CHAPTER 23

"Thank you for explaining," Belinda said.

We were in bed together, Belinda's head on my shoulder. I had just told her about Rose and Jane.

"I wish you'd explained all this last week," she added, nudging me with her bare foot.

"Then it was just one of my many cases." It wasn't quite the truth, but it was close. "And on Saturday, Harry was here. I didn't want to talk about it in front of him. Besides, you were busy quoting Shakespeare at each other."

She ignored my gibe and propped herself up on her elbow. "I think your Mr. Haverling is right about the spectacle. Like the way Le Loup arranged the women with their arms overhead."

I grunted.

"Tell me, was their hair loose, or tied back?"

"Rose had her hair done like you do yours sometimes, over your shoulder in curls. Jane's looked like it had been pulled down."

"And they were both lying on their backs?"

The insistent tone in her voice made me roll onto my side, resting my head on my palm, so I could see her face. "What are you thinking, Bel?"

"I'm thinking it sounds like the Lady of Shalott."

I must have looked mystified, for she added, "I read it to you once. It's a poem by Tennyson about a royal lady, who's imprisoned in a tower. She is cursed, so she can only look in a mirror and weave a tapestry instead of living in the world. But when Lancelot appears, she looks at him directly, and her mirror breaks. Knowing she's going to die, she climbs in a boat with flowers and floats down the river to Camelot. Lancelot recognizes her because he's heard stories. Don't you remember?"

I shook my head. "You've never read that to me."

She gave me a teasing shove, then reached for a silken wrap and put it on. "Yes, I *have*. Don't you listen when I read you poetry?"

"Not if you're dressed like that, I don't."

She gave a soft laugh, took up the candle, and left me in darkness.

I put on the dressing gown she'd bought for me and followed her to the library. She stood in front of a shelf, candle raised, scanning. "Here it is."

She paged through the volume, then passed it open to me.

"'The Lady of Shalott, published 1833,'" I read and looked up. "So it's about a lady who's ruined by a man?"

Belinda shook her head. "I think it's about a woman's desire to exist in the world. To be more than a story."

"So you think the murderer fancies himself doing that for Rose and Jane?" I asked doubtfully.

"I think you should read it," Belinda said. "Let's go back to the fire."

Sitting on the divan, with her next to me and a candle at my elbow, I silently scanned the first stanza.

"Read it out loud," Belinda said. "I like it, even if it's tragic."

I began at the first line, my tongue moving clumsily around the rhyming phrases:

"'On either side the river lie / Long fields of barley and of rye / that clothe the wold and meet the sky; and thro' the field the road runs by / To many-towered Camelot . . .'"

I read the poem all the way through and looked up to see Belinda's eyes sparkling with tears. "Bel," I said in surprise. "It's just a poem."

"But the poor woman is locked away her whole life and falls in love with someone who has no idea she exists." She blinked her tears back with a laugh and a sniff. "It always makes me cry."

"Well, I can't see what it has to do with the murders." I closed the book and laid it aside. "Although if he knows the poem, he's probably educated. That's something."

Belinda dabbed at her eyes with her sleeve and gave one last sniff. "There's also a painting, done several years ago by a French-woman named Sophie Gengebre Anderson."

"Is it famous?"

"It's well regarded. It was one of the first purchases of the Liverpool collection. In Anderson's version, the lady is in a boat, covered by her tapestry, so that's not the same. But she's beautifully dressed, with long hair, and there are flowers." She frowned. "Although there's a man in the boat, too. Someone of humbler birth."

"Well, I don't think the women were killed because of this poem."

"Not *because* of the poem." She gave a gentle slap to my arm. "Indeed, the murderer may never have heard of it. But the figure of a woman in a boat surely means something to him."

I allowed that was true.

Her expression was pensive. "Have you talked to James? He might see some link between how the women died and what would cause a man to do this."

I made a noncommittal noise.

"And I can send round to my bookseller," she offered. "He keeps prints, and he might have one of the painting."

I nearly refused before I noted her earnestness. She was as loyal as Rose or Jane, and I didn't want to hurt her feelings.

"That would be easier than going to Liverpool," I admitted.

In her eyes appeared a glint of surprise, and then an impish smile came over her face as she reached for my hand. "But I won't ask him for anything unless you come back to bed."

CHAPTER 24

The next morning, Vincent called me to his office and handed me a note from Blair: "No markings on the second boat."

I brushed aside my regret that I'd probably wasted hours on the wharves and told Vincent everything I'd discovered so far, leaving out only the Lady of Shalott. In the light of day the connection seemed less substantial that it had by candle glow.

He listened silently, and when I finished, he nodded in what I thought was a dismissal.

"Corravan."

I took my hand from the doorknob and turned back.

"The Review Commission is following this case closely." He paced to the window and looked out. "Particularly Quartermain."

I bit down on the inside of my left cheek.

He turned to meet my gaze. "He isn't our enemy, you know. He's mistrustful by nature, but his wariness regarding the Yard isn't without foundation." His expression grew rueful. "There was an interview in this morning's *Times*, further to the Daniels case. Quartermain reiterated his opinion that the man would still be alive if you'd been in uniform. That he ran because he didn't know."

Resentment rose like a hot wave inside me. "That's not true! Daniels knew perfectly well who I—"

Vincent put up a hand. "Whether it is true or not, Quartermain has influence, which the newspapers only reinforce.

Naturally, the Commission's future decisions don't depend solely upon your solving this case. But if the papers get hold of it before you *do* . . ."

I flinched, imagining the headlines. "I know."

"I don't want to be required to take you off the case to satisfy Quartermain." He rested his fingertips lightly on the back of his chair. "Do you need more assistance?"

"No. I'm all right with Stiles."

He gave me a doubtful look, and I swallowed my resentment, shoving aside the thought that this man had never solved a single case himself.

He moved a paper on his desk an inch to the right. "There's one more thing. Quartermain wants you to speak to a man named Nate McLoughlin."

Tightness twinged my spine, but I kept my voice easy. "He's of interest?"

"Last year he was convicted of kidnapping a girl and hiding her along a wharf near a boatworks. She escaped with scars on her wrists." He paused. "Are you familiar with the case? He was from Whitechapel."

"Don't think so, sir," I replied, as if I'd never heard the name before now.

He eyed me skeptically, but I kept silent, and after a moment, he nodded. "All right, then. Please do what you can to find him. Court records should have an address."

That was my dismissal.

I knew enough about Nate McLoughlin to set the suggestion aside, where it belonged, and went out into the main room to find Stiles. He was at his desk, frowning at a piece of paper with some notes in a masculine hand. As I came close, he looked up and murmured, "Madeline's recovering nicely."

I drew a chair to his desk and sat. "Is she talking?"

"Mostly at night. But she smiles now, and she held my hand yesterday."

I snorted. "Claws at me, clings to you."

He gave me a look. "It's not her fault. She was being dosed with laudanum."

"Laudanum," I repeated. A potent concoction, a tincture of opium in alcohol.

He nodded. "According to the apothecary near his office, Dr. Willis prescribes laudanum for many of his lady patients to treat their nerves." He looked dubious. "I asked Dr. Everett what would happen if Madeline took laudanum nightly and then stopped all at once. He said that would cause everything from involuntary tremors and spasms to maniacal raving." I heard James's phrasing in Stiles's voice. "Eventually, those symptoms diminish. So that explains her behavior when she first arrived at the asylum, like your notes said, and why she went quiet afterward."

I have to admit Stiles's insight pulled me up short. I'd put Madeline fairly well out of my mind, but he'd pursued the case faithfully, and he'd made headway. I felt a jab of shame that I hadn't asked Dr. Willis whether he'd been dosing Madeline.

Stiles continued, "If she didn't even stop to fetch her coat, she wouldn't have brought along—"

"I know," I said shortly. Stiles looked suddenly uncertain. And I despised myself for it. I stood up. "It was clever to check with the apothecary," I said gruffly.

He shrugged aside my praise. "She said something new yesterday, when she was awake, in English. It was just muttering about something happening in a lane, and there's two of them less than a hundred yards from her house—Willis and Kinsley. So I've been visiting them in the evening, to talk to sweeps and such, anyone who might have seen her the night she left."

"Ah. Another good idea."

He began to nod his thanks, then suddenly groped for his handkerchief and sneezed into it.

I noticed his nose was already red from wiping. A spring cold, no doubt.

"Bless you," I said and headed out.

CHAPTER 25

At the Dorstones', a grim black wreath concealed the knocker, so I used my knuckles.

When I asked for Mr. Dorstone, I was shown into the library. He didn't rise from his chair. On a table beside him was a tray with toast and a cup of tea, both untouched.

I came close and saw the redness in his eyes, the puffiness underneath them, and the wrinkles in his clothes, as if he'd slept in them. I didn't blame him for being distraught. To lose his son to mental disease and his daughter to murder? It seemed like hell on earth to me.

Though uninvited, I drew up a chair. "Mr. Dorstone, I'm sorry. I've a few more questions for you. Nothing too difficult."

His eyes met mine hopelessly.

"Is it possible that your daughter secretly engaged herself to Mr. Eddington?" This would be a similarity with Rose.

He gave a barely perceptible shake of his head. "Last week she told me in confidence she was worried he wasn't as sincere in his affections as he once was. I told her it was nonsense. He'd be a fool to lose her."

"Do you or any of your family have ties to Yellow Star Tea Company, Terrington's, or Preston's?"

His head tipped. "No. Why?"

"What about the Baldwin company? Or connections to the Home Secretary?"

He sat back, a look of befuddlement on his face. "Not at all. Has someone told you we do?"

"No."

"Then why are you asking?" he burst out, and suddenly his face was in his hands and he was sobbing uncontrollably.

I sat in silence for several minutes until his tears slowed and he drew out his handkerchief and blew his nose.

"Please stop," he begged. "These stupid, useless questions."

"Mr. Dorstone, I'm sorry. Only one more. We have reason to believe Jane may have intended to visit your son."

At the last word, his lips parted and he licked them. "Jane went to see him every month or so. She's the only one he wanted."

"Would you give me permission to see him?" I asked.

He hesitated. "I can write a letter, of course. But there's no possibility he had anything to do with . . ." His voice faded.

"I'd appreciate it nonetheless."

He unfolded his limbs from the chair, crossed to a desk, sat down, drew out a sheet of writing paper, and dipped his pen. For several minutes, there was no sound but the slow scratching of the nib on the paper.

Suddenly he looked up, panic-stricken, as if he'd been shaken from a stupor. "But you can't tell him about Jane. The doctor told us that any sort of shock could kill him! His nerves are shattered."

I stared at him for a moment in astonishment. "He doesn't know Jane is dead?"

"No. And you must swear you won't tell him, or I won't give you this!" His two trembling hands took up the page as if to crumple it.

I stifled a groan. Then how the devil was I supposed to discover anything about Jane's murder?

But I gave Mr. Dorstone my word.

He laid the paper flat again, signed his name, and pushed it a few inches across the desk, as if the act of writing had depleted his energies entirely. "There. You have what you want. Much good it'll do." Then he dropped his elbows onto the desk and put his head in his hands.

"Thank you," I said quietly and left.

I boarded a train at Charing Cross heading toward Surrey, settled into my seat, and began the business of considering how to ask Sidney about Jane—and of drawing a sharp line in my mind between what I might tell Sidney and what I couldn't.

The train drew into the station, halting with a burn of brakes. As I disembarked, I saw a sign for Seddon Hall Sanatorium directing me to the left, one quarter mile. Once there, I found the pedestrian gate open, and I started up the curved drive toward an imposing building of pale stone, its rigid lines softened by trees spaced at decorous intervals.

I entered the square foyer, which was decorated with oil paintings depicting medical men ministering assiduously to bedridden patients. Each image included a table with a shiny bottle, and, with a prick of suspicion, I approached one picture and examined it closely. There it was—"*Seddon*"—clearly on the label, and a snort escaped from my chest.

"Good afternoon," a man said behind me.

I turned and adjusted my gaze downward. The man was just over five feet tall. "Good afternoon. I am Inspector Corravan from Scotland Yard. I am here to see one of your patients." I drew out the letter.

"And I am Mr. Harper, the facility administrator." He opened the letter deliberately and read. His face stilled. "Ah. Hm. Mr. Dorstone." He folded the letter and returned it. "I am afraid he is unavailable for visitors."

"I only need to see him for a few minutes—if that. It's urgent police business. His father—"

He drew himself up. "His father has no authority to grant permission for visitors here."

I held my temper. "Is Mr. Dorstone not here?"

"Of course he is here." He wrapped his fingertips around the edges of his waistcoat. "But he cannot speak to anyone who will upset him. That certainly includes the police."

In a lowered voice, I asked, "Do you know who Tom Flynn is?"

He dragged his lower lip between his teeth, twice. "Yes."

Last March, Flynn had done a series of articles on the abuses of the Cortwell Institute, a sanatorium that had been found to be conducting experiments with magnets and injections of iron on its patients, causing their deaths. It had resulted in a widespread scandal and the eventual replacement of most of the medical staff.

"He's a very good friend of mine," I said.

I was stretching the truth, but I maintained my gaze without wavering.

His mouth hardened into a bitter line, and he made a gesture to imply he was washing his hands of the matter. "Very well. But that patient has inflicted injury on himself before. If he does so again, after your visit, we will hold you to blame!"

"I'll take care not to upset him," I replied. "But tell me, when in the past several months has he left the grounds?"

He gave me a sour look and disappeared into an office. After a moment, I heard the faraway ring of a bell before he returned with a file. A nurse—a pleasant-looking woman of about thirty-five—appeared at the corner.

"Yes, Mr. Harper?"

"Mrs. Newcomb, please give the inspector what he needs from this file and then take him to the patient's room for a brief visit." He laid emphasis on the last two words.

He left us, and she opened the file. "What would you like to know?"

"When did Mr. Dorstone last leave the premises?"

She hesitated. "We do not call him Mr. Dorstone here, you understand. The family asked that we refer to him as Mr. Drew."

An alias. Well, that wasn't surprising.

"When did he last leave?"

She ran her index finger down a page. "Six weeks ago. On the fourteenth."

If that was true, there was no possibility that he could have committed either murder. "Are you certain?"

"Oh, we're very certain," she said earnestly. "Mr. Harper and another nurse, Mrs. Winn, signed him out together. It's required."

And they couldn't be paid to look the other way? If Sidney's last name was being altered, couldn't other information be changed as well?

"Has he had any visitors lately? His sister, or his aunt?"

She consulted another page. "His sister was here three weeks ago; his aunt twelve days ago. No one since."

"What about his correspondence? Do you keep track of his letters?"

"Certainly," she said. "He receives letters from Jane, and he writes back. She is the only one."

"What sort of man is he?" I asked.

Her expression softened. "I think he's a fine young man. But he's troubled." She closed the file and turned toward the stairs. "You'll see for yourself."

We climbed to the second story and walked down a hallway ominous in its stillness. The nurse knocked at a door, and when there was no reply, she took out her key and opened it. A man sat in a wheeled chair by a window. His face turned toward us with hopeful expectancy that faded when he saw me.

Mrs. Newcomb said pleasantly, "Mr. Drew, you have a visitor."

We observed each other in silence. He was thin, almost gaunt, with his legs bony inside his well-pressed trousers. His dark hair reached his shoulders, but he was clean-shaven.

"I'll return in fifteen minutes," she said. "That is the allowed time." Then she closed the door and turned the key in the lock.

"I saw you," he said abruptly. "Walking up the drive. Are you always in a hurry?"

A small laugh escaped. "I suppose I am."

He gestured toward a chair. "What do you want with me?"

I sat down, recalled the dividing line I'd drawn in my mind, and began slowly: "My name is Michael Corravan, and I'm looking into the matter of a letter your sister Jane received recently."

He looked suddenly wary. "A letter? From whom?"

"We're not sure." I drew out my pocketbook, just for something to do with my hands, as I began to spin my fiction. "When did *you* last write to your sister Jane?"

"I'm not permitted to correspond with my sister," he said stiffly. "My mother forbids it."

I gave him a look. "I'm aware Miss Levering has served as messenger. But I won't tell anyone." I paused. "Your mother doesn't know I'm here."

He studied his hands clasped in his lap. "Two weeks ago Tuesday," he said finally. "I sent her a poem I thought she'd like."

"Nothing this past Monday?"

"No." He looked at me curiously. "Why?"

"A message was delivered to her that evening, after she and Miss Levering attended the theater. It indicated that you wanted to see her."

He sat up straighter, alarmed now. "You mean someone forged a letter from me? What did it say?"

"I don't know. It was misplaced."

He snickered. "My mother probably threw it straight into the dustbin, if she thought it was from me."

I let that alone. "Who, aside from your parents and Jane, knows that you're here?"

"The servants, of course. My uncle. My aunt, who lives nearby. Isabella and her family. No one else." His mouth twisted. "It's not something my mother wants bandied about."

"When you write to Jane, you do it here?" I pointed to the desk in the corner.

"Sometimes. Or I take my portable desk out of doors."

"May I see the stationery you use?"

He rose from the chair, rather unsteadily, drew a key from his pocket, and unlocked the top. "Here it is."

I took the sheet he offered. A fine white linen blend. "May I keep this?"

"Of course."

"And is Miss Levering your only messenger?"

He nodded, a frown forming. "But look here. This is very strange. Why would someone impersonate me? Is Jane all right?"

"She's fine." I folded the paper and put it in my pocket. "There was something about the letter that didn't seem right to her."

"Well, she'd have known if it wasn't my handwriting," he said. "I have an awful scrawl, as she says."

He was right; however, the letter might have been made to look as if it were signed by Mr. Harper or one of the doctors here.

"You can lock the desk again." I watched as he did so. "Do you know a young woman named Rose Albert?"

He shook his head. "Why?"

I had my lie ready: "Apparently, she came to the house on Monday, distributing pamphlets for women's rights." I shrugged. "I'm sure it's unrelated."

He snorted again. "My mother probably would have thrown *her* in the dustbin, right after my letter, if she had the chance."

"Your mother isn't in favor of them?"

"No. Jane is, though." An affectionate smile came over his lips.

"You're fond of her, aren't you?"

"Of course. She is the only true friend I have."

I felt a sick pang at the thought of what her death would mean to him, and the words came out before I thought: "If you don't mind me asking, why are you here?"

He flushed and ducked his head, his face full of shame. "Weakness, Inspector." His voice flattened. "Weakness of mind and constitution."

"Was that a medical opinion?"

"Yes," he said dully.

I rose from the chair. "Mr. Dorstone, there will always be people who are ready to tell you what you should think of yourself." I did up the buttons of my coat. "Frankly, I was once told I was too bloody stupid to do anything but haul grain sacks and fight in a boxing hall."

His face lifted, and his lips parted.

"I'm telling the truth," I said, for in fact I was. "But you strike me as observant and clever. Miss Levering had only good things to say about you. I'm quite sure she thinks of herself as your friend."

His expression softened.

I continued, "I'm no doctor, but if you've been here a while," I gestured toward the window, "you might consider changing your view. Bestir yourself. *Do* something. How old are you?"

"Twenty-five."

"So they cannot keep you here against your will, so long as you can find a doctor to sign your papers." I took out my pocketbook, tore out a page, and wrote my name and James's name and address. "Here's the name of someone you might write to. He's a doctor of mental disorders, a friend of mine."

With an astonished look, he accepted the scrap of paper.

I plucked my hat off the chair, said goodbye, and left the sanatorium without seeing either Mrs. Newcomb or Mr. Harper.

One thing was certain: Sidney hadn't killed his sister. Not with a look like that on his face when he spoke of her. So who had written the letter, and how had he known how to write it, so she'd be convinced to get into her father's carriage, alone, at that time of night?

And what would Sidney do when he heard of Jane's death?

The thought made me feel very low.

★ ★ ★

I continued to pursue what leads I had, though with each day I lost confidence that I'd find a meaningful connection between Rose Albert and Jane Dorstone. I spoke with friends, family members, clerks, and clergy, who were variously tearful, horrified, and obliging. From this, I gathered that Rose and Jane had never met; they had no friends or instructors in common; the families worshipped at different churches. The judge had sold most of his wife's shares in Baldwin's, so he had no significant controlling interest; and neither the judge nor Mr. Dorstone knew anyone in the Home Secretary's office. The women's suitors, Thurgood, Gordon, and Eddington, pursued different professions, and Thurgood and Eddington belonged to different gentlemen's clubs, while Gordon belonged to no club at all; and none of them had any notable ties to tea or textile companies or Baldwin's. Judge Albert belonged to the Adwaller Club, for members of the legal profession, whereas Mr. Dorstone's family had belonged to Clavell's for three generations. None of the Dorstones knew Lyvina Baldwin. I examined the boat Jane had been in, but as Blair said, there were no marks: It was like watching water seep between my fingers.

I think part of me was waiting for Tuesday morning and a third dead woman.

CHAPTER 26

I woke from my dreams with a feeling of dread heavy upon my chest. As I dressed, I realized that if I went to the Yard, I'd only sit at my desk fidgeting until word came.

Or until it didn't. But somehow I couldn't imagine that happening.

So I headed for Wapping, though it was still early.

It was one of those rare mornings when the Thames looked more silver than filth, more lifeblood than cesspool. The river was busy, but the traffic moved with pragmatic steadiness, settled in its rhythm.

At the edge of the wharf stood Blair. Something about his posture told me there had been no report yet of another body. Yet he was out here all the same, watching. Despite everything, I felt a twinge of affinity for him. This case was beginning to claw at his nerves, too.

I walked down to where he stood. His hat was slouched in the back, his hands shoved in his pockets.

He gave no sign of surprise at my appearance. Nodded briefly and put his eyes back on the river.

"No news yet?" I asked.

"Nah." A sideways glance. "You saw the papers this morning?"

I tensed. "No. Why?"

"*Reynolds's* says a young man at Seddon Hall tried to kill himself last night, after a visit from Inspector Corravan of the Yard."

His nonchalance ran heat down my spine. I forced out the word: "How?"

"Threw himself off the roof."

I knew he was aiming to hurt me, but his words only made me sick for Sidney. My visit must have stirred Sidney's suspicions, and somehow he found out about Jane. Into my mind sprang the image of that poor man in his chair, and the look in his eyes when I'd told him to bestir himself, to *do* something.

I thrust my shaking hands into my pockets so hard the lining tore. "Did he survive?"

"Didn't say." His face was impassive, but I heard the satisfaction underlying those two words.

This time his malevolence stopped me cold. The fact that Blair could take any sort of pleasure from a young man attempting to destroy his own life roiled my insides like an eddy at the river's edge. It came to me, as I stood beside him, that Blair had changed in five years. He'd always been tough and brusque, but now he was harder. Hateful, even. Perhaps more toward me than toward the world generally, but suddenly, with the finality of a door closing, I realized I didn't like him anymore, or admire him. The realization startled me, and in its wake came the feeling that our old connection had been severed as irreparably as a snapped line.

I digested this for a few moments in silence, which Blair eventually broke: "Vincent has a lot of friends who work for the papers from his time at the *Telegraph*. And he owes them for all that good publicity after he was made director."

The idea that Vincent leaked my name in this context was absurd. Vincent might be beholden to the papers, and he didn't owe me any special allegiance, but making me look bad would damage the Yard.

I let Blair's insinuation go unanswered and watched a long flat steamer whose upstream progress sent a rumble through the boards under my feet.

"You don't need to stay," Blair said. "I'll send a message if there's another one."

"I'll give it a little longer," I said, and we stood in silence. When I heard the church bells strike half past nine, I felt a cautious ripple of relief.

Both Rose and Jane had been retrieved by this hour—and no doubt Blair had his men out looking. With any luck, it was only the two women.

And then we saw it. A boat, moving fast, straight for the wharf.

"Damn," Blair whispered.

Two constables were on the boat, and one of them waved furiously, hollering something I couldn't make out over the boat traffic. Then Blair shouted back: "Alive?"

The constable nodded furiously.

I raced back into the station. "Find a cab! We need to go to the hospital! She's alive!"

There were six men in the room, and all of them stared open-mouthed for a moment. Then one yanked open the front door and vanished, his whistle blowing three ear-piercing blasts, followed by three more.

I returned to the dock and watched as two constables placed the woman on the stretcher, sodden flowers and leaves dropping from her dress onto the pier. They bore her toward the station, lurching in their haste, and I held the door open as they approached.

"Someone's going for a cab," I called to Blair. But my eyes were on the third victim.

She was older, perhaps twenty-five or thirty, with dark hair and features that lacked the prettiness of the others. She wore a gray dress, without much ornament, and unlike the others' it was cut down the front, from the collar to the hem. A sharp wind blew at it, and for a moment her right breast was exposed until one of the constables called for a halt and drew the fabric back over her. Her hair had been fixed in a modest style, although it was a dark drenched mess at the moment. Her hands were bound with rope, and I glimpsed a ring on the third finger of her right hand. The other differences were her face had more bruises and cuts than the others, and her skirts weren't bloody. She had no shoes, and her feet were bare and bony.

She looked dead.

"You're sure she's still with us?" I asked of no one in particular, as I followed the constables and Blair through the station and out onto the street.

"There's a pulse," the constable offered.

Then there was a chance.

Together one of the constables and Blair lifted the woman into the cab and laid her on a seat.

"Denmark Street Hospital!" Blair called to the driver. "Up Nightingale, right on St. George! Quick as you can."

Before I could step in, Blair pulled the door closed, and the cab drove off, the wheels jouncing against the uneven stones.

I'd been so focused on the victim before us that I'd set aside whatever ugly swamp of distrust and resentment lay between us. But Blair hadn't.

I turned to find the other constable looking at me uncertainly. "Fetch me another, would you?" I asked. He blasted his whistle three times, and within a few minutes, another cab appeared, and I climbed inside.

Had the murderer meant to leave his victim alive this time? The tied wrists and the boat, that much was the same. But the dress cut open? The plainness of it, compared to the garb of the other women? And she was older and married. Why her?

I hoped she lived long enough to tell us.

★ ★ ★

One of the oldest hospitals in London, Denmark Street was a cluster of buildings with mismatched bricks cobbled together into a rectangle. The first cab departed as mine drew up.

I headed for the entrance, but at the sound of another cab racing up behind, I halted with a sense of foreboding. There were two newspaper offices near Wapping, and we'd been lucky to avoid them as long as we had. Of the newspapermen I knew, many had a way of looking out from under their hats, stooping as if they wanted to avoid notice—or felt ashamed of themselves. Possibly both. But some were decent blokes who'd helped me on occasion.

A sturdy figure in a shapeless hat emerged from the cab, and I blew out my breath in relief.

Tom Flynn of the *Falcon*.

Though he wasn't quite the "very good friend" I'd told Mr. Harper, Tom was more than an acquaintance, and the *Falcon* wasn't like the scandal-mongering *Beacon* or *Reynolds's News*, which gleefully made the police look like bumbling bounders. Tom was a good writer, bold as brass, smarter than most, hard to shake. He'd check his facts twice, wouldn't betray his informants, and—unlike

Fishel—would hold back on publishing something if I told him why. We'd first met when I was in the River Police, and he was asking imprudent questions about dockworkers and unions. He ended up with some broken ribs and a lost phalanx on one finger, so I'd offered some guidance about people to avoid, and he'd reciprocated with information.

But how had he known to come here? Was it the constable's whistle? Or had Tom been on the river? He was up and about early. That much I knew.

Tom started toward me, his hands jammed in his coat pockets. He was a full head shorter than I but broad of shoulder and sturdy. He had a round face, bright green eyes that could look hard as stones, a small nose, and a bald spot that was hidden by his hat.

"Tom."

"Corravan." He gave me his twisted smile, wry and yet easy as a nudge, as if we understood each other. As I suppose we did. We both were after the same thing—assembling an orderly series of events—though for different reasons.

"What brought you?" I asked.

He squinted up. "Saw the boat making for the dock and watched them lift her out. This is the closest hospital."

Fair guess, I thought and headed for the door.

"Who is she?" he asked, keeping pace with me.

"We don't know."

"Where'd you find her?"

I dragged the door open. "Downriver by the docks."

He eyed me askance. "What were *you* doing at Wapping?"

I gave him a look.

"Blair here?" He tipped his head toward the corridor.

I nodded, and his nose wrinkled. Tom didn't like Blair.

"I know you have to write something," I said. "But for now, can you omit that she's alive? And I'll share what I can." I paused. "With you first."

His mouth pursed. "Don't wait too long, Corravan."

"I won't."

He settled his hat more firmly on his head and went back outside, while I headed in to find Blair in the foyer. Blair scowled at my presence, and this time my own annoyance flared. "Vincent will want to know," I said shortly. "And Tom Flynn was outside.

He saw the boat come in. He promised me he won't release details for now."

I'd done Blair a favor he couldn't have asked of Tom himself. He nodded a grudging acknowledgment and muttered, "Have to wait while they're settling her."

At last a young, dark-haired nurse approached. "Come with me, please." Blair and I followed her down the hallway, past several wards full of patients, and entered a large room partitioned by gray curtains into private areas. At the far end a doctor stood making notes on a chart. A matronly nurse slipped out between two panels. She saw Blair, one step ahead of me, and shook her head firmly. "She's in no state for visitors. Certainly not the police."

In the shape of Blair's shoulders, I read him waiting for me, the younger, less formidable underling, to step in. I took up my old role as easily as I'd have walked one of my former patrol beats. As Blair headed toward the doctor, I answered the nurse in an apologetic undertone, "We're here to protect her—though, to be honest, I'm worried about you as well."

She looked doubtful. "About me?"

"Whoever did this may try to attack her again. And," I hesitated, "hurt anyone who tried to stop him."

The starched white apron over her uniform rose and fell with a breath. "Do you truly think he might follow her here?"

"Honestly, I don't know. I hope not. But if we could have a chair placed here," I pointed, "a constable will keep watch until she leaves the hospital. Could you give us permission for that?"

She nodded. "I'm the head nurse. Nurse Hayes."

"And keep her identity—" I began.

"Secret, once we know it. Of course."

I noted down her name in my book. "So often people think we're just a bother."

She gave a small, sad smile. "There are plenty of people who don't want to believe in malevolence. We know better." With that, she left me.

I watched Blair with the doctor. They were having a conversation of some import, and suddenly Blair's posture altered in a way that told me the doctor had said something unexpected. Blair replied; the doctor was professing his thanks. Only a few minutes, and we had two allies in the ward.

But our most important ally was being kept from us.

My hands itched to pull aside the curtains, just wide enough to see our victim. Nurse Hayes was out of sight, and I inched closer to the curtains, close enough to part them.

Blair was at my side. "Corravan." He had me by the elbow and steered me out of the ward.

I muttered under my breath. "I'll stay here until she wakes up—"

"No. I'll leave the constable." He led me into the hallway. "I have her name. Charlotte Forsyte Munro."

I halted mid-stride. "The doctor knows her?"

"Knows the family," he replied. "Husband's away for work in Paris, father's another doctor. I told him we'd notify her parents."

"Did he think she'd been left alive on purpose?" I asked.

"Could be. Thinks she might be with child." He saw my surprise and added, "Only a few months along."

"So that stopped his hand?" My voice cracked in disbelief. I remembered her dress, cut from neck to hem. "Is the baby all right?"

"Can't tell yet."

A groan escaped my mouth.

"I'll give Constable Hartley instructions," he said. "Meanwhile, you see her family. Purdy Street, number 12. Marylebone."

My hackles rose at his peremptory tone.

Blair rubbed a hand over his face. "And stop in at the Yard and let Vincent know what's happened."

"It's not on the way—" I began.

"I know," he snapped. "But damn it, Vincent doesn't like being kept in the dark. And I don't want him barking at me again."

Again? I wondered.

We'd reached the foyer, where the constable had materialized, and the two of them started back toward the ward.

I hailed a cab and told the driver to take me to the Yard.

But after a mile, I banged on the cab ceiling and asked to be taken to the Forsyte house instead. I didn't much care if Blair had to endure some barking, and I'd have more to tell Vincent after I saw her parents. Besides, if Vincent was occupied, stopping in to see him could take an hour, or even two. Mrs. Munro might not live that long.

CHAPTER 27

The house in Purdy Street, just outside Mayfair, was more modest than those of the other victims. The couple who entered the parlor, where I'd been put to wait, were dressed well but not expensively. Mrs. Forsyte seemed a delicate sort, with a timid manner, while her husband clearly resented my interruption of his day. They both remained standing.

"Dr. and Mrs. Forsyte," I began in my most respectful manner. "I'm Inspector Corravan of Scotland Yard, and I'm afraid I have some unfortunate news."

Her father pinched the edges of his waistcoat. "Well, I don't imagine your sort brings any other sort of news."

I curbed a retort. "It concerns your daughter, Mrs. Munro. She is alive and at Denmark Street Hospital in Wapping, but she was attacked last night."

Mrs. Forsyte's eyes became black pools of panic, and her hand groped feebly for the high back of an upholstered chair.

Her husband took a step toward me. "Look here, are you sure? You Yard men are known for your wrongheaded reports—"

"Dr. Masterson recognized her and sent me here to tell you," I interrupted, spreading my hands in a gesture meant to calm him. "Your daughter is being cared for, but she's not able to speak yet. I was hoping you could tell me where she was last night."

The two of them looked at each other. Mrs. Forsyte's face was full of despair. Dr. Forsyte's expression was a mix of fear, shock, and consternation.

"She was here," Dr. Forsyte said abruptly. "All evening."

"Until just before nine o'clock," Mrs. Forstye whispered.

"*After* nine, Margaret," he snapped.

"Did you see her home?" I asked.

He drew back as if insulted. "Why—what do you think, at that hour?" He scowled. "How was she attacked? And where?"

"Someone assaulted her and put her, alive but likely unconscious, in a small boat. She was discovered this morning downstream from Wapping Division."

"In a boat!" gasped her mother. "Why would someone put her in a boat?"

"How badly was she hurt?" Dr. Forsyte demanded.

I hesitated. "He bound her hands and mouth. She may be concussed. That's all I know as of now."

Mrs. Forsyte crumpled into the chair and began to sob. Dr. Forsyte stalked to the mantel and seized it, bowing until his forehead nearly touched his hand. Despite his unpleasantness, I pitied the man, full of anguish for his injured daughter.

But then he looked up, and I saw I'd been mistaken. His eyes glittered not with grief but with fury. And he was looking not at me, as I'd expected, but at his wife.

His voice was a snarl. "I *told* you she'd get hurt. All those nights with that filth on the street—of course this happened! We should thank God she wasn't killed for her foolishness—and yours!" He hovered over her, his voice heavy with contempt. "All along, you encouraged her, just so you could be her favorite. See what it has earned you!"

She didn't look up. She only rocked, sobbing, her palms flat against her temples. His arms were clenched to his sides, as if in restraints. Then he stalked out of the room, slamming the door so hard it flew open again.

Whatever reaction I had expected, this wasn't it.

From behind me came a strangled moan.

I went down on my knee beside her. "Mrs. Forsyte."

A young maid with reddish hair materialized in the doorway and rushed to her mistress's side. Her hand rested on

Mrs. Forsyte's shoulder, and her voice was soothing in the older woman's ear.

She met my gaze. "She's very upset," she whispered. "You should go."

I stood and stepped away. Poor Mrs. Forsyte's face was a ghastly gray. Reluctantly, I let the maid herd me out of the room and toward the front door. "What did he mean?" I muttered. "His daughter spent time with filth on the street?"

Dr. Forsyte appeared, buttoning his overcoat, no doubt on his way to visit his daughter. "That will be all, Inspector."

"Doctor—" I began.

He drew himself up. "That is all." The words came out between his teeth. He turned to the maid, his voice hard. "Don't speak to him. I will put you out—and anyone else who is indiscreet."

The maid bobbed her head and opened the door. "Yes, sir."

I stepped aside, allowing him to precede me. "Dr. Forsyte, she could have died last night. But she's alive."

He paused at the threshold. "Don't you dare tell me she's lucky."

The maid averted her eyes. As Dr. Forsyte stalked out, I saw the resentful look she directed at his back—and then her eyes locked on mine.

She could tell me things. I could see it. But I would have to wait to find out what they were.

CHAPTER 28

For the second time, I hailed a cab and asked to be taken to the Yard. I was grateful for the twenty minutes to reflect and arrange my thoughts.

Vincent must have been watching for me because I hadn't been inside my office ten seconds before he entered. He pushed the door closed behind him and looked at me expectantly. "Were you at Wapping?"

I sat in the chair behind my desk as he took the one opposite. "Yes. There was a third this morning."

His eyes closed, and his fingertips rubbed at his forehead, leaving it red. "Every Tuesday, another woman."

"There were differences," I said quietly. "The most important is she's alive."

His eyes opened. "What?"

"She's at Denmark Street. And we were lucky. One of the doctors knows the family. Her name is Charlotte Forsyte Munro, her husband is in France, and she might be with child."

"With child," he echoed hollowly. "Good Lord." Vincent stood, paced the two steps my office allowed, and then stepped behind the chair, curling his long fingers around the top and meeting my gaze. "And then you went to see her family."

"Her parents, yes. In Purdy Street."

A pause, during which he studied his hands on the chair. At last he looked up, and his expression and voice were composed.

"Corravan, in the future, I would like you to communicate your whereabouts." He raised a hand to forestall my protest. "I understand why you went to Wapping first. But it would have taken you only a moment to send a message from there, so I knew what had happened."

"Yes, sir."

My tone was dutiful, but he heard a note that brought a spark to his eye. "You mistake me. It is not merely a matter of courtesy, Mr. Corravan. We—the Yard—cannot be caught flat-footed if someone inquires."

"I thought it best to have more to report, sir."

His eyes held mine. "I understand. But next time, send a message. In a *timely fashion*. Will you, please."

It wasn't a question.

"Yes, sir."

"Now, continue."

I recounted everything, saving Tom Flynn's appearance for last. Vincent's expression was chagrined.

"At least it's the *Falcon*, not the *Beacon* or *Reynolds's*," I said. "And Tom won't purposefully publish something that'll hurt our investigation."

"But if he writes anything up tonight, it'll be in the other papers by tomorrow," Vincent said—and he wasn't wrong. "Uncanny the way Flynn appears, just when something's happening. Like those burglaries last month in Westminster."

"He's clever," I acknowledged. "But Blair left one of his constables at the hospital. He'll let us know as soon as Mrs. Munro wakes up. Her testimony could be all we need to stop this."

Vincent pinched his lower lip between his thumb and forefinger. "We absolutely cannot let Tom Flynn—or anyone—learn about the other two women. It would unleash an uncontrollable panic throughout London, and the man might alter his methods. Although leaving her alive is already a marked difference."

"I want to find out what her father meant about the filth on the street," I said.

"It sounds as if he's beside himself," Vincent said. "Perhaps give him a day or two before you see him again."

I made no answer, and Vincent crossed to look out my window. When at last he spoke, his voice had an odd, remote quality.

"I think our country sinks beneath the yoke. More suffer, and more sundry ways than ever."

I stared at his back. "Beg pardon?"

"Malcolm's prophecy in *Macbeth*." He remained staring out the window. "Just some days it seems there's new kinds of evil out there. More vicious."

His words were an eerie echo of my own worry about a new, modern sort of crime, but I pushed them aside, not least because I don't place much stock in uselessly quoting the words of dead playwrights. Besides, I was hopeful. Charlotte Munro could change everything, if we could talk to her in the next few days.

Vincent headed for the door but paused with his hand on the knob. "Did you look into Nate McLoughlin? The Whitechapel case?"

I winced inwardly. "Not yet, but I will," I promised. "I have someone who might know where I can find him."

He opened his mouth to say something but thought better of it and merely nodded.

After he left, I should have spent an hour recording the day's events in my diary. But suddenly weary, I shrank from the task. Instead, I wrote a letter to Seddon Hall, inquiring about Mr. Drew, and posted it with a feeling of dread. Then, for the first time in over a year, I stopped at a pub on the way home, and—shouting to make myself heard over the singing—I found myself asking for a shot of whiskey.

Why? I still can't say. Might have been that Vincent's hopelessness reminded me too closely of my own. Might have been because I knew I was responsible for Sidney's second attempt on his life. Or because I balked at going back to Whitechapel as an inspector to lean on people I loved for information about one of our own.

Never mind that I hadn't had spirits in months. My body knew how the cheap whiskey would unfurl a warmth that would make my nerves stop twitching in a matter of minutes.

Sure enough, by the end of the next verse of the bawdy song, it worked.

CHAPTER 29

As I reached my house, I saw firelight flickering through the front window, which meant Harry was home. I considered walking about until Harry went to bed, but it was too dank and cold. To my surprise, when I opened the door, I found not just Harry but James, too, drinking coffee by the fire. Harry looked at me apprehensively, and his eyes fell on the evening *Falcon* sitting on the table. The modest headline, just below the fold, made me cringe: BRUTAL ASSAULT ON THE THAMES. But I saw it was only a short notice, and I unbuttoned and hung my coat before I took up the paper.

James gestured with his pipe. "You're mentioned by name."

I turned up the lamp, so I could read.

This morning, the Thames witnessed a brutal, bloody assault on a well-dressed woman of approximately twenty-five years of age. She was found by the River Police among the shallows in the Lower Pool near the London Docks. She had been placed in a lighter boat, with flowers and leaves, as if in a tableau.

A group of police, including Chief Inspector Michael Corravan of Scotland Yard, is investigating. Readers will no doubt recall that Mr. Corravan solved the Beardsley murder in January. Surely he will discover the man responsible for this wretched crime.

I dropped the newspaper back on the table, mentally sending Tom a nod of thanks. Not only had he reminded people of a recent success of mine. He'd neglected to mention that the woman was still alive and the name of the hospital where she'd been taken, which was decent of him. Yet I knew he'd included my name as a nudge, meaning, *Do you see this favor I've done for you?* I could almost hear his gravelly voice, a sing-song in my ear: *I'm waiting.*

James took a pull on his pipe. "So this is the second." Seeing my puzzlement, he added, "You told me about the first, and I said it reminded me of a Viking funeral."

"That's right," I said, remembering. "But it's actually the third. Each of the past three Tuesdays."

"Sequential murders," James breathed. The firelight reflected off his spectacles, but I knew if I could have seen his eyes, they'd be bright with scientific interest.

"What would cause a man to do something like this?" Harry asked, his face screwed up with revulsion.

I looked at James. "You always say it's one of four motives."

"Four?" Harry asked.

I sank into the remaining chair, the least comfortable of the three. "Fear. Revenge. Passion. Greed."

James nodded. "But the violence together with the flowers suggests a peculiar mix of brutality and an almost romantic attentiveness to spectacle. My mind jumps to a disease—syphilis, or childhood scarlet fever—an organic derangement—"

"That hardly matters," I retorted. "For God's sake, I just want to catch him before he—before he assaults someone else."

James wore an injured expression, but Harry said thoughtfully, "I noticed the paper used that word, 'assault.' It doesn't say she died."

My eyes flashed to him in surprise. *Damn, he was quick.*

James peered at me. "Corravan, is Harry correct? She's alive?"

I felt a mix of irritation, shame, and annoyance. If I hadn't stopped for that drink, I'd have managed this better. But there was no help for it now. Both Harry and James were waiting expectantly.

I gave them an account, being careful to omit the women's names. By the end, Harry's eyes were round, and when a log snapped, he flinched as if a spark had singed him.

"And the first two were sent down the Thames in a boat as well?" James asked.

I nodded. "With leaves and flowers. Sort of like the 'Lady of Shalott.'"

James looked incredulous. "When did you take up reading poetry?"

"You know damn well I don't. Belinda told me about it."

"I don't know that poem," Harry ventured.

"You wouldn't have studied it," James replied. "It's modern. Tennyson."

"There's a painting of her, too," I said. "In Liverpool."

James turned to Harry. "It's about a beautiful woman who spends her days weaving a tapestry, under a fatal curse that she may never leave the tower in which she's been imprisoned." He waved the pipe, as if gesturing to something in the distance. "One day, through the window, she sees the knight Lancelot and promptly falls in love. Desperate for him to see her, she puts herself in a row-boat with some flowers and sails down to Camelot."

"And dies of grief," I added.

Harry looked indignant. "That story's not modern! It's from *Morte D'Arthur*. Tennyson must've poached it!"

"Morta what?" I asked.

"*Morte D'Arthur*. It's French. It means—that is, it—it means—er, *Death of Arthur*," Harry muttered, evidently expecting me to snap at him for showing off.

"So a Frenchman wrote it?" I asked, my voice neutral.

Harry's expression eased. "Actually, Sir Thomas Malory was English, born in the fourteen hundreds. He was imprisoned in Marshalsea for murder, and to pass the time he gathered legends about King Arthur and put them down in English. Most came from old French poems and stories. I had to read some at school."

"What's Malory's version?"

"It takes place in Astolat," he replied. "Lady Elaine's father organizes a jousting tournament, and all the knights come, including King Arthur and Lancelot. Then Elaine meets Lancelot and asks him to wear a token—a handkerchief, I think—"

"Wait," I said. "Her name is Elaine?"

"Yes. Lady Elaine of Astolat. Why?" Harry looked at me oddly.

There was something about the way Harry had pronounced "Elaine" that drew up a recent memory of Stiles's mild voice: "A lane." I doubted Mrs. Beckford's troubled mind was occupied with an Arthurian legend. But perhaps she'd been saying "Elaine" instead of "a lane." So far as I'd heard, Stiles hadn't had any luck in his inquiries on either of the lanes near the Beckfords' house. I'd have to remember to mention the possibility to him.

I shook my head. "Go on. Elaine gave him a handkerchief."

Harry obliged. "Well, Lancelot knows if Guinevere finds out, she'll be jealous, so he has to joust in disguise. Lancelot wins the whole tournament, but he's wounded, and when Elaine nurses him back to health, he offers to pay her. She's insulted, and that's when Lancelot realizes she loves him. He's rather an idiot," he said, wrinkling his nose. "When he leaves, Elaine dies of a broken heart. So the villagers put her in a boat with a letter that explains everything and send her floating down to Camelot."

"Now I recall." James drew gently on his pipe. "I read some of the stories last year when they were published in *Westly's Miscellany*—in present-day English, of course. But why would a murderer re-create a scene from an Arthurian legend?"

"He could be a writer, trying to bring the story to life," Harry suggested.

James nodded thoughtfully. "He might have delusions of being Lancelot."

"Or he hates beautiful women, like that man in Carpenter's book," Harry added.

I found myself gaping at the pair of them. "God help me." I rubbed my eyes with the heels of my hands. "Now that the papers have it, we have a week before London falls into a panic about another Le Loup."

We were all silent for a minute, and then James rose. "You should go to bed, Corravan. You look exhausted."

"You can sleep here," I replied. "You might not find a cab at this hour."

James looked at me oddly. "We brought the hospital's. Didn't you see it outside?"

I stared. How had I missed a horse and a carriage outside my door?

The whiskey was partly to blame. But it had worn off, and I was so tired the room was starting to swim before my eyes.

I went to bed with half my clothes on. It was midnight. I'd be up in six hours. What was the point of changing?

CHAPTER 30

The next day I went to the hospital, walking in just as Tom Flynn walked out.

"She's gone," he said bluntly. "Went home last night. And Masterson won't be in for another hour."

So Dr. Forsyte had not come to visit his daughter; he'd come to retrieve her. *Damn*, I thought. I should have guessed he would.

Tom eyed me. "What's so special about this woman? She's not even dead."

I shook my head. "Can't say yet."

He shoved his hands into his pockets. "You know, I *could* use this."

"I know. But I'm asking you not to." I paused. "I won't talk to anyone else, I swear."

"This case could matter. To more than just her family. To London. Maybe even the nation."

"Why do you say that?"

He shrugged. "A respectable middle-class woman, a strange attempted murder? It'll catch the public's eye. And after the trial last fall, people need reassurance. It'll reflect badly, if you don't solve it."

"Believe me, I know. Vincent feels it. Makes all of us feel it, too."

He gave a short laugh. "I'll bet he does."

Vincent's dire words still hung in my ear. And despite myself, the question slid out. "Do you think there's a new kind of crime in London now? More vicious? Or am I imagining it?"

To his credit, Tom didn't scoff. "I'd say there is. Natural result of too many people fighting over too little, it seems to me."

That wasn't what I wanted to hear. I grunted and took a step back. "I'll come see you soon."

"Yah." He walked off down the street, the ends of his coat flapping.

I went inside, where the desk clerk confirmed Dr. Masterson wouldn't be in until ten o'clock. But there was no point in going elsewhere. I fidgeted in a chair near his office for the entire hour plus nine minutes, until he finally appeared.

"You let her go home," I said without preamble. "Was that wise?"

A resigned look came over his features. "Her father insisted." He opened the door and unbuttoned his coat. "In truth, it doesn't matter, so long as she has a nurse at home. She has no internal injuries; her contusions and bruises will mend. She needs rest more than anything."

I took a seat. "I had an unusual interview with her parents yesterday."

He took his time hanging his coat, fussing with the collar, as if he were trying to avoid looking at me.

"Her father said the attack was a result of her association with the filth on the street," I said. "And he blamed his wife for encouraging it. What did he mean?"

He sat and rested his elbows on his desk, rubbing his hands over his face, roughly enough to pull at the flesh. At last, he met my gaze wearily. "Mrs. Munro is an unusual young woman. Ever since she was young, she has taken an interest in social causes."

"Do you mean philanthropy?" I asked.

He leaned back and clasped his hands at his waist. "She doesn't just donate money. She works at Our Lady of Perpetual Help's Home for Fallen Women."

I stared. "Do you mean the church on Underwood Road, in Lambeth?"

"Yes. The home was added five years ago, in a building nearby."

Now I understood. "She was trying to reclaim prostitutes."

He nodded. "She'd go out in the evening to find them. Then she'd give them food and bring them back to Our Lady. She helped them find respectable work."

"Admirable," I said, and I meant it. "And she continued after she was married?"

"Oh, yes. Her husband is a crusader for social reform as well, although his interest is in abolishing slums and improving sanitation. But I'm not certain Mrs. Munro would have continued the work for much longer." He paused. "Being that she was with child."

Was.

My mouth went dry. "You mean she lost it?"

His eyes widened. "Oh, God—no! I simply meant when she was attacked. So far as I could tell, the child is unaffected."

"Dr. Masterson," I said, "this is important. Is there any sign that she was raped?"

His head tipped forward. "No. Why?"

"Her dress was cut open."

He took a deep breath. "My good man, I'm sorry I wasn't clear. Mrs. Munro was struck in the face, and her mouth and hands bound, as you saw. But there was no sign he outraged her."

Relieved, I asked, "How did you know she was with child?"

"When I examined her, I detected a swelling in her abdomen. She confirmed it."

My heart leaped. "She spoke?"

He shook his head. "I asked, and she nodded. That was her only communication all evening."

"Is she able to talk now?"

"Well." He looked dubious. "She's still in shock, but there is no *anatomical* reason she can't speak with you. I'd only ask that you be patient and tactful. She is a woman of strong character, but she's undergone a terrifying ordeal."

As I rose, preparing to bid him goodbye, he cleared his throat. "Don't be surprised if you're turned away."

"What? Why?" I asked. Dr. Forsyte had made clear his lack of respect for the Yard, but surely he would want me to find the culprit. "Because he doesn't trust Yard men?"

He studied his fingernails. "Mr. Corravan, Dr. Forsyte and I were colleagues until recently, when he sold his practice. He is a difficult man, rigid in his thinking, highly suspicious of others' motives, and obsessively aware of his standing in social circles. He was mortified about his daughter's work." His eyes met mine. "He will consider this act against his daughter as something that must be silenced, lest it become yet another piece of shameful gossip attached to her—and to him. My guess is he'll try to keep her from speaking to you."

The muscles across my shoulders tightened. "I'll keep that in mind."

CHAPTER 31

When I knocked at the Forsytes' door and explained my errand, I was admitted by a butler, taken to the parlor again, and asked to wait.

Wait I did, for nearly half an hour, during which I inspected the room more closely. Green baize paper on the walls. Four paintings, two of stern men in their dotage and two of hunting scenes, all in heavy gilt frames. A large mirror over the fireplace. At the hearth, wrought iron pieces, recently blackened. Silver candlesticks. The buttery smell of wax, not cheap tallow. A curious box made of brilliant green jade with a lion carved into the top.

"I told you yesterday I didn't want you here," came a man's voice behind me.

I turned. "Dr. Forsyte," I said calmly, "I understand your anger at what happened to your daughter—"

"Don't patronize me. Your repeated appearance here only serves to provoke gossip."

"But surely you want to know who hurt her," I said, spreading my hands. "I only want to ask a few questions. She could provide a description—"

"She's not speaking to you."

"Because she can't? Or because you won't let her?" Despite my best efforts, my voice rose with frustration.

His face flushed with rage. "My daughter wishes to put this unfortunate episode in the past, and I shall respect her wishes!"

"If your daughter won't speak with me, then will *you* answer some questions on her behalf?"

He looked at me askance, taking my measure. "If you promise this is the end of it."

I assented and sifted my thoughts quickly for the most important matters. "Has she said anything to you about the attack, how she—"

"No. I gave her a sleeping draft, and she hasn't awoken since I brought her home."

Home? I wondered. This was his home, not hers. Did the doctor dislike his son-in-law? Resent her marriage?

I opened my pocketbook. "On Monday, when did your daughter arrive?"

"At tea time. Around half past four."

"And she remained for dinner?"

"Yes. Then she began to feel tired. She left just after nine o'clock." Color came into his cheeks. "As I told you yesterday."

There's something here, I thought. Some uncertainty. Some guilt.

"And why is her husband in Paris?" I asked.

"He's an engineer for the Thames. He believes he has something to learn from the French about drainage."

That is a strong connection to the river, I thought. "Was Mrs. Munro ever attached to another man, before her husband? Engaged, or married?"

"No."

"Can you think of anyone who would be angry enough to attack her? A spurned lover? Someone she's hurt somehow, without meaning to—"

"My daughter is a kind, Christian woman. She has never hurt a soul in her life."

I let that dubious statement pass. "Does your family have any particular connection to the river?"

He stared blankly. "Such as?"

"Shares in a joint-stock company—a shipping concern or a metalworks company such as Baldwin's?" A decided head shake in the negative. "A warehouse such as Terrington's or Preston's?" More shakes of the head. "Or the Yellow Star Tea Company?"

"No, nothing like that."

"What church do you attend?"

"Our Lady of St. John's Wood."

Different from both the Alberts and the Dorstones. "And you were a medical man?"

"I *am* a physician." His mouth tightened. "University trained."

"Ah. Still practicing?" I asked innocently.

"I retired several years ago." He tilted his head back, so he could look down his nose. "I received an inheritance from my father. No doubt you'd like to invent some pernicious history, but he died of a heart attack, in his sleep. I had nothing to do with it."

"I'm sure you didn't." To keep up the pretense of calm, I feigned writing a note, though my meaningless penciling carved the page. "And your daughter. Does she speak or read French?"

"Some," he said irritably. "Like any properly educated English-woman."

I sensed his patience coming to an end, and though I knew Vincent would never have approved, I asked, "Have you ever heard the name Rose Albert? Or Jane Dorstone?"

"Who?"

I repeated the names more slowly.

"No. Why?" He sneered. "Were they prostitutes?"

"No. But speaking of them, I understand you didn't approve of your daughter's work at Our Lady."

"Of course not!" His eyes flashed. "Let me speak plainly, Mr. Corravan, and then perhaps we can be done. My daughter is fool-ish and idealistic, and from the first day she went to that place, she was put in deadly peril for the sake of depraved women who choose to abandon their God and live a life of sin—and now they want to be taken care of, to have their pillows gently smoothed and hot soup spooned into their dirty maws. Bah!"

I bit the inside of my cheek, hard. God knows most pros-titutes did lead indecent lives. But I'd known good women in Whitechapel who'd had little choice when they had hungry mouths to feed.

"They're *diseased*." His face was hard, his eyes glittering. "Cor-rupt in mind and body, and that corruption nearly destroyed my daughter."

Usually I keep my cards close, but there are moments when it's suitable to show one or two.

"There's something you don't know, Dr. Forsyte." I paused. "After I tell you, if you still want me to go, I will."

"And you'll promise to leave us alone."

"Yes." I tucked my pocketbook away. "Your chief concern is your daughter, of course. But others are in danger as well. Your daughter is the third woman to be assaulted in recent weeks."

"The *third*?"

"Yes," I said. "The two other women died. So for the safety of all women in London, I *must* speak with her."

An expression crossed his face too quickly for me to catch. It might have been relief, but it gave way quickly to condemnation. "Do you mean to tell me that had you caught him, my daughter could have been spared this?"

Damn. That wasn't the direction I hoped his thoughts would go.

His jaw was tense, the muscles working. "What does my daughter have in common with these other women?"

I let the second card fall: "Both of them were young, quite beautiful, and nicely dressed. The assaults all happened on Monday night. The other details—the boat, the flower petals, the bound hands—are all the same."

"Flower petals. Bound hands," he repeated.

"In five minutes, your daughter could tell me everything I—"

"No!"

"What if she were to speak to me *sub rosa*?" I asked persuasively. "Not in any official capacity. No one would ever hear her name—"

His eyes became slits. "She's been through enough. I will not have her become an object of gossip. Don't ever return, to speak with her or anyone else." He reached for a velvet pull to call a servant.

"We *will* catch whoever did this," I said.

He gave a short, mirthless laugh. "Given your rates of failure? They're higher than they've ever been. And every one of you with dozens of cases?"

How had he heard that?

My anger mounting, I played a last, terrible card: "What if he intended to *kill* your daughter and he comes here to find her?"

He drew himself up. "What sort of fool do you think I am? I have a guard stationed outside her room."

"But she can't stay in there forever! Besides, think of what *she* would want you to do. She has devoted herself to helping others—"

"And look where it brought her!" His mouth was wet with spittle, and he took a menacing step toward me, one hand raised to point at my chest. "That's enough!"

A maidservant arrived, and he commanded her to escort me to the front door. All I could do was leave, my fury and frustration burning. Not for the first time I wished I could use physical force to make people act the way I wanted.

As I followed the maid past the stairs, I looked up. *Five minutes,* I thought. *Five damn minutes.*

But as James often reminded me, a woman is the property of her father or her husband. And both of them trumped my rights as an inspector.

I needed to find a way to convince Dr. Forsyte to let her talk to me.

I needed a walk.

★   ★   ★

I stopped into a pub for some stew and ale. Usually, I make short work of lunch, but I decided to record recent events in order. It took nine pages of my pocketbook and the better part of two hours.

As I finished, I found myself thinking about the red-haired maid at the Forsytes'. She hadn't appeared today. How could I reach her, aside from returning to the house, which I'd promised not to do? She didn't like Forsyte, and given that servants often know a good deal about their masters, perhaps she could tell me something that I could use to convince him to cooperate.

Well, I reasoned, every servant must come out of the house sometime.

I've always appreciated the value of a back door.

CHAPTER 32

One item I omitted from my written record was Dr. Forsyte's snide comment about our failures. It rankled, I admit, not just because what he said was true. It disgusted me that someone in my division had talked out of turn.

As I entered the Yard, Vincent stood in his doorway watching me. I pretended not to see him and headed straight for my office. I had only hung my coat before Vincent pushed open my door without knocking and closed it behind him.

"Did you attempt to see Mrs. Munro again?" His question sounded almost rhetorical, which should have been my first clue of something amiss. But my thoughts were running in a different direction.

"Yes. But her father isn't letting her speak to anyone."

"You aren't certain of that," Vincent said. "It might be Mrs. Munro who wishes to put this episode in the past—or she might dread becoming the object of gossip."

He wasn't joining me in my indignation. And his words were an eerie echo of Dr. Forsyte's.

I swallowed and proceeded with more care. "But she could help save the lives of other young women."

"That is not her responsibility," he said pointedly. "That is *our* responsibility."

"But how am I supposed to do that if crucial information is withheld from me?"

"You will find a way, or I will find someone who can." He raised his eyebrows. "You do not go back to the Forsyte house. Do you understand? They want to be left in peace, and nothing is to be gained by another attempt."

Suddenly, I realized what he'd left unsaid.

"You knew I'd been to the Forsyte house this morning," I said slowly. "You knew she'd been removed from the hospital."

That's when I finally took a good look at Vincent's eyes. They weren't his usual calm gray. They were as flinty and furious as Dr. Forsyte's.

Vincent drew a cream-colored envelope from his pocket and held it so I could see the slanted black writing on the cover. "I received this half an hour ago." He flipped it to reveal the monogrammed red wax that had sealed it shut. An elaborate "Q."

I looked up.

"Quartermain is apparently a distant cousin and friend of Dr. Forsyte's."

Anger flicked along my nerves at the thought of Quartermain telling Forsyte about our caseloads and our rates of failure.

Vincent returned the envelope to his pocket. "If you ever force your way into Forsyte's household again, he will have you arrested for trespass."

I stared incredulously. "I didn't force—"

"You were asked yesterday to leave." His voice was clipped. "And if you'll remember, *I* asked you to give him a day or two. You ignored me. Quartermain reports that you were abominably rude and insulting."

"I *wasn't*." He looked skeptical, and I added, "Oh, I know I can be, but I was civil. I reminded him that his daughter cared about others, and—"

"And you told Forsyte she was the third victim." His jaw was taut. "You had no right to reveal that information."

I felt the validity of that accusation. "I know. But I thought it would make him understand the gravity—that it concerned the safety of London."

He looked incredulous. "Why would he care about the safety of London? The only thing that man cares about is his daughter." His eyes darted upward, as if she were on the floor above us. "And now I have to try to compel Quartermain to influence Dr. Forsyte to keep quiet, or even more details will end up in the papers."

I opened my mouth, and his hand went up. "For once, listen to me. Do you understand what you've done? You have given Quartermain—a man who already has profound doubts about the Yard—legitimate reasons for thinking my senior inspector is both rude *and* indiscreet. On top of that, you've had this case for nearly three weeks, with no certain results, and now Quartermain knows *that*, too."

My voice rose. "But I *have* learned something about—"

"Have you spoken to Nate McLoughlin?" His eyes were piercing.

"Not yet. But—"

The muscles in his jaw were working, but he kept his voice low. "Corravan, if Quartermain wants us to look into something, we do it. What's more, I think you've heard of McLoughlin, and for whatever reason you're protecting him, or you're being deliberately defiant. But I want an end to this. You question him. Do you under—"

"It's a waste of time, I tell you!" I burst out.

"That's enough," he said, his tone cutting as a blade. "From now on, Stiles takes the lead on the river murders. This case requires tact, discretion, and a willingness to follow orders." I stared open-mouthed in disbelief as he stepped back from the desk. "Let him read the file. And you find Nate McLoughlin."

"You're putting Stiles in just so that you can tell Quartermain you're punishing me!" My shout strained my throat. "You're earning political coins at my expense!"

Two white points appeared near the corners of his mouth, and his lips barely moved as he said, "Corravan, go home before we say things we will regret." When I didn't move, he added very softly, "I command you."

I snatched my coat and flung open the door. As I stalked through the central room, I saw others averting their eyes. They'd heard the entire thing.

It was only when I reached the street that I realized Vincent had never raised his voice. The only person they'd have heard shouting was me.

I was in a pub downing a shot of whiskey before I even knew what happened.

Chapter 33

When the morning post brought no message from Seddon Hall, I had a feeling I knew what it meant. Proceeding to the Yard in a foul humor, I found Stiles, and we divided up the tasks. He'd speak with Mrs. Munro's servants, and any friends or acquaintances they mentioned, and I'd go to Our Lady first and then to Whitechapel to find Nate McLoughlin. I took the cab only as far as Waterloo Bridge, so I could go into Lambeth on foot.

Our Lady was one of the older Catholic churches in London. Established by Queen Anne back in the 1750s, it was a spare church, the sort I like, without all the fancy furbelows and stained glass, and with a heavy bell that only tolled the hour, not wasting its breath on the quarters. A chiseled marble sign by the front door directed me around back to "Our Lady's Home." Nothing anywhere about the place being for fallen women. I appreciated that. These women didn't need it etched in stone.

I tugged at the bell pull, and the door was opened by a young nun in a black and white habit. I explained my errand, and she lisped, "Oh, you'll need to thpeak with Mother Louitha, and thee's in contemplathion for another hour."

I stifled a groan. "Could I talk to someone else?"

Her blue eyes were large and round. "I'm thorry, thir. You have to thpeak to her. But you can wait in her offith." She led me to a white room with no ornament except a wooden crucifix on the wall. A good-sized window opened onto a courtyard with gardens full of plantings. There was a plain desk, three wooden chairs, and a shelf with books about martyrs and such. Seeing as the nun left me alone, I might have nosed about, but there was nothing to see.

I sat down to wait.

Finally, an hour later, Mother Louisa entered, greeting me with her hands clasped at her waist as if in prayer. Perhaps it was their accustomed position, although I saw some callouses on her thumbs and first fingers, as if she'd spent time grasping a shovel. We studied each other from our respective chairs. It was impossible to guess her age any nearer than above forty, for her wimple covered all but an inch of her forehead and her face. Her eyes were intelligent and her gaze keen, though her voice was mild:

"What can I do for you, Inspector?"

"Have you heard about Mrs. Munro?"

"Oh, yes. We are all very glad to hear that she is alive."

I shifted. "Who told you that?"

Her eyes widened.

"I don't mean that she isn't," I added. "Only that was supposed to be kept quiet. We don't want another attack, if he intended to kill her."

She crossed herself involuntarily, a minute gesture with the fingertips of her right hand. "Dr. Masterson told me in confidence, and I've told no one. I wouldn't do anything to hurt that angel."

"Of course." I sat back in my chair. "The difficulty is she is still in shock and unable to speak. I'm afraid I must ask questions of you, if we want to keep her safe." I didn't want to overplay that card, but I needed Mother Louisa's help. "I hope you don't mind."

"Of course not."

I drew out my pocketbook and pencil. "What can you tell me about her work here? And do you remember any times when she was in danger?"

Her expression cooled. "I expect Dr. Forsyte blames us for what happened."

"He hinted as much," I admitted. "*I* only blame her attacker—but if she's ever been threatened or injured here, it's possibly relevant."

She brought her hands together and raised her forefingers to her lips, closing her eyes. At first I thought she was praying, but after a moment she said, "You must promise never to tell her father."

My pulse jumped. "I promise."

She opened her eyes. "She was assaulted once, the week before Easter. It came to nothing because Mrs. Munro always takes Mr. Bell, our gardener, with her. She'd walked ahead of him, and a man clutched at her and tried to push her into an alley. But Mr. Bell was there in a minute to stop him."

"What did the man look like?"

She hesitated. "Mr. Bell might remember."

"Were there any other incidents? Any threats by people who disapproved of her?"

"We receive threats all the time, Inspector."

"Yes, of course. But anything directed specifically at her?"

She gave a dry little smile. "Not unless you count the tirades of her father."

"You've heard them?"

Her eyebrows rose and the skin on her forehead buckled against the edge of the wimple. "He's come here several times, to tell her what a fool she was being and how we were nursing vipers in our breasts." Her head tipped. "Where did you spend your childhood, Inspector?"

"Mostly in Whitechapel."

"I thought so. You don't have a look of disgust." Her expression was regretful. "But I think people are afraid. Disgust is often the handmaiden of fear, don't you think?"

I made a noncommittal sound.

She smiled gently. "You'll find Mr. Bell rather simple, but he's a good man." She went to the door, where she rang a bell. Another nun—this one with an unfortunate plum-colored birthmark below her eye—appeared promptly, and Mother Louisa asked her to fetch Mr. Bell.

A few moments later, his silhouette filled the doorway. He was about my age, but even stooped, he was nearly a full head taller than I and several stones heavier. He had a round tanned face, strands of brown, greasy hair threading across his forehead, and a bashful expression. Yes, he looked rather simple, but his hands were like slabs of beef. No wonder Mrs. Munro could go anywhere in his company.

"Mr. Bell, this is Inspector Corravan," Mother Louisa said pleasantly. "He wants to know about the night you were out with

Mrs. Munro, when that man tried to hurt her. Could you tell him what you remember?"

His eyes drifted back and forth between us, and he dipped his head uncertainly. "You want me to tell 'im now?"

"Yes, please."

He turned to me, his hands opening and closing into loose fists, as if he longed to have them around the handle of a rake. "We were 'bout four streets from the river, after dark." He squinted. "Mebbe nine o'clock. She was a mite ahead o' me, you see. We were walking down a street where we found the . . ." He looked at Mother Louisa.

She nodded encouragingly. "It's all right."

"The fallen women." He spoke carefully, as if it were a phrase he'd learned by rote. "Some of 'em are just young 'uns, see, and Mrs. Munro always tries to git them to come back with 'er, offerin' food and such. We wuz talkin' to two of 'em, and then another one was down a ways, so she left 'em with me, and then a man came lookin' and grabbed Mrs. Munro, mebbe thinkin' she was one of 'em. She screamed, and I hauled him off o' her and she warn't even touched, she said, just her bonnet a mite mussed."

"What did he look like?"

"Ach." He strained to remember. "Mebbe thirty years old, with dark hair. Not a big man." He gestured to the middle of his chest, to indicate the man's height. "'E 'ad a cap on."

This probably wasn't the same man the livery drivers had seen.

"Did he say anything?" I asked.

"Not that I 'eard. Might'a said sumpin to 'er."

"Did you bring any women back that night?"

He bobbed his head. "Two of 'em."

"Are they still here?" I asked.

Mother Louisa spoke up. "One of them died here, poor thing; we found work for the other as a servant. Just a moment." From behind some books, she drew out a narrow clothbound ledger and paged through it. "Yes, she went to an estate about an hour outside of London. The Treadwells."

I turned to Mr. Bell. "Thank you."

He pulled at an imaginary cap and backed out of the room.

"He's a good man," I said.

She inclined her head. "We are all God's children and good in our hearts, Inspector."

"Everyone?" I couldn't keep the skepticism out of my voice.

"Yes, everyone," she said firmly.

I made a few more notes and put away my pocketbook. "One other question. Did Mrs. Munro ever quarrel with her father, for reasons other than her work here?"

Her face stilled. "Not that I know of."

She was lying. I waited, but her eyes didn't drop.

Vincent's warning be damned, I thought. "Mother Louisa, Mrs. Munro is not the first victim to be attacked by this man. There have been two others. But they were both killed."

She caught her breath and traced that tiny cross with her fingertips again.

"Now, he might try to find Mrs. Munro again, but even if he doesn't, God knows how many other women he will try to hurt. Whatever it is you're keeping from me might be precisely what I need to prevent that from happening."

Her chin lifted. "She told me things in confidence, and I won't break a confidence—not hers, not yours, not anyone's."

I squirmed in frustration. "But isn't she the kind of person who would want to save other women if she could? I'm sure she is!"

I saw the uncertainty in her eyes, along with regret. But she shook her head. "You must wait until she can speak with you."

"There may be another woman dead by then."

It was a shameless attempt to make her feel the weight of blame, but she saw it for what it was. Her eyes sparked, but her voice remained cool: "Then God bless you in your attempts to find him, Inspector."

★ ★ ★

As I reached the street I heard a hoarse whisper behind me: "Inspector!"

I turned. Under a tree stood Mr. Bell, peering anxiously in the direction of Our Lady's Home.

I approached him. "Yes, Mr. Bell. What is it?"

"I 'eard what you asked about 'er father."

"Yes?"

"Well, Mother Louisa cain't tell you anything, but I kin, 'cos I ain't made any kind o' promise. And it's import'nt to tell the truth, ain't it?"

"*I* think so, yes."

"There was a time once, when I told a lie about sumpin." He held the shovel in his large hands, turning it left and right as easily as I'd fiddle with a fork. "And Mrs. Munro tol' me her father 'ad told a lie once, swearing on the Bible, that ruined a poor girl for life. She said 'ow we *haf* to tell the truth, all the time, not just when we wan' to."

"Swearing on a Bible," I repeated.

His eyes widened. "I 'ad to go to a trial wit' Mother Louisa once. She 'ad to swear, too, only she tol' the truth."

"When was this? When did Mrs. Munro tell you about her father?"

A panicky look came over his face. "A—a while back. I—I dunno."

Talking to me had been difficult for him. I rested a hand on his shoulder. "Mrs. Munro would be grateful that you helped me."

A look of relief settled over his features, and as I reached the pavement, his off-key whistling mingled with the scrape of his shovel against gravel.

What did Dr. Forsyte lie about in a court of law? And how would it ruin a poor girl for life? Given Mrs. Munro's work, it was probably a trial having something to do with a prostitute. But why would Dr. Forsyte be present for that?

I'd had every intention of going to Whitechapel to find Nate, but that was before I heard from Mr. Bell. Now I needed to talk to that red-haired maid.

I spent the rest of the afternoon and night on the curb outside the Forsytes' home, waiting for her, or anyone, to exit or enter. But though shadows moved among the rooms, the house was closed up tight.

CHAPTER 34

The following morning found me back at the Forsyte house, early. I kept my hat low and lingered where I could watch the back door.

For three hours, I watched deliveries arrive. It was astonishing, all the things a house like this took in, just to keep itself going. Milk, groceries, packages wrapped in brown paper, a telegram. Every so often, I looked up at the windows. One of the curtains was plucked aside by invisible fingers, then released. Who was up there, watching? And where was Mrs. Munro's room?

Finally, I gave up waiting and knocked at the back door. I must've been the sixth man who'd knocked that morning. The door was opened by a short maid, harried and damp about the brow, with pink cheeks. "Oh! I was 'specting the butcher's boy. 'E's late," she said breathlessly. "What ye be wanting?"

"I need to speak with one of the maids. She's young, with reddish hair."

She looked indignant. "You don't know 'er name?" The door began to close, but I put my hand out.

"I'm from Scotland Yard," I said quietly, "and I don't want to embarrass her in front of the Forsytes. There's no cause for that."

Appealing to her sense of loyalty worked. She glanced around uncertainly, then whispered, "Come in. I'll fetch Maud for ye, but don't keep 'er long."

Soon I heard shoes tapping hurriedly over the stone floor. Maud halted when she saw me, and her eyes widened. "Oh! You can't be here!"

"Just a few questions. Then I'll go."

She fingered her apron nervously. "What?"

"What happened on Monday night, before Mrs. Munro left?"

Her eyes darted to the corner, then she leaned close, speaking quickly and quietly. "She and her father quarreled. Not in front of the Missus, mind you, because it upsets her." She shook her head. "'Twas after dinner, when the Missus was with the housekeeper."

I felt a prickle at the back of my neck. "Over what?"

She spread her hands. "Dr. Forsyte said it was all her fault that her mother's so poorly because Mrs. Munro hasn't visited."

"Why hasn't she?"

She twisted her apron. "She hasn't been here since the trial."

"When was that?"

Her brow creased in concentration. "Six months ago, mebbe?"

"Was the trial about her work at Our Lady?"

"It was about a maid, but I don't know the particulars."

"And did her father take Mrs. Munro home Monday night?"

She shook her head. "He'd taken too much wine at dinner, so she didn't want—"

"Maud," came a hiss, and the first maid was around the corner, snatching at Maud's arm. "Get upstairs! Hurry! Mrs. Beale's lookin' for you!" She whirled on me. "The doctor's seen you lurking around! You're going to get us all dismissed." She hustled me toward the door and dragged it open. "Get *out*!"

Three long strides and I was out the door and hurrying along the street. I kept my head down and rounded the corner—

And a hand came out and grabbed my arm. I looked up, half expecting Dr. Forsyte, his face red with fury.

But it was Stiles, his expression troubled.

I pulled out of his grip. "What are you doing here?"

"Please, Inspector." He took my arm again and kept me walking away from the house. "Dr. Forsyte saw you outside and came in person to the Yard."

"So Vincent's angry at *me*." A hard laugh came from my chest. "Keeping Mrs. Munro from us is like tying our hands behind our backs—and then whipping us for losing!"

"You know I'm with you all the way," Stiles said earnestly, "but the man nearly lost his daughter. He's not thinking straight right now. Would you be?"

In silence we crossed the street at the corner. I stepped absently over some horse droppings as I remembered Maud's words. I wanted to think about them while they were fresh in my mind. "Stiles, I need to find out when Dr. Forsyte stood trial or appeared as a witness."

"For what?"

As we strode along the crowded pavement, I told him what Mr. Bell had said and how the maid had confirmed it.

"Perhaps Dr. Forsyte bore witness against a prostitute," Stiles said. "That might upset Mrs. Munro enough to keep her out of the house for a while."

"It might." We stepped off the curb, our strides matching as we continued down the street. "But I think Dr. Forsyte lied under oath. Mr. Bell seemed certain on that point." I dodged a boy hawking a broadsheet. "What did you find out at the Munro house yesterday?"

"There were a few odd things," Stiles said. "First off, Mrs. Munro's maid said her mistress hadn't been to see her parents in months. But her mother asked her to come for dinner—begged her, in fact. Made a special visit last week to ask her. Then, on Monday afternoon, a cab came to pick Mrs. Munro up, but she'd already left, walking. Now, her father might have sent it without asking—"

"But that fits with the others. He could have abducted her then, only she foiled him," I interrupted. "So he simply waited outside the house. Dr. Forsyte lied about seeing her safely home. Did she ever arrive?"

Stiles shook his head. "The maid didn't know. She'd been told not to wait up."

Our discussion had brought us all the way to within sight of the Yard. As we crossed the street and stepped onto the cobblestones, he put his hand on my arm and drew me to a stop so that we faced each other. "Inspector, I've never seen Vincent as angry as he was today." His eyes were dark with concern. "Forsyte was *shouting*, and when he left, Vincent called me in."

I didn't envy Stiles having to deal with the aftermath of that storm. "Well, if anyone could handle Vincent in a fit, you can."

He winced. "It's not something I like doing."

It was the closest he'd come to a rebuke. "Sorry," I said. "What did he say?"

"He told me he was taking you off the case—and hinted he might send you down."

I stared. "Send me down."

"But he only said it to me," Stiles added hurriedly. "To my mind, that means he'll let you stay, if you apologize. Explain to him why this case weighs so heavily on you. He'll listen to that."

I drew back. "What do you mean, why it weighs so heavily?"

"Le Loup," Stiles replied, surprised. "I know that's what's plaguing you. It bothers me, too. All the time."

"Why would that make a difference to Vincent?"

"Because he'll understand why it would make you act like this."

"Like *what*?"

A pause, and then reluctantly: "Ruthless."

I was silent for a moment. "You think if I apologize, he'll let me stay?"

"I hope so."

"Then I'll try." And then, as an afterthought, "Don't tell him anything I found out from the maid. He'll only see that as me trying to justify why I went back to the Forsytes'."

He looked at me uncertainly. "All right."

★ ★ ★

I'm not one to shrink from an inevitable confrontation, so I went straight to Vincent's office, my hat in my hand, in both senses of the phrase. But he didn't want just me. He wanted Stiles, too.

"Give me a reason I shouldn't suspend you," Vincent began. His voice was toneless and his eyes were like stones. I stayed quiet because I was fairly sure I didn't have an answer that would satisfy him.

"He knows more about this case than I do, sir," said Stiles.

Vincent took that in.

Then it was as if a cork had been yanked out of a bottle.

For half an hour, Vincent ripped into me every which way, not minding at all that Stiles was there to hear. He never raised his voice, but I heard how the Yard was taking a different direction and the cloddish, bullheaded methods that I'd used in Lambeth and the River Police weren't befitting this division. I heard how police work was changing—that with the rising number of newspapers and the growing number of people who read them, we were on public view, for every Londoner to see, every day. Even before he came, he'd heard I was temperamental and explosive, and I made other Yard men nervous. It seemed I thought that being considerate of others was a sign of weakness and my way forward was to run roughshod over anyone in my path. In fact, I had all the finesse of a rabid bear barreling through the woods. He'd never held my past in Whitechapel against me, until it seemed that I took real pride in behaving as if I were still in a bare-knuckles boxing club. But I wasn't the only one who had something to prove, and not only the Commission but the public at large was keeping a close eye on the entire Yard.

I don't remember the rest.

I kept my feelings to myself, said not a word in my defense—though it nearly killed me—and stayed quiet and apologetic, until eventually Vincent had spent his fury and waved Stiles and me out of his office.

Vincent had made himself clear. The only reason he wasn't throwing me off the case—and perhaps out of the Yard entirely—was because Stiles was vouching for me. One more misstep, and I would be sent down.

The truth was, I couldn't argue with what Vincent said. The Yard *was* changing. The whole bloody world was changing. But I wasn't sure I had it in me to be different than I was.

*   *   *

I pushed the pub door open with a little more force than necessary, so it hit the wall and swung back hard enough I had to stop it with my palm. A few men looked up from their tables, startled, but the amiable rumble of conversations resumed as I crossed the floor and scraped a stool back from the wooden bar. The barkeep had a round face, a meager thatch of brown hair, and slow beefy hands. He appeared ready to offer me an affable greeting, but a quick look at my face made him think better of it. "What'll y'have?"

"Whiskey," I said.

He upended the bottle and poured the spirit in a glass, then swiped a rag across a splotch of grease on the bar and put the glass down in front of me, without meeting my eye. Not as if he was afraid. More as if he hoped I wouldn't cause trouble, but he'd cope with it if he had to. Then he turned to the bar's only other occupant, a burly man seated two stools to my left, whose hands encircled a pint pot of ale. "So what'd she do when she saw it was gone?"

For some reason, the barkeep's imperturbability irked me to no end. I downed the whiskey in two quick gulps and dropped the glass back onto the bar with a clunk loud enough to sound like a demand. He met my eye and silently poured another inch into my glass. Feeling the sideways scrutiny from the other customer, I glowered but sipped this glass more slowly.

Eventually a third man appeared, taking a seat to my right. To my surprise, a heavy hand landed on my shoulder blade. I turned, grasping my truncheon, and the man's hands came up.

"No need for that, Corravan."

John Fishel. Of the *Beacon*.

I left my hand where it was. "What do you want?"

He removed his hat, revealing his rumple of dark hair running to gray, planted his elbows on the bar, and gave me an ingratiating smile. "What do you think? I want to know about the attack on Mrs. Munro."

I stiffened. He didn't use the word "murder." Did he know she was still alive?

"You know damn well I'm not going to tell you," I replied. "Besides, you'll write what you want, no matter what I say."

"Now, that's not true, mate," he countered, pointing a finger, first at me and then at the bartender. "A pint, if you please."

The bartender handed it over with a brief smile.

Fishel's voice lowered, became oily. "I know something about your victim's father. The medical man. And there's no reason I won't share it, providing you trade."

"What is it?"

He shook his head and took a long draft from his glass. "Has to be an even exchange. Like prisoners, Corravan."

I barked a laugh.

"Ah, don't be sore," he said, a quick hand resting on my arm, like the friend he wasn't. I resisted the urge to shake it off. "Just because we're trained as good as your lot at putting together a story."

"Bascoe got away because you printed his address, Fishel. Two more people ended up dead. *That's* what you're trained to do. Muck it up."

That finally pierced his breezy demeanor, and his face twisted into a sneer. "I'm not the one who made bollocks of the Le Loup killings—"

I rose from my stool, towering over him. "Get the hell away from me, you little rat!"

He glared up at me and snatched his hat. "You just sit there on that stool, you drunken sot. See how you far it gets you!"

I raised my voice, so he'd hear it even though he was nearly to the door. "Do you know why you write for the *Beacon*? Because you were thrown out of the police for running away from a man with a knife! You bloody coward!"

The shot told. He whirled to retort, but everyone began to guffaw. Softly at first, more heartily as Fishel's face reddened. He turned back toward the door. By the worst sort of luck a dog was crossing his path, on the way to a table, to beg for scraps. I saw the dog out of the corner of my eye, and I was already moving when Fishel gave a fierce kick to the dog's side, right into the ribs visible under her thin coat. She gave a yelp—a small one, as if she were used to blows and knew it was no use making a fuss. But before I could make my way through the tables to the door, Fishel was gone. I wrenched the door open, but he'd vanished into the crowd. With an oath, I turned back, closed the door behind me, and stood looking down at the dog. She was a sweet thing, not a pup but still young, with brown eyes, a scar along the side of her muzzle, and ears that didn't quite match. I bent down, and she shrank from me, rousing a wave of shame at my part in the kick.

"I'm sorry, girl," I muttered. "I shouldn't've riled him."

I retreated to my stool and ordered another whiskey. Or two. I don't remember. The ugly truth was that Fishel might very well find out who attacked Mrs. Munro before I did. I started home, but even in my mind's sloppy state, there was an uncomfortable sense that Fishel, of all people, had given me something I could use. But what the devil was it? Clumsily, I retraced our exchange and found it: he knew something about Dr. Forsyte worth trading for.

The medical man, Fishel had called him.

I should see James. He might know.

★   ★   ★

The hospital felt uncomfortably warm. In the foyer, I unbuttoned my coat, flapping it to create a breeze across my shirt, which stuck damply to me. Finding James's office empty, I headed to the women's ward, and then the men's. At the far end, James and Harry stood together over a bed that held a man whose feet hung well past the end. James was asking him some questions, and Harry was diligently taking down notes. Watching the boy, I congratulated myself. I'd brought him to the right place.

At last a nurse approached with a tray, and James and Harry stepped away. As they caught sight of me, James nodded a greeting, but Harry's eyes dropped back to whatever he was writing. Then he moved on to another patient, while James came near. "Good evening, Corravan."

"Hullo." I jerked my head back toward the ward. "What's wrong with him?"

"Inchoate paranoia," James said.

I stared in astonishment.

James sighed. "He believes people mock him because he's very tall, so last night he tried to cut his legs."

I forced down the laugh that bubbled up as I realized James was talking about the patient, not Harry.

"It's a terrible delusion," he continued as we walked toward his office. "He thinks that being shorter will make him less noticeable, and yet, of course, cutting his legs brings about the very attention he dreads."

"Poor bloke," I said sincerely. "But I meant Harry."

He looked at me askance. "Harry?"

"He ignored me just now."

We reached James's office and sat in our usual chairs. "I expect he's feeling put out." He peered at me over his spectacles. "You know, Corravan, the boy is a lot like you."

"That's what Belinda says." I heard the slip on the second "s" and felt a spike of wariness. James didn't seem to have noticed, but I knew what he'd say about my drinking. I bit down on the end of my tongue, hard, knowing from experience that pain would sharpen me up, keep my words crisp.

"Well, she's right, as usual," he said. "He's clever, and he cares about doing some good in the world." He rubbed his fingertips along the edge of his desk. "He's also prickly as a thistle when he thinks someone finds him a burden, and that trait alone makes him more like you than anything else. You've taken no time to get to know him."

"What does he need me for, when you're so fond of him?"

He glowered at me. "Don't be an idiot."

"I'll get to know him after this case is over, all right? There'll be time then."

"He doesn't need a nursemaid," he protested. "But he shouldn't have to beg for simple acceptance."

"Oh, for God's sake! Don't *you* start! You think I should feel guilty? He's nearly sixteen! Do you know what I was doing when I was that age? I was loading cargo on the bloody docks! And you know how hard I've been working—"

He threw up his hands in protest. "Don't vent your spleen at me! You asked why he's ignoring you, and I told you. Why must you always, *always* explode?"

That last word, a near-echo of Vincent's, made me slouch back into my seat.

He broke the silence: "In happier news, Mrs. Beckford seems to be coming around. She trusts both Stiles and Harry."

"Well, that's something," I said. A thought swam up into consciousness. "By the way, did Stiles mention that the Beckfords have a private inspector looking for her? His name's Taft, in case he comes your way."

"Yes, Stiles made a special trip to tell me. Taft hasn't appeared, but if he does, he certainly won't be admitted." He gave a flick of his hand, as if the man were an insect, easily brushed away. "Mrs. Beckford spoke again last night. Harry heard the name 'Rachel,' very distinctly."

"Rachel?" The word slurred out as "Ray-shell." I wasn't so far gone that I didn't hear it.

James studied me for a moment, and his expression grew dismayed. "Have you been drinking spirits?"

"No. I'm just exhausted." I carefully enunciated the lie. "And frustrated. Quartermain has been complaining about me not being tactful, and Vincent's not happy with how the case is going, so today he told me I have the manners of a Whitechapel bully, among other compliments. And then he passed the lead to Stiles. I'm being allowed to assist."

If I hoped to be seen as the victim, I should have known better.

"Ah. Well." James turned up a hand, as if to suggest it was no more than he expected.

My annoyance flared, but I needed his help, so I changed the subject. "Do you know a doctor by the name of Forsyte?"

"I've heard the name." He gave me a keen look. "Why?"

"It was his daughter who was our third victim, this past Tuesday."

"Ah." His eyebrows rose. "How is she?"

"Recovering, I presume. But she won't talk to us. Or, rather, her father won't let us talk to her. He's got her locked away upstairs in his house, like that lady in the tower." I leaned forward, resting my elbows on my knees. "There's something bloody odd about that family, James. Mrs. Forsyte seems scared to death of her husband. And Mrs. Munro hasn't been to see her parents in months."

"Munro?" he repeated. "So Forsyte's daughter is married?"

"Yes. Charlotte Munro. She tries to reclaim prostitutes . . ." My voice faded at the stunned look on his face.

"I know who she is." His voice rasped as if something had caught in his throat. "Two of my nurses are women she sent to us."

I sat back in my chair. "Well, that's a coincidence."

"Not really. Mother Louisa knows doctors at all the London hospitals. She asked me last year if I'd be willing to give a chance to two decent young woman who'd been driven to desperation. Mrs. Munro brought them here." He added slowly, "I didn't know Forsyte was her father."

I frowned. "Is there any chance you might convince him to let his daughter talk to me? As a fellow medical man? Nothing I said carried any weight. I even told him that his daughter wasn't the first victim—that this murderer was out to hurt other women in London as well. He didn't care."

"Of course not. This section," he tapped the front right area of his head, "cares deeply about protecting kin. As I've told you, it's a core element of the mind, and when it is preoccupied, nothing else matters."

"Do you know anything about him? Anything I could use to bring him around?" His look of surprise made me pause, but I kept on. "Someone hinted there was a scandal he'd taken pains to hide. Could be something involving a trial."

His expression grew incredulous. "You intend blackmail?"

"No." I waved a hand. "Influence."

He drew back. "My God, Corravan."

I leaned over the desk. "Mrs. Munro probably doesn't even know what happened to those other women—and what might happen to dozens more if she doesn't talk."

"Well, she knows what happened to *her*. That might be as much as she can consider right now." His voice carried a warning. "You can't force her to speak before she's ready. You'll end up with someone like poor Mrs. Beckford, unable to speak at all. You need to be patient."

"He kills on Monday nights, and it's Friday," I retorted. "It's bloody hard to be patient when five minutes with her would make all the difference."

"Badgering her and her family isn't going to help," he said sharply. "You can't just issue commands to people! You can only ask—and respect their decisions."

"I don't issue commands!"

"Yes, you *do*! I've been on the receiving end!" His hand slapped the desk. "I've known you for ten years, Corravan, and you're like a dog with a bone—which is an asset most of the time. But right now that bone belongs to a *person*—a woman who has just experienced a threat to her *life*. Get hold of yourself!"

"For God's sake, you sound like Vincent!"

"Perhaps he's right for once. Did you ever think of that?" he blazed back. And then, as he looked at my face, the fight seemed to go out of him. He passed a hand over his eyes wearily. "There is no point in this. And I don't have the wherewithal to cope with your intransigence today."

His voice dropped off, and his face was heavy with more than fatigue. I saw despair mixed with guilt and revulsion. James had worn the same expression the night he had come to me, fearing for his nephew Maurice's life. Following a hint from one of the boy's friends, I'd combed half a dozen of the worst brothels in London before I found Maurice and carried him out, naked and covered in blood but alive.

Oddly, recollecting what I'd done for Maurice softened the hardness in my chest more thoroughly than remembering anything

James had done for me would have, and my voice was mild when I asked, "What's the matter?"

He fiddled with some tiny pins on his desk, gathering them into a pile between his thumb and forefinger with the same delicacy and precision as he wielded his surgical instruments. "I lost a patient last night. I thought his condition was improving. And—well, there's someone I should have consulted. It's my fault."

"I'm sorry, James. Truly."

His sigh stretched the black buttonholes of his waistcoat. His exhalation returned them to their proper location behind the pearl buttons.

The mantel clock chimed the half hour, and James stood and reached for his coat. "I'm going home," he said. "Don't start up drinking again, Corravan. It leads nowhere good."

"I'm not drinking," I said. "I have work to do."

I kept the slur out of my voice, but he looked at me with a mix of resignation and disappointment.

I stalked out and found a pub with a stool very much like the one I'd inhabited earlier. Part of me knew James had a right to his disgust.

But by the third whiskey, I didn't despise either of us anymore.

CHAPTER 35

In the past I'd always been able to hold my liquor, but I was out of practice, and it took me three tries to slide my key into the lock. I pushed the door open and stumbled over the threshold. Cursing, I started to undo my coat.

The light from a fire on the hearth flickered across the wall. Harry? Here? That would be strange, given the way he behaved at the hospital.

Still, I called out, "Harry?" as I hung my coat and walked toward the sitting room.

"No," said a woman's voice.

Belinda was in a chair by the fire, her feet tucked up under her skirts, a cup of tea at her elbow. Despite my being drunk and surly and spoiling for a fight, the sight of her brought me to a standstill. Belinda's beauty had never been the sort that she made up at her dressing table. It was in the curve of her cheek, the angle of her jaw, the arch of her brow. Bone-deep. Tonight, she'd dressed with care. Her hair fell in waves across her shoulders, and her dress of pale sea-green was one of my favorites. Her eyes were dark and sparkling in the light from the flames. She looked as lovely as I'd ever seen her.

I should enjoy this, I thought dully. It might be the last time I'd see her for a while, if she caught on to the fact that I'd been drinking.

"Are you all right?" she asked.

"What are you doing here?"

Her eyes widened. "I might ask what *you're* doing here, given that you were supposed to be at my house last night." She paused. "It's Friday, Michael."

"I know what day it is." I sat down to remove my boots.

"You didn't come, and I was worried," she said softly. "And you smell like a pub. Where have you been?"

Head down, I unbuckled the second boot and drew it off. Drunk as I was, the working part of my brain knew that if I spoke more than a few words, she'd realize I'd had more than a pint. I wanted to hide it. Stupidly, I just shook my head.

"Michael."

I sighed and sat up. "I'm tired, all right?"

She eased herself out of the chair and came toward me, cupping my chin so I had to look up at her. Her expression changed instantly. "You've been drinking spirits." She dropped her hand, and the light of surprise in her eyes dimmed to disappointment.

The room spun clockwise, and I fought to turn it in the other direction.

"I'll make some coffee," she said and vanished.

I groaned and closed my eyes. I didn't want coffee. I wanted to go to bed. But back she came, with a hot cup, which she put in my right hand. She drew an ottoman near, so she could sit beside me.

"Why?" she asked.

"Why what?" The two words slid together.

"You haven't had a drink in months. Is it because of what was in the paper?"

I halted the cup at my mouth. "What'd it say?"

"That young women of means are being murdered. And . . . the Yard is covering it up."

So Forsyte had talked. "Jaysus." The curse came out the way I'd have said it in Whitechapel. I stared at the black liquid inside the cup.

"What happened today?" she asked.

"What happened?" I snorted. I took a gulp of the coffee and plunked the cup on the table. "Well, the third victim's father won't let me talk to her because God forbid *anyone* help the police put away a murderer. And Vincent ripped into me for my bad manners. And James accused me of mistreating Harry. And now *you're* going to start in—" I was being unfair, but something ugly was pushing me on "—and I don't need another bloody lecture!" My voice had risen to something close to a shout.

Her body stiffened. "I'm not going to lecture you. My God, Michael. After all this time, you still don't know me."

Through the haze of the drink, I felt a sense of alarm, and a knowledge that I needed to try to be rational, to not say something blitheringly stupid. "Of course I know you." I heard my voice slur over the words. "I've been drinking, but I haven't lost my mind."

She laid her hand against my cheek, and her eyes, wide and serious, held mine. "Do you remember the story you told me once? About the time you were boxing in that horrible place, for O'Hagan, and you looked around and realized that everyone in the whole place wanted you to lose because they'd bet against you."

I nodded dumbly.

"Sometimes when things aren't going well, you act as if you're right back there," she said softly. "It's you, all alone, against everyone else. You even fight with your friends. But you're not in a boxing hall anymore, and I'm not your adversary."

The image of her with her small fists raised called up a short laugh. "Bel, don't be ridiculous. I know that."

Her hand dropped from my cheek. "Do you?" she asked, without a hint of a smile. "I don't think you do. What's more, I don't think you want to. So long as we're all on the other side, you can be the lone rescuer of the world, can't you? The invincible Perseus to every desperate Andromeda chained to her rock." She spread her hands. "And that makes you feel better."

I opened my mouth to argue—though I had no coherent thoughts in my head and only the vaguest idea who Andromeda was—but she stopped me. "No, let me finish. I've known you for years, Michael, and tonight I finally realized something. Being the rescuing hero means you don't ever have to face your own weakness." She was shaking her head. "You don't have to sympathize with anyone who's powerless or afraid. All you have to do is save them."

I bristled. "So saving them is *wrong*?"

"It's not wrong. But not being able to admit your own humanity is almost . . ." The word came out reluctantly: "Cowardly."

"*Cowardly?*" I jabbed a thumb toward the door. "There is *nothing* cowardly about confronting people out there who are trying to murder and—"

"That's not what I mean." Her voice was keen with exasperation. "But it's as if you have only two ways of being with people. You're either fighting them or rescuing them, and neither allows for your humanity—or—or feelings of loneliness or fear or uncertainty! Thus far, in your life, it has served you because whether you're fighting or rescuing, you usually win, either by strength or sheer—" She shook her head, struggling to find the word, "—*relentlessness*. But it means that when you find yourself afraid that you might not be able to solve a case, or to save a young woman from dying, or to save a dozen young women from dying"—she spread her hands again—"you won't let me, or anyone or anything, help you. Except whiskey. And when someone *does* manage to help you, you can't even say thank you." She shook her head hopelessly. "You mean well. I know you do. But why can't you be a little humble, stop acting as if you and you alone are saving the world? Walk around on the ground like the rest of us? Can't you see that a shard of uncertainty, a trace of fellow feeling for someone who's desperate or—or vulnerable—would make you a better inspector, a better man?"

Suddenly I couldn't stand it anymore. "I'm not some character in one of your novels, Bel. You can't just write me to be different than I am. And I'm a bloody good inspector—no matter what Vincent or any of you think."

She opened her mouth and shut it again with a sigh. "Never mind," she said and stood, gathering the cloak she'd laid across a chair. She paused, looking down at me. "Your problem with Vincent is you can't fight him, and he doesn't need rescuing. But I can't have this conversation with you. Not now." She wrapped the cloak around her shoulders and said, with some satisfaction, "You're going to feel rotten tomorrow morning."

Her logic was all wrong, though I couldn't say how. So I plucked out a piece of the fight I knew I could win. "I do walk around on the ground," I muttered. "Because I wasn't born with a carriage to keep my pretty slippers out of the muck, remember?"

It was a low jab and wholly unfair. Even through the haze of drink I knew that. She'd been born wealthy, but she'd never cast my beginnings up to me. And Belinda's family had seen their share of unhappiness. Money hadn't kept it away.

Her face went still, and she opened the door. "Come outside with me." Her voice was cold. "I need a cab."

"You didn't bring your carriage?"

"I didn't think I'd be leaving."

I heard the rebuke, but rather than trying to undo the mistake I was making, I shoved my feet back into my boots without buckling them and stalked beside her to the corner, where I hailed a cab and put her inside—God, I'd done this a thousand times, felt the warmth of her fingers through her gloves, had never liked the sensation of cold loss when she withdrew her hand from mine—and gave the cab driver the address. I had to repeat it three times. I could feel my mouth forming the words badly. But finally he understood me.

As the cab pulled away, I went back inside and locked the door, kicking off my boots and swearing savagely as one stayed on my foot. I pulled it off and hurled it against the wall before I thrashed my way upstairs and sank onto my unmade bed.

We'd argued before. But even in my stupor, I knew this time was different. The ache in my chest told me that.

CHAPTER 36

I was woken around midday by a persistent banging in my skull. I ignored it for as long as I could, until I realized the pounding wasn't in my skull. It was at my front door.

The knocking halted as I sat up to an aching head, a sour taste in my mouth, and a queasy stomach. Belinda was right about one thing. I felt rotten. With a groan, I held my throbbing head between my palms.

The knocking started up again.

For God's sake. If Harry had forgotten his key, it was going to just about kill me to be civil.

I pushed myself to standing, eyed my wrinkled clothes, descended the stairs, and opened the door.

It was Timmy, one of the messenger boys from the Yard. His face was red, and a shine of sweat coated his forehead. "Mr. Stiles sent me," he gasped. "Said to tell you there's been a fourth."

"A fourth," I repeated stupidly.

He rounded his back, rested his hands on his knees. "Another lady in a boat."

Darkness seemed to close in on me from the left and right. "But—but it's Saturday." Or was it? How long had I slept? "Isn't it?"

He looked at me uncertainly. "Aye, it's Saturday. But—er, Mr. Stiles wants you to come back with me to Wapping, straightaway."

"Did Stiles mention if she's alive or dead?"

"Oh, she's dead." He spoke with the certainty of having seen for himself.

My heart dropped like a stone into a well. Even given the pathetic state of my brain, the blame was easy to trace. I'd revealed the pattern to Forsyte, who'd leaked it to the press, and the killer hastened his next murder by three days.

I beckoned Timmy inside. "Then I have time to change."

★   ★   ★

By my quick count, nine reporters crowded the vestibule where a sergeant vainly tried to keep order. Tom Flynn was one. John Fishel another. I stood outside the room, beyond Vincent's line of sight. But I could hear everything that was said.

There were no identifying marks and no jewelry. Charlie Dower was sketching, although I was beginning to feel that knowing her identity wouldn't help us understand why she'd been chosen.

Then someone muttered, "Her wrists are cut bad."

The image of bloody flesh formed in my mind, and with it came a wave of heat followed by a cold sweat. I bolted toward the door, barely reaching the alley before what little I had in my stomach came out of me. My left hand clung to the rough brick, and I remained where I was, doubled over, my eyes tearing from the effort, waiting to see if there was more.

A steady hand on my back made look up to find Tom Flynn. I half expected him to mock me. But his expression was sober and concerned. "When's the last time you ate?"

I didn't reply.

"Come on." He led me to a pub two streets away and pushed open the door, waving me toward a table in the corner. I sat, still tasting the bile in the back of my throat. He returned with two steaming mugs and a plate of food, and he sipped and watched as I alternated bites of potato with hot coffee.

I sensed his questions accumulating, but he waited until I set down my fork before he asked, "Why weren't you in the room?"

I gave him a wary look.

He waved a hand. "None of this is going to end up in the *Falcon*."

"Vincent isn't pleased with me at the moment."

"Why not?"

"You're worried about me?" It came out more churlishly than I intended, and I forced a grin to smooth it over.

He rubbed his hand over his mouth and didn't reply. Just watched me with those green eyes of his.

I sighed. Tom was discreet. Decent. He didn't deserve me being surly. Especially since I'd waited too long to talk to him, and another paper had broken the story. I owed him. "Vincent told me yesterday I have all the finesse of a rabid bear barreling through a forest." I saw Tom's lips twitch. "Because I did something stupid. I told the third victim's father there were two others, to convince him to let me talk to his daughter. He told the press."

His gaze sharpened. "The *Times* only said the Yard had been covering up murders of well-to-do young women in London. Were the previous two found on the river as well? In boats?"

I nodded. "It's one man."

Tom mulled that over. "Curious how the victim's father leaked only enough to discredit the Yard. Didn't mention the boat."

That *was* odd. Then again, in his irate state, he might not have taken in that piece of information or regarded it as important.

"His name's Forsyte," I said. "A doctor, retired. There's something dodgy about him."

He grunted. "I could inquire, discreetly."

I shook my head. "If Vincent got wind of it, he'd guess you were asking on my behalf and . . . well, he'd toss me for good."

"What if this man kills again?" Tom saw me flinch. "I could do some searching in our archives. Vincent would never know."

Belinda's rebuke about me not accepting help came to my ear as clearly as if she were standing in the room.

I managed a smile. "Give me a day or two, Tom. And then I may ask you to look. All right?"

He turned his mug in slow circles. As I drained mine, he said, "I understand barreling through the woods. I do it myself. But sometimes you need to make like an owl."

"Make like an owl," I echoed.

A rueful grin appeared and then faded. "I had an editor—brilliant man, died last year—who gave me that advice." He circled his head with his finger. "Owls can turn their heads all the way round, did you know? And they listen when the forest gets quiet."

"So if I stop tearing around and just perch somewhere, the answer'll come?" I said it lightly but smiled to show that I knew he meant well.

He set his elbows on the table and rubbed at his truncated finger. "Couldn't promise it. But for me, the final piece usually comes from someone I stopped to talk to instead of rushing past."

"You've made your point." We were silent for a minute before I added, awkwardly, "By the way, thanks for your piece. You didn't mention Mrs. Munro was alive."

One shoulder rose and fell. "You asked me not to."

My indebtedness weighed heavily on me. "I feel rotten not telling you more, all right? But I will, soon as I can."

"Yah." He tipped his mug toward me to show there were no hard feelings. "Well, you buy my coffee next time."

★   ★   ★

After I left Tom, I stood on Blackfriars Bridge for hours, watching the river clench and release like a muscle, until the afternoon glow faded and the haze held the golden pinpricks of light from the gas lamps along the Victoria Embankment. At last, I turned toward home. Newsboys were already shouting the headlines, printed in the bold letters that were usually reserved for railway disasters or assassination attempts on the queen. I sought a copy of the *Beacon*, knowing it would be the worst. The urchin who sold them was bellowing, "Murders! Murders! Read it now!"

I thrust a coin at him and stood in the middle of the pavement, tilting the front page toward a gas lamp. As usual with Fishel, there was no byline.

LONDON LADIES MURDERED, SCOTLAND YARD SHIRKING, NEW DIRECTOR FLAILING

In recent weeks there have been up to a dozen attacks on ladies in London, and Scotland Yard is once again cloaking its ineptitude!

I forced myself to read on. Naturally, Fishel made it sound as if every woman in London was in danger, that we at the Yard had made no progress despite giving priority to wealthy victims, that we were deceiving the public, and Director Vincent's leadership was foundering. To round it off, he retold the story of the Yard detectives' trial from last fall, as if the public might not remember.

I dropped the paper into a dustbin, and my feet found their way to Belinda's street.

★　★　★

Saturday was the night she was usually at home to her friends. She had invited me, repeatedly, to attend as one of the many, but I'd always refused. I wouldn't have been comfortable, and I knew that Thursdays were ours alone and safeguarded. That was what had mattered.

As I stood and watched from under a tree across the street, one carriage after another drew up to her door. Well-dressed people climbed the steps as the drivers pulled away, and her butler Robert invited them inside. The melody from a quartet of strings wafted out each time the door opened.

The selfish part of me wished she were unhappy enough about our quarrel to cancel her soiree. But there was a better part of me that admired her for keeping to her usual plans. She valued steadiness in character, manner, and habits, and she had told me enough about her mother that I understood why.

The last carriage deposited its passengers, and the door closed behind them.

In a wash of regret, I closed my eyes and let myself remember how it felt to bury my face in her hair, to feel so deeply entwined that the very words I used meant something different when spoken in her presence. And indeed, there might be times when I wanted to fight with her or rescue her, but that's not all there was.

On my way home, I did not stop in at any of the dozens of pubs I passed. Perhaps it was getting through my thick skull that it was time I did some things differently.

I put the key in the door and opened it. Just as on Tuesday night, Harry was sitting by the fire. But he was alone, and this time there were several newspapers on the table.

Harry looked at me, his dark eyes wide and worried. "Do you know who she is yet?"

I shook my head. "They've circulated portraits. They'll probably learn tomorrow."

"And she was dead?" he asked softly.

I sank into a chair. "Yes."

Worry lined his young face. "Are you getting close?"

I sighed. "Not really. We've no idea how these four women are connected—if they are. It doesn't seem to be about money or love."

"If it isn't passion or greed, Dr. Everett says it's fear or revenge," said Harry.

"But fear of what? Revenge against who?" I asked reasonably. "I can't see why he'd be *afraid* of these women. And what could the four of them, individually or together, have done to him?"

We were silent until the fire began to burn low.

Finally, I admitted, "I'm so tired, I can't think about it."

"I thought I might as well sleep here," Harry said with manufactured nonchalance. "Mrs. Beckford isn't saying anything new."

Harry's attempt at camouflaging his concern for me caught at my heart. He wanted to show he was my ally without making me feel I owed him for it. *Damn*, I thought. *I must make it a delight for people trying to help me.*

"That's good of you," I said. "I'd appreciate the company."

A flash of surprise appeared in his eyes, and he gave a shy, close-mouthed smile. "Good night, then," he said and headed off to his room.

Though I was tired, I remained by the fire, thinking. James had said Harry and I were alike, in that neither wanted to be considered a burden. Something about Harry's kindness tonight reached deep inside me and drew me back in time.

The first few days after my mother vanished, I ran the streets, searching for her desperately. Later, as despondency and fear overwhelmed me, I took daily refuge in one of the hundreds of wretched nooks and crannies in Whitechapel, where I crouched motionless for hours, often until dusk, when someone found me. Out of kindness, my mother's friends fed and sheltered me for weeks, or even months, perhaps. I don't recall. Until one night when Mrs. Tell, with three children and a babe of her own, fed me supper, same as she had before, but this time I saw the way her mouth tightened minutely as I reached for a second piece of bread, and I snatched my empty hand back as if I'd been burned.

That night after all of us were in bed, I listened to her hands thumping the dough for tomorrow's bread onto the kneading board. And I realized, suddenly, that my mother had no doubt worked after I went to sleep, trying to keep me from seeing the truth, that in Whitechapel there wasn't nearly enough sleep and food and safety and work to go around. I was overcome by hot waves of mortification and shame that I'd been a useless burden on mothers like Mrs. Tell for so long. How could I have been so stupid and selfish?

That night I lay in the bed next to Charlie, staring at the ceiling, resolved to discover how other boys did it, how I might earn a shilling or two to pay my fair way. The next morning, I watched as Mrs. Tell divided a crust of bread into five bits. I watched as she chewed hers for a long time, not wanting to swallow it because then it would be gone. And when I left the Tells' rooms in the morning, I decided that would be my contribution: I'd bring home some bread. But a nice loaf, big enough that each of us could have a thick slice, would cost at least half a shilling. What could I do? I went to a dozen different shops, asking if I could run errands or sweep up or do most anything, and the owners all shook their heads. And then I came to the bakery. From across the way, I watched people arrive and depart, pale golden loaves of bread poking out of sacks. I saw a boy attempt to draw a loaf out of a woman's bag, only to have his ears boxed. *That's a warning to me,* I thought. A small crowd of people entered the shop ten minutes before closing—enough people to form a distraction, and I followed them in and, brazen as could be, took one of a dozen loaves from a basket, slipped it under my shirt, and walked out. It was still warm from the oven, and when I finally arrived at the Tells' with my offering, I was greeted with cries of surprise and excitement from Charlie, Betty, Danny, and even the baby, and a grateful "Thank ye'," from Mrs. Tell. "How'd you come by it?"

I'd prepared my lie: "Toted some potatoes for a costermonger with a bad back."

She eyed me sharply, but that night before I climbed in with Charlie, she pulled me close and kissed the top of my head. "You're a good lad, Mickey."

I understood she wasn't only thanking me for the bread. She was thanking me for doing what I could to pay back her generosity. From then on, I knew that being weak won me a measure of tolerance, but eventually it ran out. The virtues that brought lasting appreciation were strength and certainty, decisiveness verging on brashness, and self-reliance.

Those traits had served me well until now. But given that my approach to the case had thus far yielded no good result, perhaps, as Belinda said, remembering what it was to be powerless and desperate might help me understand the man I was trying to find. The fire was down to ash when at last I rose from my chair. Upstairs, I nudged the door open to look in at Harry, sleeping, and felt a wave of tenderness, and something like sadness, too, at the way he had curled his long legs up to fit the length of the bed.

CHAPTER 37

Sunday's church bells woke me at seven, and I would've sworn I was lying awake, but I must have fallen back into a doze, for suddenly there was Harry, leaning over me, his hand shaking my shoulder.

"Mr. Corravan, wake up." His eyes were sober, his thin cheeks flushed as if he'd been running. I smelled the dampness of his woolen coat; he'd already gone out somewhere.

I sat bolt upright. "Is there another dead woman?"

"No, no," he said hurriedly.

My heart dropped back down to somewhere near its usual location, and I squinted toward the window. Rain blurred the houses opposite. It could have been any hour of day.

"Dr. Everett wants you to come to the hospital," Harry said.

"Is he all right?"

His eyes met mine. "He's fine. He just told me to fetch you. I couldn't be sure, but I think he had someone in his office."

I grunted. "What time is it?"

"Half past ten."

I pushed myself to standing and picked up my clothes from the hooks. "Give me a minute."

Harry left the room, and I dressed and then dunked a flannel into the basin and ran it over my face. I examined myself in the mirror. For the first time in several days, my eyes didn't look red-rimmed. I entered the front room and put on my coat.

"Might want your umbrella," Harry suggested tentatively, his hand on the wooden handle.

Despite everything, a wry laugh broke out.

The pinched, hurt look that came over his face stopped me in my tracks, and I hastened to correct the misunderstanding.

"I'm not laughing at you, Harry. Honestly, I'm not." I held out my hand for the wooden handle. "Stiles says the exact same thing to me. Tries to keep me from catching my death."

"Oh, I see." His expression eased to a grin of acceptance that faded shortly afterward. "I'm not sure he's taking his own advice, though."

"Why do you say that?" I shut the door behind us.

"It's just that he's been looking poorly. Last night at the hospital he insisted he wasn't ill, but he was coughing and looked feverish to me."

"I'm sure he'll be fine," I replied. "He's a sturdy sort."

We opened our umbrellas against the drizzle and walked in silence to the next street. As we paused at the corner, waiting for a carriage to pass, Harry spoke up: "Were you and Mrs. Gale arguing about me the other night?"

I turned. "What?"

He tipped his umbrella back, and his face looked resolute. "The night we went for dinner. I could tell you'd been quarreling. Was it about me?"

It took me a moment to remember—because *that* quarrel with Belinda wasn't the one uppermost in my mind. "No, Harry. It was something else."

"Oh." The flat monosyllable held disbelief.

"She wanted me to tell her about this case, and . . ." My voice dwindled.

"You didn't want to tell her?" His tone was curious.

"No. Not because I don't trust her," I added. "I just tend to keep things to myself until I have at least an idea of a solution." A dozen steps on, I added, "As she recently pointed out, I don't like admitting my failures, even to her."

He gave me a measuring look.

"It had nothing to do with you," I assured him.

"All right."

We walked on, while I mulled over the fact that misunderstandings occur all the time, and I probably don't know half of them. At least Harry had the decency to ask.

"Mrs. Beckford is better, you know," he broke into my thoughts. "She's still not talking much, mostly just nods or shakes her head. But at night, she doesn't thrash about. She sleeps like a normal person."

"James told me you heard her say the name 'Rachel.'"

He nodded. "Clear as anything. Before that, she said the same words three nights running. A table and a knife, a fire and a red stone. The way she said it made me think it was something she'd memorized, like a poem." He frowned. "But it's not in any poem I know. And it's not in 'The Lady of Shalott' either. I looked."

"What about Pierre?"

He looked puzzled.

"James said that she spoke his name, early on."

His eyes lit with comprehension. "Oh, I don't think it's a man's name. *Pierre* means 'stone' in French. She always says *une rouge pierre*. 'A red stone.'"

"Ah." I paused. "Speaking of the poem, Stiles told me Madeline once said something about 'a lane,' and he figured she meant one of the lanes near her house. But I was wondering if she might have said 'Elaine.' What do you think?"

He frowned. "Perhaps. But I've never heard her say it."

"Hmph. Well, I'm glad she seems better." We neared the hospital gates, greeted Owen, and entered the courtyard. "I could buy you dinner tonight, after you're finished here."

"Oh—you don't have to."

I sighed. "Harry, I'm sorry I haven't been particularly welcoming." He gave a wry sideways look, which I deserved. "But you arrived a day after this case began. Every week a woman dies, and I'm damn frustrated. But I'm not frustrated with you." I rested a hand on the doorknob but waited to turn it. "Can you see that?"

He gave a few nods, a boy's awkward attempt at grace. "Yes." But a smile brought warmth to his eyes, and as I opened the door and we parted in the foyer, I felt a sense of relief. It might be the only thing I'd do right today, but at least I'd done one.

★　★　★

When I entered James's office he was standing beside his desk, talking to a woman dressed in a maid's gray dress and a drab bonnet. With the light coming in from outside, I saw them both in profile.

Only when they turned toward me did I realize the woman was Belinda in disguise.

I halted in mid-stride, stopped by twin waves of surprise and shame. It's a wretched thing to face the woman you love after behaving like a drunken ass. But at least she was here. I felt as if I'd slipped my hand into a pocket and found an unexpected pound sterling.

"Good afternoon, Michael." Belinda's face was calm, her voice restrained.

James's gaze flashed between us.

I avoided his questioning stare and asked Belinda, "What's the matter?"

James handed me an envelope, and Belinda said, "It was under my door this morning."

The envelope was cheap, the kind a shopkeeper might use to store receipts, and the front held only her name, in jagged letters, as if someone had drawn them with his off hand. I opened the flap and pulled out the single sheet of paper:

Mrs. Gale

Tell your inspector to stop looking into the murders of the ladys in the boats. If he don't, you'll come to harm, and I spect he loves you. I don't want a do it, but I will, same as I done to the others. Jist tell him to wait. He'll find out later what it's about.

A painful tingling swept from the crown of my head down my arms and into my hands.

James said, "It must be the murderer. His tone seems earnest."

But I barely heard him. I looked at Belinda, imagined this man doing to her what he'd done to the others and felt fear vining rapidly around my heart and constricting my lungs.

I heard her voice, as if from far away: "Michael. Stop it. *Stop it!* I'm *fine.*" My eyes refocused on her face. Though her expression was anxious, her voice was determinedly practical. "Nothing's happened."

"You need to get out of London," I said.

"No," she said. "But as I already told James, I'll go to Catherine's."

I didn't want her at her sister's. "I want you out of London."

Her chin tilted up stubbornly. "I have commitments here."

James gave a cough. "We were just discussing how this man might've discovered your friendship." He paused. "Once the newspaper named you as the inspector on the case, he'd be able to locate you easily enough."

"But that doesn't explain how he connected me with Belinda," I objected.

James raised an eyebrow. "I assume he followed you to her house."

Before I could say a word, she said, "Michael hasn't been to visit me since Thursday before last."

One of my knees suddenly buckled. "That's not true," I said hollowly. "I went to your house last night. Watched people go in."

She appeared disconcerted, and I turned away to see James's eyebrows forming two semicircles over his spectacles. "Who else knows about your—connection?"

"Hardly anyone," Belinda replied. "A few of my most trusted friends."

"And Harry," I said slowly. "But I can't imagine how this man would have found him."

"Where is he now?" Belinda asked.

"Here at the hospital." A shiver ran over me at the thought that Harry had spent last night with me. What if the murderer had been watching my flat? He'd know who Harry was—could follow him from my door—threaten him—

Suddenly my mind jumped to two nights before when Belinda had left. "Friday night," I said. "You came to my house. What if he followed you home?"

Belinda caught her breath. "He wouldn't even need to do that, Michael. You spoke my address several times to the driver."

"But you'd notice someone hanging about," James said to me.

Not in the state I was in. My eyes met Belinda's, and she said, "The street was dark."

I closed my eyes, and in my mind I watched her carriage pulling away, this monster shadowing her. I supposed I should be grateful he didn't hurt her then and there, but all I felt was a growing rage so wild that I opened my eyes to get away from it.

Belinda was watching me, her expression soft.

"Please don't go home," I said quietly. "Not even to collect your things."

"I'll go straight to Catherine's until this is over."

"I'm sorry, Bel. I swear—"

"Don't." She shook her head. "I'll manage."

There were a dozen things I would have said if we were alone.

"The one good thing to come of this," Belinda said, "is you may have learned something important about this man."

James assented. "His handwriting and education, unless he intended to deceive."

"Or he must have an accomplice," I replied, "to write the messages that lured the women away."

"Well, yes," Belinda allowed. "But I wonder if it isn't really the women he wants to hurt at all." Her eyes, large and thoughtful, shifted to James and back to me. "Perhaps he wants to hurt the men. Killing the women they love injures them worse, and for longer."

The truth of it hit me like an uppercut to my chin.

James recovered more quickly, nodding as if it was an obvious truth. Which it was. Of course. Otherwise the murderer would've sent the threatening letter to *me*. If Belinda was the same as "the others," and if the logic of the letter extended to the four women, at least three of them had men who loved them dearly.

Dear God, we'd been thinking about these murders all wrong.

"The connection isn't among the women." My voice sounded breathless and peculiar. "It's among their husbands and fiancés."

"What do the men have in common?" Belinda asked.

"Thurgood is an architect. One of Jane Dorstone's former suitors is at university, and the other works at a bank here in the city." I recalled each in turn. "Munro is a civil engineer, working on sanitation projects on the Thames, so there could be a connection to Thurgood, and to the river."

"He's not giving them a warning first," Belinda interposed, nodding to the letter still in James's hand. "The way he did for me."

"But I'm not one of his original targets," I said. "I'm only an incidental obstacle."

James was studying the letter again. "It seems he anticipates you catching him, but *later*. The notion doesn't seem to concern him."

"He might have nothing to lose," I said, recalling the barkeep's description of the man's cough. "I wonder if he's dying."

"That could explain why he altered his pattern from Monday night to Friday," James said. "His time is running short."

"Or perhaps he feels resigned because he has nothing, or no one, to live for," said Belinda gently. "Perhaps he's alone, and this plan is all he has left."

My eyes met hers.

There was a knock at the door, and Harry poked his head in. "Mrs. Gale, there's a sergeant here to collect you."

"I sent for someone to escort her to her sister's," James said.

"A good idea," I said. I wished I could take Belinda myself, but the less we were seen together, the better.

Belinda gathered up her umbrella.

I longed to say something to her—an apology for drawing her into danger and for my idiocy the other night—but she turned away and preceded Harry out the door without looking back. I swallowed my guilt and regret and general wretchedness and watched the door close behind them. And I swear at that moment, something inside me broke for good. If I had to change every damn assumption and habit and procedure I'd ever used in detection in order to solve this case, I would.

I could do without any of them sooner than I could do without her.

CHAPTER 38

I drew close to the Yard and heard the sounds of a gathered crowd. As I came through the stone arch, I saw a mob, much like the ones that had gathered the previous autumn. Men and women were shouting, shoving, raising their fists.

"You've buggered it again!"

"Some o' ye probably murdered 'em y'selves!"

"What are ye hiding?"

"You're liars, all o' you!"

Stifling a groan, I edged my way around them to get inside. As I started up the steps, two men grabbed at me, but I squirmed away as Sergeant Wicks opened the door to let me in and dragged it closed, throwing the bolt. Inside, the atmosphere was grim. We could all still hear them. They began a chant I'd heard before: "Bungling ain't so very hard, when you're in sodding Scotland Yard!"

A scan of the room revealed everyone making a dogged show of going about their business as usual. Vincent's door was propped open, as if to say he wasn't locking himself away from the furor but was in it with us. I made my way straight toward his office, Belinda's letter in hand. It was all I had to offer, and I hoped it was enough.

Stiles's desk, unoccupied, reminded me of what Harry said about Stiles looking poorly. But I kept on and knocked at the doorframe.

Vincent looked up. His lips tightened, and his gray eyes were flat and unwelcoming.

On his desk lay two newspapers, one with a headline RAIL-WAY DISASTER SABOTAGE and the other MANCHESTER RAILWAY DISASTER.

I felt a prick of chagrin as I remembered that the river murders weren't the only highly public cases Vincent was overseeing.

"Begging your pardon, sir," I said, my voice subdued. "I know you told me not to come back until you called. I know—" My voice broke. "I push too hard sometimes, and I've not handled this well. But you need to know about this." I offered him the envelope. "It's a letter my . . . good friend Mrs. Belinda Gale received this morning."

His eyebrows rose. "Mrs. Gale, the authoress?"

"Yes."

He read the letter twice, then left it unfolded on the gleaming wood of his desk and looked up, a question in his eyes.

"I think we've been looking at this case the wrong way, sir," I said. "It's not the women who have something in common."

It took a moment, but then understanding lit his eyes, and slowly he leaned back in his chair. "You think it's the men. The men who love them."

The tension in my spine ebbed as he seemed to accept the idea without a fight.

"I was thinking, sir," I continued, "that we—that is, someone should talk once more to Anthony Thurgood, Rose Albert's secret fiancé. She was the first, so I imagine he is the most important. If we find someone who wanted to injure *him*, then perhaps we can start making a connection to the others."

He nodded slowly. "He's an architect, so he and Munro are both engaged in civic projects. And the banker might be involved in financing them," he said, as if my notes were right in front of him.

I did my best to conceal the surprise he'd have taken, rightly, as an insult.

He stood and went to the window, staring toward the river. "What do you know about McLoughlin?" He turned to meet my gaze. "I assume you haven't spoken with him. But you recognized his name."

"Yes, sir," I admitted. "My family knows him, and while I don't know all the particulars, they say he's a good bloke and was wrongly convicted. The girl said he'd held her for three days, but after the trial it came out she'd been seen at some shops during that time." Vincent's eyes narrowed, and I added, "Could be they were mistaken. But he was convicted on her word alone."

His brows lowered. "I read the transcript. He tried to hide that he'd worked on that wharf."

"Being scared, he might've done that," I said. "But I know someone who can help me find him." I paused. "Whitechapel boy or not, sir, if there's even a possibility he had something to do with this, I'll bring him back with me."

He nodded. "His address at trial was a boardinghouse in Brook Street. Number 16."

I stifled my disappointment. I wanted to talk to Thurgood first. But I reminded myself I was lucky Vincent was even considering allowing me to do this.

"Perhaps Stiles could go speak with Mr. Thurgood," I suggested.

He shook his head. "I sent Stiles home on Saturday night. He was ill."

I felt a jab of dismay. Sent home and still not at work this morning? He must be even worse off than Harry said.

Vincent's expression betrayed both regret and annoyance that he had little choice but to let me return. I wished desperately there was a way to make him feel better about it.

It was Belinda's voice that rang in my ear: *Why can't you be a little humble, stop acting as if you and you alone are saving the world?*

Awkwardly, I said, "Sir, would you like me to see Thurgood and the other men, or find Nate first? Or do something else?"

Vincent studied me for a moment. At last he said, "Go see Thurgood and the others first, Nate afterward. Tomorrow if you must. But report back to me tonight. All right?"

I nodded. "It might be late, sir."

"I'll be here."

He picked up one of the papers, and I took it as a dismissal.

At the threshold, I heard his voice behind me. "Thank you for sharing the letter and explaining your thoughts." His voice was still cool, but the words were civil.

"Yes, sir," I replied and left.

His manner certainly hadn't been encouraging, but I had a feeling that I'd at least provisionally halted my downward slide in his estimation.

CHAPTER 39

In Sackville Street, I found the building firm of Charles Barry and Robert Richardson Banks. I had to wait in the foyer for two hours until Anthony Thurgood returned from an appointment, and as he entered, the man looked pale and unhappy. He was unhappier still at seeing me, but he invited me to his office and answered my questions willingly enough. No, he had received no threats, written or spoken. No, he had never heard of Mrs. Munro's husband Andrew or either of Jane's suitors, Samuel Gordon and Robert Eddington.

"Are they suspects?" he asked.

I shook my head. "You've seen the papers? The other attacks?"

He nodded despondently. "By the same man?"

"We think so. Four so far."

He dropped his head into his hands, rubbed the heels into his eyes.

I sat down, uninvited, in a chair near him. "But, Mr. Thurgood, the four women don't have much in common. And we're beginning to wonder if the connection might be among their husbands, fiancés, and suitors."

He lifted his face from his hands, revealing an expression full of horror. "Oh, *God*! You think Rose died because of *me*?"

"We don't know if it was personal," I said hastily. "Can you think of anyone who would want to hurt you, for any reason? Have you slighted someone, or do you owe anyone money, or does anyone owe you?"

"None of that." He slumped in his chair, his elbow on the arm, and rubbed his hand over his mouth. "Oh, God, I don't know." He looked so wretched I wanted to turn his thoughts in a different direction.

"We're also looking for a tie to the river. How long have you been with this firm?"

"Four years," he said.

"What sort of buildings do they design?"

"All kinds." He gestured toward some framed blueprints that hung on the wall. "The pump house in the Italian gardens in Hyde Park. Saint Stephen's Church in South Dulwich. The forecourt of Burlington House in Piccadilly."

"Anything by the river?" I asked.

"No." Then he reconsidered. "Well, we've been contracted to renovate the Inner Temple. It doesn't face the Thames, but it's close by, east of Waterloo Bridge."

I sat back. "How did that come about?"

"Three different building firms put in plans, and we won it last month. All the materials are being ordered, some from Wales, others from Italy. We're to begin construction early next year."

"Who were the other two firms?"

"Thomas Cubitt and Walter Angstrom." He rubbed at his temple with his fingertips. "Angstrom was angry about losing because last year he renovated Gray's Inn—one of the other three Inns of Court—but he just accepted two new commissions for Mayfair hotels, so he's not suffering for work. And Cubitt always has more than he can manage."

"Would anyone be angry enough about your firm winning that they'd want to hurt you?"

"I doubt it. I was only incidentally involved in the proposal," he replied. "And Angstrom isn't the sort to do something violent. Nor is Cubitt. His passion is design. He's not a murderer, for God's sake—"

"All right," I cut him off. "But any tie to the river is of interest to me right now."

"Yes, well," he said dispiritedly. "I can't think of any other."

I felt a similar sense of futility. Nonetheless, I tried again. "Do you purchase materials from Baldwin's?"

"Of course. Everyone does. They're the largest supplier of girders in the city."

"And the Home Office? Do you obtain contracts from them?"

"Sometimes." His face revealed his misery. "Look here, when do you think you'll know why she was killed?"

"We're getting close. But regardless, you're not to blame for her death."

He swallowed hard, his expression bleak.

"One other question," I said. "Do you by chance know anyone named Elaine? Or did Rose? Could she be one of her friends, perhaps?"

He shook his head. "Not that I know of."

I didn't expect a different answer; it was just another grope in the dark.

I stood. "In the meantime, would you not mention this conversation to anyone? We can't have anyone making wild suppositions. It will only make our search more difficult."

"Of course."

I bid him goodbye. At the doorway, I turned back. He was staring into mid-air, his face set and hopeless and appearing ten years' worth of sadness older than it should. And yet there was a look of bewilderment about him too, like a child who had suffered a loss against which he had no defense.

If I thought it would have helped him, I'd have told him that I'd lost my mother, whom I loved more than anyone, and I understood his grief. The deep, heart-hollowing pain that made itself felt in nightmares, that roused a flash of hope at the sight of any woman who bore a passing resemblance to her, that made me long to howl and moan and even die as the truth of her absence took hold.

But I remembered my experience keenly enough to know that any words I might utter would have provided no comfort at all.

★   ★   ★

As it was the middle of the day, I knew I wouldn't find Mr. Eddington at his home in Dulcet Street. Reviewing the notes in my pocketbook, I found the name of the bank where he was employed as a clerk. Central Bank on Newgate Street, in the shadow of St. Paul's, wasn't far, so I walked along the embankment and turned north.

Mr. Eddington was seated at his desk. He looked thinner than before, and dark smudges stained the skin under his eyes. At the sight of me, he flinched, as if expecting another blow. But after a moment, his eyes sparked and an angry flush rose to his cheeks. "Inspector," he said frostily.

I stood behind the chair opposite, as he did not invite me to sit. A stove cast a good deal of warmth, and I unbuttoned my coat. "Mr. Eddington, I'm sorry to disturb you here."

His lips pressed together until they vanished. "I saw the newspaper account. Jane wasn't the first."

"No, she wasn't. And we've discovered some new facts," I replied. Whereas Mr. Thurgood had been despairing, this man had chosen fury as an alternative to grief. I would have to tread carefully. "We have not found any meaningful similarities among the women. So now we are looking for connections among the families and loved ones of these women."

His spine stiffened. "Well, I know one person you should look at. Jane's mother. She's hateful!"

I drew out my pocketbook and pencil. "Why do you say that?"

"Why, she made Jane miserable!" he burst out. "Criticized her for everything from what she wore to the amount of jam she spread on her toast."

While that sounded unpleasant, it was doubtful it would lead to murder and wouldn't connect Jane with the others.

"That is certainly something to consider." I made a note on a blank page. "A few more questions. Do you know Anthony Thurgood or Robert Munro?"

"No." His entire body tensed again, as if he were ready to leap up and slay them. "You suspect them?"

"No, I do not," I replied evenly. "Do you know of anyone who might be angry with you? Or bear a grudge?"

"Of course not," he said without even thinking, and then understanding dawned. "Are you saying her death might have had . . ." His hand came up as if to fend off the suggestion.

"Mr. Eddington, have you had any rows in the past year over money or debts?"

"*No.* Oh, some friendly wagers at the club have put some friends in debt to me, but only five pounds or so. It's nothing."

I knew people who'd consider five pounds worth killing for. But members of his club presumably found it as negligible an amount as he did.

"We also wonder if anyone connected with Jane might have ties to the river," I said.

"The Thames?"

"She was found there in a boat," I reminded him. "They all were."

"Well, I have none to speak of," he said irritably. "I walk by it sometimes, like anyone. I drink tea that's brought in by the ships, and our housekeeper uses spices in her cooking."

I held my temper. "I was thinking of your work here at the bank."

"Oh." His exasperation abated a degree. "Well, many of our clients have connections to the Thames. For God's sake, most every company in London does—whether they receive their raw materials by boat, or warehouse their goods there, or build ships or gas lamps for the embankment . . ."

"And do you have any connection to Baldwin's? The metalworks company?"

He nodded. "They bank with us."

I felt a pinprick of hope.

"What about your family? Any connections to civil engineering or the Home Office?"

His expression altered, and he drew away from his desk, his hands fidgeting on the arms of the chair. "Well, I can't imagine it has anything to do with this, but my mother's cousin is Sir Charles Westingford."

Westingford? The name was vaguely familiar. He saw me groping, and he added, "The Assistant to the Home Secretary."

My heart tripped, and the pinprick of hope grew.

"You look as if that means something," he said. "But frankly, I doubt Jane even met my uncle." His lip curled. "Oh—perhaps they were in the same room at one of our parties. But he isn't the sort to bother talking to ladies who are attached."

"Hmm," I said nonchalantly. "Just a few more questions. Do you or does your bank have any particular connections to the Inner Temple? Or the architectural firm of Barry and Banks? Or Cubitt or Angstrom?" He shook his head after each. "Do you happen to know anyone named Elaine? Or did Jane know anyone by that name?"

"I don't think so."

"Finally, I understand this is a delicate matter. What can you tell me about Samuel Gordon? I understand Miss Dorstone was acquainted with him."

He sighed. "Yes. Sam asked for her hand last December. But I believe he is engaged now, or nearly so, to someone else."

"Where is he now? Mr. Dorstone told me he was studying abroad."

"Oh, he's returned. Up at Oxford, reading classics."

It didn't sound likely that he'd have much of a connection to either the Thames or building of any kind.

To reassure him that I was nearly finished, I put my pocketbook away. "Where might I find your uncle?"

He tapped his fingertips on his chair arm. "Up at his country estate, in Lancashire. Take the train from Euston to Preston and ask the way to Scarsbrick Hall. Anyone can direct you."

"Thank you." I did up the buttons on my coat.

"If you'd have found him after the first one, Jane would be alive." His voice was accusing, his eyes bright with resentment. "Tomorrow would have been her birthday, you know. Mother had planned a party. With all her friends and—and pink roses. They were Jane's favorite."

Despite his manner, my heart softened. "I'm very sorry."

He snorted and averted his eyes, and I left, relieved and yet dismayed to have found some plausible connections among the river, Baldwin's, and the Home Secretary, Sir Stephen Vernon Harcourt, one of the most powerful and wealthy men in all of London.

The image of the tiger, from several weeks ago, reappeared in my mind.

★ ★ ★

It was nearly six o'clock when I returned to the Yard.

I had to wait to see Vincent, who was occupied with a visitor in his office. Over an hour later, finally, a man I didn't recognize departed, and I knocked.

He looked up from his desk. "Hello, Corravan. Anything?"

"Possibly." Like Eddington, Vincent didn't invite me to sit, and I remained standing, reporting everything I'd learned.

At the end of my recital, he nodded minutely. "So there are . . . threads connecting Thurgood, Eddington, and Munro to both Baldwin's and the river."

"Thin threads, yes, sir." When he didn't reply, I continued, "I'm planning to go to Whitechapel tomorrow first thing to find Nate. And then I could go up to see Westingford."

"That may not be necessary. I can make some discreet inquiries first, here in London."

The caution in his expression suggested he didn't trust me to manage an interview with the Assistant to the Home Secretary tactfully. Well, so long as we obtained the facts, I was beyond caring how they came to us. "Yes, sir."

He made a note on a piece of paper and slid it into one of several folders at his right hand. "Thank you, Corravan, again, for keeping me apprised. I appreciate your efforts."

Rather stilted, but decent of him to say.

"Yes, sir." I let myself out, then went to a chophouse where I ordered myself a meal.

Whitechapel, tomorrow.

I almost choked on the beef stew as I realized that the next day was Tuesday.

I could only hope that our man had committed his murder for the week, and we wouldn't have a fifth body in the river in the morning. But my sense of unease continued to grow until it ruined my dinner. On my way home, I stopped by Belinda's sister's house. It was dark, except for an upstairs window. The shadow flitting behind the curtains could have been Belinda or Catherine; it was impossible to tell. I walked the length of the street twice, keeping my eye out for anyone lurking, and saw no one. Nevertheless, I slipped into an alley and watched until the upstairs window went dark. Then I stayed another half hour, just to be sure.

Chapter 40

By Tuesday morning, we knew that the fourth woman's name was Emma Montooth, and she hadn't been seen since around two o'clock on Friday.

As Stiles was still at home ill, Vincent sent Inspector Mills to speak with her family and friends while I headed to Whitechapel. Mills and I planned to meet back at the Yard at six o'clock. That should give me plenty of time, I hoped, to find Nate McLoughlin.

★   ★   ★

Half an hour with Ma Doyle would steer me straighter than any number of hours scouting around Nate's last known address on Brook Street. I approached her shop, peered through one of the two front windows, and backed away. Too many people who'd want to say hello and ask why I was there.

I went round to the alley and slipped in the back door, where Elsie was scooping tea into packets. She gave a shriek of surprise, then came toward me to throw an arm around my waist. I drew back and studied her. She looked more like her mother every time I saw her. Same sassy tilt to her chin, same hazel eyes. A pile of auburn hair wound into braids. Damn pretty, even beautiful, at age nineteen. I wondered how many Whitechapel boys were hovering around.

"What're you doin' here, Mickey?" she asked.

I couldn't help but grin. "Nobody calls me Mickey anymore but you and Ma."

She slapped me gently on the cheek. "That's for not coming round for Sunday tea in *weeks*. And here it's a Tuesday. Are ye needin' somethin'?"

I shrugged sheepishly. "I'm looking for somebody, and I have a feeling Ma might have an idea where to start. Nate McLoughlin." Her grin faded, and I put up a hand to reassure her. "I'm not here to cause him trouble."

Her head tipped. "What do ye want with him then?"

"I need to ask if he had anything to do with the women who've been murdered on the river."

"Ach!" she exclaimed. "He would never!"

"I'm guessing he didn't. But I still have to ask. Do you know where I can find him?"

Her mouth formed a pink rosebud. "I'll fetch Ma. She might know."

She pushed open the door to the front room, and the chatter of half a dozen conversations swelled and then faded as the door shut. I upended a barrel and sat on it, just like I used to when I'd work sums for Ma on my slate.

The smell of Darjeeling—a tang that often flavored the Doyles' living quarters above—together with the purpose of my errand took me back to that afternoon when I'd come for Sunday tea and Elsie had told me about Nate McLoughlin's trial. It had taken place a fortnight before, and she was still angry about it. The gist of what I remembered was this:

There was a girl named Gemma Greene, too pretty for her own good, who loved to stir up trouble among the boys, flirting with a few at a time and relishing it when they'd fight over her. It was mostly harmless, until she set her sights on Nate McLoughlin. Nate was a good, hardworking lad who fancied another local girl named Katy Dewy, and he'd have nothing to do with Gemma, which first made her want him worse and then made her sulky and spiteful. One day, Gemma vanished. No one knew where she was for three days, and her mother had been worried enough to call the police. At last, Gemma turned up, saying that Nate had taken her to a basement near the wharf, tied her up, and outraged her. She'd managed to undo the ropes around her wrists and escape.

I'd never met Nate myself, but according to Elsie, Nate had never done anything like this before, and he wasn't the sort.

The problem was, he had no alibi. He worked on the docks by day and slept at home at night, same as always, but Gemma said he came to her between and left her for hours. She showed people the bruises and scrapes on her wrists where he tied ropes. The trial happened almost immediately, with Nate convicted on Gemma's tearful testimony and sentenced to nine months. But a few days after the trial, it came out that four different people saw her at various shops two of the days she was supposedly abducted. And no one had questioned Gemma's story of how she'd undone the knots and escaped. "Fancy a dockhand not knowing how to tie a proper knot," Elsie had scoffed, and I'd thought she had a point.

Part of the reason Elsie had related all this was because she wanted me to get Nate out of prison, and I had to explain why that was impossible. The outcome didn't seem wholly justified, I admitted, but there had been a trial and verdict, and I couldn't undo that, especially given that it took place in a borough where I had absolutely no standing or authority. I tried to console her, saying that Nate would be out of prison in a matter of months, but Elsie had a firm sense of what was fair and what wasn't, and her face had reflected her frustration and disappointment.

The door opened and Ma appeared, drying her hands on a towel. "Why, Mickey, what're you doin' back here?"

Back in the Chapel, or in this back room? I wondered. But I only gave her a quick kiss on the cheek.

"Is Harry all right?" she asked, her expression concerned.

"Oh, he's grand," I said, waving a hand. "First thing he told me was he loves Latin and wants to be a doctor, so I brought him round to James. Now he spends all his time taking patient histories and soaking up whatever James'll teach him."

She frowned.

"But I see him," I added hastily. "I admit we had a rough patch to start, but we're fine now. He's a smart bloke with a good heart. He's even helping me with an old case, seeing as I'm on a new one."

She winced. "Aye. Those poor ladies in the boats. I saw your name in the papers."

I nodded. "Remember I told you about the Commission?"

"Trying to shut down the Yard," she supplied.

"One of the commissioners has it in his head that Nate McLoughlin might be involved. Because of what happened before."

Her expression grew indignant. "But it was a lie from start to finish!"

I drew out another barrel for her and upended it. "Elsie told me about the sort of girl Gemma was, and I know it came out afterward that she was seen at some shops. What else can you tell me?"

She settled on the improvised seat, her lips pursed so tightly with disapproval that her right cheek dimpled. "Well, two weeks after the trial, she's showin'—" her hand rested on her stomach "—and trying to say it's Nate's. Now, any woman who's ever had a child knows no one shows at four weeks. Then a fortnight along, after Gemma ran off, her sister 'fessed she found rope hid in Gemma's drawer, with blood on it, like she made the marks herself."

I blew out a breath. "Where did Gemma go?"

"Ach, I couldn't say. But the damage was done, o' course." Her face took on a pinched look. "The worst of it was, the week before the trial, the rumors were so thick that Katy Dewy told Nate she didn't know what to believe and broke things off. I'd say that hurt him worse than bein' found guilty. Poor lad."

"And he's never admitted to it?"

She shook her head. "I've known Joan and her boy for years. I'm telling you, Mickey, he didn't hurt Gemma."

"Ma, I'm guessing you're right. But I still need to talk to him." I saw her begin to protest, and I leaned in. "Otherwise, somebody else is going to come looking. Better it's me, isn't it? I'll give him the benefit of the doubt."

"O' course." She thought for a moment. "Wait here."

Twenty minutes later, she was back. "Try the Golden Horn. Ye remember where 'tis?"

"Sure."

She looked at me sorrowfully. "But don't think the way you find him now is what he was. He never used to drink more 'n a pint, but Joan says he's soused most days." Her voice was sad. "He's bitter, Mickey. Like you could'a been."

I nodded in acknowledgment. "If you hadn't made me see reason."

She patted my cheek, more gently than Elsie had. "Take care o' yourself. And Harry, too."

I pulled her into a quick, grateful embrace. Then I headed for the Horn.

It had been more than a decade, but plenty of us from the docks went there, and I found it without making a wrong turn. The paint from the wooden sign had faded, leaving only the carved letters and the shape of a horn, and the door was new—probably because the old one had rotted. As I swung it open, the smell of hops and river-scented floorboards brought me back. For just that second, I could have been seventeen, with some swagger in my step and a few shillings in my pocket, and Pat Doyle could have been right behind me.

At this time of day, the men weren't here to sing or play cards or even start a fight, like those who'd come later. A dozen men, most of them alone at their tables, drank sullenly and with purpose. Only a few bothered to glance up as I entered.

I went straight to the buxom woman behind the counter and asked for my quarry.

She pointed behind me. A tight silver ring made her chubby finger look like a pink sausage in its casing. "There."

I turned to find Nate's eyes already on me, and I approached. He was around Colin's and Elsie's age, twenty or thereabouts, wiry the way dockhands are, with a good pair of shoulders, a handsome face, a thatch of tousled red hair, and a grim set to his mouth.

I sat down on the stool opposite.

"Nate? I'm Mickey Corravan," I said.

He gave me a dark look. "You're police."

I nodded.

"I ain't done nothin'," he said warningly.

"I just want to ask you some questions."

A snort. "Like you'll believe me."

"Listen." I leaned forward. "I grew up here. I know how things can be."

He appraised my overcoat. "You seem t' have done a' right."

"You know Ma Doyle?"

That erased some of the sneer, and a cautious interest lit his eyes.

"She took me in after my ma disappeared," I said. "And she says you didn't touch that girl."

He deflated, and his eyes dropped to his pint. "Well, I didn't."

"I tend to believe her." His gaze flicked up to meet mine, and I lowered my voice. "But I have to ask you. You've heard about those dead women on the river?"

"O' course." Then his expression changed. He looked horrified, first—then hunted—and at last despondent. "You think I done it," he said dully. "'Cos 'a wot they said I done before."

"Where were you on Friday afternoon and evening?"

He thought for a few seconds. "Here."

I stood and approached the barmaid. "Was Nate here on Friday?"

"Shore." She wiped the inside of a glass with a rag. "He's here most every night, drinking until he's too blotted to stand."

"When did he arrive?" I asked.

She twitched her full mouth to the side, held it there while she thought. "Came around one in the afternoon, just after I come. Left mebbe midnight."

"You're sure?"

Her eyes drifted to him, and to my surprise, her expression softened. "Poor fool. Warn't fair what she did to 'im." Her gaze returned to me. "Whatever somebody done that day, it warn't him. He was so soused he couldn't walk straight."

"You're certain it was Friday."

"Friday was last day I worked." She turned to a man with the jowls of a walrus who was perched nearby, pretending not to listen. "Dick, you was here Friday. Was Nate here?"

"Aye. I started playin' cards around three. He was here" —he directed his thumb toward the corner where Nate sat brooding over his pint— "in his usual spot."

So Nate had two alibis.

"And your names?" I asked. If she demurred, I'd doubt her, but she obliged instantly.

"Margery Flaxwell." She tipped her head toward the man. "Dick Connelly."

"Thanks." I pulled some coins out of my pocket and dropped them on the bar. "A pint for Dick, if you would." The man nodded his thanks, and the coins vanished under her plump hand before I'd turned away.

I returned to Nate's table and scribbled the names in my pocketbook. "You're clear. I promise," I said, looking down at him.

He gave a doubtful look and lifted his tankard to his mouth again.

There was something in me that wanted to sit back down, to try to convince him that as rotten as he felt right now, his life wasn't over. That things could change. That ten years from now, he could find himself with work he liked, a woman he loved, maybe even one who loved him back enough to forgive him when he acted like an ass. Friends who cared enough to argue with him when he was steering himself wrong.

The scowl on his face told me he wanted to be left alone.

Still, I tried. "My name's Corravan," I reminded him. "I'll help you if you want. Find you something to do, get you away from here. You can reach me through Ma Doyle. You hear me?"

"I don't need help from the likes o' you." His resentment was obvious, but I might have missed the note of shame, the need for something beyond rescuing, except that Belinda's reproach had taken root in my mind.

"It's true that I've done all right for myself, Nate. But only because someone helped me, back when I left Whitechapel." I thought of Mr. Gordon, the superintendent in Lambeth. "Helped me more than once. And I needed it. I was young and stubborn, and there was a lot I needed to learn," I said frankly. "If it hadn't been for him, I'd probably be dead."

That penetrated his mistrust, however briefly. He looked at me searchingly, but he said nothing, so after a moment I said, "Offer stands, any time. All right?"

He nodded, and I had to be satisfied with that.

I reached the street and considered what to do next. The offices of the *Falcon* weren't far—no more than a ten-minute walk. I turned in that direction and reached the large door, pushed it open, and mounted the stairs to the second floor, where dozens of men were laying type, their fingers quick and deft, plucking the lead bits from their wooden compartments.

I approached the nearest man. "Where can I find Tom Flynn?"

His eyes never left his task. "Upstairs."

I thanked him and climbed a flight of rickety wooden stairs that I wouldn't have wanted to navigate in the dark. An oblong rectangle of light lay across the floor at the end of the hallway, and I reached the open door and looked in. He was bent over a table covered with old newspapers.

"Tom."

He looked up, and his expression brightened. "Corravan. Hullo."

Before I even had time to settle into the chair, Tom pushed a page of newsprint toward me. "I may have found your trial."

My jaw dropped. "You shouldn't have spent—"

"Oh." Tom waved a hand. "I'm looking for some other articles. Kept my eye peeled for it, and—well, you can see why it stood out."

Yes, I could. The headline, in one-inch capital letters: WEST END DOCTOR ACQUITTED.

Tom leaned forward, elbows on the rough table, his thumb rubbing over the shortened finger on his left hand. "You can read for yourself, but about four years ago, Dr. Forsyte was called to a case and diagnosed a kidney stone." He touched his lower right side, beneath his ribs. "However, it was actually appendicitis, and the woman died. There was a question of Forsyte being drunk when he saw her, but the case was dismissed. Barrister knew what he was about. Bartholomew Griffiths."

I could imagine Forsyte, like Mr. Bell said, swearing on a Bible, trying to save himself from jail, from having to sell his practice. I scanned the article, but Tom had omitted nothing important from his rapid synopsis.

I blew out my breath. "You're a good man."

He brushed the compliment aside. But I wasn't so much a fool that I didn't know the effort he'd taken on my behalf. I owed him more than a pint now, and I pay my debts. So I told him everything I'd discovered so far, with the proviso that he couldn't use it yet, and I'd have more for him soon.

He walked me down the back stairs and whistled for a cab. The sky darkened as I rode west, and I fit this new information about Dr. Forsyte into what I already knew. As I passed St. Paul's Cathedral, I recalled the barrister's name: Bartholomew Griffiths.

The feeling that I'd heard the name before—and recently— was like a shard of metal under the skin in my palm. Trying to dig the circumstance out of my memory occupied me all the way back to Whitehall, where I climbed out of the cab. I still couldn't remember where or when I'd heard of him, but I knew if I stopped trying, it would come to me eventually.

CHAPTER 41

Mindful that I hadn't eaten all day, I stopped in a pub to wolf down a slice of shepherd's pie before I returned to the Yard. Vincent's door was open, with Inspector Mills inside, and Mills must have noticed Vincent spotting me, for he turned as I approached.

"Any luck?" Vincent asked.

"It's not Nate," I said to both of them. "He has an alibi for all of Friday. Two of them, in fact." I handed over a piece of paper with their names and the address of the Golden Horn.

Inspector Mills's cough rumbled in his throat. "I was just saying that I met the fourth victim's father—Montooth. Furious, of course, that we haven't caught the man. Railed at me for a good ten minutes before I could get a word in."

"Was she married?" I asked.

"Engaged. Emma was eighteen. Her fiancé is named David Cobb, who's at university, reading history."

I had the fleeting thought that he might be connected somehow with Jane's suitor Sam Gordon, or Rose's brothers at Cambridge. "Which one?"

"Oriel. One of the Oxford colleges. But her father says Cobb wouldn't have anything to do with this. Called him a 'weak-minded ninny.'" He curled his lip in imitation of Mr. Montooth.

"What does Montooth do?"

He sniffed. "He's a gentleman. Collects art. Serves on a few railway boards."

"And how did Emma go missing?" I asked.

"That's the strange thing," Mills said. "I know all of the others were taken at night. Seems Emma was intending to go to the bookshop and the milliner on Friday afternoon."

That *was* different. Perhaps the man was merely guided by opportunity. Perhaps the three Tuesdays were coincidental.

Inspector Mills took out a handkerchief and wiped at his nose. "The milliner says Emma stopped in at around three o'clock. But after that, nothing."

Vincent sighed. "All right. Well, I suppose we should find out if Mr. Cobb has any connection to the river, building, or engineering—although it doesn't seem likely."

I heard the flatness in Vincent's voice, and by the gloomy look Mills gave me, I could tell he felt just as discouraged.

"Thank you, Mills," Vincent said and nodded. Mills turned away, and I made to follow, but Vincent said, "Just a moment, Corravan. Please close the door."

I stiffened. I hoped he wasn't still fixed on Nate McLoughlin. Even Quartermain should be satisfied with two alibis.

Vincent gestured toward the leather armchair opposite. "Please."

Well, this invitation was noteworthy.

Warily, I drew the chair away from the desk far enough to accommodate my knees and lowered myself into it.

His gray eyes met mine. "What is your opinion of Chief Superintendent Blair?"

The question hit me like a bucket of ice water, and it took a moment to recover. Vincent's expression was bland, but there was a prickling along my spine, and I sensed I was being tested. I began cautiously, searching for words noncommittal enough that I'd only confirm whatever Vincent already knew.

"I worked under him for four years," I replied.

"Yes." He waited.

"He knows nearly everything about the river," I said. "The depth of water at various places, the tides at different times of the month, heights of the bridges, the foremen and managers of the warehouses, men who own the shipping lines and work at Custom House."

"A knowledgeable man." He folded his hands across his waist-coat. "Could you tell me why you left?"

Again, I had the sensation—stronger now—that this was a test, and a critical one. I couldn't imagine Vincent rewarding me for disparaging a former superintendent. It was on the tip of my tongue to say that I'd merely wanted a change, to let him think I was capricious or overweening or even disloyal, when Vincent said, "We have it on good authority that Blair leaked information about the first two murders to the press."

I flinched, knocking my elbow into the chair arm.

"You're surprised." A look of relief crossed his face.

"Of course," burst from me, but I fell silent as questions rose to my mind in a wave. What would Blair gain by sabotaging the investigation? Was this out of spite toward me? Toward Vincent? Or out of general resentment that the case had been turned over to the Yard?

"Corravan, I need an answer."

His words jerked me back to the present.

"Why did you leave?" he asked again, patiently.

I coughed to clear the thickness in my throat. "I had concerns about some of Blair's actions, sir."

"Specifically?"

Vincent's tone told me he knew something, and I resolved to say only what I knew for certain.

"He was overlooking some of his men taking bribes from officers at Custom House," I replied.

He unclasped his hands to turn over a palm. "And?"

He was looking for an allegation that I couldn't give him. "Sir, there's nothing else I could say with certainty. And I don't guess. Feels too much like slander."

"Very well." His eyes were sober. "Were you acquainted with a Custom House officer named Walsh?"

So he knew.

My heart tripped, and my spine cleaved to the upholstered back of the chair.

A second wave of questions: Was this the reason Stiles and I had been sent to Wapping that first day? Not because Blair had requested me for the lighter boat, or because I happened to be available, but because Vincent knew I'd watch Blair with extra care?

Yet another wave of questions formed behind this one: What else did Vincent know? And did he blame me for not speaking up about my suspicions years ago, for dodging the mess and moving to the Yard?

Vincent sat with his spine straight, his left elbow resting lightly on the chair arm. "Mr. Corravan, I have a particular reason for wanting to know. And I shall keep your confidence."

I was silent for a long minute. I had never told anyone the whole story, not even James or Belinda. But the look in Vincent's eyes told me that if I didn't tell him now, he'd never ask me for the truth again.

"As you probably know," I began slowly, "there are some merchants and shipping companies who give bribes to customs officers to avoid paying the proper duties on goods. The customs officers in turn pay the River Police men a portion of it, to guarantee safe passage and no trouble. This has been going on for years." Vincent's expression suggested he knew all this, and relieved, I continued, "But a few years ago, the penalty for accepting bribes rose from a moderate fine to five years in prison. So some of the customs men stopped taking them. Still, some of the River Police men were wanting their money, so they'd threaten them—or beat them. One of the River men discovered that Kevin Walsh was planning to report them, and he and another man went to talk to Walsh, convince him to keep quiet."

"Who were they?"

The names stuck in my throat. I remembered how low I felt when everyone thought I'd ratted out O'Hagan. Only this time I was actually being a rat. But I'd left the River Police for a reason.

"Jonas Pye and Steve Wick," I said. "Wick's the sort who goes along with things, but Pye's clever as they come."

He nodded. "Go on."

"Walsh turned up dead two days later. His body washed up on the bank near Scully Dock. A new man at Wapping named Tom Finney was assigned the case and didn't seem to be making much headway." Young Finney had been chosen for a reason, and Vincent's face told me he understood that. "But I learned enough to realize what had probably happened."

"How?"

This was another question whose answer stuck in my throat. But at last I said, "Kevin's brother Liam saw Pye and Wick and Kevin in a pub together two nights before his body was found."

Vincent's chest rose, as if with a quick inhalation.

"But Liam was a drunkard," I continued. "And he'd had some run-ins with River Police men over the years."

"An ax to grind, perhaps," Vincent supplied.

I nodded. "So I had no real proof that Pye or Wick, or any of the River men, had killed Walsh." I took a breath. "Still, I was all set to go to Blair with what I guessed. I wanted to do the decent thing, so I met Pye at a pub to tell him ahead of time." A small snort escaped, as I remembered how Pye had laughed at me. "He told me that Blair already gave them an alibi for that night and Finney made it official, putting it in his report."

Even as I spoke the words, I was back there in that pub, with Pye's words carving a crater in my chest. "Blair looks after his own, Mickey." Pye had laughed a second time, no doubt at the stupid expression on my face, at my disbelief that Blair would cover up a murder. Pye was always cocksure, but I sensed he wasn't bluffing. And as much as Blair had watched out for me for four years, as much as I'd grown to admire him and even love him, I couldn't say for certain that he wouldn't lie, under oath if necessary, to protect his own men.

"You believed him?" Vincent asked.

"I tended to, yes," I said. "Blair's loyal. And it's not as if losing two good River men would bring Kevin Walsh back."

Vincent leaned back into his chair, and it was then that I realized he'd held himself motionless since I began. The times when I'd unfolded a story like this to Blair, he'd stand behind his chair, fingers curled around the top, rocking forward and back until I concluded.

"You never confronted Blair, even in a roundabout way?" Vincent asked.

"I had no proof that would stand up," I said.

Vincent's gaze sharpened in a way that told me he noticed I'd dodged the question. When I remained silent, he inclined his head as if waiting, but this was where I drew the line. There was nothing else he needed to know, no good that could come of replaying that last, wretched, curse-filled conversation between Blair and me.

"Then you transferred to the Yard," Vincent concluded.

My eyes dropped to my hands clasped at my waist. They were quick, strong hands, but they'd been powerless to obtain any sort of justice for Kevin Walsh, or to hold Pye or Wick or Blair himself to account. Powerless to do anything but leave the whole mess behind. The shame of it flared so hot that sweat broke out along my scalp.

"You couldn't stay," Vincent said. "Could you?"

"No," I said.

Vincent steepled his fingers, touching the tips to his chin. "When I first mentioned Blair just now, you looked as if you wanted to ask something."

"Did you send me to Wapping, the morning we found Rose Albert, because I'd know to keep an eye on him?"

His eyebrows rose. "No. It's only recently I learned most of this, although you've filled in some gaps. I sent you because you know more about the river than anyone here. Or so people tell me."

I didn't dispute that. "Do you think Blair squealed to the papers to discredit you, or me? Or both of us?"

"I'd say both of us," he replied. "I imagine he resents my oversight, and this was his way of trying to get out from under it. He's also probably scared of this." His index finger pointed to me and then back to himself. "That you'd trust me enough to explain why you left."

Yes, Blair had done what he could to undermine that trust, implying Vincent leaked my Seddon Hall visit.

"Kevin Walsh's case was five years ago," I said. "I'm surprised anyone would still be thinking about it."

"Some members on the Commission have long memories." Vincent gave his quiet smile. "That's why the River Police was discreetly tucked within my purview when I was brought on."

"I see." It was on the tip of my tongue to ask what Vincent would do with this information, if this would have repercussions for Blair. But it was really none of my concern. And with that thought came an unexpected wave of relief.

"Thank you for telling me," Vincent said. "Though it certainly took some prodding."

There was a glimmer in his eye that reassured me. "Yes, sir. Beg your pardon."

"I also appreciate you going to find Nate today, though it must have seemed a fool's errand." His left elbow on the chair arm, he touched two fingertips to his chin and rubbed.

"I know why it was necessary."

A knock at the door, and a sergeant appeared. "Beg pardon, sir, but they just came in, and both said they were urgent."

To my surprise, the sergeant held out two messages, one to Vincent and one to me.

Vincent opened his, and I unfolded mine.

I recognized Tom Flynn's scrawl: "Griffiths has served as counsel for several large companies on the river—shipping, ware-housing, manufacturing—including Baldwin's. Try Cecil Lowell, member of the board."

My heart tripped. So Griffiths, Dr. Forsyte's barrister, was linked to Baldwin's.

"Damn," Vincent whispered. "It's Stiles."

I tore my thoughts away from Tom's message. "Is he worse?"

"Yes. He's in hospital and asking for you," Vincent said.

"In hospital?" I stared.

"St. Anne's."

So he was with James. My worry, which had flown high, dropped a notch.

I handed over Tom's missive. "Sir, I think I should try to find Mr. Lowell."

He passed the message back. "I'm acquainted with the man," he said. "You may find him at his club. Boodle's in St. James's Street. But see Stiles first. He's cool-headed, not the sort to ask for you if it isn't important."

I wondered if this were a veiled criticism of myself, but I let it go. Vincent turned his message, so I could read the three lines. The terseness of James's message, so unlike his usual eloquence, was warning enough:

Dear Mr. Vincent, Your man Stiles is here at St. Anne's, very ill, but asking for Corravan. I've written, but he has not replied. Please send him with all haste.

★   ★   ★

At the hospital, I went straight to James's office. "How ill is he? Is it influenza?"

He looked at me with an expression equal parts exasperation and anxiety. "Where the devil have you been? I sent for you hours ago! It's pneumonia in both lungs." He rose from behind his desk and stalked past me through the door I'd left open. "I wanted to give him something to alleviate his cough and help him sleep, but he *insisted* on staying awake to see you." He spoke those words over his shoulder as he hurried along the corridor. I caught up to him on the stairs, and he led me to a curtained corner.

Stiles's fair curls were shining with sweat at the temples, and his face was gray against the pillow. The curtained area reeked of the onion poultice on Stiles's chest. Stiles saw me and smiled weakly, turning his head. The very movement caused a series of coughs to explode out of him, and his entire body shuddered with the effort to suppress them.

I stepped toward the bed, laying a hand on his shoulder. "Stiles. I had no idea."

"Alone," he whispered, closing his eyes.

"Be quick about it," James said as he stepped outside the curtain. "Every cough damages his bronchial tissues."

"What can I do, Stiles?" I asked.

His hand came to his chest, as if to hold his lungs steady while he tried to speak. "See Rachel tonight."

My breath caught. "You found her?"

"Maid . . . at Beckford's." His coughs convulsed him, and it was a minute before he lay back on the pillow. "She left . . . same night Madeline went missing."

I took a cloth and wiped the spittle from his mouth. Mindful of James's warning, I didn't ask how he knew. "Where is she now?"

"New position. With Mrs. Sudbury," he whispered. "Harriet had to convince her to talk to me. Skittish. If I'm not there . . . won't be another chance."

"What's Rachel's surname?"

"Wells."

Briefly I wondered how she'd found a new place without a written character. But there were men in Selwich Street who forged one for a price.

"S'posed to meet outside the house. Tonight's . . . only night . . . could get away." He closed his eyes, exhausted.

Outside the window, it was beginning to rain. The last thing I wanted to do was stand outside a house waiting for a maid, especially when I wanted to find Mr. Lowell at his club.

But I'm more potato than rot.

"I'll see her," I promised. "I'll tell you everything she says, and if you want to talk to her later, you can."

He winced. "Tell her . . . sorry I couldn't come. Explain."

"Of course."

He gave me the address. "Wait on the street . . . near servants' door . . . seven o'clock."

I repeated the address to reassure him, then stepped outside the curtain. "Is he going to be all right?" I asked James in a low voice.

His face was tight with worry. "I don't know. He should have come in days ago."

"How did this happen? I thought it was just a spring cold."

James shook his head. "Apparently he's been out every night, walking about London in the rain. He's worked himself nearly to death, literally."

The nurse parted the curtains and stepped inside.

"Why was he out walking?" I whispered. "Did he tell you?"

"He was following someone," he replied, his murmur nearly drowned out by Stiles's hacking cough.

Following Rachel? The Beckfords?

But no case was worth this.

Perhaps James saw the depth of my worry, for he touched my arm in a rare gesture of rapport. "I'll send word if he takes a turn. One way or another, the fever should break within the next forty-eight hours."

From behind the curtain came the sound of retching, and bile rose in my throat. I swallowed it down and sent one of Ma Doyle's short prayers heavenward, on the off chance it might tip the scale.

"I'll see Rachel, just as he asked," I said. "Don't let him worry about that."

He nodded and stepped inside the curtain.

I climbed into a cab. Naturally, I'd forgotten my umbrella. My heart twisted, thinking of how Stiles would've made sure I had it, and I felt a pang of remorse. He wasn't just a skiff bobbing in my wake. What rubbish. If I thought of him that way, it was only because it allowed me to shore up a particular vision of myself. No, Stiles was his own boat, making his own wake.

Damn it, he couldn't die.

"Where to, guv?"

Whatever Stiles wanted me to find, I'd do my best for him.

I gave the driver Mrs. Sudbury's address in Thurlow Street.

CHAPTER 42

It was a pleasant road, and though it was not yet dusk the gas lamps were lit when I arrived at a quarter to seven. With the rain coming down in earnest, I strode along the iron fence to a side alley. Between the bars, I studied the back door, in shadow under an awning, before I retreated to the meager shelter of a nearby tree to wait.

For half an hour, I stood in a rain that ripped down through the branches and chilled me to the bone. The muscles down my back ached from clenching them against the cold.

Finally the rain thinned to a mist.

The shadows had thickened, and the gas lamps hissed and flared, casting a weak, wavering glow on the wet cobblestones. A few pedestrians hurried by, their umbrellas lofted. A lone cab churned the puddles, sending ripples along their surfaces. A scrawny gray dog sensed my presence under the tree, gave me a wide berth, and slipped around the corner. Still I waited, and still Rachel didn't come. When the church bells tolled half past, I began to worry: Had I missed her? Had she gone out a different door? Left early? Changed her mind about talking to Stiles?

Damn everything twelve times over. But there was nothing to do but to wait and hope she'd come. I'd give her until eight o'clock, at least.

Finally, as the church bells tolled three quarters, the back door opened and a young woman appeared and exited the gate. Of medium height, she wore a dark hooded cloak around her shoulders, with skirts showing underneath. By the light of the gas lamp, I could see her peering up and down the street. Her black hair was pulled back from her young, pretty face.

I came out from the shadows. "Rachel Wells?"

She drew back distrustfully. "You're not Mr. Stiles. Harriet told me he was young and fair."

Another time I might have minded, or laughed, that she thought of me as old.

"Please don't be afraid," I said, using my gentlest voice. "I'm from Scotland Yard. Mr. Stiles is in hospital, so he sent me."

"How do I know tha's true? Harriet said he was to come hi'self! Stay away from me! Stay away—" Her voice trembled, and with her eyes fixed on me, her left hand groped for the gate latch.

I drew out my warrant and held it up, my other hand palm forward, in a gesture of surrender. "This is my police warrant. If you'd like, we can go to the nearest division, where they'll vouch for me."

I walked toward her slowly, offering it.

She hesitated and shook her head. "I cain't read it, and I ain't going to a division." Her face was pale, but her chin was up, and her eyes searched mine. "Is Mr. Stiles really sick?"

"He has pneumonia in both lungs. He's very sorry he couldn't come himself." I replaced the warrant in my pocketbook. "Did Harriet tell you why he wanted to talk to you?"

Her hand clutched at the neck of her cloak. "About—the Beckfords."

"Could we go somewhere quiet?" I asked.

Her expression was instantly wary again. "I ain't goin' nowhere alone with ye."

"Of course not. I just want to get out of the wet. Is there a tea- or coffeehouse nearby, perhaps, where women are allowed? Or a pub? Somewhere you'd feel safe."

She studied me. Then she nodded, cautiously. "I know a place. 'Tisn't far."

"Wherever you like."

She led me down the street and turned right onto another. She passed the King Henry, from which came the sounds of raucous laughter, and pushed open the door of the Blue Swan, a smaller place at the corner. The wooden sign had weathered, and the poor swan was missing her tail feathers. But the room was sedate, with a dozen people at scattered tables. I bought us two tankards of ale, and we found a quiet corner. The table wobbled, sloshing my ale over the rim. I drank enough so that it wouldn't spill again and watched as she removed her hood. In the light from the lantern above our table, I could see her delicate complexion, her large dark eyes, the curve of her cheeks, a few dark glossy brown curls that escaped their pins. She wasn't just pretty; she was lovely.

I felt a warning prickle down my arms.

"What d'ye want to know?" she asked.

"Rachel, when did you leave the Beckford house?"

Her eyes slid away from mine. "Near six weeks ago now."

"The same night Mrs. Beckford did."

She gave a cautious nod.

"Did they ask you to leave, or did you leave on your own?"

She said nothing, merely studied me with a distrust that brought to mind Madeline in the cab on the way to the hospital. The similarity in their expressions was unnerving—and it planted a suspicion that twisted the soft place under my ribs.

"What happened, Rachel?" I kept my voice gentle. "Did something frighten you?"

She gave a low snort but kept her voice just above a whisper. "Why do you want to know *now*, when it's too late? How do I know this isn't some sort of trap to—to—catch me out for sum-mat else?"

Something like forging a character? I thought. "I've no desire to catch you out," I assured her. "But I've a feeling you're a sensible girl, and you wouldn't leave unless you had a good reason."

Like an ebbing tide, some of the wariness left her. But still she didn't speak. And why *should* she trust me, after all?

I leaned forward. "I found Mrs. Beckford, Rachel. She's alive."

Her eyes lit with surprise and relief. "But Harriet told me she's still missing! Where is she? Is she all right?"

Rachel's concern seemed genuine. Whatever had happened in that house, Rachel didn't blame her mistress.

"She was in Holmdel Asylum," I said. "I don't know how she ended up there, but she was wretched. Half starved and unable to speak. I took her to a hospital where there's a doctor I trust. But she's so overwrought that she only talks in her sleep. And she says the same words over and over again. Something about a table and a red stone and a knife." Rachel's eyes widened, and her lips parted. The skin on my arms prickled anew. She understood the significance of those words. "And your name," I concluded.

Her eyes dropped down to her hands in her lap, and a shiver shook her whole frame.

"She spoke mostly in French," I continued, "so it took us a while to understand." I sat back. "I'm gathering something terrible happened. Was Mr. Beckford part of it?"

"I'll say he was."

The way she said that, low but with such loathing, I was gaining a sense of what he'd done. But still, I needed her to tell me. "What happened, Rachel?"

She looked up. "After Mrs. Beckford said my name, how'd you find me? You didn't ask *him*, did you?"

"No. Mr. Stiles only talked with Harriet. She's a loyal friend, Rachel. He had to do a fair bit of work just to convince Harriet to relay a message to you." I saw her jaw soften. "Now, I want you to assume I know nothing. I don't even know the right questions to ask. So go back as far as you need to, and—and take your time. I've all night for you, if you want it."

She sat still, gnawing at her lower lip so cruelly I thought it might bleed.

I changed tack. "What can you tell me about Mrs. Beckford? Was she going mad, the way her husband said?"

"Course not!" she said witheringly.

"He told us he was worried about her. He wanted to protect her."

A hard snort. "He hated her. Married her for her fortune. I heard him say so." The door opened, bringing in a gust of cold air, and Rachel watched a family of three find seats near the fire.

"Rachel, the doctor—Dr. Wallis—who'd been treating her, agreed with Mr. Beckford. And Mr. Spear, and Mr. Beckford's brother."

"They're *all* liars," she spat out.

Liars who had orchestrated their stories well, I thought, remembering how neatly their accounts had folded together with only minor inconsistencies.

For the third time, I asked, "What happened?"

Her gaze was full of accusation. "Why would you believe me?"

"Do you see this?" I pointed to the small scab that remained on my cheek and pushed my hair back from my forehead to reveal the bare patch. "When I tried to take Madeline home, thinking that's where she'd want to go, she fought me so hard she pulled my hair and drew blood. Struck at me with my own truncheon. She would've killed me before she went back inside. So I'll believe anything you tell me about what happened in that house."

At last she spoke, her voice low: "He come at me."

"Stephen Beckford?"

She hesitated. "The first time, it was his brother—Robert. He come at me with a knife in the kitchen."

I knew better than to pull out my pocketbook and pencil, but I had to remember every single word of this; she wasn't going to say it again.

"He—he'd grab me, mean like, and kiss me and touch me, and then he'd give me a pound and laugh afterward." Her lips trembled. "I tried to be careful so I warn't *ever* alone, and mostly I could, but he'd catch me coming or going sometimes, or if it was late and no one else was about. And he—he did more each time."

"How many times?"

"Four." Her expression was at once pained and pleading. "You prob'ly think I'm no better than a—a—common whore, but it warn't like that. My parents are dead. I didn't have anywhere else to go."

"I don't think you're a whore," I said tightly. "I think he's a bloody *savage*."

She started at the venom in my voice.

"Go on," I said. "What happened the last night you were there? What did he do?"

"Not just him. Both of them. Mr. Beckford and his brother." She swallowed. "Close your eyes."

"What?" The word slipped out.

"Close your eyes," she repeated, her voice breaking. "I can't have you looking at me when I tell you this."

I'd never been asked that before, but I understood. There had been times in my life when I'd wanted the same.

"All right." I shut my eyes and put my palm across for good measure. My hand smelled faintly of Stiles's onion poultice. "I won't look until you say you're finished."

"Oh, you'll know," she said.

Every nerve of mine was strained toward her, to catch every word and nuance of tone.

She began haltingly: "That day, the chimney—the one in the library, I mean—it had been smoking, and we'd had a sweep in to clear it out. It took him hours, so I didn't get to clean that room till after dinner. It must have been near ten o'clock. When I finished, I came into the kitchen to eat the supper Cook left, and Mr. Beckford and his brother came in and found me at the table. I'd stupidly lit a lamp." Her voice thickened with anguish. "They were real quiet like, but I could smell the drink on their breath . . ."

She told me then, the things they did to her, things so vile that waves of heat and ice ran from the top of my head down every nerve. My heart thudded sickeningly inside my chest, and I longed for the end. But I'd asked, after all. So I clamped my teeth on the inside of my left cheek until at last it was over.

I took away my hand to find her eyes full of fear that I'd doubt her.

"I believe you," I said hoarsely. "I believe every bloody word, Rachel."

Her lips parted and tears sprang to her eyes. She dashed them away with her fingertips.

"Did Madeline—Mrs. Beckford—did she know about this?" I asked.

Rachel sniffed. "That's why they stopped. She came down to the kitchen. She must've heard summat, or knew . . . somehow. She opened the door and saw—everything—and screamed."

I could imagine it. Rachel atop the kitchen table, the men assaulting her—and Madeline at the doorway, her mouth open wide.

"What happened next?"

Rachel exhaled so deeply I smelled the ale on her breath. "Mr. Beckford—Stephen, I mean—he let go o' me and went toward her, but she took one of them big knives from the wood block by the sink and kept him away. She told them to let me go, or she'd kill them—and she might not be big, but she looked scary then, like a witch, her eyes flashin', and her hand waving the knife, screeching to raise the dead. It warn't enough to scare 'em after the first startle, but they let me go, and I got myself over to her. She told me to run, so I collected my things from my room and took off out the back."

Her words silenced me. But at last I understood the depth of Madeline's terror at the thought of going back to that house. Her husband was a monster. And what would he have done to her, knowing she'd witnessed his crime?

Rachel added, "I've thought about it, over and over since then, and I think she suspected. Don't you? Else why would she come looking for me?"

Why indeed? Unless it had happened before.

I made my voice very quiet. "Rachel, did Madeline know any-one named Elaine?"

Her eyes were incredulous.

Hurriedly, I added, "One day Madeline muttered something about 'a'" —I exaggerated the pause—"'lane,' and we thought she meant a street. Only later did I realize it could be 'Elaine,' and when you said just now that Madeline suspected—"

She shook her head in bewilderment. "How could you not know? You're police!"

"We have hundreds of cases, and if it wasn't one of mine, I wouldn't have heard." I leaned forward. "What is her surname?"

"Price," she said. "Her name was Elaine Price."

"*Was*," I repeated, and she nodded unhappily. "Who was she?"

"The other kitchen maid 'sides Harriet. 'Twas last summer, ages 'afore his brother and him started on me. Only she accused him." She took a breath. "See what it got *her*."

Suddenly I remembered; Stephen Beckford had listed Ellie Price among the servants who'd left.

"What did she get?" I asked.

"Nothin', o' course!" Her voice was disdainful. "She went to trial, though she shouldn't ha' bothered. We all said so. Beckford had the doctor and all the rest on his side. The judge gave her two pounds ten and sent her away."

I didn't answer. I couldn't. My breath quickened as my mind began to rearrange the pieces, working them all in. The judge—Albert? A doctor—Forsyte? Elaine—the Lady of Shalott? The river. The boats. The rope around the wrists. The torn, bloody skirts. The red stone? Robert's ring.

In that moment, I felt the case change course, as surely as I'd ever felt the tide turn under my oar.

"Tell me more about Elaine Price," I said. "What happened to her after the trial?"

She looked askance. "If I tell you, you won't tell him, will you? He'd just laugh."

"I promise."

With a sigh, she ran her thumb along a ridge in the glass. "Elaine knew she wouldn't find another place, not here in London, anyway, with Beckford sayin' she was trouble. Besides, she'd start showin' soon."

"She was with child?" I asked sharply. "You're certain?"

She nodded. "She told Harriet. They stayed friends, even after she'd gone. Elaine's monthlies had stopped, and she was sick every morning. Only the baby came too early, and it died. Near six or seven weeks ago, not long 'afore I left. Elaine kept bleeding after it came, and she died, too." She rested her elbow on the table and fidgeted with her hair. In doing so, her sleeve slipped off her wrist, revealing scars from the ropes one of the Beckford brothers had used.

I found myself staring at the skin, thin and red and puckered.

She caught me looking and pulled her sleeve down. "Sometimes I think mebbe Elaine's the lucky one," she muttered, averting her eyes. "At least she don't remember anything."

"I'm so sorry, Rachel. For you and for Elaine."

She nodded without looking at me.

After a moment, I asked, "What about the other servants? Beckford told me two others left last summer as well. A footman and another maid. I think her name was Annie. Did he assault her, too?"

"No, but he dismissed them 'cause they knew what he did to Elaine. They both had families to take 'em back in."

Unlike you, I thought.

Rachel wrapped her cloak more closely around her. "The Beckfords hired someone to root them out."

"Root them out?"

"Scare them out of London, so they couldn't make trouble." She sniffed. "A detective, or summat like one."

My breath caught. "Was his name Taft?"

"I dunno. But Harriet said he come to the house again, a few weeks back."

Yes, that was likely Taft. If the servants had been run out of town, they'd have left without a character, like Rachel. Whether they had families or not, they'd have diminished prospects of employment. So these were yet more people Beckford had left injured in his wake. But for a man like Beckford, there would always be more.

"And Harriet? Did they ever come after her?" I asked.

She shook her head. "She's the butler's niece. Quincy would never stand for it."

"Did Quincy know? And the housekeeper?"

Her lip curled. "They know what side their bread's buttered on."

I leaned back into my chair and blew out a sigh at the wickedness of it all. "Rachel, you need to make a formal report. Or it'll happen again. If not to Harriet, to someone else."

Her eyes widened, and panic came over her face.

"It would be different this time—" I began.

She leaned over the table, her hands wrapped tightly around the edges. "I told *you* because I thought it would help Mrs. Beckford. But I'd hang myself before I speak of it to a group of men who'd laugh at me, or worse! And just when I've settled into a new place? No, I won't do it! I won't!"

Her voice had risen to a shrill pitch. People were staring. I muttered, "All right, Rachel. I won't make you."

"Swear it!"

"I swear!" I replied, my voice as vehement as hers.

The room had gone silent. We sat quietly until all the stares drifted away, and I added softly, "I will never make you speak of it again, anywhere or at any time."

A sheen of sweat had appeared on her beautiful face. Tears filled her eyes again and ran down her cheeks. "I thought you understood!"

"I do. I do." I dug in my pocket for a handkerchief, relieved that I'd put in a fresh one the night before.

She looked at the folded square uncertainly.

"It's clean," I said.

She took it, opened it to its full size, and pressed it to her eyes.

At last she took it away. "I mean it," she said slowly and distinctly. "I will take my life rather than repeat that story in court, just to be laughed at."

Again, I believed her. Every bloody word.

★   ★   ★

We parted at the doorway of the pub. I thanked her, put one of my cards into her hand, told her that if she ever needed anything, ever, to call on me, and turned away, my mind churning.

The Thames wasn't the river in the poem, and London was no Camelot. But it was Elaine's story just the same.

The two cases were flip sides of the same coin. Elaine—the maiden, Elaine—the maid . . .

Thank God Stiles had convinced Harriet to trust him, I thought fervently.

I crossed two streets before I realized my stupidity. I'd been so damned swept up in Rachel's wretched story, I'd forgotten to ask. I spun and raced back to the pub, then kept running, shouting her name.

"Rachel!"

At the end of the street, I found her, put my hand on her shoulder—

The face was that of a much older woman, pale and fearful.

I apologized profusely and turned away.

Dear God, where was she?

"Mr. Corravan," she said, hurrying toward me from across the way. "For mercy's sake! What is it?"

Between gasps, I asked, "Did Elaine have a suitor? A fiancé?"

She shook her head. "Don't think so. She was shy."

My heart sank. I'd been so sure.

Then who would have taken revenge on her behalf?

The image of Sidney Dorstone popped into my head.

"What about a brother?" I asked. "Or—or a father?"

Her expression changed. "Oh, a father to be sure. She met him every other Sunday for a walk, on her afternoon off."

A father.

My heart jolted. "Do you know where they'd go? Or where I can find him?"

She shook her head.

I took a breath. "All right. Thank you again."

She nodded. And then, reluctantly, "And thank you. It don't fix nothing, but I'm glad you know."

We parted again, and I turned for home, my feet moving of their own volition. Like easing a boat into its berth, I was slipping into Mr. Price's mind. It might have taken longer if I hadn't been in Whitechapel that very morning. But my experience years ago with O'Hagan had driven into my bones how it felt to be at the mercy of someone cruel and infinitely more powerful. It was nothing for me to imagine Mr. Price's feelings, as he sat through a mockery of a trial, and then endured his poor daughter's death.

The transcript of the trial might have Elaine's former address, which might lead me to her father. But that wasn't the only reason I needed to see the document. A trial required more than a judge and a doctor and a witness or two. God only knew how many other daughters Price was planning to kill.

CHAPTER 43

The next morning, I was out the door early to see Vincent. The walk to the Yard gave me time to organize my thoughts afresh, and they weren't comforting.

First off, from the beginning, Beckford had taken me in as surely as a street trickster plays his mark. Belinda had said I longed to rescue people. Thinking back to Stephen Beckford's initial visit to the Yard, I wondered if he had sensed that tendency in me. But whether he had or not, he'd produced every sign of helpless uncertainty and despair, of being the victim in desperate need, and I'd risen to the bait like a fish.

Second, Vincent still didn't know that Madeline was hidden in James's hospital. My heart sank as I realized I would have to tell him today. He'd be furious with me, again, rightfully so, for skirting the law and keeping this secret. But perhaps if I knew *precisely* how Madeline Beckford and the river murders were related, he'd be more forgiving. In the cold light of morning, the certainty I'd felt last night about Mr. Price had faded some. I needed to be sure of my facts.

My steps slowed as I approached the Yard. It would take hours to find the trial records, but I could at least keep Vincent apprised of my whereabouts, in a timely fashion, as he would say. I scrawled a few lines on a page from my pocketbook and folded it over. I hovered near the stone arch until I saw Sergeant Cole approach, and I greeted him.

He came toward me. "Mr. Corravan, what are you doing out here?"

"I have to go to the Home Office and the Old Bailey. I'll be back soon. But could you ask the desk sergeant to deliver this to Vincent?"

He looked at me oddly, no doubt wondering why I didn't want to walk the hundred yards and deliver it myself, but he slid the paper inside his pocket.

I'd only reached the next corner when I heard my name shouted behind me. It was the sergeant, and his face was pink from hurrying. I met him halfway, and he handed me an envelope. "This just came for you."

It was addressed in a feminine hand: "Mr. M. Corravan, Scotland Yard."

It wasn't Belinda's writing, but my hand shook as I opened it and read: "Yesterday afternoon, we noticed a man who appeared to be keeping his eye on the house from across the way. He remained until evening, though he is gone this morning. In addition to bolting our doors and drawing our curtains, we've taken the precaution of hiring an armed man for protection. We felt you should know." The note was unsigned. But it was clearly from Catherine.

"Something the matter?" Sergeant Cole asked, his expression worried.

"This came just now, you said?"

He nodded. "Some chap left it on the front desk. I figured it might be important."

I thanked him, shoved the message in my pocket, and turned away.

No one but me had known where Belinda was. So Price had followed me to Catherine's, and I'd endangered Belinda yet again. The rabid bear barreling through the woods. What a damned fool. I reached up and gave my hair a vicious tug, relishing the pain in my scalp, feeling it was the least I deserved.

I strode along the pavement, imagining the worst possible outcomes. In my mind, the hired man had been shot and Belinda had been abducted and tortured and taken out of London in half a dozen ways by the time I reached the Home Office. But the civil greeting from the guard, the usual protocol of entering signatures, dates, and times in the record book, and even the warm, musty air brought me back to the present, and I marshaled my wits. The fact that they'd noticed the man lurking meant that Belinda and Catherine were on their guard, and they had protection. There was nothing to do but put my head down and find Mr. Price; it was the only way Belinda and any other women connected with the trial would be safe.

It took nearly an hour for the clerk to find the notation in the Criminal Registers, which held the trial calendars for both the Central Criminal Court and the Sessions Courts for London. Making a note of the indictment numbers, I headed for the Old Bailey.

I made my request, and it was another tortuous hour before the documents were delivered. I sat by a window and began to read the trial transcript for one Stephen Beckford, a gentleman, accused of rape by Elaine Price, a maid in his employ.

Presiding judge: Hon. Judge Albert.

I'd expected it, yes. But still, I read only that far before my hands started trembling so hard I had to lay the pages on the table in front of me.

★　★　★

Half an hour later, I'd read the entire transcript through, some parts twice over. The gist of it was that Judge Albert had presided over a trial that, on the face of it, seemed quite ordinary. Had I not heard Rachel's story—had I not seen how the thought of returning to the Beckford house had driven Madeline into a frenzy—I might have believed the verdict because the evidence of Stephen Beckford's innocence and of Elaine's supposed deception was assembled so convincingly. I, too, might have believed, as the jury did, that Elaine had falsely accused her employer, in order to extort money. That she needed it because her father had lung disease and medicines were costly, and she was beautiful enough to tempt any man. I would have been convinced by all the witnesses assembled by T. Bartholomew Griffiths, Esq.—the man who'd had the hospital wing named for him, thanks to the Beckfords, but who was a barrister, not a solicitor, as James thought. Dr. Forsyte had testified that Elaine had never been forcibly raped but must have offered herself willingly. Three witnesses, Sidney Morris, Alan Montooth, and William Speare—of course, I realized grimly, remembering how he'd embellished upon Madeline's "peculiarities"—had verified that Beckford was at their gentleman's club, Clavell's, the entire evening that the rape was alleged to have occurred.

I made a list of the names:

Judge Albert
Dr. Forsyte, medical witness
Alan Montooth, alibi
Sidney Morris, alibi
William Speare, alibi
T. Bartholomew Griffiths, barrister
Gordon Trask, foreman
And the eleven other members of the jury

I dropped my forehead into my hands, feeling the horror coming at me from both sides. Four daughters had been cruelly used and murdered, to avenge Price's own daughter's death. He was monstrous, depraved, ruthless.

But if what Rachel told me was true, these pages hid the truth about a group of wealthy gentlemen who had conspired to create a perfectly crafted, cohesive lie, in order to shield a different kind of monster—one who had committed the most brutal sort of attack upon an innocent girl.

It was just as Beckford had done before, calling upon his brother and Speare and Dr. Willis to spin a web of lies about Madeline.

The proof took shape like a line tethered to shore, and I could pull myself in, hand over hand toward certainty. Where else would Rachel get those indelible scars? And knowing what her husband had done, of course Madeline would be tormented to near madness. And how else could so many of the details in Rachel's story about what the two Beckfords had done to her correspond to those in Elaine's testimony?

The worst of it—a fact that struck like a blow to my chest—was that Beckford couldn't be retried for the same crime. He could never be punished for what he'd done to Elaine.

Legally, we could try him for what he and his brother had done to Rachel. That would at least provide a modicum of justice for Elaine, and Madeline as well. But Rachel would never testify in a courtroom. As for Madeline, a wife could not be forced to testify against her husband. So the only witness to the assault on Rachel was ineligible to appear.

With a cry of frustration, I picked up my pocketbook and flipped backward to review all the names I hadn't found in the trial transcript: Anthony Thurgood, Andrew Munro, Robert Eddington, Samuel Gordon, David Cobb. Clearly it was the women's position as daughters, not wives or fiancées, that had caused Price to go after them.

Suddenly I realized another name that was missing: Mr. Dorstone.

I scanned the transcript again to be certain.

Strange. Why had Jane Dorstone been murdered?

I sat back in the chair. My appalling lack of insight regarding the Beckfords' characters notwithstanding, I believed I'd read the temperament of Mr. Dorstone accurately. He would have broken down rather than be co-opted into such a scheme. But if Mr. Price was going after daughters, then Jane's father must be involved in the trial somehow.

Unless there had been a mistake. Or a different family member had been involved.

The fourth name on my list was *Sidney Morris*. Was this the error? Was this Jane's brother by a different name—perhaps his first and middle names?

He'd been called Sidney Drew instead of Dorstone at the sanatorium, and one change of surname could point to the ease with which he might adopt another, if the need presented itself. But Sidney didn't seem the sort to lie under oath in order to ruin a woman's life, any more than his father did.

I flipped to the last page of the transcript, where the men's names were listed with their residences, and my heart sank. There, next to Sidney Morris, was the Dorstones' address on Marlton Lane in Mayfair.

I'd need to see Mr. Dorstone again. In the meantime, we had to look at these other men, to discover if they had daughters. Particularly Speare and Griffiths. Also the foreman Mr. Trask. I could imagine Mr. Price blaming those three more than the other jurors. Hastily, I began to copy the entire first page of the trial, including the accusation and verdict.

I needed to tell Vincent all of this. But first I needed to see Stiles.

★   ★   ★

I went to the hospital and found James coming out of the conta-
gious ward.

"You can't see him," he said without preamble.

"I have good news—"

"He's not conscious, Corravan." James's face was pale, and the
sagging skin under his eyes told me he'd been up all night.

I fought down the shock and fear that his words planted inside
my ribs. I had expected James to work one of his usual miracles.
He had done it so often before.

His expression was despondent.

"I know you're doing everything you can," I said.

"Yes," he said simply. There was a long pause—unusual for
James—and then he said, "Did you talk to Rachel?"

"She was the key to everything." We walked together toward
his office, and I summarized our conversation. By the end, James's
eyes were like flint, and he cursed the Beckfords under his breath.

"I know," I said. "The devil of it is they're going to get off scot-
free. Both of them. There's no chance Rachel will go to court,
given what happened to Elaine."

James gave a hard knot of a smile. "Perhaps not," he said as he
closed the door behind us. "I told you Stiles had been out in the
rain all those nights."

"Yes. Following someone." Even as I recalled the words, I
could see it in my mind's eye: Stiles trailing the brothers at all
hours. "Was he following the Beckfords?"

James's expression raised a flicker of hope that Stiles had found
something damning.

"The brothers go to their club on Tuesday and Friday nights,"
James said. "They go to their club and the theater on Wednesday—"

"I know," I broke in.

James peered at me. "And they visit a brothel on Thursday
nights."

The flicker of hope dimmed. "Well, that's not illegal. We can't
charge them for that."

"One of Mary Jeffries's."

My breath caught. Yes, that made a difference. Since the early
1870s, Mary Jeffries had run four brothels that catered to the rich,
the titled, and the royal. It was rumored that King Leopold II

of Bavaria was a patron, as was "dirty Bertie," the Queen's heir apparent. One of the brothels had specially designated rooms for flagellation and another had rooms for men who liked to do things with animals.

"Which one?" I asked.

"Rose Cottage, two weeks in a row." His voice was flat. "It has girls as young as seven."

The thought brought on a wave of disgust, but my hope flared anew. The Metropolitan Police might turn a blind eye to some forms of depravity, but not that one. If we could catch the Beckfords there, it would ruin them. The legal age of consent was thirteen; the sentence would be prison for years. And I knew enough of life in prisons that I could make sure they received what they deserved.

"You're right," I said. "That would hold up. But why wouldn't Stiles tell me before now?"

"He said Harriet made him *swear* not to tell anyone at the Yard about the Beckfords until after he talked to Rachel." James shook his head. "I think she was afraid the Yard might not care about what Rachel said, if you already had a crime you could prove."

Fair enough, given what the public read about us in most of the papers.

"Stiles only told me last night after you left, and he made me swear not to tell you unless you talked with Rachel. He's the most honorable bloke I've ever met." James added grimly, "Much good it's done him."

The fear inside my ribs sharpened to a physical pain. The worst of it was I could do nothing for Stiles, other than to set his mind at ease.

"When he wakes," I said, "tell him that without Rachel, we'd still be flailing in the dark. He did everything right."

★　★　★

Vincent took my confession better than I thought he would. Perhaps it had something to do with the note I'd sent him, explaining my whereabouts for the morning, which lay open on his desk, proof that I was trying to abide by his instructions. I began by relating how I'd found Madeline Beckford in Holmdel, and when I described how she'd attacked me as we reached her house, I saw him making the connection to the scratches he'd observed on my face a few weeks back. I took all the blame for installing Madeline at the hospital and gave Stiles all the credit for finding Rachel. I detailed the attacks Rachel had experienced, concluding, "She was telling the truth, sir. I saw the scars."

"I believe you." His voice was brittle. "Do you think that one of the Beckfords is killing these women then?"

"No." I shook my head. "I might have thought something like that, too, but Rachel told me that there was another maid—eight months ago—who was forced to endure the same thing. The difference was, she accused Stephen Beckford, and it went to trial." I handed over the copy I'd made of the first page of the transcript and a few select paragraphs of testimony. "In September."

He scanned the pages, his face blanching as he read Elaine's account of the assault and the vile words Beckford hissed in her ear as he did it. At last, he looked up, his face full of stunned, horrified comprehension. "This is why you went to the Old Bailey."

I nodded. "My guess is Beckford was acquitted because he called in favors or bribed everybody from the judge to the witnesses. I'm trying to determine the extent of it. The maid received a couple of pounds and no justice at all. Then she died giving birth to the baby about six weeks ago."

"Just before the murders began," he said slowly.

"Sir, Elaine's father used to pick her up for a walk every Sunday."

"Elaine," he echoed.

"Like Elaine of Astolat," I added.

"The Lady of Shalott." His jaw went slack. "That accounts for the pageantry of it." A curse I'd never imagined I'd hear from him slid out under his breath. "So he's killing these women to punish the men who helped to acquit Beckford." He swallowed hard. "That's a twisted sort of revenge."

I paraphrased Belinda's words: "The death of someone we love injures us worse, and for longer, than dying ourselves."

Vincent licked his dry lips and thought for a moment. "And Beckford couldn't be the first victim because Elaine's father would be one of the first people we'd look at, as having the best motive."

I agreed. "He'd never have had a chance to hurt all those others. We'd likely have found him by now."

He leaned back in his chair. "What do you think should happen next?"

I knew from experience what Stiles would have wanted to do. But I hoped Vincent would see it my way. "I don't think we should warn those other families."

"Absolutely not," Vincent said. "We'd only set off a panic. People can't keep quiet about something like this."

Relieved, I added, "And if one newspaperman hears about it, the world'll know." I took a breath. "But I do think we need to find out if Mr. Speare or Mr. Griffiths or Mr. Trask has a daughter."

"I'll set sergeants in plain clothes to watch their houses," Vincent replied. "Meanwhile, you find Price. Like last time, he may not wait until Monday night."

"What about the Beckfords?" I asked.

Vincent nodded. "We should have someone at their houses, too, for protection."

I stiffened. That wasn't what I'd meant.

Vincent's mouth tightened. "I know. Allowing Mr. Price to punish the Beckfords might make you—make us all feel better, but the law must mete that out. Set a watch on the Speares, Griffiths, Trasks, and the Beckfords. But until I say otherwise—don't tell anyone." His eyes held mine. "Is that agreed?"

I nodded. Dare I ask for protection for Belinda?

Damn it, I had to.

"There's someone else's house we—" I broke off, remembering what James said about issuing commands. "Would you consider one more house?"

Vincent raised an eyebrow.

"Catherine Weatherby. My friend Mrs. Gale took refuge with her sister after she received the letter. It seems there was a man watching the house yesterday." I hesitated, wondering whether to own my fault in that, and decided I should. "I went to check on them. I may have been followed. They've hired a man for protection, but . . ."

Vincent's brow furrowed at my mistake, but he said only, "Very well."

I gave him the address, watching him make a note of it on a blank page.

"Now." He set down his pen. "How is Stiles? Is he any better?"

"No, sir. He's worse. Unconscious. I went to the hospital just before this."

Vincent gave a minute shake of his head, but I was beginning to recognize that his gestures and expressions were smaller than most people's—and smaller still when he was upset. "He's a good man," he said at last. "And fiercely loyal to you."

"Sir?" slipped out before I thought.

He pulled a face. "The day you went to the Forsytes' for the third time, I was ready to suspend you. Stiles asked me not to because your instincts were the best he knew." His eyes narrowed. "He told me about the moment you first saw Rose and you asked where her jewelry was. Granted, that turned out to be irrelevant. But Stiles told me that it didn't occur to anyone else to notice what was missing." He seemed to be waiting for me to confirm it, and I nodded. "Last year, when you were trying to figure out who was smuggling guns, he was checking bills of lading against records of weights and shipments. It was you who suggested starting with the boats that were riding low in the water."

I shook my head deprecatingly. "That's just experience."

He continued, "One of the first stories I heard when I arrived was how you solved the Bodney case your second week here, when the case was two months old and everyone else had given up."

I wanted to squirm, as if I were a schoolboy being praised in front of a class. "I knew someone in Lambeth, from when I was in uniform. And I sat at the door in that back alley for two days. So it wasn't instincts or expertise. It was just stubbornness." I paused. "And coffee. I paid a maid on the next street over to bring it to me every two hours, hot."

A smile flickered over his features.

"Stiles is cleverer with people than I am," I said, "and he does it without even thinking."

His eyes held mine, and there was a moment of sincere affinity, for both of us appreciated Stiles's worth and desperately wanted him to recover.

Then he shifted in his chair, and the moment was gone. "Please write up your notes promptly. Keep them concise because we need the details to be readily apprehensible. This case is breaking quickly, and I don't want to be caught out. All right?"

I nodded. "There's one more thing, sir."

He sat back.

"The Beckford brothers go out most every night together, and Stiles found a pattern. I was wondering—" I swallowed, "—how would you feel about a raid on Rose Cottage on Thursday night?"

His face stilled. "Thursday night, you say?"

"Two weeks in a row."

Vincent let out a small groan, and I understood his initial reluctance. Depending on who was in the brothel, it could create a political and social maelstrom. But Vincent was as disgusted by the Beckfords as I was. He might find a way to manage this. I held my breath and waited for his answer. At last he said, "I'll think on it."

At least he hadn't dismissed the idea out of hand.

CHAPTER 44

At the Dorstones', I was shown into the parlor by a maid. I'd never received an answer to my inquiry to Seddon Hall, and dreading the answer, I asked whether Sidney had survived his fall from the roof.

She looked surprised that I knew about it, but she nodded. "Sprained both his ankles and broke an arm, but he's alive. The doctor said he was lucky."

The relief made my standing knee wobble. I caught myself and thanked her, and for a quarter of an hour, I stood at the window, feeling grateful. At last Mr. Dorstone appeared at the threshold.

"What do you want?" Mr. Dorstone asked dully as he entered. His eyes were still red-rimmed, either from lack of sleep or crying.

"I'm sorry to bother you. I just had a few last questions." I met him on the carpet in the middle of the room. "I know your son is called Sidney Drew at Seddon Hall, but has he ever been called Sidney Morris?"

He looked perplexed. "Well, Morris is his middle name, a family name, but he rarely uses it."

"Does he belong to Clavell's?"

"We all do. But he hasn't been there in months." He began to fidget with the ends of his coat sleeves. "Why?"

"To your knowledge, has he ever testified at a trial?"

"A trial?" He started. "What sort of trial?"

"The rape of a young woman. It occurred about eight or nine months ago."

"Rape!" He gaped in disbelief. "Of course not! He wouldn't— he—of course not! Besides, how could he get out of his sanatorium to testify? You saw for yourself! Most days he can barely—"

"What are you doing?" came a shrill voice from the doorway.

I turned to see Mrs. Dorstone, her eyes glittering and her cheeks pink.

"I beg your pardon," I said evenly. "But a man named Sidney Morris testified at an important trial last fall. We're trying to locate him."

"Well, it wasn't *our* Sidney," she retorted. "Surely it's a common enough name!"

"Perhaps," I said. "But this Sidney Morris is a member at Clavell's and gave his address as this one."

Her face paled.

"Dorothy—" Mr. Dorstone began tentatively.

"Nonsense! Sidney had nothing to do with any trial!" She glared at me. "We've had a wretched fortnight. Now leave us alone!"

I picked up my hat and left, taking a backward glance at Mr. Dorstone. He had the look of a turtle pulling back into its shell.

God help that poor man, I thought.

Mrs. Dorstone's defensiveness had me fairly well convinced that Sidney had, in fact, testified at the trial—though it seemed her husband had no knowledge of it. But what a strange bundle of contradictions she was! On the one hand, she felt such contempt for her son that she couldn't bear to visit him—and on the other, she sought to protect him from being questioned. I put it down to the fact that maternal instinct dies hard and took the next available train out to Seddon Hall. I had the luck to find a pleasant nurse in the office instead of Mr. Harper. I told her my business; I didn't need to see Sidney Dorstone, but I did need to see the log of his comings and goings.

She produced the records for me, and I looked them over carefully. Sidney was at the sanatorium on the day of the trial.

But how?

Was it possible that Mr. Price had found the wrong Sidney? And that Jane Dorstone was unconnected by even the slimmest thread to Elaine's trial? Amid all the injustices at hand, that seemed doubly brutal.

I asked the nurse if I could visit Mr. Drew for the usual fifteen minutes, and she took me to his room. "He tried to destroy himself not long ago," she murmured as she inserted the key in the lock. "His sister was murdered in London, and he's utterly despondent."

Feeling the full weight of my guilt, I assured her I would be careful of what I said and entered the room.

Sidney lay in his bed. His legs were underneath the blanket, and his arm in a cast on top of it. When I spoke his name, his eyelids fluttered.

"Sidney."

He rolled away from me. "Go away, you pig."

I'd probably have said the same thing.

"Your father made me swear not to tell you," I said to his back. "I'm very sorry about your sister. I knew it would be hard on you. We're doing all we can to find the man who did it."

A sniff.

"How did you find out?" I asked.

"How do you think?" He rolled toward me, his expression disgusted. "Your friend the newspaperman told me."

Tom had betrayed me? The thought sent me reeling. "What?"

"Pike, or whatever his name was."

"I don't know anyone named Pike. What did he look like?"

"Fairly tall. Stocky. Brown eyes and hair, graying here." His fingertips went to his temple.

Damn it. Fishel must have followed me. And then leaked my visit to the papers.

"His name isn't Pike," I said. "It's Fishel. And he's no friend of mine."

"Well, he said he was. He told me Jane was dead. And you suspected *I'd* done it." He shuddered. "Then he tried to make me talk about her. I told him to get out."

I thought briefly of what I'd do to Fishel next time I saw him, and, uninvited, I dropped into the chair beside the bed. "He was probing for what you knew. I'm going to tell you the truth, all right?"

He eyed me warily, his right hand lying protectively over his cast.

"Your sister is one of four women who have been attacked during the past few weeks. They're abducted by someone who pretends to deliver an urgent letter from someone they love." Dismay creased his brow. "But we found a connection among the women—and it has to do with a trial last fall in which Sidney Morris, residing in Marlton Street, is named as a witness for the accused. Can you explain this?"

"Naturally," he said with a shrug. "You're looking for my uncle. *His* name is Sidney Morris. I'm named for him—to his disgust as well as mine."

"Your uncle," I repeated.

"Yes. My uncle. My mother's brother," he said with a show of patience.

Of course. Mr. Dorstone said Morris was a family name.

Chagrined, I asked, "Your mother's fond of him?"

"Dotes on him." His slender fingers twitched against the bedsheets. "Jane and I hated him. Made my childhood hellish."

In a flash, the outlines of a picture began to emerge: a young boy, sensitive by nature, abused by his uncle, with the approval of the boy's mother.

"Do you think I might find him at Clavell's tonight?" I asked.

"Probably."

"Is he married? Any children?"

"No. He's a bachelor."

I drew in a breath. If Sidney Morris had a daughter, Price would have taken her. Failing that, he'd taken Jane. My skin felt as if it were shriveling over my bones.

"Why would your uncle give your father's address as his own?" I asked.

"Because he lived with us for a year, when he had to give up his own rooms." Disdain twisted his mouth. "He gambles. Dogs and cocks, mostly. He likes the blood."

"When did he leave?"

"I don't know. Last fall sometime. October, I think."

My pulse quickened. That would be right after Elaine's trial.

"Were you aware of him testifying at a trial any time around then?"

He shook his head. "Frankly, I'm shocked he'd bother, unless there was something to be gained by it."

I rose. "Did you write to my friend? The man whose name I gave you?"

His eyes veered away. "No. Not yet."

"Mr. Dorstone, I *strongly* advise you to leave here and make something of your life. There's a young woman who loves you. Isn't that a good enough reason?"

He did not answer, only tugged at the sheets with his good hand.

A soft knock sounded at the door, though it didn't open. "Time to go, sir," came the nurse's voice.

Was there anything I could say that would convince him to get out of this bed?

I extended my hand and spoke slowly. "Mr. Dorstone, you've helped save innocent women's lives by what you've told me. Thank you for having the strength of character and the decency to do that for them."

Perhaps I was spreading the jam a bit thick, as Ma Doyle would say, but Sidney needed to hear it.

A look of surprise crossed his face. My hand was still before him, and he lifted his own hand from the bedclothes to shake it. "Goodbye, Mr. Corravan. And good luck to you."

I arrived at the station in time to see the down-train pulling away, which meant my return would be delayed by three hours. But I wasn't sorry I'd remained that extra minute with Sidney. I spent the time at a pub, eating a wedge of pie and looking over the papers. Mindful of my promises to Vincent, I also sent a telegram, explaining briefly what I'd discovered, as I'd try to find Morris at his club and wouldn't return to the Yard tonight. At last, I boarded the train for London, still thinking hard.

★ ★ ★

It was dark as the train drew into the city, and I went straight from Charing Cross Station to Clavell's, where I gave my name and was told to wait in the foyer. Wait I did, for thirty minutes—so damn tired I nearly fell asleep in the chair—before the doorman returned and told me that Mr. Morris wasn't at the club after all.

It was a lie. I could see it in his face. But he wasn't budging, and I was too worn down for a fight. It was nearly ten o'clock. I dragged myself out the side door, into the alley that led back to the well-lit street of Pall Mall.

I'd go home and find him tomorrow.

As I passed a large dustbin, the muted click of a gun's hammer being drawn back made me freeze. Out of the corner of my eye, I saw three of them.

"What do you want with Sidney Morris?" The man's voice was slurry with drink.

"I just want to ask him a question," I said and began to turn, palms out, painfully aware that the men stood less than ten feet from me, my revolving pistol was at home, and my truncheon was of no use.

There was a pause, and then—God knows why—I dodged to the right, lunging low. And in that instant, the weapon fired. I felt the bullet graze my left shoulder, a sharp burn that made me cry out. But I was already whirling, finding my feet, coming in toward the man with the gun. I struck his jaw before he had time to fire again. His head snapped back and he fell, but the second man was already plunging toward me and tackled me hard, driving my spine into the ground. My right foot in his gut drove him away when the third leaped toward me. I rolled away into a crouch—

Then something hard hit the side of my head.

I heard the shrill whistle of the Metropolitan Police.

Footsteps. Shouts.

Someone saying, "Christ. It's Mickey Corravan, all right."

Mickey, like I was back in Lambeth, in uniform. Or in the River Police. Who was it?

I tried to open my eyes. Tried to sit up. Put my hand up to my temple, and it came away sticky.

And then everything went black.

CHAPTER 45

I woke to the smell of coffee and the softness of a bed.

At first I wondered if I'd dreamed everything. But as soon as I moved, my left shoulder throbbed and my head ached. I gave a soft groan.

"Hullo."

Harry's voice.

My vision was so blurred that it took a moment to realize I was in my own bedroom, and Harry stood beside me, holding a white cup whose outlines moved strangely.

"That for me?" I asked. The words didn't come out as I intended, but he caught my meaning.

"Sure."

He bent down, helped me sit up, and put the cup in front of me. He didn't let go until he was sure my hand was steady around it. "Careful, it's hot."

"Yes, doctor."

He gave a lopsided grin in response.

I gulped at it. "Ech. Sugar."

He looked stricken. "Sorry. I forgot. I'll get another."

"No. It's all right. Probably medicinal." I took another sip. "How did I get home?"

His eyebrows rose. "You don't remember?"

"No."

He pulled a wooden chair close and straddled it, resting his fore-arm on the top bar. "Two police from Lambeth division brought you in a cab. Said they'd been watching for you at Clavell's, and when they heard a shot, they came running. I sent for Dr. Everett, but he wasn't home, so I did what I could. I imagine he'll come round when he gets the message."

Watching for me at Clavell's? I wondered. It took me a moment to recall the telegram I'd sent Vincent. He'd sent men who would recognize me on sight. I felt a wave of gratitude toward the man. And toward Harry.

I squinted at him. "It can't have been easy, coping with me by yourself."

He shrugged. "No real harm done except to your shoulder."

My memory was returning. The voices and footsteps. The dark alley.

"Do you know who it was?" he asked.

"I have a guess, but I didn't see them, and they could find half a dozen witnesses to say they never left the club."

He nodded toward my shoulder. "You should probably have a fresh bandage this morning."

I pushed the bedclothes off. The left sleeve of my shirt was gone, and blood traced the edge of a bulky bandage. Carefully I began to raise my arm, to see how far it could go without hurting.

"Can I cut it off?" he asked.

"What? My arm?"

Harry stared. Then he saw I was joking and let out a genuine laugh. "Your shirt."

I grunted. "Not likely I'm going to wear it again."

"No. I think it's beyond repair." He rose and went to fetch the scissors.

When he returned, I was examining the bandage. "You did this?"

He looked embarrassed. "As well as I could. You're rather dif-ficult to maneuver."

I couldn't help but chortle, imagining the scene, though I sti-fled a groan as he raised my arm a few inches to cut the shirt away. The pain shot around my shoulder and down my spine. Using water and a towel, he removed the bandage, his hands working carefully enough that it didn't hurt, and I said so as I examined the gash. It wasn't deep but it was jagged.

"Dr. Everett has me stitching now," he said hopefully.

I didn't much care for the way he was looking at me, as if I was a specimen. "Just a fresh bandage is fine."

Deftly he cut a four-inch ribbon and wrapped it around the wound. It was throbbing worse than before, but I stayed very still, and after a few moments, the throbbing dulled to an ache. The bandage was neater, too, small enough to fit under a fresh shirt.

"I understand if you don't want me stitching, but you should go to the hospital to see Dr. Everett this morning," he said.

"I need to go to the Yard."

"You're not going to be any use if it gets infected and you get a fever," he said officiously.

I glowered at him.

"You really don't look well," he said.

"For God's sake," I grumbled. "If you're so concerned, fashion me a sling out of that old pillowcase."

★   ★   ★

By ten o'clock I was in my office with my door closed, feeling sick.

Much as I didn't want to admit it, the journey by cab had been an ordeal. My head ached with pain that came in waves. I shouldn't have rushed; Vincent wasn't even in yet. I put my head down on my desk just for a minute, hoping the nausea would pass.

When I woke, the left side of my face felt numb and there was the feeling of spittle at the corner of my mouth.

"Inspector?" A warm hand rested on my good shoulder. "Inspector?"

I sat up and looked blearily around me. My God, I'd fallen asleep at my desk. My eyes sought the clock on the wall. Half past eleven. I'd lost an entire hour and a half. I rubbed the heel of my right hand into my eyes.

"Sorry," I muttered.

"Inspector." Sergeant Baird's voice was still tentative. I looked up. Those muttonchop whiskers were too old for his young face.

"What?"

"There's a woman here for you, sir."

I took a deep breath. "Is she alive or dead?"

"What?" He started at my grim jest.

"Nothing, Baird. It's just most of the women I'm seeing these days are dead."

He replied uncertainly, "Well, this one's alive. But it looks like someone tried to make it so she warn't. Says her name's Miss Martin, or some such."

Marvelous. A beaten woman case. "Can't someone else—"

"She said she'd only talk to you." He shuffled his feet. "I told her you were busy, but she's insisting. Says she's in a hurry. Has to get back somewhere."

"Of course she is." I used the desk edge to heave myself to standing and was relieved to find my headache mostly gone. That extra bit of sleep was what I needed. Gingerly I adjusted the makeshift sling, settling the weight of my arm into it.

"Here," he said, extending his hand. There was a cup of coffee in it, and that small act of kindness nearly unraveled me. That morning, I needed reminding that the world was a decent place, and I needed coffee to put some warmth back into my blood. Somehow the sergeant had known. I finished the cup in three long swallows, and as I came from behind my desk, I said, "Thank you, Baird."

"O'course, sir," he replied, and I made my way toward the rooms we used for conferring privately with witnesses.

I peered through the window. The woman was dressed in good but plain clothes, with a hat that hid most of her hair. Neat gray gloves, a small reticule. Decidedly middle class. But she was turned away, so I couldn't observe even her profile.

When I opened the door, she turned, and I saw bruises on her face and scratches along her cheek. She was between twenty-five and thirty years old and vaguely familiar. I found myself struck by her expression. Resolute and intelligent. Her eyebrows rose. "Goodness, what happened to *you*?"

"Nothing."

She looked disbelieving but didn't press. "I don't have much time."

No doubt she wasn't used to being kept waiting. "My apologies. I've had a busy morning," I said, stifling the urge to explain that she wasn't the only person in London with a problem. "What can I do for you?"

She winced. "I beg your pardon, Mr. Corravan. It's just that, as I told the sergeant, I have to get back. My father doesn't know I've come, of course, and it's best for all of us—you especially—if he doesn't." She shook her head, her expression forlorn. "Honestly, I've given up trying to reason with him, but for my mother's sake, I don't want to provoke another quarrel."

Well, this was an unusual beginning. Mystified, I sat down opposite. "Ma'am, I'm sorry. Who are you?"

Her expression changed to understanding. "Oh! I told the sergeant when I came in; perhaps he didn't hear me." She took a deep breath. "I'm Mrs. Munro. Charlotte Munro."

My head snapped back. If I wasn't wide awake before, I was now.

How could I not have recognized her? The answer was in her present attitude. She was no longer an unconscious half-dressed woman in a boat.

The thought that I'd seen her bare breast gave me a twinge of embarrassment, and I coughed to carve out a few seconds to recover. "Mrs. Munro, of course," I said. "Well, I'm—I'm surprised to see you. Your father said you wouldn't speak to me."

"My father never asked me," she corrected me. "He thinks I'm at the stationer's. That's why I don't have much time."

"Now I understand. I'm sorry. I'm being stupid." I sat back and added sincerely, "I'm very glad you're here."

She leaned forward, her expression earnest. "Last night I overheard two of our servants talking, and my maid smuggled me one of the papers. That's when I realized—I could have been killed."

Slow as my mind was, one thing was clear. I remembered what others had said of Mrs. Munro—that she was aware of the dark deeds done in London, and her mission was to help women in danger. A river of hope was rising in me, for she might be able to provide everything I needed. The question was, how much should I tell her, in order to elicit what she knew? She might know details that were essential to finding Mr. Price—and not even know she knew them.

She continued, "One of the papers said it might be the work of a deranged man who will keep killing until he is caught. Is that true?"

"We do think he will kill again, unless we prevent it."

"I want to help, if I can," she said softly. "But first, I wish to know—that is—do you know why he chose me? Was it something I did?" She was fighting back tears. "Could I have prevented it?"

My heart went out to her. Despite being a married woman, she looked vulnerable and very young.

"No." I was emphatic. "It was nothing you did."

She looked unconvinced. "You see, I work at a house for fallen women, and—"

"Mrs. Munro, truly. You did *nothing* to bring this about." I chose my words carefully. "In fact, I rather think your work may be why he left you alive." A pause. "That, or your condition."

"My condition," she echoed.

"You're with child, aren't you?"

She gasped and looked at me in amazement. "Mr. Corravan, he asked me the same thing, in almost those same words. How did you know?"

So Mrs. Munro being with child, like Elaine had been, had stopped Price's hand.

I took a deep breath as I absorbed this. The pieces of the puzzle were coming readily to hand. It was on the tip of my tongue to ask if Mr. Price had said anything else when Mrs. Munro said in a strained voice, "Please, Mr. Corravan. What else do you know about him? You *must* tell me."

I did as she bid, revealing not everything but enough about the trial and Mr. Price and Elaine to reassure her that she wasn't to blame for the attack and to help her understand the importance of the questions I'd ask afterward.

Her blue eyes were fixed on me the entire time. Clearly, she had practice in confronting ugly truths, but I saw the rising horror, and as I concluded, her eyes brimmed with tears.

She covered her face with her hands. "To think my father participated in this." I kept silent as she fought to regain her composure. At last she looked up. "That poor young woman," she whispered. "And her poor father."

I am not often surprised to speechlessness, but her compassion toward a man who'd nearly killed her silenced me for a long moment.

At last, I said, "It's a tragedy for everyone. But our difficulty is that we don't know how many other women he intends to hurt.

There are at least three other men who could be seen as directly accountable, but if he decides to hurt the jurors, there could be more. Or he might stop and go after Beckford himself."

She sat quietly for a moment, and when she spoke, her voice was strained but practical. "You said the first three attacks were on Monday night. But this last was on Friday. So the next attack could happen at any time, couldn't it?"

"Yes," I admitted. "We think he might be worried that we're getting close to finding him, and he's hurrying. But we need to know how he found you, where he took you, anything else he said to you—anything at all. Because *that* part of the pattern may remain."

"Of course." She straightened her spine, and her eyes focused on a point in midair, almost as if she was seeing him there. "He was an older man, perhaps forty-five." Her eyes flicked to me. "Not quite as tall, but broad like you. His hands were calloused across the palm, as if he worked with them. His hair was dark and thick and wavy. He wore it long, and he had muttonchops." She put her own hands up to the sides of her face.

That coincided with the description of the man outside the Dorstones' livery.

"Thank God you had your wits about you," I said. "Did you notice a cough?"

"To be sure," she said. "But he looked like any other cab driver."

I fit this with what I knew. Mr. Price must have followed her to her parents' house and waited until after dinner when she emerged. He hadn't needed a written message this time.

"Is Mr. Price a driver by profession?" she asked.

"I don't think so. But anyone with a cab and a horse can set himself up. Please, go on."

"He paused at an intersection, saying that his horse had caught a stone. Then he begged my pardon and said he needed a tool from under the seat. He stepped inside, and I smelled chloroform." She paused, remembering. "When I woke, my hands were bound, and my mouth as well, so I couldn't cry out. I was in a boat, and I think the cold water at the bottom roused me. We were inside a shed with some broken panels, and the light was coming in—moonlight, I think—so I could see him above me. He looked almost mad. His eyes were wide and staring. Then he drew out a knife—a horrible thing, with a heavy blade and a wooden handle, and then—then—he asked me if I knew what it was to suffer."

The directness of the question made me draw my breath. "What did you say?"

She shook her head. "I couldn't speak, he had the gag so tight on my mouth, but I moved my hands over my belly." Her voice altered. "It wasn't consciously done. It was merely my first thought. But he saw my hands, and he asked if I was with child. When I nodded, he had the most peculiar look on his face—grief and hatred and despair all at once. And indecision."

I must have looked dubious, for she rebuked me: "Mr. Corravan, I've become practiced at noticing changes of expression. Often, they tell me whether a young woman has become hardened to her fate—or is still willing to believe that the world holds something better for her than prostitution."

I nodded. "Of course. Er—so he stopped his knife."

"Yes. And instead of cutting my throat, I suppose, he sliced open my dress—the—" she averted her gaze in embarrassment "—the entire bodice—and laid his hand on my belly. And just then, as if on cue, the baby moved." Her eyes met mine again, and her voice softened. "The man felt it, Mr. Corravan. Then he put the knife away, struck me across the face, and I remember nothing else until I woke in the hospital with Dr. Masterson."

My heart was skipping beats.

So Price watched his victims, knew where they lived and where they went. After that, it was simple. A cab and some chloroform. And a boat.

"What can you tell me about the shed and the boat?" I asked. "Do you remember anything at all? Noises or smells?"

"We were near the docks in Lambeth," she said. "I recognized the bells of Christ Church because they ring 'Oranges and Lemons' on the hour. I smelled the timber yards and ammonia."

Ammonia.

I had an idea what that smell might be from. "And you're certain it was the Christ Church bells."

"I sometimes visit the almshouse east of Holland Street." Her head tipped. "Is this what happened to the other women?"

"It's similar."

"And you think this is revenge."

"We can't be certain. But Elaine's trial is the only thing we can find that links all of the victims." I drew out one of my cards and passed it to her. "Not everyone has your mettle, Mrs. Munro. If you think of anything else, get a message to me, would you?"

"Will you catch him?"

"Believe me, I'm doing nothing else with my days."

She nodded and looked down at her hands.

"What is it?" I asked.

She met my gaze. "Would—that is—would you consider me tainted?"

I sat back in my chair, surprised.

She flushed a mottled red. "I don't know what my husband will say."

"My guess," I said, "is he is going to be horrified. But he isn't going to think any less of *you*." I thought about how I'd felt when Belinda received that letter. "On the contrary, I think he's going to feel terribly guilty for having left you alone in London."

She gave a gasp, and her eyes widened. "Why, you're right, of course! He's going to blame himself, though he shouldn't." She extended her hand to touch my sleeve. "Thank you. I wouldn't have thought of it—but that's exactly how he'll feel." She tucked my card into her reticule. At the threshold, with her hand on the door, she turned and looked at me as if she wanted to say something else. But then she merely gave a brief smile and left, closing the door behind her.

I put my right hand to my face and rubbed.

The door opened, and Vincent slid inside. "Who was that?"

"Charlotte Munro."

Vincent shut the door. After I relayed everything she said, a frown gathered on his brow, and I sensed why.

"I'm sorry I didn't fetch you, sir. But she asked for me, and I was in the room before I knew who she was."

He waved a hand.

Awkwardly I added, "And—thank you for sending the men to Clavell's last night. I'd have been dead if you hadn't. As it is," I dropped my chin toward my left shoulder, "the bullet just nicked me."

"Yes, I heard." He rested his fingertips on the back of the chair Mrs. Munro had vacated. "Emma Montooth's father is on the board of directors at Beckford shipping. And Judge Albert and the barrister Griffiths are both members of the Adwaller Club."

I nodded. "The Beckfords belong to Clavell's like Morris does. And Griffiths served as barrister for both Forsyte and the Beckfords."

He let out a sigh. "It's a snug little web the Beckfords have spun, isn't it? The difficulty is, I don't know how that helps us find Price."

A fortnight ago, I might have merely headed for Lambeth to follow my hunch.

Instead, I said, "When Mrs. Munro mentioned the smell of ammonia and the bells, I thought of McOwens wool works. They're just north of Christ Church, and they use alkaline baths to clean the wool. They'd also have their own lighters for moving the bales onto ships."

Vincent's eyes lit up. "Do you think that's where Price might be obtaining the boats?"

"Could be. I know the dock supervisor, and he'll tell me if any boats have gone missing. Price may even have found work there at some point, so he'd be familiar with the place. Should I go to McOwens? I can ask Mills to come along."

He studied me for a moment. "No need for Mills, unless you think it's necessary. But Quartermain wants to send you down to division after this case, and I would prefer not to. Please don't give him even a thread of an excuse."

"No barreling through the woods, sir," I said.

A tiny reluctant smile pulled at one corner of his mouth for an instant before it disappeared. "Good luck, Inspector."

Chapter 46

McOwens was the largest and oldest of the wool merchants with manufactories on the river. When I reached its wharf, I slipped in the side door and approached one of the workers rolling an empty wheelbarrow up the dock. He couldn't have been more than twenty, but the signs of labor already told: his shoulders were bulky and rounded, his hands rough and reddened. "Where's Wooster?" I asked.

He raised his chin toward the smaller of two buildings. "Top floor, most like."

I nodded my thanks and headed for the staircase. It opened onto a large second-story loft with a bank of leaded windows overlooking the river. Wooster stood surveying the wharf below, and as my boot scraped the top step, he turned, his expression pleasantly bland. He'd seen me coming.

"Corravan," he said, walking toward me with an outstretched hand and an air of false geniality.

I accepted his hand. "Wooster."

"What can I do for you today?"

"Nothing much. Just wondering if you've had any lighter boats go missing."

A look of surprise. "Did you find one of ours somewhere?"

"Might be."

"Well." He headed down the stairs. "Let's look."

On the ground floor, he unlocked a cabinet, took up a book, opened it, and ran a finger down the margins. Then we went outside to the loading area, and he pointed. "Here's our main boathouse. Should be twenty in here; four are being used."

"Are they marked or numbered in any way?"

"Of course."

My feet halted. "Really?" The River Police had found no identifying marks on any of the boats except the first one with the "T." My heart sank. Perhaps Price wasn't using McOwens lighters after all.

"Not where anyone can find it, though. I'll show you." He took a set of keys from his pocket and unlocked the door.

The air inside smelled of damp wool, lanolin, and ammonia. The boats were stacked bottoms up, and I made a quick count: twenty present, and four racks empty.

"We had a problem with boats going missing a few years back, people changing out the numbers. So we hid them." He gave me a look. "I'd take it as a favor if you didn't mention it."

He tugged one of the horizontal thwarts out of place. I'd never seen one that was meant to be removed, but clearly this one was. He flipped it over, so I could see the bottom. "MCO 28" was burned into the plank, black and deep enough that it couldn't be removed without sanding half the wood away.

"They're all marked?" I asked.

He nodded.

"And these are all of your boats?"

"Well, there's another twenty or so upstream. We've enough here without them. Most of the time, this is enough."

Another boathouse. My heart skipped a beat. "Same sort of shed?"

"Like enough."

"Who's watching it?" I asked.

He drew back at my sharp tone. "Nobody. It's locked."

A shed, rarely visited and left unwatched. "Might I have the key for it?" I asked, keeping the excitement out of my voice. "I'll bring it back in an hour or two."

With a clink, he removed a key from the ring. I reached, but he closed his fist around it. "Look here, are we getting blamed for something?"

I shook my head. "Not at all."

His eyebrows rose. Cautiously, he added, "And I've bought some goodwill?"

I nodded. "A good deal, actually."

"Return it to Bowen, my foreman. Red shirt." He put the key in my hand, and I headed west.

★   ★   ★

The padlock wasn't in regular use, and it took work to turn the key. I went inside the shed and saw that several of the boards were pretty well rotted. The boats were dusty and the place stank, but every slot was occupied by a boat. I searched carefully for any sign that the place had been entered recently but found none.

Damn. I was sure this would be it.

Stepping outside, I locked the door behind me, dropping the key into my pocket. I stood there, staring at the river, the traffic going upstream and downstream. Hundreds of boats, thousands of people, millions of tons of cargo. It was hard enough to find something that was *present*. How were we to find a few lighters gone missing? I felt the rumble of fast-moving water under the wharf and turned away. My eyes skidded along the shore.

And stopped.

On the next wharf, a shed, with a faded sign: "Beckford Shipping Co."

Rarely do I feel like a complete bumbling idiot. But I did then.

I was already running down this wharf and onto the next, stumbling over the uneven planks in my haste.

This shed was in bad repair. I could tell that much already. I circled around the side, hoping I could find a way in. Below the roofline was a gap about eight inches square where the wood had rotted away. There was black mold along the crevices between the wooden planks, and brownish-green slime where the wood met the waterline. I walked around to the back, ran my eyes and then my right hand over the weathered planks.

I found one loose board. And another. And another. My heartbeat rising, I studied them carefully. They were held together not by nails but by rough brackets. I jiggled them, pushed at them, searched for a way to remove them easily.

And then I saw the hinges, fashioned out of rope and tied with a stevedore's knot. I slid my fingers into a hole where the boards had rotted through and pulled it open so I could step inside. Enough light was coming through the square above that I could count five empty berths. One more than I'd expected, but still.

Looking for signs of struggle, I found a smear of mud from a shoe and a scrap of dark blue brocade caught on a splinter in the floor. And then came the peal of "Oranges and Lemons" from Christ Church.

I backed out, leaving everything exactly as I found it, so as not to alarm Mr. Price if he returned.

I started back toward McOwens to return the key. Had Mr. Price worked at Beckford Shipping, either before or during the time Elaine had worked for the Beckfords? That would be an awful coincidence. Or had he merely used their boats? I knew no one at Beckford Shipping whom I could ask. But if Price knew about Beckford's shed, he'd probably worked in this part of the river. Perhaps he *had* worked for McOwens at some point.

When I gave the key to the foreman, I asked him, "Have you ever had a man named Price working here? He'd be about forty-five or so now, strong, with dark, thick hair."

To my surprise, he nodded. "Sure. Bernard Price. He worked here for a long time."

My breath caught. "He did?"

"'Aven't seen him in two or three years, though. Was a good man, knew the river."

"Any idea where I could find him?"

He sniffed. "'E used to go to the Grouse and Gander on Brunswick Street."

"Thanks."

I'd already headed back toward shore when he called after me, "'E had a daughter. I remember that. Pretty little girl."

I turned back. "That's right. Elaine."

"Yah, used to come here sometimes with her ma, to bring him supper. She could prob'ly tell you where 'e is, if you kin find 'er."

The knot under my ribs tightened. But I merely thanked him again and left.

★   ★   ★

First I went to the Yard to arrange for a plainclothes watch on the boathouse.

Then to the hospital, where James told me Stiles was still hanging on. Where there is life, there's hope, he said. While there, I asked him to look at my shoulder, and he praised Harry's bandaging, put four stitches in, and gave me a proper sling to wear.

Then to the Grouse and Gander. But no one there remembered seeing Price recently.

So I did what I do when I know I won't be able to sleep. I walked. Methodically, like I was on my old beat in Lambeth, walking and bearing right, again and again. Back then, it often turned up something.

I couldn't say how many miles I trudged that evening, stopping into pubs and lodging houses on the south side of the river. Long enough that I got a blister in the same place I used to, on my left heel. But I chanced upon an apothecary that was open late, strapped on a dab of plaster, and kept going. On I walked, past midnight, then one, through the squalor and smells, the gas lamps and garbage. I knew Price would return to the boathouse, but I wanted to find him before he took his next victim. And he might be just around the next dark corner.

Finally, it was nearly two in the morning, and every street was quieting down. So I went home.

But all night, in my dreams, I walked. Only I wasn't looking for Price. With the deranged logic of nightmares, I walked because so long as I kept moving, Stiles would be alive in the morning.

★　★　★

For three days, I worked feverishly, searching for Price, stopping in at the hospital each morning and evening to check on Stiles, and resting my shoulder, which was mending nicely. Harry was home at night, and it was thanks to him I ate and slept. James was wrong about Stiles's fever. On the third day, it still hadn't broken.

And then it was Monday.

I didn't even wonder if Price was finished. I knew he wasn't. Couldn't be.

I sent a note to Belinda via a delivery of bread to Catherine and received a brief answer. "I'm fine. Don't worry." It wasn't signed, but I knew her hand. I tucked it carefully into the pocket at my breast, as if by keeping it safe, I could keep her safe, too.

CHAPTER 47

Monday night, I went to wait outside the home of the Griffiths on Candall Street. Call it an impulse, but he was the Beckfords' barrister, likely the presiding genius at the trial, and I could imagine Price wanting to be sure Griffiths was dealt with. Through discreet questions, we knew that in addition to the man and his wife, a son and a daughter lived at the home, as well as several servants, including two maids.

I stayed buried in the shadows and didn't reveal my presence to the sergeant in plain clothes, who must have been pulled from the Mayfair division, for I didn't recognize him. He did just as I would have done, standing at the corner opposite the house, just outside the ring of gaslight, where he could observe the street as well as the front door. We'd had men stationed here for days, and I sensed from the sergeant's posture that he was doubtful it could possibly be worth all this time.

I watched the inhabitants of the house moving through the lit rooms, soft-edged silhouettes behind the curtains. Finally, at eight o'clock, Mrs. Griffiths and her daughter, dressed in fancy garb, came out of the house. My pulse quickened as they approached a cab that drew up to the door. From where I stood, I'd seen that cab loitering around the corner, as if in wait, for perhaps a quarter of an hour.

I leaped forward and hollered at them. "Stop! Stop! Don't get in that cab!"

Mrs. Griffiths turned and stared at me in alarm. "What on earth?"

"Did you order this cab?" I demanded.

"Cab?" She looked at me as if I'd lost my mind. "This is our carriage!"

"Your family's carriage?"

"Who else's would it be?" she retorted.

I looked up at the driver. He was a young man, pale, slender, with short fair hair. The exact opposite of Mr. Price. "Look here—" he began with a frown.

"Never mind," I muttered. "I'm sorry. A misunderstanding."

The sergeant was beside me then, breathless, though he said not a word.

The daughter was clutching her mother's arm, her expression fearful. I realized the irony of it—that in trying to protect them, I had probably frightened them half out of their wits.

"I'm an inspector with Scotland Yard," I explained swiftly, "and we've had reports of unethical cab drivers in this part of London. May I ask, where are you going?"

"We're visiting friends for dinner," Mrs. Griffiths snapped. "And as I said, this is a private carriage, not a cab for hire."

I looked up at the driver. "Will you wait and bring them home?"

"Of course he will," Mrs. Griffiths said. "He always does. Now, get in, Anna. We don't wish to be late."

Mrs. Griffiths and her daughter climbed in, and the carriage rattled off down the street.

The sergeant was looking at me with a mix of uncertainty and resentment.

"I'm sorry," I said wearily. "I had a feeling the man we're looking for would be here tonight."

He frowned. "Well, I've been watching the house since four o'clock." He pointed in the direction of the vanished carriage. "They're the only ones who've left, through the front door, leastwise. Some servants have left, too, but I was told it was the daughter he'd be after."

"That's right." I put a hand on his shoulder, to soften any sense that I hadn't trusted him. "You're exactly right."

He looked mollified. "Well, that driver ain't going to hurt 'em. He don't look like he could fight off m' sister."

A driver and a private carriage. Price could never convince the two women to get into his cab afterward—unless—

Suddenly, belatedly, the sergeant's words sank in.

I spun on my heel. The sergeant stepped backward with a look of alarm.

"That's it!" I burst out. "He's going to get rid of the driver! Throw him off the box! That's how he'll get at her!"

His eyes went wide and his mouth opened.

"I need a cab!" I spun around and darted toward the nearest cross street.

The sergeant shouted, "One just turned up that street, going north!"

"Find out where they're going!" I threw over my shoulder. "I'll be back!"

To this day, I couldn't say how I caught up to a London cab. I'm sure I must have looked mad to anyone watching, but I don't recall seeing a soul. All I perceived was the yellow lantern, appearing to grow as I ran. I pulled abreast and waved frantically at the driver. "I need you to drive down Candall Street! Hurry, and I'll give you double!"

At his nod, I leapt inside, and he turned the carriage and whipped up the horse. We were rattling over the stones when we reached the Griffiths' house. "Hold up here!"

I leaned out of the carriage and shouted out the window, "Where?"

"Twelve Wigmore!" the sergeant called out. He took a few running steps toward me, but I ordered the driver to go, and he did.

"Fastest way?" he asked.

"Yes—no—however a private carriage will go."

"Aye, then."

The wheels churned against the stones, and I clung to the strap inside, all the while scanning each cab as we drew up from behind and passed it, looking for the young man with the fair hair and the delicate hands. I was so bent on finding him that I almost didn't see the carriage coming toward us, the driver a dark, hulking man.

Was it Price?

He'd thrown the driver off already?

I twisted round to stare at the carriage. It looked the same—the same sort of wheels—but there were thousands of them in London.

I made a split-second decision.

"Driver, follow that carriage we just passed," I called. "But don't let him know."

He turned obligingly. "Aw right, guv'nor."

"That man means harm, but we need to confront him somewhere quiet."

Then I fell silent, so the driver could muster all his concentration for the task at hand. I craned my head out the window and didn't take my eyes off the carriage for a moment. Staying back a ways, we followed it east and south by the smaller roads, across Regent Street, across Charing Cross, toward the Strand, parallel to Fleet Street, across Blackfriars Bridge, and then down toward the wharves. With each turn, I felt more certain it was Price driving. The Beckford boathouse was close, and as I watched, the cab ahead drew into a darkened lane and vanished.

And the lantern vanished, too, as if it were suddenly extinguished.

I swore under my breath and jumped out. "Follow me."

He didn't even pause before he clambered down.

"Good man," I said, then ran around the corner and down a narrow alley. Stopped and listened, trying to contain my breath.

Then came the scrape of a wheel, the clop of a horse's shoe on stone. I dashed forward, followed by my driver, and there was Price, climbing down from the box. Silently, sliding along the shadows, I came up behind him, and put my revolving pistol to his back.

The metal found his spine, and he froze.

I said, "Mr. Price, don't resist."

He took one rasping breath, and another. Then his shoulders softened and slumped forward, as if he were dropping a burden at his feet. Was it my imagination, or did I sense a peculiar relief? A weariness that was far beyond physical exhaustion?

"Put your right hand behind you." He did so, and I slid one of the metal cuffs around his wrist and clicked it shut. Without my asking, he brought his left hand back, and I had him, my fingers wrapped around the connecting chain. I put my gun away and turned.

"Driver! Look in the cab and tell me what you see."

He stepped forward warily and peered in through the window. He turned to me, his face filled with horror. "Two ladies, both dead as doornails!"

"I think they're drugged. See if they're breathing."

He swung open the door, and in a moment, he reappeared, relieved. "Aye! They're just sleepin'."

"Good. Drive them to Candall Street and leave your name and address with the sergeant there. You'll be well paid for your time and trouble. And I'll drive your cab back myself."

"A' right." He eyed Mr. Price uncertainly. "What are you goin' to do with him?"

"Never mind that," I said crisply. "Go on, now. Take the ladies home. Tell the servants to fetch a doctor. They've likely had chloroform, but they should be all right."

He climbed onto the box, and I waited until he'd vanished around the corner. Then I prodded Mr. Price, who had the resigned air of a beast of burden under a yoke.

"Head toward the bridge," I said.

With Price ahead of me and my hands on the cuffs, we walked along the pavement in silence, until I asked, "Where's the driver of their carriage?"

"Side of the road," he muttered. "Not far from the house."

So the sergeant will find him, I thought. "Alive?"

"Yah. I've nought 'gainst *him*."

We reached the bridge with its stone parapet, and about twenty steps along, I turned him so the light of the moon shone on his face. I needed that.

He gave a series of phlegmy coughs into his shoulder. When he'd finished, he wiped his mouth against his lapel and said, "You're Corravan, ain't ye?"

"Yes. And you are Bernard Price."

"Why're y' bringin' me here?" he asked.

"I know why you did it," I said quietly. "I read the trial transcript."

A tremor shook his entire frame, and then he went still again. His breathing was strained, but his shoulders bunched powerfully underneath his coat, and I was glad I had taken the precaution of cuffing him. His dark eyes were pinned to mine.

"That trial was a bloody mockery," I said.

"Damn right."

"But why hurt those women?" I asked. "Why not Beckford?"

"I'd'a kilt him, too." He shook his head, the black hair going every which way in the breeze that came and went. "But not until I got t' others first. I wanted justice. Was I wrong to want that for my girl?"

"Mr. Price, this isn't justice! Those poor women didn't deserve what you did. And their friends and their fiancés are devastated because of you. Do you understand?"

An expression of uncertainty crossed his face before the anger returned. "But it was the only way to teach those men anythin'!" By moonlight, his eyes were black and glittering as the water below. "There are some folks wot have a *heart*. They understand a poor man's pain, even if they ha'n't felt something like it 'afore. But there are some who can't imagine anythin' they ha'n't felt themselves." His chin gestured toward all of London north of the Thames. "The only thing that lot understand is meanness."

I didn't say so, but yes, I'd felt that way sometimes.

"You're a Yard man," he said accusingly. "You should know better 'n anybody how people only think about themselves and their own."

"It's true of many people," I admitted. "But not everyone."

He snorted. "So you don't hate 'em? Wot—you think you can change 'em? You're more fool than I took you for."

"I loathe men like the Beckfords," I replied. "But there *are* truly kind people in the world, who look beyond their own."

He grimaced in disbelief.

A tug steamed through one of the arches below us, and the vibration penetrated the soles of my boots. I waited until the boat had passed before I answered. "After my mother died, a woman named Mary Doyle took me in because I needed a home. But her bigger kindness was the *way* she did it, for she never let me see what a burden it was, never made me feel ashamed of being an extra mouth to feed. She thanked me for whatever I could contribute, instead of making me feel like it was the least I owed her."

He shrugged. "You were lucky."

Yes, I was. Unbelievably so. Not just because Ma Doyle took me in. But because day in and day out, she showed me what human decency and compassion looked like. I'd never thanked her for that. But now I was endlessly grateful to her for providing an example that might help me here.

"Bernard, tell me about Elaine," I said gently.

He sagged his left hip against the stone. "Le' me ask you somethin'. Do you know a girl? A good girl. A sister, mebbe, or a niece?"

Part of me wanted to resist entering into the scene he was sketching. But Elsie's pretty face rose unbidden into my mind, and I nodded.

His chin lifted in reply. "Aye. So imagine your girl, workin' in a house where she's just trying to earn her wage. Every day, up at six, staying up till ten or eleven at night to finish her work, and her only break a half day on Sunday." His voice broke. "Now imagine a brute, coming home drunk, and taking her one night, in the kitchen, threatenin' her with a knife and tyin' her down and plantin' his seed in her, all the while laughing that his wife ain't so nice as she is. And her getting up the courage to stand up in court, when speaking it is near as wretched as livin' it again! My sweet girl—those men smirkin' and mockin' her—and hearin' those terrible lies told about her *wantin'* him to do what he done so she could blackmail 'im after—my sweet girl—"

His voice had gone hoarse, and his whole form trembled. "To give her two pounds ten, as if that was enough to live on, 'cause she has no chance of findin' another position, no chance of a decent life for the rest of her days! And carrying a babe inside her, by a man wot'll never give her a farthing toward its care. And you know you cain't help her."

His eyes were dry—but mine were stinging with tears, sharp as needles. I wasn't just picturing Elaine but also Elsie and Belinda, too, as a girl, and Rachel, all of them overlapping like a series of waves.

"But you *could* help her," I managed.

He shook his head. "I'm dyin'. Black lungs from workin' in the mines as a boy, 'afore I found work on the river. Cain't you hear it?" He studied me for a minute. "Aye. I see what you're thinking. That I killed because I might as well, seein's I have nothing to lose. But what else could I do?" he burst out. "Think on it, man! Haven't you ever been at the mercy o' men who care no more for you and yourn than if you was a pebble in their way?"

It was as if he had some uncanny power to see into my past. Rattled, I said nothing.

He leaned forward: "If it was your daughter, what would you do?"

Another fair, and brutal, question. *Dear God*, I thought. I hoped I wouldn't murder young women for the purpose of teaching their fathers a lesson. But yes, I'd want to see the Beckfords hurt. What would stop me is the knowledge that there was no point in trying to teach men like Beckford anything.

Again, I couldn't answer. Perhaps he thought I was unaffected, for he sighed, and his voice became flat, toneless. "I held Elaine in my arms the night she died. She warn't crying out. Hadn't been the sort to squall, even when she was a babe."

"A good girl," I murmured, and he nodded. "Did you let Charlotte Munro live because of the baby she was carrying?"

"Yah. Warn't fair not to."

So despite everything, he had a shred of decency, an unwillingness to harm the innocent unborn child.

"And you began with Rose Albert," I said.

His chin lowered. "He war the judge. At the end, he talked to the jury like he hadn't heard a word Elaine said."

A foghorn sent its mournful note from upriver. I waited until the echoes had faded. "And where did you get the idea for putting the women in the boats?"

His chest heaved, and he fought down a cough. "I only learnt to read and write some, and I can't see the little type in the papers. But Elaine could read as good as anybody." He wagged his head. "Each week, she brung a paper with stories 'bout King Arthur and his queen and the knights joustin' and all to read out loud. And then, one Sunday, she says there's a special story 'bout a girl named Elaine, except it's sad. She was cryin' by the end of it, with the maid lovin' that bloke and him not even knowin'. Elaine liked a good cry over a story."

There were tears running down his rough cheeks, but he didn't seem to notice.

"So when she died, that Monday night, after bleedin' so, I took her poor body down to the river and found a boat for 'er. Steered past the docks in the dark. Stayed with her all the way past Blackwall Reach."

No wonder we hadn't found her. From there, the tide would have taken Elaine all the way to Sheerness and the sea, unless the boat was caught in some of the marshy land along the river.

His voice grew tender. "Till I kissed her for the last time and let 'er go."

His words were harrowing my heart, but there was more I had to know. "How did you write the letters?"

"I've a friend who c'n write proper. And it don't take long to find out from servants what's happening in a house."

"And then you used chloroform and cut the women's wrists."

His chin came up. "Only after they was dead. That warn't half what that man did to my girl." His voice became pleading. "It was just to show 'em! I did it so's they could see for themselves."

The image of Elaine prone on the table, with Beckford looming viciously and hissing in her ear, rose again in my mind as clear as a painting, and, God help me, my horror at what Bernard Price had done to his victims was momentarily outweighed by sympathy for his daughter, the shift as evident as the movement of scales at the docks when one too many sacks of grain landed on the plate.

But there was no way to balance this scale. Nothing Mr. Price could do, and nothing anyone could do to Mr. Price, could make amends for the deaths and suffering of his victims. And nothing could be done to make amends to Mr. Price for what had been done to Elaine. I felt the futility of it, and for the first time in my life, I understood what Ma Doyle meant once when she said that finding folks innocent or guilty is sometimes a poor way of righting the world. What could possibly be a just end to all of this? What could be done in the courts? I could think of no result that held justice or even decency, much less atonement. I stood in the path of the cold wind racing down the dark river and felt a profound sadness, for all of them, and a desperate wish to do no further harm.

As if he were following the train of my thoughts, Mr. Price asked, "What're ye going to do wi' me?"

Quartermain's voice erupted into my ear: *"If you let him go, I will punish you to the furthest extent of my reach."*

"Mr. Price," I said quietly. "If I do my duty and bring you in, you will stand trial. You'll have to tell Elaine's story. To men who will care even less."

Horror swept over his face, and I saw the whites of his eyes. He threw back his head and let out a howl. "I can't do that. I won't— I'll be damned if I—I won't—I won't—" His voice rose to a shout, and he broke into a spasm of coughing.

I had to come close to make myself heard. "But I can't set you free either."

He clamped his mouth shut, and his black eyebrows lowered in bewilderment.

"I've heard that if you hit the water from this high, you don't feel anything else," I said.

After he drew a quick breath, a gurgle came from the back of his throat. His expression was a mix of wariness and wonder. "You'd—you'd be—lettin' me—" He fell silent. Then he leaned over and studied the water. "Here's one of the deepest parts."

"Yes."

His shoulders straightened as he moved his bound wrists. "No cause t' worry. I cain't swim with these."

"No."

He licked his lips. "You could be hanged you'seln, if they don't believe I got away."

"You're a large, powerful man. When I tried to take you into custody, you smashed me in the head and flung yourself over the wall before I could stop you."

He considered that. "Why're you lettin' me go?"

I chose my words carefully, to be sure they expressed the truth as I saw it. "What you did to those innocent women was wrong— terribly wrong. Rose Albert, Jane Dorstone, Charlotte Munro, and Emma Montooth were loyal friends and daughters. Decent, kind people who took care of others, who tried to do some good in the world. And there are people who loved the dead women dearly and who will never, ever recover from the loss."

He flinched.

"But making you go through a trial isn't going to bring them back, and the courts have injured you enough."

His breath came in quick pants. "What about Beckford? I can't—"

"He'll be dealt with. He and his brother go to a brothel on Thursdays."

He nodded. "Yah. In Hampstead."

"The police raid it on occasion." I paused. "The next time may be on a Thursday."

His panting halted.

"Once word gets round what they've done, they won't survive prison." My voice was thick with feeling. "Trust me on that."

Relief flashed over his features, and one deep, ragged breath and then another swelled his chest. Then he stepped on a stone beside the parapet.

"Wait." I came close. "You need to knock me on the head."

"That's right," he said and began to draw back to do so. Suddenly he stiffened, the shoulders of his coat bulging, as though he had tried to free his hands. "Do you have a knife?"

"A knife?" I shook my head. "I can't—"

"No," he said impatiently. "Not for *that*. I want you to take what's round my neck."

"What is it?"

"It's a medal. Used to be hers." He tipped his head sideways, revealing a narrow strip of leather against his throat. "I don't want it to go down with me."

I drew out my knife and ran the blade underneath the thong. It clove in two, and I caught the ends. Threaded onto the leather was an oval bit of pressed tin. My thumb detected bumps and ridges. A saint's medal, perhaps. Like the silver one Belinda had given me, of Saint Michael, patron saint of police, that I refused to wear, leaving it in a box at home. It came to me, in a flash of insight, how pathetic that was, that I wouldn't even accept a *symbol* of assistance.

"Who is it?" I asked.

"Saint Zita. Patron saint of maids and servants." His voice was low. "Not that it helped her any."

Dear God, if only it had, I thought.

"Will ye keep it?" he asked. "I ain't worth rememberin'. But she was."

His words made my throat constrict. "Of course."

I put the medal carefully in my pocket, so he could see I had it safe. Then I stood still, ready for the blow.

He made a good job of it, his forehead smacking mine hard enough that everything went black and pain razored from my neck down my spine. Anyone looking would have seen me stumble backward, fall, and take time before I stood. Through a blur, I saw his bulk lurch sideways and vanish.

By the time my vision cleared, I was alone.

I struggled to my feet and leaned over the parapet. Below, a dark shape disrupted the moonglow that flickered over the river. Then the shape sank, and the surface ripples recovered their rhythm, running the pale silver light all the way to the shadowed shore. A fierce uncertainty hollowed out a space in my chest.

I wished I knew if I'd done the right thing.

CHAPTER 48

The next morning, as the bells struck six, I sent a message to Catherine's to say the man had been found, and she and Belinda were safe. I reached the Yard early enough that I found only the desk sergeant and a constable.

It was yet another Tuesday. But this one would be different.

I stood in the doorway of my office and watched as Vincent entered. In all the months he'd been at the Yard, it was the first time I'd taken the opportunity to study him as he made his way through the main room. His very stride and gaze bespoke prudence, evenness of temper, and intelligence. Perhaps from the beginning he hadn't given me enough credit for my virtues, but I hadn't acknowledged his either. That morning, I fully recognized how well suited he was to the task at hand—rebuilding public trust, fending off the Quartermains of the world, taking a position of civility with the newspapers, and managing men from all sorts of backgrounds.

His eyes caught sight of me, fixed on the bruise on my forehead, and he said, "Give me ten minutes, Mr. Corravan."

"Of course, sir."

My subdued tone, perhaps more than the words, made him pause before he disappeared into his office, closing the door. I returned to mine where I simply sat. Sometimes waiting is what must be done. At the prescribed time, I knocked, and he bade me to enter.

Vincent stood behind his desk with an opened letter in his hand. Although I'd given him his full ten minutes, he was still in his overcoat. My entrance roused him from his reverie, and he exhaled audibly through his nostrils as he greeted me.

He folded the paper. "It's from the hospital. Stiles is all right. His fever broke."

A profound sense of gratitude wiped all other thoughts from my mind for a moment. "Thank God," I said fervently.

He nodded toward another written message on his desk. "And the body of a large dark-haired man in handcuffs was found near Blackfriars Bridge this morning."

I kept my face expressionless as he hung his coat on the creaking rack.

Vincent sat, gestured for me to follow suit, and folded his hands across his waist. "I heard that you were at Mr. Griffiths's last night. The sergeant stationed there said you ran after the family cab and sent the two women home."

"Yes, sir. The young man was watching the house conscientiously. And it was he who alerted me to how Price would capture the two women."

"But you caught him."

I gave him a clear and concise account of the exchange between Mr. Price and myself, up to a certain point.

"He confessed all of this to you," Vincent observed. "Where were you standing?"

I had my answer ready.

"On the bridge, sir. I'd put him in cuffs. He told me he would talk, but I'd have to keep my distance. He said he'd throw himself into the river otherwise."

His gaze sharpened. "You believed he was so casual about his death?"

"He was already dying, sir. Black lung. He worked in the coal mines as a child, and at times he could hardly speak for coughing."

"Hm." Vincent looked thoughtful. "Letting Charlotte Munro live for the sake of her child. Strange bit of decency, wouldn't you say?"

"I think he was a decent man before his daughter died. Some of it remained, I suppose."

Vincent went very still, and I had the feeling, suddenly, that I had revealed too much of my ambivalence. But he only asked, "What happened next?"

"I explained that he would have to stand trial for the murders. He said he would rather die. That he had sat through Elaine's trial, had seen her disbelieved and laughed at by the judge and barrister and the rest, and he was damned if he'd repeat the experience."

"I see."

"It became clear to me that I'd have to seize him in order to bring him in alive," I continued. "I came toward him as he finished speaking, and he smashed me in the head so hard I fell backward." I touched my forehead, where the bump was purplish and very evident. "And then he flung himself sideways—so quickly that I didn't have time to grab him."

A frown creased his brow. "Is it your belief that he planned to do so all along, after he explained himself?"

"Yes."

"But why would he do that when Beckford is still free?"

I took a deep breath. "I told him we knew about the brothel, and it was a prosecutable crime." Vincent's expression was inscrutable, and I added, "So long as we keep mention of Mr. Price out of the papers, the Beckfords won't be alerted. They'll go to Rose Cottage as usual on Thursday."

Vincent pushed himself out of his chair and went to the window. Into the closed room filtered the morning murmur of other men's voices, the muted blare of boats on the river, the banging of a door in the corridor upstairs.

"I'll authorize the raid," he said finally. "But I want Mills to handle it. Especially given what happened with Mr. Price, there can be no appearance of you meting out justice to the Beckfords."

Relief blazed along my nerves.

"And the Beckfords will be the only ones Mills captures," he continued. "Unfortunately, it's not unlikely we'll find men of prominence at Rose Cottage."

"Yes, sir," I said and began to stand, hoping he would not ask.

"Mr. Corravan."

I sat back down.

"You left the sergeant at Griffiths's and went after Price alone." His eyes—intent—met mine. "Did you *seek* that private interview?"

I had spent most of the night honing my answer—an honest one for myself, but also an honest one I could give Vincent. Had I wanted to confront Price alone because, as Belinda said, I always wanted to be the sole rescuer? To affirm my own strength? So I never had to admit my own weakness? Perhaps. But the closest I could come to the truth was that from the moment I spoke with Rachel and heard Elaine's story, my revulsion toward Price had been tempered with understanding. Certainly, I wanted to hear Price's story to bring a successful close to the investigation. But there was another reason, too: I wanted Price to tell Elaine's story, just once, to someone who would listen.

I gave Vincent the truthful reply that would serve him: "I was afraid seconds would matter, sir. I didn't want to lose the carriage, and if, as I suspected, the driver had been thrown off, I thought the sergeant should find him and ascertain he was all right."

Our eyes met and held for a long moment. I could have sworn I saw a flicker of approval, even admiration. It seemed both of us felt justice had been served—though neither of us, for different reasons, would ever say so aloud. He could report a successful result to the Commission, and perhaps it would keep the Yard whole for the time being.

Vincent tapped his fingertips lightly on the desk edge. "Your handling of this has been . . . adroit. I would suggest that next time you do your best to have a witness to a confession. But your explanation accords with the sergeant's." He cleared his throat. "It is not lost on me that you are making an effort to tamp down your . . . tendency to barrel." The shadow of a smile appeared. "Please write the account exactly as you've described it." He nodded to dismiss me. "That is all."

"Thank you, sir."

I left the room, closed the door, leaned against the frame, and breathed.

There would be a next time.

CHAPTER 49

That afternoon, I went to the hospital to visit Stiles. He'd recovered sufficiently to be wheeled by chair into the sunroom. The golden warmth cast its light over half a dozen patients seated or walking with the assistance of a cane or a nurse. To my surprise, Madeline was there as well, sitting beside Stiles, in a rocking chair. A nurse stood nearby, and Madeline held a tiny baby in her arms. Not wanting to disturb them, I kept out of sight.

The nurse nodded in approval. "This is such a help, Mrs. Beckford. Mrs. Kipp needs her rest."

Her words put a sweet, gratified expression on Madeline's face.

Stiles leaned forward in his chair, and Madeline looked over at him with a shy smile before returning her gaze to the infant. I had a curious feeling then, looking at the three of them. They could have been a family. Though Stiles was thinner than usual, pale and unshaven, he had something of the attitude of a doting father, and Madeline looked like an affectionate mother. It was a false picture, of course, but true in a way; the kindness the nurse and Stiles had shown Madeline, and the tenderness she was showing the baby, were very real. My heart lightened. Madeline would be all right and Stiles was on the mend.

I turned away to find James, to tell him that the case was finished and that eventually, Madeline would be able to go home to her house without fear.

★   ★   ★

The raid at Rose Cottage went off perfectly under Mills's supervision. Twenty-four men were caught in situations that left them open to scandal and incarceration. Through a remarkable amount of bumbling and fumbling in the dark, twenty-two of them managed to escape out the back door, many of them in embarrassing states of undress. Two of the men, however, were caught and put on trial for committing sexual acts with five girls younger than eleven. Stephen and Robert Beckford were sentenced to thirteen years in prison, with no possibility of parole.

★　★　★

As Mills was preparing the raid on Rose Cottage, I made two calls. The first was to Tom Flynn, which took the better part of two hours. The second was to Mrs. Munro.

Earlier in the day, I'd sent a note asking if I could visit at her convenience. She sent back a reply asking if I might come that evening, as she was most eager to speak with me.

I could understand that. When I arrived, we sat in the parlor, and she offered me tea or coffee. "We don't have spirits in the house," she apologized.

Given her father, I could understand that.

"Coffee will be fine. Thank you."

As she made the request of her maid, I couldn't help but think of the day when I was sitting in a different parlor with Lucy Marling, scribbling in my pocketbook. It seemed months ago.

After the maid brought in the tray, and we were left alone, Mrs. Munro smiled at me. Her face still bore traces of bruising, and the gown she wore covered her neck and her wrists. But she had a glowing, joyful demeanor that I've noticed in other women who were with child, and I wondered how I'd ever thought her plain.

"My husband is on his way home," she said. "He arrives next Saturday."

There was a brief, awkward pause. Not for the first time I thought, *There is no easy way to begin a discussion about a murder.*

"I'm here," I began, "because the case has come to an end."

Her hand set the teacup into the saucer with a gentle clink. "I imagined so, when you asked if you could visit. Although I've seen nothing in the papers."

"No, we won't be releasing it until tomorrow, for various reasons. Some parts of this story are very distressing," I said cautiously. "But I'd like you to know it, so you can see just how important a role you played."

"I'm glad I could be helpful." She settled back in her chair, the cup and saucer in her lap. "Was it the trial, as you thought, that drove him?"

So I told her the end of the story, omitting little.

Her manner remained calm—until the very end, when I explained that Price had flung himself over the side of the bridge.

Despite my careful narrative, she discerned the truth: "Why, you let him go," she said in astonishment.

It was on the tip of my tongue to defend my action—but then I realized she was looking at me not angrily or even uneasily, as Vincent had, but with admiration.

I looked at her in perplexity. "How is it that he hurt you so badly—he threatened your life, and the life of your unborn child—yet you wouldn't want him punished?"

"Oh," she said gently as she set her cup and saucer on the table. "In my experience, it is only deeply unhappy people who seek to hurt those around them. And at some point, we all struggle with pain." She looked thoughtful for a moment. "Do you read poetry, Mr. Corravan?"

Thinking of the last time I'd read a poem, with Belinda in her negligee, I felt a stab of longing. God, I hoped I might do it again one day. "Sometimes."

"Matthew Arnold wrote a very beautiful poem called 'Dover Beach' in which he speaks of this struggle. Do you know it?"

I shook my head.

"In the final stanza, he says, 'Ah, love, let us be true / To one another! For the world, which seems / To lie before us like a land of dreams . . . / Hath really neither joy, nor love nor light, / Nor certitude, nor peace, nor help for pain.'"

A small snort escaped me. "That sounds hopeless."

"Oh, but it isn't!" she replied earnestly. "He means that the world is full of confusion and strife, but love is a true balm for it."

Her words, together with the intelligence and serenity in her expression, brought Belinda to my mind for a second time in as many minutes. And inside my chest, I felt a shift as palpable as a strong wave under my boat, forcing me to adjust the weight in my feet.

"You understand what I mean, don't you?" A smile hovered about her mouth, and unconsciously she rested her hand on her belly. "Without love, what is the point of it all?"

Chapter 50

It was nearly nine o'clock the next morning when I arrived at Catherine's house. Her maid Sarah peeped through a window beside the door, and her hand rose to cover her mouth when she saw me.

A moment later, the door opened.

"Hello, Sarah. Do you remember me?"

She bobbed, her eyes bright. "Of course, Mr. Corravan. And we all saw the *Falcon* this morning, about the man being caught. Mrs. Gale was so pleased! We all were."

"She's here?"

She gestured to an open door. "I'll fetch her."

"Thank you."

I entered the parlor and stood by the window, observing the street. The morning sun was dropping its warm golden light down the sides of the buildings across the way.

A rustle made me turn.

"Hello, Michael," Belinda said quietly.

My throat constricted as I took her in—her expressive eyes, the smooth curve of her cheeks, the delicate lines around her mouth.

I took a tentative step toward her. "I've been all kinds of an ass, Bel, and I'm sorry. But I need—that is, I want to tell you everything that happened. You deserve that much."

She gestured to the sofa, and we sat at either end, facing each other.

"You were right, you know," I began. "When you said I was a coward."

She flinched. "Oh, Michael. I shouldn't have said that. I was angry and hurt, and—and upset—"

"But you weren't wrong," I interrupted, and she waited while I tried to find the words I wanted. "When I ran out of Whitechapel all those years ago, I made up my mind that if I got away, I'd never again let myself be that scared, never again be so desperately at someone else's mercy."

She nodded.

"And you're right that being an inspector lets me pretend that I have the power to undo evil and brutality." I shook my head. "But really, I don't. None of us does, except in small ways. And despite all my efforts, I *was* that scared again. The day Price threatened you."

"Michael—"

I held up a hand. "Let me finish, please. The newspaper account isn't anywhere near complete, and it can't be, until after certain things happen. But I want to tell you why Mr. Price attacked those four women. The story really begins with his daughter, a girl named Elaine."

She sat silent and wide-eyed through my entire recital. I omitted the ugliest details from the trial transcript and from Rachel's account. I didn't want to put those images in her head. God knows, I wished they weren't in mine. But even so, as I finished, her breath was coming in small gasps, and her fingers were clasped together and bone white.

At last I concluded, "After I heard what Price had to say, I realized we weren't all that different."

She looked aghast. "Michael! What he did was unforgiveable! You'd *never* do such a thing."

"I hope not," I replied. "But I know for certain I'd want to hurt people very badly, if anyone did to you what Beckford did to Elaine and Rachel and God knows how many others."

She reached a hand for mine, and I gripped it tightly. "I've felt the same outrage he felt," I continued. "The same feeling of coming up against someone who had more power than I, who cared nothing for my pain."

"I know," she said.

"That's why I understood him. He wanted to make those men experience the pain they'd caused. He had to put them in his position, so they'd know what they'd done."

"Revenge isn't always just about hurting someone back, is it?" Belinda said slowly. "It can be a way of conveying something. When words don't compel someone to admit their wrongdoing . . ."

"And the law courts fail," I supplied. "It's a way of calling people to account."

Her face was troubled. "It isn't justice, though."

"No," I admitted. "But the courtroom wasn't the place to resolve this. The story that would be told there would be all about the fathers."

A flash of comprehension lit her eyes. "That's why you told Mr. Flynn about Rose and Jane and the others, and the kind things they did while they were alive. He devoted half of the article to them."

"Yes."

We were silent together for a while, until she sighed. "It's so dreadfully sad. All of it."

"I know. And I'm still not sure I acted properly. But I've turned it over and over in my head and can't see a way that justice was possible."

"Perhaps it wasn't," she replied. "Perhaps in this case there was only mercy."

I studied our clasped hands where they rested on the sofa between us. "Is there any mercy left for me?" I tried to say it lightly, but too much hinged on her answer. When she didn't reply, I added in a low voice, "Bel, you were right in everything you said." I swallowed. "But I'll keep trying. I swear I will."

"Michael." Her voice was tender, and it gave me the courage to raise my gaze to meet hers.

"I don't deserve to have you take me back," I said hoarsely. "But I'm yours, however you'll have me."

Her eyes sparked with perplexity that softened to understanding, and the faintest smile curved her mouth as she gently shook her head. "How can I take you back, when neither of us ever left?"

It took two ragged breaths before I could reply. "Bel," I whispered, and like quicksilver on glass, she was in my arms.

And we did not say another word for a very long time.

ACKNOWLEDGMENTS

I began this book nine years ago, in 2012, after reading a true story about a young woman who was treated with terrible unfairness in an American court of law. The injustice clawed at me, and when I first hesitantly proposed the idea for this mystery to my wonderful agent, Josh Getzler, of HG Literary, I warned him that this was different from my other books. Instead of a young, thoughtful woman amateur sleuth, it featured a prickly Scotland Yard inspector who was a former bare-knuckles boxer and dockworker from seedy Whitechapel. Josh replied, "Wonderful! I can't wait to read it!" So I began writing.

As with all my books, this one is steeped in Victorian tea and history. People often ask what parts of my book are true, so here is a brief account. (For a more complete answer, please visit my website.) First, yes, in 1877, four Scotland Yard inspectors were tried at the Old Bailey for corruption and taking bribes, with three convicted and sentenced to hard labor and prison. The public's trust in the Yard was shredded, and the Departmental Commission on the State, Discipline, and Organisation of the Detective Force of the Metropolitan Police (the Victorians loved their long committee names) embarked upon a two-month investigation, after which the Yard was reorganized into the Criminal Investigation Department under a new supervisor, Frederick Adolphus "Dolly" Williamson, and a new director, C. E. Howard Vincent, in 1878. I have omitted Mr. Williamson from my novel and kept Mr. Vincent as the man more likely to challenge Michael Corravan. The real Mr. Vincent, like my fictional character, was a young man, well educated, the second son of a baronet, and a former *Daily Telegraph* correspondent, who had never served in police uniform. The conversations and conflicts between him and Corravan are, naturally, fabrications.

People often think of Jack the Ripper as the first serial killer (the crimes were called "sequential murders"), but there were dozens all over Europe before 1888, including Gesche Margarethe Gottfried (1785–1831), who murdered fifteen people by arsenic poisoning in Germany; Martin Dumollard (1810–1862), a Frenchman guillotined after having been arrested and charged with the deaths of twelve women from 1855 to 1861; Hélène Jégado (1803–1852), a French domestic servant who murdered as many as thirty-six people with arsenic; and Mary Ann Cotton, a British dressmaker who poisoned more than twenty victims (most of them her own husbands and children) and was hanged in 1873.

As suggested by Corravan's interactions with Tom Flynn (of the fictional *Falcon*) and John Fishel (of the fictional *Beacon*), the Victorian police had a fraught relationship with the newspapers—so much so that in 1879, Howard Vincent felt obligated to write in his new handbook, *A Police Code*, "Police must not on any account give any information whatever to gentlemen connected with the press relative to matters within police knowledge, or relative to the duties to be performed or orders received, or communicate in any manner, either directly or indirectly, with editors, or reporters of newspapers, on any matter connected with the public service, without express and special authority. . . . The slightest deviation from this rule may completely frustrate the ends of justice." As I've depicted in my novel, *Reynolds's News* often presented the police in a negative light: "Scotland Yard persists in holding out every inducement to policemen to trump up charges in order to obtain the rewards that are given to those who procure the most convictions" (1880).

I have included historical figures throughout, including the brothel owner Mary Jeffries and the vicious Jack "Bones" Brogan in Seven Dials. Annie Besant, whose notorious presence at Belinda's evening soirees causes the burglary that brings Corravan and Belinda together, published a book on birth control, for which she and her coauthor stood trial in June 1877. The jeweler Marie-Étienne Nitot and the House of Chaumet, which he founded, are real. The adulteration of tea and other comestibles was a huge issue, addressed (not entirely successfully) in a series of laws passed 1860–75. And the double-jeopardy law was in place for eight hundred years, rescinded only in 2005.

Elsewhere, I have taken liberties. While the River Police are based on Wapping Street, and Blackfriars Bridge links the north and south banks of the Thames, the church Our Lady of Perpetual Help is actually in Fulham, not Lambeth, and was not built until 1922, but I liked the name for a church that attempts to aid young women trapped in poverty. Seddon Hall is based on Holloway Sanatorium in Surrey, which was built between 1873 and 1885, so it would have still been under construction at the time of my novel (1878). As for gentlemen's clubs, Pemberton, Clavell's, and Adwaller are fictional, but the other clubs named are real, with many still in existence on Pall Mall. Hatton Garden is (still) the jewelry district, but I have invented many of the street names.

For those interested in true history, I want to share some of the resources I consulted, which provided the historical basis for much of this novel. All errors are my own. These include Haia Shpayer-Makov's essential and brilliant book *The Ascent of the Detective: Police Sleuths in Victorian and Edwardian England*; Gilda O'Neill's *The Good Old Days: Crime, Murder and Mayhem in Victorian London*, full of primary source material from the *Times* and other publications; Carolyn A. Conley, "Rape and Justice in Victorian England," in *Victorian Studies* 29.4 (1986): 519–36; "The Medical Evidence of Crime," *Cornhill* 7 (1863): 338–18; Henry Mayhew, *London Labour and the London Poor*; Peter Ackroyd, *Thames: The Biography*; Lara Maiklem, *Mudlark: In Search of London's Past Along the River Thames*; Charles Dickens, "Down with the Tide," in *Household Words*, 1853; and Judith R. Walkowitz, *City of Dreadful Delight: Narratives of Sexual Danger in Late-Victorian London* and *Prostitution and Victorian Society: Women, Class and the State*.

My thanks to Nigel Taylor, of Advice and Records at the National Archives, for information on Old Bailey and court records, and to Susan Fenwick, Administrator to the Clerk, The Company of Watermen and Lightermen of the River Thames.

My profound thanks to Jessica Renheim, Melissa Rechter, Madeline Rathle, Rebecca Nelson, and the entire team at Crooked Lane Books who fell for Michael Corravan and helped me complete this book. They have been a dream to work with—organized, generous, wonderful communicators, and true fans of historical mysteries. Thanks to Priyanka Krishnan, my first editor, who took a risk on a new author, and huge thanks to Josh and everyone at HG Literary for their unflagging support over the years.

One of the (largely) unsung rewards of being an author is meeting people from all over the world who love books the way I do. My gratitude overflows toward all those who responded warmly to the publication of my previous books, *A Lady in the Smoke, A Dangerous Duet*, and *A Trace of Deceit*. These include innumerable readers, authors (mystery and otherwise), publishers, booksellers, book clubs, librarians, bloggers, bookstagrammers, reviewers, conference organizers and attendees, and members of professional groups including Mystery Writers of America and Sisters in Crime. A special thanks to Barbara Peters and her entire staff at the Poisoned Pen Bookstore in Old Town Scottsdale, which I think of as my literary home. Thanks also to Phillip Payne and KT Tierney at Anticus Gallery for their lovely, constant support. Gratitude to all the book club and group leaders who have graciously organized author events for me and those who helped make events a success, including Debbie Arn, Patty Bruno, Jules Catania, Peggy Chamberlain, Robin Chu, Donna Cleinman, Lisa Daliere, Bill Finley (of Tucson Festival of Books), Ann Florance, Denise Ganley, Hank Garner, Amanda Goosen, Nancy Guggedahl, Allison Hodgdon, Denise Kantner, Ruth Lebed, Christie Maroulis, Melissa Orlov, Phyllis Payne, Rebel Rice, Laura Schwartz, Lori Stipp, Mb Thomas, Ellen Trachtenberg (of Narberth Bookshop), and Dana Tribke (of Arizona State University). Thanks to all the bloggers who have welcomed me, with special thanks to Dayna Linton, Melissa Macarewicz, and Cindy Spear for tirelessly championing my books. Thanks also to my fellow authors who have supported my work, especially Shannon Baker, Rhys Bowen, Donis Casey, Susan Elia MacNeal, Anne Perry, Rosemary Simpson, and Judith Starkston.

As with all my books, this novel started as one thing and shifted shape, depending in great part upon feedback from my beta-readers and experts I consulted along the way. A special thanks to all who advised or read drafts of this book: Ann Marie Ackerman, Susanna Calkins, Kate Fink Cheeseman, Wendy Claus, Masie Cochran, Mame Cudd, Tami Dairiki, Julianne Douglas (Sister Witch #1),

Andrew Fish, Mariah Fredericks (Sister Witch #2), Jane Garrett, Kristin Griffin, Claudia Gutwirth, Julie Larrea, Evan Leibner, Jennifer Lootens, Mimi Matthews, Kathy McAvoy, Nevine Melikian, Barry Milligan (who caught me mixing up wolves and rabbits, among other things), Anne Morgan (my title wizard), Stefanie Pintoff, Roger Ruggeri (with a special thanks for helping me name my protagonist), Nova Sun, Anita Weiss, and Anne Wilson. A special thanks to my web designer Amanda Stefansson for creating a beautiful website and helping me navigate it. Thank you to Bill Polito, my high school English teacher who told me years ago that I could write; my straight-talking newspaperman Tom Flynn is a tribute to him. A heartfelt thanks to my mother, Dottie Lootens, and my mother-in-law, Nancy Odden, for their loving support.

Lastly, as always, my deepest gratitude to my husband, George; my daughter and always first reader, Julia; my son, Kyle; and my ageing beagle-muse, Rosy, who naps in my office chair. I could not do this without you. You are as steady under my skiff as the river tide to the sea.

READING GROUP QUESTIONS

1. Under the legal doctrine known as "coverture," most English-women in the 1870s were profoundly disenfranchised. They could not own property, initiate divorce, or vote, so they had no (legal) voice in their own finances or marriages, much less in government. In this book, Madeline, Rachel, and Elaine are victims of violence and sexual abuse, but they also speak and act in ways that shape events. What do you think of Rachel's decision to speak her truth to Corravan but to refuse to testify in a court of law? What does it mean that Madeline can only find her voice in French? What are some examples of female characters demonstrating their strength, through their speech and otherwise?

2. Price and Corravan have some aspects in common—they're physically similar, and both have worked on the docks and have struggled with loss. How do you account for the differences in their characters? To what extent do you think their similarities cause Corravan to feel some empathy for Price during their scene on Blackfriars Bridge in chapter 47?

3. Today we think of Scotland Yard as the elite unit of the Metropolitan Police, but in 1878, after the trial of the detectives, there was profound distrust of the Yard and plainclothesmen that took years to rebuild. In this book, how do the acts of the Parliamentary Review Commission, the newspaper reports, and the behavior of the various inspectors have repercussions for the Yard's reputation? How does the political and social climate dictate the

possibilities for the Yard regaining public trust? Do you see any similarities with situations today?

4. As a professional author who earns a living, Belinda Gale may seem a bit of an outlier, but in Victorian England, quite a few women were writing novels, including George Eliot (born Mary Ann Evans), the three Brontë sisters, Elizabeth Gaskell, Margaret Oliphant, Geraldine Jewsbury, and Mrs. Henry Wood (whose sensational novel *East Lynne* sold more books than any of Dickens's). What does Belinda's writing career do for her? How would she be different if she were merely an heiress? At several points, Corravan ascribes certain aspects of her character to her being "a novelist." Do you think her profession shapes the way Belinda thinks and acts? If so, how?

5. In Victorian England, the roles of the police and the press were intertwined. Then as now, newspapers reported the news, and they could also create it and shape it. Corravan, Tom Flynn, and John Fishel all have different methods and different purposes for assembling their stories. What are the different models of arriving at "truth"? Does Corravan recognize his own biases and purposes and how they may shape the story he's trying to build? What are the ethics involved in building a story? Do you see any parallels with situations today?

6. River Police Superintendent Blair and Corravan have a difficult history. Do you think Corravan was right not to have been honest with Blair before he left the River Police? Is Blair justified in his bitterness toward his former protégé? Given that Corravan is five years older and presumably somewhat wiser and more experienced, might he handle the situation around Kevin Walsh's murder differently now?

7. After nearly 250 years of British rule, the Irish Republican Brotherhood (later nicknamed "the Fenians") was formed in 1858 with the goal of achieving independence and home rule for Ireland. Amid rumors of armed uprisings, in 1867 (a decade before the events in this novel take place), the Fenians bombed Clerkenwell prison in order to break one of their members out of jail. The bombing killed a dozen Londoners, injured 120, and was described as "a crime of unexampled atrocity" by the *Times*. Some

historians have called it the first act of modern terrorism, and it provoked fear and outrage in Londoners and exacerbated anti-Irish sentiment. How do you see this prejudice playing out with respect to the social hierarchies in the novel, in Whitechapel, the Yard, and elsewhere? Are there similarities with particular situations today?

8. With its meandering curves and tidal ebb and flow, the Thames River has been used variously in literature as a metaphor for human life, rejuvenation, and modernity. Early in the novel, Corravan comments that while some people see it as "the life-blood of the city," he usually sees it as a "cesspool, a receptacle for the entire city's detritus," and "a live serpent, filthy and slithering at my back." How do you see the river functioning in this book as a unifying element or a symbol, perhaps for aspects of Victorian life, values such as mercy and justice, ways of thinking, or feelings such as hope and fear?

9. In chapter 35, Belinda rebukes Corravan for being "cowardly," not in the physical sense but in the emotional one. Do you think she's justified in saying so? Why or why not? Corravan admits later that she has a point, but have other events in the novel contributed to his ability to internalize her advice?

10. Belinda and James both mention that Corravan and Harry are alike in some ways: they're clever, they're orphans, they're coming out of Whitechapel with very little, and both resent being a burden. Do you think Harry helps Corravan evolve over the course of the book? And does Corravan help Harry mature?

11. In this novel, there are three different facilities for the ill: Holmdel Lunatic Asylum for the Poor, James Everett's ward in St. Anne's Hospital, and Seddon Hall Sanatorium (based on Holloway Sanatorium in Surrey, built circa 1873). Medical science was still in its infancy. From our present-day perspective, what do you make of the different kinds of treatments meted out to the different patients at these institutions?

12. Gentlemen's clubs in London were powerful ancillaries to professional organizations such as the law, medicine, and parliament. They were part of what we'd now call the "old boys' network."

Women didn't have clubs, but do they find other ways to gather? How important are physical spaces such as pubs and shops and even streets in establishing micro-communities and facilitating events such as social change?

13. In many ways, Director Howard Vincent (based upon the real C. E. Howard Vincent) is a foil for Corravan. They are both intelligent and the same age, but Vincent is the second son of a baronet, was educated at public schools (equivalent to our private schools), previously served as a newspaperman, and had no experience in uniform. By the end of the novel, their relationship has evolved from a fairly adversarial one to one based on mutual respect. What enables this to happen? Do the two men change each other?

14. In the climactic scene on Blackfriars Bridge, Corravan thinks of what Ma Doyle once said to him: "finding folks innocent or guilty is sometimes a poor way of righting the world." Torn, he opts to act in a way that he thinks will at least cause no more harm. Was Corravan right to let Price escape by dying? What else could Corravan have done that would have been in keeping with his values or the values of the Yard or society? What roles do empathy, restitution, punishment, and forgiveness play in achieving justice? Where do justice and mercy intersect? What factors shape justice in a given culture or time period?